C000154091

Copyright ©2022 Rob J. Hayes
(http://www.robjhayes.co.uk)
Cover image ©2022 Felix Ortiz
Cover design ©2022 Shawn King
Edited by Sarah Chorn
All rights reserved.

THE WAR ETERNAL

SINS OF THE MOTHER

ROB J. HAYES

FOR PAT
BEYOND BLOOD AND BIRTH
BROTHERS IN MISADVENTURE

PROLOGUE

I WAS THERE WHEN THE SECOND CATACLYSM changed our world forever. And what happened after it... Well, that's all on me, I suppose. It should come as no surprise that in the midst of those great events, I stood in the centre of the storm. Or perhaps, I was the storm. The world changed around me. I changed the world around me, because without that change, we all would have died. Then again, we might still. All things end. All life ends. But I will be damned before I go quietly!

I was there. Floating above it all. Watching the end play out. I saw a plume of brilliant alabaster fire against the silver sky. A river of blood painting the muddy ground crimson. Pallid flesh erupting from the earth, crushing the rock around it, tearing down the sky. Monsters and horrors and creatures plucked straight from our nightmares. Terrans, pahht, even the garn had quit their ceaseless strife to die upon the battlefield facing their end together. United. For the first time in history, united. But not by me.

I was there. I saw my friends fall and knew I could do nothing for them. We each had our parts to play, our battles to fight. We fought together and apart. Sourcery tore across the battlefield from a hundred different places, the combined might of our world brought together by an adversary none of us could hope to fight alone. There was a pitiful force left to us, but then that too is my fault. Lightning burst to life as a Sourcerer died in rejection. An Arcstorm wreaking havoc in both friend and enemy lines all at once. The enemy pulled its flesh back from the storm, leaving smouldering chunks of itself behind. But it had flesh to spare. We did not.

I was there. My children fought their own battles, both those without and within. I had prepared them as much as I could, but it was not enough. It could never be enough. We can never adequately prepare our children for what the world will throw at them. Their lives deviate from ours in unfathomable ways and in the end, all we can do is hope that the strength we have nurtured within them is greater than the weaknesses we have inflicted upon them. My children fought their own battles. And I watched them fall.

I was there. A portal opened nearby and a pahht Sourcerer leapt through, streaking past me. An Aeromancer at the height of their ability, with the power of flight at their command. Two Hellions caught sight of the pahht and dived after him, their wings beating, churning the smoky air. Perhaps I could have stopped them, saved him, but that was not my struggle. I was ignored, and there I hovered, above it all, gathering my strength. That's not entirely true. My strength has always been close at hand. I was gathering my courage, waiting for my opening.

"I see it," I said as our enemy finally revealed itself. The war went poorly for both sides. My forces were dying, crushed or worse beneath a monstrous foe they didn't understand. Couldn't hope to beat. Our enemy suffered too much damage. It could no longer hide beneath the rock and earth. It had finally shown its true self. It had finally revealed its heart.

"I'm ready." A lie, though spoken with the best of intents. We are never ready for the big events in our lives, and anyone who says differently is either a fool or a charlatan. The big events and truly momentous occasions sneak up on us like assassins in the night. You might plan and prepare, even steel yourself for the pain you know is to come, but you can never really be ready. We are born into this world unprepared for the horrors of it and for the wonders of it, for the trials it places before us and the sacrifices required to survive them. We leave it the same way. I know. I speak from experience. I have already died once and I had no wish to go through it a second time. But the world does not care about our wishes.

I hung for a few moments longer, searching the battle for any sign of those I loved. They were gone. All of them gone. Everyone I loved, fallen beneath the crushing mass of our enemy as it emerged from its hiding place. If only those I hated had gone the same way, but of course, they all survived.

"I know!" I snapped. Time was not on my side. Not on our side. I was delaying, procrastinating, scared to meet my fate. And every moment I hesitated, more of us were lost. I was out of time. We were all out of time.

I was there. I closed my eyes, drew in a deep breath, and fell. Towards the earth, towards the battlefield. My battlefield. My war. They called it the Corpse Queen's war. What a load of shit! It wasn't mine; it was ours, all of ours. It was the battle for everything. The Second Cataclysm. It was the end of everything. I didn't start this war, and I didn't fight it for myself. I fought it for them. For my friends and my family. For my children. For all the people of Isha. For the terran people and the pahht, the garn and the mur, and all the others. Even the Damned and the ferals. For all the people of both Ovaeris and Sevorai. I fought for everyone. For everyone!

And I was going to die for them all, too.

CHAPTER ONE

SHADOWY WINGS CARRIED ME THROUGH THE great rift into Sevorai. The Other World. Created by the Djinn, populated by the Rand with monsters and nightmares pulled straight from terran imagination. I had never been to Sevorai, not physically, only ever as a psychic projection of myself. I was not prepared for the experience.

In many ways Sevorai is a dim reflection of Ovaeris. Colours are less vibrant, the air is thinner and cooler, the sky is endlessly grey. The ground appears rocky and barren of life, though that is a lie. It is actually teeming, but the grass often mimics the rock around it, and the trees do not leaf or flower, but are skeletal things with bleached white claws for branches. Many have needles that are sharp as razors.

Look again, Eska, Ssserakis said in my head. After so long apart hearing my horror's voice in my head was like music. Discordant, screeching music, but music all the same.

We floated down to a rocky outcropping a few
hundred paces from the rift. I staggered when we touched
down, my feet unsteady and my body exhausted even
with the strength my ancient horror was lending me. My
wings faded as Ssserakis retreated inside my shadow and
I immediately turned back to stare at the portal, back into
Ovaeris. The rift fizzed at the edges like foam washing up
on a beach. Beyond it, I saw only the swirling orange storm
Sirileth had created when she crashed our moon onto our
world. I could see nothing of my daughters.

They will be fine, Eska. Look down.

I did. I saw grey rock, brown grass, shapes wriggling
through the foliage. There were tufts of something like
orange moss clinging to the side of the cliff face below.
Beyond that, on the stony ground, I saw small animals
darting through the undergrowth nestling in the shade of
the cliff. A river flowed in the vast canyon below, the waters
dark and murky, the rapids white and crashing. Near the
base of the cliff, the river fell into a fathomless crack that
split the ground.

"What am I looking at, Ssserakis?" I asked.

*You have been to my world before with your magic. What
looks different?*

"Just tell me." Ssserakis always did like to lead me to
conclusions rather than point them out to me. I had not time
for it. I was worried about my daughters back in Ovaeris.

*My world is not as populated as yours, Eska. Yet it teems
with insignificant life, too primitive to provide anything but scraps
of fear.*

It is a strange truth that sentient peoples fear
differently than beasts and insects. Or perhaps we just
fear more intensely. Whichever it is, I long ago learned

that Ssserakis liked the taste of more complicated fear. But
that was not what my horror was getting at. I had been to
Sevorai before through use of Impomancy. It was a mostly
barren place with pockets of life in large acropolises, across
expansive plains, in jungles made of bone and caves made
of glass. But close to the rift, it was thronging with foliage,
undergrowth, minor beasts, insects, flies, snails, odd beetles
with oversized horns. Everywhere I looked was life.

"Is it because of the portal?"

*No. It was like this before you opened the way to your
world. They are fleeing, Eska.*

"Fleeing what?"

The Beating Heart of Sevorai.

"Norvet Meruun?"

I will show you.

My shadow twisted, wings bursting from my back
again. Ssserakis gave them a single beat and then another
and we lifted off. We had never been able to fly before, only
glide, but something was different now. Perhaps it was
because we were physically in Sevorai, but Ssserakis was
more real, less insubstantial.

We flew swiftly along, climbing higher into the
featureless sky. My body ached from the strain and my limbs
dangled uselessly like a pup picked up by the scruff of its
neck. Below, the world passed by in a dizzying blur of greys
and browns. The occasional splash of a more vivid colour
where beasts and monsters darted about. I saw a copse of
creakers crawling between a forest of bone-white trees. They
were moving towards the portal. Fleeing, as Ssserakis had
said.

*What has happened since we parted? How have our
daughters grown so? Why are you so frail?*

"You've been gone twenty years, Ssserakis." In truth, we had been separated for far longer than we were ever together. But there was a rightness to our reunion. Like I had found the missing part of myself. A friend once lost and now found, the presence both comforting and easy. But even that was too separate a distinction. We weren't friends. Ssserakis and I were closer than that. In each other we had found completeness. Two souls resonating as one. Stronger, more harmonious.

Is that a long time?

I laughed and the wind took my breath away. Ssserakis beat our wings a little harder, not understanding my sudden joy. Of course an immortal being with no body or age hadn't any concept of time.

"Twenty years is a very long time, Ssserakis. Especially for me." I was an old woman. I had only been alive for maybe forty years, but the Chronomancy had wreaked its terrible curse upon me. Back in the Pit, so long ago now, when I was fighting Josef I swallowed a Chronomancy Source. The rejection had hit hard and fast and in one minute I aged ten years. That was bad enough. But I had somehow absorbed some of the Chronomancy just as I had the Arcstorm and Geomancy. That innate Chronomancy continued to age me unnaturally fast. Alive for just forty years, but in the body of woman closer to seventy.

"Sirileth said she could feel you, Ssserakis. She's always known about you. What did you do to her?"

Ssserakis was silent for a while. I heard the leathery beat of our wings, watched the grey world zip by below. Saw a pack of khark hounds nipping at a yurthammer's legs. The yurthammer belched out steaming orange fire, but the pack

split and nimbly dodged away before dashing back in to
harry the monster some more. Then we were past them.

*I spoke to her. When she was a part of you. I showed her my
world.*

Is there any wonder Sirileth turned out how she did?
Before she was born, my horror tormented her with visions
of a world formed of nightmares. I was supposed to keep her
warm and safe. But I was never warm inside with Ssserakis
possessing me. I could not protect her from myself.

*Our daughter is stronger than you give her credit for,
Eska. I did not break her, only showed her what she deserved to see.
Sevorai is as much her world as Ovaeris. She is mine as much as
yours.*

I considered that. Ssserakis might not have had any
hand in creating nor raising Sirileth, but it had been with
me the entire time I carried her. As closely bonded as we
were, maybe it did make Ssserakis a parent to Sirileth.
Certainly, she never knew her father. I barely knew the man.
I wondered if my horror had filled that void.

*Such foolish concepts. Parents. The child is yours and the
child is mine.*

"She's not a child anymore."

Below us, a wide plain streaked with deep crevices
stretched out for as far as I could see. Patches of pale
shrubberies clung to the soil here and there, but the cracks
in the ground were too common, like veins of fat in abban
steak. I saw the start of a great skeleton. Small, at first,
though perspective made that a lie. It was massive. A
monstrous skull like that of a tiger but elongated and much
much bigger. The skeleton stretched behind it like a serpent,
winding along, ribs and bones buried half in the dirt and
half reaching for the sky, all the flesh long since eaten away.

At places, the skeleton had fallen into the crevices, but it was so long and large I found myself staring down at it for minutes as we flew above. And then recognition dawned on me.

"Is that Hyrenaak?"

It was. There was a strange edge to Ssserakis' words. I think it might have been fear. It takes a lot to scare the living embodiment of fear.

"What happened?" I couldn't quite fathom it. Hyrenaak was as timeless as Ssserakis. One of the lords of Sevorai. Almost as old as the world, the giant serpent had never touched the ground. Now it was nothing but half buried bones.

The enemy happened. Norvet Meruun is more cunning than we believed. She infested a pack of terrablooms with her children and waited for Hyrenaak to feed on them. Once he had swallowed them, they erupted from the flesh and tore the serpent apart from the inside while he still flew. He thrashed and screamed, ripped chunks of himself free, but Norvet Meruun's children clung to his body and consumed him. I heard him crawling, screaming, begging, Eska. But there is no mercy in Norvet Meruun. Her children swarmed him, ate the scales from his back, the flesh from his guts, the eyes from his head. He took a long time to die.

We passed the tail of Hyrenaak, the Landless. A bony protrusion half buried in grey dirt, half erupting, the final spike at the end pointed towards the sky it had once ruled. We flew on, Ssserakis beating our wings harder, gaining more speed as if eager to be away from the sight of the dead serpent.

"Why?" I asked, still trying to comprehend it. "You said Hyrenaak took no part in your war against Norvet Meruun. Why would she kill him?"

Don't be a fool, Eska. It is what she does. Norvet Meruun consumes everything. She is the death of Sevorai given form. The beating heart and eventual end rolled into a mountain of pulsing flesh. Ssserakis fell silent for a few moments. I felt it brooding over its next words. *And she no longer fears me.*

We glided towards a waterfall that flowed upwards instead of down. The water somehow rushed up the side of a cliff and burst free in an azure spray before gathering into a roaring river and flowing down the mountainside.

Prepare yourself, Eska.

In the distant sky I saw hellions and wind thrashers swarming, buzzing through the air. The hellions, bat-like in appearance though each as large as one of those awful horse creatures, were carrying things in the claws of their back legs, though I could not make out what. The wind thrashers were more insectile, with six overlapping iridescent wings that beat against each other creating an awful buzzing sound that hurt the ears. They had squat bodies with no legs, but eight arms, some ending in claws, others in suckery tentacles, and others still with hands. They also had terran-like faces with goggling black eyes and mouths full of serrated teeth. I will remind you that all the inhabitants of the Other World were ripped straight out of the nightmares of terrans, pahht, and tahren.

As we touched down next to the top, or bottom, I suppose, of that waterfall, I stared into the valley beyond and finally understood the depth of what Ssserakis had been trying to show me. Norvet Meruun dominated the horizon.

Pallid flesh the colour of maggots with red veins running through them extended as far as I could see. It pulsed every ten seconds or so and I felt a heartbeat thrumming through the earth at my feet. My innate

Geomancy came alive and tried to convince me a quake was coming. The maggoty flesh rose out of the cracked ground, splitting it where the mountainous body of Norvet Meruun could no longer be contained even by solid rock. Gargantuan tentacles, each the length of the great chain of Ro'shan I had once climbed, flailed in the air, occasionally falling and lashing at the ground.

I looked to my left and saw only Norvet Meruun. To my right and she was all I could see there, too. She was everywhere. Plastered across the horizon, clinging to Sevorai like a pestilent tumour breaching the skin, roots sunk so deep they clung to bones of the world.

This is only the barest glimpse of her. She has already consumed half my world.

Creatures swarmed around her. The hellions and wind thrashers above, and others below. Some were her children, the Abominations slithering slowly along, searching for more to consume. I watched a smallish one, probably the size of large dog, split off from her flesh and start undulating its way forward like some pale, rubbery slug. A few minutes later, a huge Abomination the size of ten abbans, blobbed forwards and re-joined Norvet Meruun's flesh, becoming one with its mother once more. There were other land bound monsters too. I saw a pack of imps digging at the riverbank, slowly altering its course for some reason I could not fathom. Their skin writhed, little worms poking out of their flesh all along their arms and necks, waving, wriggling at the air like blades of grass in a breeze. Further back, a pack of ten ghouls, some small as a terran, others large as a house. They were dragging a dead yurthammer along by its thick, scaly tail. They deposited the dead creature near the line of pulsing flesh and backed away, yipping and cavorting, the smaller ones scaling the larger and leaping off their backs in apparent glee. Norvet Meruun pulsed again and the flesh touched the yurthammer and immediately began dragging on it, pulling it in and absorbing it into the disgusting mass.

There were other monsters too, large, and small. Some I couldn't even name, had never seen before in all my studies of the Other World. I saw a giant creature many times the size of an abban, with curved horns and a mouth that drooled an inky black fluid. It had those little worms infesting its back and skull, tails wriggling in the air. Then it reared onto its jointed hind legs and strained against a huge cart full of rock, pulling it away from the expanding border of hideous flesh.

"What happened?" I stepped closer without thinking, slowly ambling down the hill alongside the flowing river.

The Iron Legion happened.

"Of course it was that sceptic bastard."

When he took me from Sevorai, he upset the balance.

"What balance?"

The balance, Eska. Since our creation by the Rand, we lords of Sevorai maintained the balance. We positioned our territories around Norvet Meruun. We kept her small. Each of us carving off bits of her. Not letting her grow. Her fear was an exquisite thing I could have feasted on forever.

"You penned her in like an animal? Like cattle?"

No. We caged her like a memory too painful to bear. She is the Beating Heart, Eska. From the moment of our creation, we knew she would be the death of our world if we let her. Only through our combined efforts could we hold her back. We each took our places, built our territories, cultured our minions. I had the grandest city of all, you have seen it. My horror fell silent for a moment and I felt it brooding. *You have seen how it once was. How it should be.*

Hyrenaak took the sky, tearing apart any of Norvet Meruun's minions that dared to leave the ground. That is why she killed him first. Without his guardianship, the skies belong to her creatures now.

As if in answer, one of the wind thrashers buzzed closer, the racket of its wings beating against each other a persistent drone that crackled in my ears. It stared at me, two hands twisting around a barbed spear that appeared hewn from rock. I ignored the monster and paced on.

Kekran and his army of imps served a similar purpose on the ground. He could not stand against Norvet Meruun's tide of flesh, so hunted the minions she sent out past the lines of her territory.

I had met Kekran once. A strange creature almost terran in appearance, but a twisted version of my people with skin that seemed to swirl, eyes that glowed with malevolent red light, and limbs that didn't quite match his body, as though he had pulled them from another creature and grafted them onto himself. I was told he had fought Hyrenaak once, had lost an arm, but had taken an eye. That was enough to convince me that though Kekran might look terran, he was far stronger than any of my people.

"Is Kekran dead?" I asked as I walked on. Another wind thrasher flew closer, wings buzzing. I now had an audience of two. They darted about above me, watching, never staying still for more than a second or two.

Not quite. Norvet Meruun tore off an arm, both his legs, and half his torso away. He fled to recuperate. That Kekran could apparently survive being ripped to pieces was terrifying in its own right.

"What about the other lords of Sevorai."

Ssserakis chuckled bitterly in my head and my shadow writhed beneath me. *Brakunus was supposed to hunt Norvet Meruun's minions just as Kekran did, but the ghoul is a coward and a fool. I should have taken him long ago. For all his failings, he would have made a powerful host.* A pause. *Not as powerful as you.*

"I don't need flattering, Ssserakis. The other lords."

Aire and Dialos. The one that is two that is many that is two that is one. Ssserakis laughed again. *We call them the twins and they hate it. They have their own territory and try to keep Norvet Meruun at bay, but they are fated to fight each other for all their lives. Recently they have let that fate distract them from the greater task.*

Lodoss wanders Sevorai and cares nothing for its problems. His torment is unending. He cannot die, and yet wishes for nothing but. As powerful as he is, he is useless.

Flowne has always taken her task the most seriously, but since the balance was disrupted she cannot hold back the tide. She blames me and has sworn to tear me apart if I approach her territory again.

"Could she do it?"

Ssserakis sulked for a few moments. *Yes. I am weak, Eska. I have been weak for too long. When the Iron Legion took me, the balance was disrupted. Norvet Meruun surged forward and took my territory, consumed, or enslaved my minions. By the time you sent me back, it was too late. My cities were destroyed, my minions gone or too mindless to fear anything. Norvet Meruun herself has grown so great she no longer fears me.*

"Slow down." I was still trying to grasp it all. The buzzing of the wind thrashers wasn't helping. We had an audience of five now, their wings creating such a drone my ears hurt. Each of them had those same worm-like extrusions poking out of arms and torso and head, waving in the air.

"You're saying you're too weak to fight Norvet Meruun because nothing fears you anymore?" I had long known my horror fed on fear, grew fat with it. But starved of fear, or when too much of the energy that terror provided was expended, Ssserakis grew small and weak and lethargic.

Yes. Watch.

My shadow shifted beneath my feet. A spike of inky black shot out, upwards, skewering one of the wind thrashers through the eye. It died immediately, its wings falling still, its arms going limp. Ssserakis withdrew my shadow and the monster dropped to the ground, twitching its final spasms. The worm-like extrusions embedded in its skin wriggled for a few more moments, then writhed free. And I sensed nothing. The other wind thrashers continued to watch. Wings buzzing, they flitted about above me.

They did not fear me. Always, through Ssserakis I had been able to sense the fear of those around me. The horror drank it in, fed on it. It often used me to scare others, providing it a hearty meal. But from these creatures there was nothing.

One of the gargantuan tentacles reached out from the main mass of Norvet Meruun, stretching the vast distance between us, towering above me. My wings burst from my back and Ssserakis beat them hard, pulling us back and up into the sky just as the tentacle fell, slamming onto the ground where I just stood, cracking rock and sending dust pluming up around it. The remaining wind thrashers darted easily out of the way and approached me once more, not attacking, just watching. The tentacle slowly withdrew, dragging along the ground, tearing a new furrow in the earth.

You feel it. There is no fear. I grow weak without it. There is nothing for me to feed on. Norvet Meruun no longer fears me. I could hear my horror growing panicky. It was not something I had ever felt from Ssserakis. It was an ancient horror, as old as Sevorai itself. But when faced with an implacable enemy, it didn't know what to do.

"Why don't they fear you?" I asked as we hung there in the sky, rising and falling to the steady beating of my wings.

Norvet Meruun has grown too large to care. Her body is sluggish to react but does so on instinct alone. She knows I cannot do any significant harm to her growing flesh, so does not care. Some of her minions follow her willingly. The ghouls are cowards and place their bets on the monster most likely to win. Others are enslaved.

"The worms infesting their skin."

Ssserakis made a sound in my head like a snort of disgust. *They are little more than puppets. The infestation controls them. They feel nothing. I can slaughter a hundred of them and still, they will not fear me!*

I stared down at the vastness of the enemy Ssserakis was fighting. It overwhelmed me. How could anyone hope to fight something so huge, so all encompassing? It stretched from horizon to horizon. Ssserakis said Norvet Meruun had already consumed half of Sevorai. Did that mean half the world was already covered in her pulsating flesh? I turned to stare back in the direction we had come, as though my failing eyes could pierce the distance and see the great rift. The first stable portal between our two worlds.

"Oh fuck!"

Yes. In connecting our two worlds, our daughter has

doomed Ovaeris along with Sevorai. Once Norvet Meruun has
consumed everything here, she will do the same to your world.

"What do we do?"

Fight! Swallow your Sources. We were always stronger
together. We'll carve her flesh apart and slaughter her minions. If
we hurt her enough, she will learn to fear me again.

It was all too overwhelming. To vast to comprehend.
Too big to fight. "I can't, Ssserakis. I'm old. Tired." I didn't
need my horror to whisper the next bit in my head, it was
a fear I had tormented myself with for a while now. "I'm
weak."

A wave of disgust poured over me. Ssserakis finally
realising the state of the body it had possessed.

You have let your body wither. Your magic rots within you.

I laughed bitterly as we hung there in the sky, wings
beating slowly. "Age will do that, yes."

Again, the sharp sense of disgust crashing against me.
This is not age. The Iron Legion was old, but he was strong. You
have ALLOWED yourself to become weak.

"I'm tired, Ssserakis. I have been tired for a long
time." I didn't say the next bit. I didn't need to. I was tired
and I was alone.

You're not alone anymore.

I couldn't help it. I couldn't fight. I was despair made
manifest. The inevitability of failure turned my limbs to
stone, weighing me down. Even my wings beat slower and
we glided down to the ground. I collapsed next to the top
of the waterfall, staring at the enemy stretching before me. I
knew we had no chance against it.

"I'm tired, Ssserakis," I said. The words came unstuck
and flowed from me. I finally admitted the truth to the only
creature in existence who could truly understand me. "I've

made so many mistakes. I'm tired of making mistakes."

The call of the void surged and dragged me out to sea with it. Trying was so hard. The effort too great. The inevitable failure, the consequences were too high. The horrible truth was in front of me. Just like Imiko, I wasn't strong enough to bear both the weight of the world and my conscience. Life was so much pain and it would be easier to not be. I was so fucking tired of being me, of making the same mistakes, fucking everything up. So much easier to just let it end.

Stop wallowing, Eskara! Listen to me. I know you. You are not tired of being you. You are stronger than that. You are not ground down by your mistakes, you are sturdier than that. You are tired of facing them alone. But you are not alone anymore. I am here. I am with you. We are each other's strength.

"What if we're each other's weakness?"

STOP IT! This self-indulgent whining is unlike you. It will not help my world or yours. It will not save your people. It will not save our daughters. Snap out of it and help me. Or shall I crush your heart in your chest, flee your carcass, and find someone who will. Perhaps I should have gone to our daughter after all.

"Don't you dare." As much as I loved Ssserakis, I would not inflict the torment of carrying it on another, especially not Sirileth. She might think she wanted the possession, but she didn't understand what it would cost her. The cold inside, the nightmares. The need to cause fear in others to feed it.

Then stand up. Swallow your Sources. Shed this useless notion of weakness. Together we will carve Norvet Meruun apart. We will make her fear us.

I stood unsteadily. My legs were weak, but the leaden feeling had passed. The wave of despair retreated, and the

call of the void no longer drowned me. It was always this
way. When it rose it seemed insurmountable, a towering
monstrosity that I could never hope to fight. Despair and
disgust and pain, and over it all the need to be free of it
once and for all. But then, like the tide, it ebbed and left me
feeling raw. Raw, but no longer beaten. Despite that, I didn't
swallow my Sources. I didn't leap into battle as Ssserakis
demanded. Instead, I turned back towards the great rift.

"Take us back, Ssserakis." I was unused to the horror
inside my body. I had not yet regained enough control to
summon my wings myself.

But the enemy—

Once, both long ago and perhaps not so distant,
I would have done as Ssserakis wanted. I would have
swallowed my magic and leapt into the midst of Norvet
Meruun and dashed myself upon its insurmountable flesh.
But I was older, weaker, and wiser. I knew we would lose.

"If we strike at it now, we'll die."

Ssserakis grumbled but didn't argue. My shadowy
wings boiled out of my back and Ssserakis took us into the
sky, flying swiftly towards the great rift.

"I need time, Ssserakis, to recover from… Well, a lot
has happened recently."

I hung limp as my wings beat to a steady rhythm,
carrying us above the Other World and its myriad greys.
Such muted colours, but there were colours. Like a reflection
of Ovaeris seen through a dusty mirror. I crossed my arms
and bent my mind to the puzzle of how we could hope to
defeat a creature such as Norvet Meruun. Then I realised
how much I had missed being able to cross my arms.

I had gradually come to accept the little annoyances
of having only one arm. There was no sense in grumbling

over something that was done and could not be undone. I learned to cope, adapt. Less crossing of arms, more holding my left shoulder, or thrusting my hand into a pocket. But now I didn't have to adapt. Thanks to Ssserakis, I had a second hand again. It was formed of shadow and skeletal like all the flesh had been stripped from the bones. Each finger ended in a sharp talon. Just like my wings, it was Ssserakis' power, but my shadow. They were a part of me and a part of the horror. Two beings from separate worlds working as one to a common goal. Just like the Auguries, those ancient prophecies that claimed I was the one who would end the eternal war between the Rand and Djinn.

A plan was beginning to form in my mind. "We can't kill Norvet Meruun alone, Ssserakis."

We cannot kill her, Eska.

"What?"

She is the heart of Sevorai. As long as my world exists, so will Norvet Meruun.

"So what is this all for? How can we win?"

There is no winning this fight. Only prolonging it. The balance, Eska. It is about the balance. We need to cut her flesh so it withers and dies, beat her back until she can be contained once more. She must learn to fear me again.

Our fucking stupid, mindless, arrogant, arsehole gods! So enamoured with their petty squabbles, their vaunted war eternal, they reproduced it here in Sevorai. A war that can never be won but must be fought for the sake of that world. Fucking Rand! Fucking Djinn! Idiots, all of them.

"We can't do it alone, Ssserakis," I said, staring at my shadowy hand again. "You say Norvet Meruun covers half of Sevorai, there is no way we can prune back that bush alone. We need help. Allies. An army. Two armies. Five.

What happened to yours?"

She ate it. Ssserakis fell silent. I basked in the quiet beating of wings, the rush of cool air against my face.

You wish to rally your world against mine?

"Can you think of a better plan?"

No. Nor can I think of a worse one.

CHAPTER TWO

ABBANS STRADDLE THAT LINE BETWEEN wonderful and terrible. On the one hand, they are hairy monstrosities as large as a house. These were females, each of the beasts sporting six legs instead of the male four. They have great shaggy coats that stink of piss and they plod along at a pace akin to walking. And the ticks they sometimes carry are the size of my fist. On the other hand, abbans make wonderful steaks.

It only took a few hours to reach New Picarr, and we spent it in relative silence, though the marshal's pointed glares were as loud as a newborn crying out for the tit. Arex, the old soldier with only one good eye and a sword as rusted as his skills, sat behind me and played with a deck of cards, constantly shuffling and then picking one, only to sound disappointed. It takes a special kind of stupid to play against yourself and somehow lose every time. His bad eye kept sliding to the side and occasionally he'd bash a hand against the side of his head to get it to focus again.

New Picarr was a boil on the landscape that nestled beside the once-great city where I had been trained to use Sourcery. Picarr was nothing but ruins and ghosts now. Crumbling buildings aged before their time, like me. Invisible traps set by the defenders just before the old Orran-Terrelan war was lost. Monsters summoned by the Iron Legion to guard his lair. Yes, he called it a laboratory, but I call it a lair. In the stories I used to read, the villains always had lairs and the Iron Legion was an evil fucker, make no mistake.

Picarr brought back a host of ill memories for me. My time at the academy was often unpleasant enough to be considered torture. I had gained enough distance and perspective over the years that I could look back at my time there and see all the things the bastards did to me. They trained me to be a weapon and I almost died so many times from the rigours. They conditioned me to be loyal above all else, to think of the Orrans as saviours and the Terrelans as evil beasts. It took me many years to realise the truth of that conditioning, and still, I sometimes find myself falling back into the old patterns they seared into me. I am the weapon. Yes, that is what the tutors at the Academy made me. A weapon. A tool for killing. I am not sure I have ever been anything else.

But that was just what the tutors did to me at Picarr, and they were supposed to be the good guys. The Iron Legion, evil shit stain that he was, experimented on me, along with a few of the other students, and changed me, injected Necromancy into my body. Another curse my time at the Academy left me with, though the Iron Legion called it a blessing. He was a deluded monster.

Lesray Alderson, a fellow student, tried to kill me on no less than three occasions. She would have managed it too, if not for my old friend Josef. Worse than her attempts though, was that she left me with an unbound desire to unmake myself. I can never truly rid myself of that seed she planted inside me. The call of the void, the desire to commit suicide, to end the pain and the suffering and my brutal existence. I have learned to live with it, to ignore it, but I still have my dark times when I'm alone and I think about how easy it would be to slit my wrists and find relief in death. A sharp pain, a slow aching throb, and then peace. Quiet. Numbness and nothing.

What else? I absorbed an Arcstorm in Picarr. I wore a crown of fire and almost burned up in the Djinn's flames. A lot of painful memories around that city, and yet I settled down for my new life just a few hours away from it. Perhaps I thought there was still some mystery hidden in its depths I was yet to find. More likely it was just that advancing age makes us crave the familiar.

We waddled into the fledgling town of New Picarr, leaving the abbans at the stables before continuing on foot. Marshal Araknar led us to the town inn and said we would be leaving in the morning. With that, he gave a flamboyant bow and rushed away. It did not escape my notice that he had not offered to pay for our rooms.

I took the opportunity to bathe in private. Back in Wrysom, bathing was done in the river, and it was not often a wholly private affair. The villagers had long since gotten used to seeing my wrinkled, scarred arse, but that didn't mean I didn't bristle at showing it to them. At least they had finally stopped asking questions about my numerous scars.

That meant I could stop lying to them about one thing, at least. Once bathed and with a meal inside me, I spied Arex in the common room of the inn, making friends with kind words and failed magic tricks. I had no wish to join him. I wanted to get out and see what had become of New Picarr.

The streets were wide, the buildings tall and constructed largely from scavenged stone, much of it crumbling. New Picarr was a town built from the corpse of the old city. It was also filled with ghosts. They flocked from the ruined city, drawn by the emotions of people. Ghosts have ever been that way. They are largely formless things; ethereal blurs drifting about, untethered emotion that is drawn to its tethered counterpart. Some ignorant fools often believe it is only fear that draws ghosts. Idiots. They are drawn to strong emotions. Believe me, it's quite unnerving to be in the throes of passion with a competent lover only to open your eyes at the moment of heated release and find a couple of ghosts floating above you, watching like incorporeal voyeurs. Sucks the passion right out of the moment.

In New Picarr, ghosts were everywhere. Drifting down the streets, floating through walls, following behind passers-by, gathering at shops or stalls. Most of the inhabitants ignored them, long since used to their ineffectual presence. You could tell the out-of-towners by the way they startled when a ghost drew near, or tried to hide their purses from ethereal eyes. The ghosts were different around me, though. They gained form when I moved close. My innate Necromancy brought out the person they had once been. Instead of floating blue blurs of haze, they became people again. They had faces and hands and clothes and, judging by the looks on some of those faces, even memories. It faded once I passed, though. I can't help but feel I tortured the poor wretches just by being near them, offering them brief glimpses of the person they had once been and could never be again. I could have unmade them. I had long ago learned how to pick ghosts apart, unweave them and allow them to move on with their death. But honestly, there were so bloody many of them, who has the time?

I stopped at a shop with a sign outside that claimed it sold magical artefacts and curios. Curiosity has always been one of my greatest strengths and weaknesses all at once. A bell above the door rang as I entered. The shop was filled with shelves and crowded with items both mundane and wondrous. I have always had the strange ability to sense enchantments, though I cannot tell you where the ability comes from. Augmancy is the Sourcery of enchanting items with magic properties and it is a school of Sourcery that rarely works alone. To enchant a lantern with fire so the wick never burns out, the Sourcerer would need to be attuned to both Augmancy and Pyromancy. It is because of this that enchanted items are rare and expensive to make. Despite that, the shop was filled with them. I could feel the familiar tingle of enchantments across my skin like a lover's gentle touch tracing lines up and down my arm.

"Can I help you, elder?" said a pretty woman of middling years and extensive smiles. She appeared from a back room, her hands resting in the front pocket of her work apron.

"I doubt it," I said, "but you're welcome to try." I leaned close to a shelf and peered at a tankard. There was a little hand-written note below the cup that claimed any liquid poured into it would taste of fireberries. Wonderful fruit when pressed into a sauce, but you'd never want to drink it. Starts off tasting like honey, then suddenly your tongue is on fire. I'd never heard of such an enchantment before, but I knew very little of Augmancy or what it was truly capable of.

The woman with the apron stepped forward, the smile still warm and fixed to her face like it was pinned there. "How about a mirror enchanted to show you your youth?" She plucked a little hand mirror from a nearby shelf and twisted it around to face me.

The girl who stared back at me from that mirror broke my heart. She was young, smooth-skinned, and bright-eyed. Her hair was short and so dark it was almost black. And her face was unmarred by scars. Even the ugly, jagged line of puckered flesh that stretched across my left cheek was gone. I would like to say it didn't bother me, but Chronomancy had stolen so much of my life. That mirror made all that I had lost too clear. Much like the ruins of Picarr, it reminded me of times I would prefer forgotten. That girl who stared back at me from the mirror had yet to experience the worst bits of life. Had yet to experience true loss or the betrayal of those she loved most. She had yet to become a monster.

"Do you really think I'd want to spend my time staring at how things used to be?" I hid the pain from my face and cocked an eyebrow at the woman. "Useless bloody trinket." A ghost drifted into the shop behind me, floating through the wall. It was a tall man with long hair and childish dimples. He stared down at himself in wonder.

"Oh!" The shop owner drew back from the ghost. "How strange. Go on. Shoo! Away with you." She waved her hands at the ghost, but it ignored her and started perusing aimlessly about the shop as though it were an actual customer.

I browsed the shop a while longer and the owner seemed delighted to parade items in front of me as though she expected me to buy something. There was a silver dagger inlaid with gemstones that glowed in the dark. The woman claimed the edge never dulled. I rolled my eyes until she got the hint. Next was a length of rope that would slip out of any knot tied into it. I failed to see how and why such an enchantment was achieved. She fetched a child's doll from high on a shelf. It was a sad little thing of faded cloth and squashed stuffing in the vague likeness of a cat. When the woman squashed the doll's nose, it produced a roaring sound that was so lifelike I almost ducked for cover. The Sourcerer who created it must have been skilled in Vibromancy. The doll made me smile but I had no wish to purchase it. I imagined giving it to Denma back at Wrysom, but I could also imagine the little girl following me around with it, making it roar until I set the damned thing on fire just to be free of it.

I think the owner could see my lack of interest, but like any good salesperson, she was doggedly determined and began making up stories to go with each of the items. The doll belonged to a rich Orran merchant who had likenesses made of the beasts he had hunted. A compass that always pointed to a specific gemstone and had been a gift from an adventurer to her husband so she might always find her way home. A scarf made of rich golden fabric and embroidered with runes would apparently change colour in the presence of strong Sourceries. The owner spun a tale about an old tutor at the academy who used it to detect various attunements within the students. It was a load of crap. The only way to determine Sourcery attunements was to shove Sources down the student's throat and wait to see whether they started dying or not.

While the owner prattled on about the next mystical trinket, I scanned the shelves. Each item was placed on its own, with a little scrap of paper detailing it. I saw one sheet of paper standing alone, that claimed the item was the personal diary of Loran Tow Orran, better known as the Iron Legion. I ground my teeth at the thought of that man, a nasty habit I've never been able to drop.

"Where's the diary?" I asked.

The owner frowned and peered at the shelf, then nodded. "Oh, I've been meaning to take that down for a while now. We had it, but a young woman bought it a while back. She seemed very pleased with her purchase, as all my customers are." She nodded and launched into a story about a silver cheese knife belonging to a demon from the Other World.

Lastly, the owner showed me a locket that could look inside a person's heart and show them an image of their one true love. Their soulmate. "Now this is one of the most storied items we have," the woman said in a conspiratorial tone, as though she were about to share one of the world's greatest secrets. I must admit, she had a flair for the dramatic. "This necklace once belonged to the Corpse Queen herself, Eskara Helsene."

I scoffed. I had never owned such a necklace, and if the woman was wise, she might have looked at me more closely, noted the missing arm and the pale danger in my eyes, and made the connection. But no one ever did. It helped, I suppose, that Eskara Helsene was supposed to be a middle-aged woman with eyes that flashed like lightning and a shadow that writhed beneath her, not a grumpy old lady with pale sapphire eyes and a perfectly mundane shadow.

"You may laugh," the owner continued. "But I have seen paintings recovered from the Academy of Magic that show the Corpse Queen wearing this very locket."

I had never sat for a painting of any kind at the academy. Mostly, I was just tortured. Besides, with all that going on I didn't have time to sit still for some fool to paint me.

"They say that even at a young age, long before she donned her morbid mantle, when Eskara Helsene wore this locket, all it showed her was darkness."

I was half tempted to put the damned thing on just to see if she was right. It wouldn't surprise me. Instead, I laughed at her fanciful tale and bought the scarf. At the very least, it would help keep me warm when winter rolled around.

The next morning, I was rudely awoken by Arex pounding on my door. I threw my clothes on, hiding my missing arm beneath my poncho, and wrapped my new golden scarf around my neck. Enchanted or not, it was quite comfortable. Arex claimed the marshal was already gathering people to depart and I had the distinct feeling he was hoping to leave me behind. I snagged half a loaf of stale bread from the tavern kitchens, thanking the boy working the oven, then made my way outside to find the marshal striding down the street with a dozen fools in tow. I plodded after them, already thinking up some choice insults I could throw the man's way. It was far more diplomatic than breaking his legs and leaving him in the dust with a venomous 'How do you like being left behind?'

The marshal had scrounged together quite a force of

nobodies. There was the two of us from Wrysom. One was an old soldier who could barely remember how to hold a sword, and Arex was there too. From New Picarr, there was Marshal Araknar, who was a Sourcerer with an attunement to Pyromancy. I knew nothing else about the man. There were also four soldiers, two men and two women who looked like they were too young to even remember the Terrelan empire. They had certainly never seen a conflict worse than a tavern brawl. There was a guard captain from New Picarr, and I kept my eye on him. He was tall and dark-skinned with sharp eyes and a way of using them that spoke of distrust.

Some people study you with a depth to their gaze that goes beyond scrutiny. They will size you up and determine if you are a possible threat. I'd seen pit fighters look at folk that way. I'd seen people look at me that way, though not for a long time. The guard captain's name was Tolster, and he stared at me hard enough I started to itch.

From the village of Burrich to the east, there were two women. I recognised one as my counterpart, a fellow hedge witch, as they liked to call us. In reality, it was just what we Sourcerers were called now there was no empire to kidnap us and force us into service. Her name was Juyi, and she was a Biomancer, a Sourcerer specialising in the healing arts. She was a middle-aged woman with plenty of wrinkles, though she wore them better than I, and a smile that put everyone at ease whether they liked it or not. I didn't trust that smile and I wondered if perhaps Juyi was attuned to Empamancy as well. I hate Empamancy and always have. No one has the right to poke around in my head and stir up my emotions but me. Juyi had a brute of a woman with her, a fighter who carried a spear longer than two of me, and an iron-bound wooden shield I probably couldn't have lifted when I was in my prime. I let my gaze linger on that one until she noticed and both of us grew uncomfortable. What can I say? Age may have shrivelled my body, but I can still appreciate a good-looking woman when I see her.

The final three members of the marshal's group were mercenaries from Polasia. One was a tall, rangy woman wearing gleaming chain armour over her chest, a metal-studded leather skirt over her legs, and thick fur sandals. She carried a small round shield on her back and had a sword buckled on either side of her hip. Her skin was bronze, and her lips were painted a deep red. I have always found Polasian customs to be quite strange. The women accentuate their lips with powders and oils, while the men all wear veils to cover their mouths. Well, they covered everything below their eyes. The Polasian woman's companions were both men. One was tall and the other short, but both were bare-chested save for a leather strap that held a large shield on their backs. They wore no armour, only leather skirts around their legs and carried no weapons of any kind. Another strange custom of the Polasians: only the women were allowed to carry weaponry. Both men had purple veils tied around their heads to cover their faces.

The marshal stopped us at the edge of New Picarr where three abbans waited, each with a spacious saddle attached. I was glad for that. Lounging in an abban saddle was like riding in a carriage with an open roof. As long as you didn't mind the lumbering gait, it was quite comfortable.

Marshal Araknar cleared his throat. "We have a couple of days' ride ahead of us. We're going west."

"You have a lead?" the Polasian woman asked, her

thick accent tripped past her red, smiling lips. "Thank the Tear!" She was, of course, referring to the great tear in reality located out in the Polasian desert, where the eye of whatever it is that gods fear stares through. Some Polasians worship it. Not the creature beyond, but the tear itself. Idiots! It's like a beetle worshipping the boot slowly descending upon it, all while completely oblivious of the foot that's about to do the actual crushing. She thumbed over her shoulder at her companions. "There is only so many times I can watch these two fuck before I become bored." The two men said nothing.

The marshal cleared his throat, his cheeks flushing red like a good little terrelan raised to be ashamed of sex. "Well, that's... Yes, we have a lead on where these attacks are coming from. My scout followed the signs from the latest attacks to Lake Lorn, though he said the tracks were unusual."

Unusual is a terrible way to describe anything as it is not a description, but rather a lack of. "What does unusual mean?" I asked.

"Not normal," one of the New Picarr guards said with a snicker. His friends joined in. Somewhat inexplicably, the earth shifted under his feet, and he was sprawling in the dirt a moment later. I snickered right back.

The young guard surged to his feet and pointed at me. "She did that. Bitch made the earth move and tried to kill me."

Marshal Araknar sighed and raised an eyebrow at me. "So, you're a Geomancer then? That is useful to know. Any other attunements?"

I shrugged. I actually had very little control over my Geomancy. It was not one of my attunements at all, but I had absorbed some of the magic in my youth when I had raised a city from the earth. It turned my arm to stone as its price but left me with some small level of innate magic that meant needed no Source to use it. Regardless, I have always liked to keep my cards close to my chest and my attunements were private as far as I was concerned. "I'll let you know if and when you need to," I said, then winked at the young soldier.

The soldier stepped forward to square up to an old woman three times his age and half his size, but Marshal Araknar cleared his throat again, wrenching the attention back to him. "In this case, unusual tracks mean they aren't terran. The scout has never seen their like before. They do not belong to any terran, nor the Cursed, and not the Damned either. Whatever we're dealing with is new, and they have destroyed two villages, and we believe they are responsible for a number of missing people from New Picarr as well." A touch of fear crept into his voice, and I had the distinct feeling the man was out of his depth and struggling to come to terms with it. "I sent word to the governor of Esvale, but she said her troops were all busy defending the borders against raiders from Tefts and Yenheim. We're on our own."

"Don't worry," the Polasian mercenary said. "We will protect you from the monsters." All bravado and smiles, she had no idea what was waiting for us. None of us did, not even me.

CHAPTER THREE

I GAVE BIRTH TO MY SECOND DAUGHTER, Sirileth, just nine months after the Terrelan Empire collapsed. I should say, nine months after I murdered the Terrelan royal bloodline once and for all, accidentally slaughtered half the city of Juntorrow, and brought the empire crashing down around me. Saying it collapsed makes it sound a little less damning. Passive almost. Nothing to do with me, honest. It just fell under its own weight. The emperor accidentally stopped breathing, stabbed himself a dozen times, then eventually hanged himself. I'm completely innocent.

I was a queen when Sirileth was young. The Corpse Queen. I took the city I had pulled from the earth and turned it into the seat of my power. I built a queendom around me and named it Yenheim after my poor friend Josef. I thought I was paying him some great respect by naming a new nation after him. In his more lucid states, when he remembers who he is and how he became what he is, he laughs about it and calls me a fool. In his less lucid states, he doesn't care. The wild Sourcery he absorbed to save me plays tricks on his body. Some days he is a statue made of stone, others he can walk through walls like a ghost. Sometimes he can see the past and the future, and others, his eyes melt and his toes turn black with frostbite. He heals through it all though. His immortality is a curse I wouldn't wish on anyone, and I have a lot of enemies.

I floundered in my first few years as queen of Yenheim. I was struggling to learn how to rule and decide what sort of ruler I wanted to be. I was also failing to be the mother I wanted to be. I loved Sirileth with all my wretched heart from the moment she was born, but I didn't know how to raise her. I tried my best. It wasn't good enough.

When Sirileth was three years old, she took to following me about everywhere I went. Her little legs weren't long enough to keep up and she occasionally tripped over her own feet, but she refused to be carried. Nor did she cry when she fell and grazed her palms or skinned her knees. I rushed to her side the first few times, determined to help her and assure her it would be fine, the way my mother had once done for me. But Sirileth just flailed her little arms at me until I backed away, then stood on her own, lip quivering and eyes wet. She dusted herself off in the same manner I did whenever Hardt put me on my back during sparring, then walked past me without a word. Her fierce independence and determination were an inspiration. Is it strange that I took such inspiration from my daughter? I despaired whenever she hurt herself, sick with worry I cried the tears she refused to but wiped them away before Sirileth ever saw them.

The halls of my palace in Yenheim were wide, bowing first outwards and then in towards the roof. An ancient Djinn ruin based upon the slug-like Garn aesthetic, pulled from the earth by my own hubris. It was easy to get lost in those halls if you didn't know the way. I stopped outside the giant doorway that led to my throne room and waited for Sirileth to catch up, smiling at the fierce frown on her chubby face. Sirileth's eyes always held a strange darklight, like the sun behind an eclipse. It was the sort of light that seemed dull, but if you looked at it too long, it would blind you. I loved her eyes.

My daughter stopped beside me. She always walked on my right side. If she ever found herself on my left side, she would make an effort to move. She looked very official in her little red dress, her dark hair, the mirror of my own, tied in two braids hanging behind each ear. Hardt did the braiding as Sirileth would let no one else touch her hair, not even me. She had a purple flower tucked behind her right ear, a gift from Tamura. The old Aspect had taken up gardening as a hobby and loved to surprise Sirileth with colourful flora. I looked down at my daughter and asked if she was ready. She gave a silent nod, staring straight ahead. I felt her hand grip mine. It was warm and soft and so comforting, my heart broke a little. I had to open the door with my foot, then we strode into the throne room, Queen and princess, hand in hand.

I always hated dealing with the day-to-day chores of the crown. Tamura assured me it was important to put an official air on things and have supplicants view me from the throne when they came to ask for judgement or favours. Though I swear, half the time people came to me just to complain about their neighbours as though it was somehow

my job as queen to care. Apparently, it was. I once helped
Horralain through a nightmare of supplicants demanding
decisions from him. At the time, I had thought it a dream he
had concocted, but it was far more realistic than I gave him
credit for. I much preferred Imiko's way of dealing with her
criminal empire. She got to hold her meetings in taverns and
discuss matters over drinks and laughter and music. I envied
my little sister for that.

My throne room was an expansive cavern that
stretched up into darkness and could easily engulf an army.
Two great pillars stood intact, glowing blue mineral seams
snaking through them. There had been more pillars once,
twelve of them, but they collapsed when I raised the city
from the earth, and the rubble had long since been cleared
away. There were people in the throne room. Most of them
waiting for my judgement or hoping for a favour, some were
in my employ with news to deliver. Tamura sat at the foot of
my throne, whistling to himself.

A tug on my hand got me moving. Little Sirileth,
more eager to do my duty than I ever was. She walked
forward with her head high, one hand clutching mine,
the other scrunching and then smoothing down her dress.
Scrunching and smoothing, scrunching and smoothing. She
was always so nervous around people she didn't know but
never let it stop her from confronting them.

My throne was a morbid thing. Black stone carved in
the likeness of corpses erupting from the earth and clawing
out towards the living. I did not commission it myself, but
rather found it waiting for me after I returned from the
dead. My subjects found my reputation a thing of pride and
sought to bolster it, and it had the desired effect. People
who weren't used to the hideous thing came before me and

couldn't keep themselves from staring at the clawing hands and screaming.

I sat upon the throne and leaned into it. Once, I might have crossed my arms as I stared down on those waiting, but it lacks the impact when you only have one arm. Instead, I laid a hand upon one of the carved skulls, drummed my fingers on it, and tried my best not to shift to find a comfortable spot in the damned thing. I invited Sirileth to join me, but she shook her head and stood on the opposite side of Tamura, with a stern expression that made me want to laugh and scoop her into a crushing hug. I wish I had.

I sat through hours of people coming to me with their problems that day. After the first few, Sirileth sat, her legs giving out, and she struggled to concentrate on what was happening. Such willpower from a little one. Eventually, she fell asleep, head leaning against the stone of the Corpse Throne. I should have called a halt to it then. I should have spared my daughter what came next.

Somewhere into the third hour, a man came forwards, escorted by two Yenheim soldiers. He was in shackles, but his clothing spoke of money and his attitude of power. He was tall and pale, and his eyes burned with conviction. He was a Diviner, trained to seek out Sourcerers. He had also been found with two young boys chained in the basement of his house. Interrogation revealed that he worked for Kottlelan to the east, and was tasked with stealing young, untrained Sourcerers to start a new Academy of Magic. It was not something I could allow. Taking citizens, children from my kingdom, stealing them from their parents like I had been taken so long ago was not something I could abide. I knew all too well how children like that were treated, the pain and torture they were subjected to, the monsters they

were turned into. I could send the man back to Kottlelan
with a message to stay away from Yenheim, but I knew that
would do no good. Some messages are better sent in blood
than words.

I lurched from my throne with a snarl, reached out
with my hand, drawing on my Kinemancy Source to force
a Sourceblade. The arrogant bastard's eyes went wide a
moment before he realised the danger he was in. He died
with a scream, my Sourceblade lodged in his chest, and fell
to the floor dead, blood bubbling from his lips. What can I
say? A ruler should always be prepared to get their hands
dirty, or bloody. And I was angry. Rage has ever been one
of my failings, and the man was trying to steal children. He
was taking them from their parents and subjecting them to
a lifetime of pain. Excuses, I know. I did what I did without
thinking of the consequences.

When I turned back to my throne, my chest still
heaving from my anger, I could feel spots of the man's blood
on my face. Sirileth was awake, staring. Wide darklight eyes
gazed at the corpse cooling at my feet, then she stared at her
mother who made it.

Sirileth was just three years old when she first saw me
kill a man. It was not the last time.

I'd like to say our journey to Lake Lorn was pleasant,
but I can't. It was uneventful, at least, and when you've lived
a life like mine, uneventful is usually the best you can hope
for. We had three abbans and thirteen riders, so the saddles
were cramped. I rode with Arex, Juyi, and Juyi's big warrior
friend who turned out to be called Shine. I asked her if it was
a nickname, but Shine chose not to answer and prodding
seemed pointless. Arex and Juyi kept up a steady stream of

conversation the first day but ran out of topics by the second. I tried to keep quiet, enjoying the silence, but Juyi had a way of pulling me into conversation I couldn't quite ignore. She'd say something blatantly wrong, like the sky was bloody well purple, and the moment I scoffed, she'd invite me to correct her. Infuriating woman. Though I will admit she made the time pass a little more easily.

By the sounds of it, our other companions fared little better. The Polasian woman was easily bored and ordered her two men to start touching each other. It made no difference to me, I'd have happily watched, but poor Marshal Araknar wasn't ready to be assaulted by the more interesting Polasian customs. At the end of the first day, he all but begged Tolster to switch abbans with him. Tolster seemed more than glad to escape the inane conversation of his four young soldiers. By the end of the second day, he too was pale and unwilling to even look at the Polasians.

A thousand years ago, Lake Lorn had once been the site of a great terran city. During the height of the Rand and Djinn's eternal war, their clashes were devastating, and they didn't give one fuck about who got caught in the fire. Well, Lake Lorn, or just Lorn at the time, got caught up in it. One moment, it was a bustling terran city as large as any we had ever built, and the next, the earth depressed beneath some invisible force and everyone who called it home was burst like an overfilled pig's bladder. Water rushed in to fill the depression and cover the crime, and Lorn, once-thriving merchant city and home to the Five Colleges of Art, became haunted Lake Lorn. The gods didn't care, of course. I doubt they even noticed. Turned up, murdered an entire city for no damned reason, then fucked off to congratulate themselves on being so high and mighty. Yes, I still hate the gods. Age may have mellowed me a little, but some things never change.

I had seen Lake Lorn once before. When I was just five years old, the recruiter stole me from my home and my family and took me to Picarr. We passed the lake. I remember it was so large I couldn't see across it, with water still as glass, and an eerie mist that clung to the surface like a man to his balls. Well, the waters weren't still anymore.

We dismounted at what had once been the edge of the lake. And by 'dismounted', I mean I tripped over the lip of the saddle and tumbled down the abban's hairy leg to sprawl on the ground. A couple of Tolster's soldiers laughed and I glared at them as I picked myself up and tried to dust myself off. There was a time I would have set them on fire and raised their charred corpses to serve me for such mockery. There was also a time when I wouldn't have tripped over my own feet trying to dismount an abban. We gathered at the water mark where the grass turned to mud and stared at the remains of Lake Lorn.

"What happened to the Lake?" Juyi asked.

"Must have dried up," Marshal Araknar said in a voice so heavy with disbelief I wondered who he was trying to convince. "It has been a hot, dry summer."

I scoffed. "We had a big bloody storm just two weeks back. Damn near drowned us all."

The marshal opened his mouth to argue, then closed it again. Lake Lorn, the largest lake in all of Isha, was gone. There were a few puddles scattered here and there, right at the centre of the crater the light still bounced off standing water, but for the most part, the lake had just vanished. In its place was a drowned city the likes of which even I had never seen before.

Our world, Ovaeris, is one of ruins. Our gods made it that way. The Rand and the Djinn and their eternal war ravaged our world time and time again. We called it their war, and it sounds as if it was a short thing. I suppose in terms of immortality it was. But their war lasted centuries. Sometimes decades would pass with no conflicts, then for a hundred years the world would be battered by magical energies that cracked the earth, split the sky, and devastated everyone they touched. When those conflicts were over, the terrans and pahht and tahren and garn would crawl out of whatever holes we cowered in and rebuild our civilisations atop of the wreckages our stupid fucking gods had left behind. The Rand and Djinn were nothing more than callous children kicking over anthills, only we were the ants. Our world is built on top of the ruins the war eternal left behind, and the city at the bottom of Lake Lorn was one of those ruins.

The city sat at the bottom of a crater and consisted of a huge sprawling mess of buildings. Some were dilapidated, crumbling as though the walls had simply given way. Others stood tall and strong despite the ages spent underwater. Some had pitted stone, eroded by whatever pressures scratched away them, and others had bizarre floral structures growing out of them, like plants or shrooms but made of rock. A greenish-brown vine-like weed clung across much of the stonework.

"Lursa's Tears!" Juyi cursed, her mouth hanging open.

"You could fit all of Old Picarr in there and still have space for more," Arex said. He wasn't wrong. The city was massive. Some of the buildings were gargantuan things.

"I have seen this before," the Polasian mercenary said

in her clipped accent. "We have ruins like this in Polasian desert. Under sand, not water. Sometimes sands shift, hidden buildings no longer hidden. The great eye looks upon them." She was referring to the tear in reality in the deep desert in Polasia, and the eye that peered through from that other world. That thing that the eye belonged to was what our gods called God. It had created the Rand and the Djinn, and it had also imprisoned them in our moons. It watched our world, picked at the tear, always making it larger. Tamura had once called it the Second Great Cataclysm, a prophecy of doom to come. I fucking hate prophecies. Especially when I'm part of them.

I stared down at the city, saw movement. Just a flash of something passing between the ruined streets and then gone. "You think whatever destroyed our villages came from here?" I asked.

Marshal Araknar glanced at me and scratched at the stubble on his chin. "Maybe? The water drained and monsters marched out? Things from the Underworld, left behind when the city fell and became a lake?" He was desperate, out of his depth, and looking to me for answers. I had none.

"Perhaps." I shrugged. "There're ghosts down there. Not like in Picarr. Those poor things cling to the world as slowly fading emotion. Down there, I feel..." I tried to search for the right words. "Dread. Whatever lives there did not want to be freed."

"Necromancy too?" Juyi asked. "You are full of surprises, Silva. I didn't think there were any left who practiced that school." She smiled as though a party to some joke none of the rest of us were in on.

I pointed to the right. "There's a drier patch of the

bank over there, might be easier going. Assuming we are heading down there?"

The marshal cleared his throat a little too loudly and started forwards. "Of course. We have to investigate. This way."

It was a long walk down a muddy slope and everyone was slogging their way through silt and sucking goo as we started towards the drowned city. I'd like to say I powered through it with the rest of them, but that would be a lie. I fell behind quickly, struggling through the muck. Sweat dripped down my face and ran down my back, and I was breathing heavily before we were halfway to our destination. At one point I tripped on some hidden obstacle, and fell to my knees, my hand sinking into the oozing filth to keep myself from planting my face in it. No one offered to help me up. No one even noticed. We were all dealing with our own trials.

The others reached the outskirts of the city first and found the footing more stable. There was still a good covering of silt, but beneath that, the streets were cobbled. I found that strange. It was more than most cities on Isha managed these days, yet this sunken city was a thousand years old, a thousand years dead.

Tolster was the first to realise I was lagging. He glared at me and said something I couldn't hear. I heard his young soldier mocking me, the one with the hook nose and dancing eyebrows. I considered opening the ground beneath him and burying him up to his neck in mud, but it was idle fancy and nothing more. I could use Geomancy to impress children with party tricks, but that was the extent of my power and control with that Sourcery. A far cry from the terror who had once pulled a city from the earth.

"Come on, grandma," shouted the hook-nosed arsehole. "Pick up those knees."

I trudged on.

"Do you need me to come back and help?" shouted the wiry guard with a disgusting brown tooth in her mouth. "Does the old woman want a piggyback?"

I slogged on, one mud-sucking step at a time.

"We're all waiting for you," Tolster said as I reached the city limits. "Perhaps you should go back."

I sucked in a deep breath and stepped up onto the first of the cobblestones. I cannot describe how much I wanted to sit down and rest for a bit. I was out of shape. Horribly unfit and suffering from a decade of easy living and a lifetime of well-earned aches and scars. I was old. Aged unnaturally by the Chronomancy rejection I had suffered through so long ago. They were nothing but excuses for my lethargy. I swore to the gods and to the moons and to myself that when I got back to Wrysom, I would start exercising again.

I trudged past Tolster and his mocking guards without a word. Past the Polasian and her men, past Juyi and Arex. I walked past them all into the drowned city. "Stop gawking," I shouted over my shoulder. "I'm not going to wait for you."

"Silva!" Juyi's voice, tight with alarm. I stopped and turned to her, sighing. Stopping was bad, I wasn't sure I'd get going again. "Your scarf."

I grabbed the end of the scarf from around my neck and held it up. The gold weave of the fabric was changing colour, deepening to a sickly ochre. From somewhere deeper inside the city, we heard a noise like a rockfall as one of the buildings collapsed. There were more than just ghosts inside that drowned city. Whatever had drained Lake Lorn had awoken something.

CHAPTER FOUR

WE WALKED THROUGH THOSE RUINED streets slowly, peering down darkened alleyways and straining our ears and eyes for any signs of an attack I was certain was coming. Tolster and his guards swarmed ahead of me, shields drawn and spears ready. Gone were the mocking jabs. Now there was the possibility of danger, they were all so professional. I wondered if that would last past the first one of them dying. You never can tell how people will react when shit hits the wall. I've seen people lauded as heroes piss themselves and cower at the first sign of true danger. And I've seen those named villains rise to the occasion and put themselves in harm's way to protect those who would condemn them. The only way to truly test the mettle of a sword is by swinging it at something.

I dropped back, walking closer to Arex, catching my breath. He hadn't bothered to unsling his shield yet. A good soldier, an experienced soldier, knows to conserve their strength for when it's needed. He held an arm out to me and I ground my teeth and took it. I was grateful for the support, at the same time I hated myself for needing it.

"What do you think happened to the scout?" Arex asked the big Polasian man as we stopped outside what looked like it had once been a temple of some kind. It was a massive building with towering spires at each corner, one of which had collapsed, and a domed rooftop. Sun-baked weeds hung all around the stonework, and the stench was overpowering even over the earthy smell of silt.

The big Polasian stared at Arex for a couple of seconds, then pointed to the purple veil across his mouth.

"What? Khark got your tongue?" Arex asked. His bad eye slid sideways and he bashed a hand against his head to correct it.

"He doesn't speak," the Polasian woman said from a step behind us. "Not in public anyway. Has a sweet voice, like honey and orgasms." She slapped the man on the arse. "But only for me." She stepped past us and strode to the head of the group. "Why are we stopping? If we spend all day staring at old buildings, night will come, yes? I have no wish to sleep here."

"I saw something," Tolster said, his voice overly gravelly. I knew that tone. I knew it all too well. Bravado used to smother fear.

A figure appeared at the temple doorway. It was a terran, a man with long dark hair, a beard to match, and a robe of curious golden design with gemstones stitched along the arms. He leaned against the temple door, breathing hard, holding one arm across his body. Then he looked up and saw us.

"Run!" the man shouted and sprinted at us.

Marshal Araknar lit his hand on fire with his Pyromancy and shouted, "Stop there!" in a very commanding voice. The robed man ignored him.

The guardsman with the hooked nose stepped in front of the robed man, his shield held up to stop the headlong rush. He braced, expecting an impact, but the robed man passed straight through the shield, running into the centre of our group, his robe flapping. The big Polasian lurched forward and wrapped his arms around the robed man, crushing him in a bear hug. That was a mistake. The robed man vanished.

The marshal sighed and extinguished his hand with a sharp shake. "Ghosts!" he shook his head. The region was swarming with them. Most spread out from Old Picarr where thirty years ago the Terrelans and Orrans had unleashed Sourceries so potent they still lingered. Lake Lorn had been created when the Rand and the Djinn unleashed even more powerful magics, so it made a certain kind of sense that ghosts would linger even after a millennium. Still, I had never seen a ghost so distinct and lifelike before. Even the ones who gained form from my Necromancy were not so... real.

The big Polasian coughed, jerked, his back spasming. Then he went painfully straight and rigid.

"Desa?" the Polasian woman said. She crept towards her man, reaching out to touch his back. "What was that?"

Desa's head snapped around to stare at her with an audible crack. His eyes were wide, blood streaming from them like crimson tears. "I told you to run," he snarled from behind his veil. He might have had a voice like an orgasm in life, but in death, it was the hollow rasp of guilt that sometimes follows such sweet release. "Get out get out get out!"

"I'm sorry, love," the Polasian woman said. Quick as a flashfire, she drew one of her swords, rammed it up into Desa's back, around the shield. Desa's shoulder cracked as it swivelled about, his big hand clamped down on the Polasian's woman's, crushing it against her own sword. She cried out in agony, already reaching for her other sword. Desa twisted his grip and snapped her wrist. She howled then, all attempts at fighting forgotten. Desa wrenched his arm around, tossed the woman away. She crashed into Tolster, and they both went down in the silt.

Most of us were frozen with shock, not sure of what to do. Even me. I had spent years honing reflexes, throwing myself at every horror imaginable, rushing headlong into fights against monsters, gods, and women. Yet I had let it all go when I left Yenheim and took Silva's name. I was gawking like the next country fool.

The other Polasian man rushed forward, grabbed at Desa. He was smaller but heavily muscled. I had seen Polasian men grapple before. They might not be allowed weapons, but they knew how to fight. He took hold of Desa's untwisted arm, pivoted to throw the bigger man over his shoulder into the muck. Flesh and tendons tore away and Desa's arm ripped from its socket. The smaller Polasian man stood slowly, holding his friend's arm. He turned to look at Desa just as the dead man's head snapped back around, the skin of his neck tearing away. He lurched forward and down, bit into the smaller man's face.

"Kill him!" Marshal Araknar screeched.

With a violent shake of his head, Desa tore the other Polasian man's nose and jaw away. The smaller man fell without a sound. Not dead, but probably wishing he was. His nose, a mangled ruin. His jaw a horror of blood, flesh, and bone landed in the mud beside him.

Juyi's guard darted forward, slammed her shield against Desa's body, stabbed her spear over it. The point ripped through the man's neck and out the other side. Shine jumped out of reach as Desa's remaining arm cracked about, flailing for her. He grabbed hold of the spear shaft instead, tugged on it, driving it further through his neck and catching the woman off guard, pulling her close. I saw a moment of fear in Shine's eyes as Desa lurched at her. Then Arex roared and swung his sword low. The rusty blade bit deep into Desa's leg and he toppled, landing in the silt with a splat. Juyi's guard let go of her spear and rushed backwards, shield held up and ready. Juyi herself was kneeling in the mud, desperately trying to use her Biomancy to save the smaller Polasian man. Foolish. Even if she managed it, she would be doing him no favours. Better to let him die quickly with an injury like that.

Marshal Araknar shouted for us to get out of the way before flames shot from his outstretched hand, engulfing Desa. He didn't cry out as his flesh burned and fat melted. In seconds, the marshal reduced Desa to a charred corpse. When he pulled back on the flames and let them die out, we stared as Desa kept moving. His limbs were gone, reduced to blackened stumps. His flesh had melted from his skull. His skin was blackened, cracked, and steaming, but still, he flailed about in the mud. One of the New Picarr guards turned and emptied his stomach into the silt. Tolster struggled back to his feet, dragging the Polasian woman with him. She spat, drew her second sword with her off hand, screamed as she drove it point first into Desa's skull.

He stopped moving then. I think we were all glad of that.

The smaller Polasian man died minutes later. Juyi tried, but there was no healing that sort of damage. Half his face had been bitten away. The sight was gruesome enough that even I turned from it. Not Juyi though, she had a healer's iron will, able to stare into the mess of a person as they died and not look away. Two of our party dead, another one injured, and even old Arex could claim he helped out. But not me. I stood and watched it all happen and did nothing. It's a humbling thing to realise just how soft and useless you have become.

The ghost didn't rise from Desa's corpse. We left the bodies there and moved on. We had hours before sunset and none of us wanted to be inside the city when that happened. Terrans have an instinctive fear of the dark. I know this better than anyone, I was once host to Ssserakis, the literal embodiment of that fear made manifest. But more importantly, it is an instinct that comes from somewhere. There is a good reason to be afraid of the dark, and the things that call it home.

Juyi healed the Polasian woman's broken wrist while we walked, though it was clear how much it cost her. Biomancy is a powerful Sourcery, but it takes its toll on both doctor and patient. I reached inside my robes and found my Source pouch, ran my fingers over the magic there. Kinemancy and Pyromancy, two of my strongest attunements and the only Sources I brought with me. I couldn't risk an Arcmancy Source. If it reignited the storm in my eyes, everyone would soon realise who I truly was. I wouldn't risk Portamancy either. The thing that watched from beyond the portals had taken an interest in me once before and ever since, portals didn't work right around me. Too often that thing, that terrible eye that also stared out from the great rift above the Polasian desert, found me through them.

As we struck our way forwards into the heart of that drowned city, the silt on the streets became thicker. There was brackish water standing beneath our feet and soon we were wading through ankle-deep slush that smelled of rot and decay. We passed a statue that had once been of a terran with an arm raised to the sky, but time and the waters of Lake Lorn had long since stolen all the finer details from it and left it a greying lump of smooth stone. The buildings around us grew larger and darker, and the noises that echoed along those dead streets were anything but natural. The sun waned, slouching toward its daily defeat, casting us all in long shadows.

The marshal called for a halt, and we scrabbled inside a large building that looked like it might have been a workshop at one time. Thick stone walls and a chimney, a large open area inside with stone steps that led up to a second storey. We lit lanterns and huddled together in the centre of that space. Outside, something howled. Even more ominous was when that howl turned to a wet gurgle and then stopped.

"We're not even a third of the way to the centre of this ruin," the marshal said. "Either we head back now and try to reach the lake's edge before sunset, or we hold up here for the night."

The Polasian woman looked up, her eyes shadowed. Her bravado had died with her men. She'd already chewed the red paint off her lips, and she kept gripping the hilt of her sword so tightly her knuckles went white. Fear and probably guilt too. They both have that effect on a person, gnawing away at them, eroding the layers of courage and wisdom that we build around ourselves until all that is left is a small child huddled alone in the dark. "What if more of those things come?"

"We don't even know what that thing was," said Hook Nose. He hadn't sheathed his sword since the attack.

"A ghost," Tolster said.

"Never heard of a ghost possessing a person," I said, looking around, hoping for a chair and finding none. All the wooden furniture had long since rotted. I found all eyes on me. "They mostly just drift around and look pitiful until they fade enough that you can't even see them. That thing..." I shrugged. "It was more likely some sort of ghast from Sevorai."

"Sevorai?" Juyi said. She was staring at me with narrowed eyes. "The Underworld?"

"The Other World, yes. Its true name is Sevorai."

"You're an Impomancer too, then?"

I could have cursed my foolish tongue. I've always been too proud of my knowledge and far too eager to show it off.

"Rare for a Sourcerer to have three attunements these days," the marshal said. "Even rarer for a hedge witch."

Shine nodded. "Most Sourcerers with that sort of power were killed off during the war, or when the Corpse Queen sacked Juntorrow."

Arex chuckled, his eye sliding sideways but he didn't seem to notice. "That's what they call her. The kids called old Silva here the Corpse Queen." Bloody idiot man! "They scream like a rat in a trap when you chase them." He chuckled again. I'm sure he was trying to defuse the situation, but then good intentions are so often the shadow that hides the knife.

"She's only got one arm," Hook Nose said.

I scoffed, desperate to not let them see how worried I was. "So do a lot of people. Especially those of us old enough to remember the war. To have fought in it." They couldn't find out who I was. If they did, they might kill me there and then and pat themselves on the back for having saved the world. At the very least, my nice and comfortable life in Wrysom would be over. I don't think I've ever been truly happy in life, and I am damned certain I do not deserve happiness, but I was close enough in Wrysom. I had left everything of my old life behind: my throne, my people, my friends. My daughter. I'd abandoned them all and found a certain peace as Silva that I never managed as Eskara. And I could see it all crumbling away before me as a bunch of country fools figured out my secret.

"I would have fought in the war if I'd been born before it," Hook Nose said petulantly.

"You'd have died in it, boy," I sneered.

"I do not give a fuck who this old lady is," said the Polasian woman. "I will not stay in the cursed city tonight." I could have kissed her for changing the subject.

"Any other surprises?" Marshal Araknar asked, his gaze locked on me.

"I'm actually a pahht, I just shave all my fur off every morning."

The marshal stared a few seconds longer, then shook his head. "If we try to leave the city now, we might not make it out before dark. Then we'll be caught in the streets with only lanterns for light. If we stay here, we can rally together and set watches. We should vote on it." From the ten of us left, five voted for leaving and five for staying. The marshal seemed at a loss, unable to make the decision. So, I made it for him.

I'm often asked why people follow me, why men many times my size, age, or experience line up behind me. Well, it's because I tell them to. There is a trick to leadership, and it is a simple one. People are sheep, always looking for someone to follow. They don't care if it's the most qualified or deserving of people. The simple fact is most folk will follow the first fool to step forward and tell them to. So, there is my trick in all its bare simplicity and astounding wisdom. Leadership is about having the confidence to step forward and lead.

I started towards the stone steps up to the next floor and waved my hand over my shoulder. "I'm going to find a dryish spot to lie down. Wake me when it's my watch."

I heard a few grumbles, a couple of insults. Then Arex, Juyi, and Shine all followed me up the steps. The rest were soon to follow.

CHAPTER FIVE

MY CHILDREN BREATHED JOY INTO MY DINGY old palace. You may remember I pulled that palace from the earth, raised a section of the ruined Djinn city to serve the purpose. At the time, long before Yenheim had the name, it served as both palace and fledgeling town. The halls were alive with both people and activity. It was still dark all the time, there were no windows anywhere and so everything was lit with lanterns and torches. No matter how many of those you light, the shadows always find corners to dwell in. It reminded me of the Pit in many ways, and I found that oddly comforting, which is strange to admit because the Pit was a detestable prison and I fucking hated it. But in my palace, there were always footsteps, the sounds of distant chatter echoing down corridors, people to stop and talk to, livestock being led here or there. I remember some old man bred cats, the little kind, each one smaller than a babe.

They hunted down vermin and got underfoot and had an annoying habit of sitting on my throne the moment I stood. Still, they brought life to the otherwise decrepit halls.

All that soon changed though. When I returned from the Red Cells, the change was already in motion. People were leaving the palace to set up a town surrounding it. Wooden homes and workshops popped up everywhere, spreading out from the palace. Yenheim was… becoming. By the time Sirileth was born, the halls of my palace no longer rang with the sounds of life. Things only got worse. More deserted, more lonely, more devoid. I lost myself in the care and love of my daughter and paid it all very little attention. But the emptiness of my halls was a truth I could not escape. I felt… deserted.

Tris and Vi changed that though, and little Sirileth too. When I brought my adopted children back from the Iron Legion's cages, I had no idea who they were or who they might grow up to be. I just saw myself in them. Josef and I all over again, and rather than a lifetime of suffering and hardship, I hoped to give them comfort and love. So, I brought them home and made them my own. It pleased Hardt. I remember him smiling at me as I sat on my corpse throne with Sirileth on my knee, Vi nestled in beside me on my seat, and Tris at my feet, hugging one of my legs. All my children were asleep. Hardt watched us, smiled, and said: You're a good mother, Eska. I always knew you would be.

Well, I sure proved Hardt a liar.

Tris and Vi brought life back to my dry, dusty halls. Tris was ever the more adventurous one, quieter, but a born leader. He formed the adventuring parties to explore the 'depths' of their new home. Don't worry, I had long since cleared the catacombs below of lingering monsters and

Damned. He recruited other children from Yenheim, too. Those from the growing town who had either never stepped foot in the palace or had been too young to remember it. Thanks to Tris, and how easily he made new friends, my palace often rang with the footsteps of cavorting children, or their squealing cries as they jumped at shadows.

He was more than just a leader of miniature adventurers though. Tris was courageous. I had rescued him from the Iron Legion's cages, he and Vi both, but unlike Vi, Tris remembered his life before those cages. I saw his dark looks and hastily wiped tears whenever I asked him about it. He never talked about his old family, his original family. Nor did he talk about what the Iron Legion had done to him and Vi. Whenever I asked, he got that look about him, all determination and fire, so strange to see on a child of just five or six years old. He'd just say It doesn't matter. We're home now. And that was that. I do not think it was for his own sake he buried that knowledge, those experiences, and pain. He did it for his sister. Vi remembered nothing of the cages or her life before them. She had blocked out everything prior to her rescue, and Tris, well, Tris was brave enough to suffer alone if it meant giving her that measure of peace.

As for Vi, she was always... well, Vi. I swear that little girl never stopped talking, an endless barrage of questions and mindless chatter. I once found her alone, staring at a plant someone had brought in to try to bring some colour to my rooms. There was no one else about, but little Vi was there, chatting away, making observations about the plant; its flowers, its leaves, the way it smelled. Always talking, even to herself. I watched her for a while, listening and wondering at the noisy little fiend I had brought into my life. She got on famously with Tamura; the two of them were a joy to watch together. Vi would ask something like why the sky was blue, and Tamura would respond with something equally foolish like why was rock hard. They would go at it for hours, firing questions at each other and never finding answers. The questions always became more and more ridiculous as the contest wore on until Vi would ask the old Aspect why fingernails kept growing but teeth did not, and Tamura responded with who invented goats and why did they pick such a wonderful word. Vi filled my palace with noise even as a child, and I loved her for it.

If Tris was courageous, then Vi was unbridled support. She always backed her brother. I don't think I ever saw her argue with him. When Tris said they were going on an adventure, Vi was always the first to line up behind him, claiming the spot of party chronicler. She never carried a notebook with her but made observations every step of the way, and her memory of those adventures was perfect. I wonder if it was a side effect, a compensation. Some part of Vi had shut down during her treatment in the Iron Legion's cages. She remembered none of it or the time before, but her memory of everything that came after was perfect. After their adventures, she would recite in great detail every step of their journey and everything they encountered from the faces carved into the walls, to the corridors that pooled with water seeping from below.

I sometimes think they both adopted the roles they did to help the other. Tris was a born leader, yes, but I wonder if he organised those adventures into the catacombs to give Vi the new experiences she craved. To replace the sad memories she had lost with happy ones of them together. At the same time, I think Vi filled the world with chatter and noise and questions in part to keep the darkness and silence from devouring Tris. From an early age, he was prone to brooding, but no one could remain a sullen grump with Vi around. It buoyed my heart every time I saw the two of them together, and yet, at the same time, it made me ache for what I had lost. For the other part of myself. I hoped Tris and Vi would never betray and hurt each other like Josef and I did.

And then there was Sirileth. My true daughter, the one I had created and carried, gave birth to. So quiet, even at such an early age. Always aloof, but also always there. When she wasn't following me about, which was rare, she trailed after Tris and Vi, a part of their little adventures, but also not. More like a watcher, distant and unobtrusive. At first, I thought she was scared. Too timid to join in with her more boisterous siblings.

I saw them from time to time. Tris with a little cadre of children, each carrying a stick or a lantern or, in Vi's case, chalk so she could mark the walls and they would always find their way home, out of the depths. Sirileth followed, a few paces behind, her little legs working harder to keep up with the older children. She said nothing to them, only followed in silence and watched the others play.

I remember one time I stopped them briefly, pulled Sirileth aside, and knelt in front of her. She stared at me, no smile on her face. She so rarely smiled. Her darklight eyes burned bright as the sun in the gloom. A clump of hair had fallen in front of her face, and I made to tuck it away behind her ear, but she dodged away from my hand. I told her she could join in with the other kids, she didn't have to stay at the back and be apart from them all. Tris, always the little leader and so happy to include, heard me and agreed, said of course Sirileth could be a part of the adventure. Sirileth was just four years old at the time, but she understood. She shook her head and told me she was where she needed to be.

I didn't understand. I thought she was too scared to join them, maybe because they were older than her or maybe because she thought they didn't like her. But now when I look at it, I don't think that was it at all. I think to Sirileth, she was a part of the group. That was just how she took part.

I waved at Tris for them to continue and he strode off into the gloom, his stick held high as he led his intrepid explorers onward. Vi detached herself from the group, ran back to me, and flung herself into my arm almost bowling me over. She hugged me tight, told me she loved me. Called me mother. Thinking back, it was the first time Vi ever called me that, and my shrivelled swelled. A dried-up river suddenly flowing once again, bursting its banks.

She ran off to join Tris. Sirileth waited behind for a few moments, watching me with her burning eyes, unmoving. Then she turned and walked away, following the little group. A part of them, but also apart from them.

The city came alive at night. The howls, I knew, belonged to ghouls. They are disgusting scavengers of the dead, though not above hunting. They have two legs and two arms, just like a terran, but they crawl along the ground instead of walking. They wear strips of cloth all over their bodies, taken from the dead, have teeth like serrated knives, and smell like an abattoir on a hot summer's day. Most unnervingly, ghouls never stop growing. The oldest are gargantuan, giants many times the size of the biggest terran. I heard a big one plodding past outside our stone shelter, each footstep promising death.

But the howls were not the worst of the noises. I have made a study of the Other World and many of the monsters

and horrors that call it home. It had been many years since
I last visited Sevorai, but my copy of the Encyclopaedia
Otheria I left back in Yenheim was the most comprehensive
edition in the world. I knew the noises that swirled within
that drowned city. The scrabbling claws were khark hounds,
huge wolf-like beasts covered in armoured spines. They
were a favourite summon of mine back in my warring days
as they are easy to control and quite deadly. The groaning
trees in the wind were creakers, giant skeletal hands that
crawled around at night and stood erect like trees during the
day, deadly ambush predators.

Yet there were also noises I didn't recognise and that
scared me. The wet slosh of something rolling through the
silt. The harsh, insistent click of a monster I couldn't name
crawling across the roof above. It was all the evidence I
needed. An Impomancer had been to Lake Lorn. I had no
idea how they drained the lake, but they had summoned a
host of monsters from the Other World.

None of us got any sleep that night. The Polasian
woman and Hook Nose huddled in the corner smoking
cigars and talking in hushed whispers. Tolster paced back
and forth so much I felt like breaking one of his legs to
give us all a few moments of peace. Juyi buried her head in
Shine's chest and by the way the woman trembled I could
only assume she wept. Worst of all my companions was
the marshal. He stared at me for most of the night, his eyes
narrowed and flames from his Pyromancy playing across his
fingers. Even I stayed awake, clutching at my little bag of
Sources, staring at the doorway and the stone steps beyond.
Every time I heard a noise, I expected to see something from
our nightmares lurching up the steps to attack us. When had
I become so meek and cowardly? There was a time I would

have stridden into the night and faced whatever horrors assailed me with my head high and my storm flashing. I would have cowed the monsters outside and forced them to serve me or die. I would have moved when the ghast went for the Polasian man and stopped it instead of doing nothing while I watched it murder him.

I didn't know if it was age or comfort that had made me so weak. Complacency is born of easy living and peaceful times. I was not made for peace. And I was damned sure not raised for it. Yet there I was, a trembling old woman cowering in the dark and praying for the light to come and save me. Well, prayers are nothing but false promises made to benign nothings, not even worth the breath they're spoken on.

Luckily for us, the attack did not come. At least, not yet.

The next morning, as the first rays of light shattered across the drowned city, we crept from our hole to find little changed. There were new tracks in the mud, a couple of gouges torn from the stone walls, a dead ghoul lying outside our building like a gift. Cats often give gifts of dead animals to others, present them with such unabashed pride; Look at me, I killed something many times smaller and weaker than I and demand recognition for my ferocity. I wondered if this was the same thing. A bigger horror from the Other World presenting us with its kill to prove its prowess. The others took it as a threat.

"We should go," said one of Tolster's guards. She had a square jaw and always seemed to be chewing something. It was an annoying habit that made me want to punch her square jaw. Her nasally voice only fuelled that desire. "Get out while we can." There were dark bags under her eyes, though we could all boast those.

"Not until we find out what caused this," Marshal Araknar said dramatically. He struck that thoughtful pose again, one hand on his elbow while the other stroked his no longer immaculate little beard. "We need to know what drained the lake and where these monsters are coming from."

"Then we get the fuck out and come back with an army," Square Jaw said.

"An army?" the marshal shook his head. "Where would we find that?"

"Send to the Fall," Square Jaw snapped. "They'll help."

Marshal Araknar gave the woman a simpering look like she was a small child who just asked a fish why it didn't just grow legs and walk on land. "The Fall have their hands full with those savages from Yenheim. Besides, we have three Sourcerers here, including me."

"Fuck lot of good that did Desa and the other one!"

"Pruto," the Polasian woman said quietly. Her jaw was set and her eyes hard. "His name was Pruto. He loved to paint and made love like a starving man devours a meal." In the silence that followed, she started walking, continuing along the path we followed the day before. I fell in beside her, rubbing at the ache in my legs and wishing she had a shorter stride.

Juyi was next, her guard Shine beside her, as always. "I think you need a better class of soldier, Captain Tolster," she said with a smile. "These ones are being shown up by an injured foreigner and a little old lady."

I glared at her. I didn't like being called little, no

matter how true it might be. I've never been tall, and age has an annoying way of shrinking us. It's damnably unfair.

We passed a small square, surrounded on three sides by crumbling buildings. I could imagine it might have been a pleasant garden once. A stone bench stood to one side, covered in decaying vines. All that beauty I imagined was certainly was gone now, replaced by a macabre mockery of all it might once have been. A copse of creakers had taken up residence. Six skeletal hands with skin like withered old bark and fingers reaching towards the sky. They stood still and looked just like dead trees, but I knew better. I could hear them creaking. And, of course, there was the matter of the dead khark hound. The furthest creaker had one of the hounds in its grasp, its fingers curled in, piercing the hound's body in four different places. Blood leaked from those wounds, dripping down the grey skin of the creaker.

Everyone stopped to stare at the terrifying sight. Everyone except me, that is. I'd seen it all before and much worse. Ssserakis had shown me many of the horrors of the Other World. Creakers were the least of our worries. "Best you move on and not get too close," I said over my shoulder. "They'll not bother us unless we bother them." It was mostly true, during the day at least.

When at last we came across the scar that had drained Lake Lorn, we all knew we had found the source of the empty lake. We saw arcs of lightning from a couple of streets away, scoring nearby buildings and reaching for the sky. Arcmancy. The storm I held inside ached to feel the electric touch of it, to absorb it. To reignite within me. It was a dull throbbing at once both painful and seductive, I could have lost myself in the sensation if I just closed my eyes and fell into it.

The scar that had drained the lake was fifty feet across and had taken half a building with it. It was a jagged tear in the ground and lightning crackled from within, striking up and out at random. I had seen its like before and I knew what caused it: Sourcery. More accurately, Source rejection. A catastrophic rejection by a Sourcerer holding more than one Source in their stomach. This was how Josef, Coby, and I had killed the Iron Legion. All that was left now was a hole in the ground, a wearing of reality, the barrier between worlds growing thin. It was impossible to know how deep it went. It gnawed at me, that thinness. Like an itch I sometimes got between the fingers of my missing hand, so subtle it turned to a maddening, raw ache.

"I've seen this before," Marshal Araknar said as we gathered a dozen feet from the scar. Lightning arced out of the hole, tracing a line of smoking fire across the bisected building.

I nodded. "In Old Picarr, where the Iron Legion died." Out of the corner of my eye, I saw him turn to look at me.

Hook Nose took a few steps forward and spat. He got a good length on it, his spittle flying over the edge of the scar and disappearing into the depths. "We know what caused this now. Let's get the fuck out of here."

Marshal Araknar stepped beside me and cleared his throat. I glanced at his shin and he took a step back. "You think a Sourcerer died here. That's what created the scar?"

"Source rejection is the only thing I've seen that can cause a wound in the world like this," I said. "What I don't understand is why a Sourcerer was out here in the centre of what would have been a bloody great lake, swallowing enough Sources to do this. Nor do I know why there are so many creatures from the Other World around here."

"Drawn to the scar maybe?" Juyi asked. All three of us Sourcerers gathered together. I was certain my knowledge outstripped them both a hundred times over, but sometimes it's not about knowledge but perspective. We are creatures of habit, and our minds love patterns. We work and think along those patterns. We are confined, held prisoner by those patterns. Luckily for us, not everyone follows the same habits. People who have learned differently will approach a problem from different angles. Collaboration becomes the essence of discovery, many minds challenging each other, breaking each other out of the established patterns.

"Why would they be drawn to the scar?" I asked.

Juyi shrugged. "I don't know, but this place is thick with wild Sourcery. Perhaps they like that. I'm not an Impomancer."

"Clearly."

The marshal struck his thoughtful pose again, stroking his beard. "Arcmancy rejection takes the form of an unleashed Arcstorm. Chronomancy rejection causes the Sourcerer to age. Geomancy turns them to stone. Is it possible an Impomancer in the throes of Source rejection would summon a host of monsters at random?"

Now there was a thought. I had to admit that I might have misjudged the man. He was perhaps not as stupid as I thought. It still felt like we were missing something though. There was nothing at Lake Lorn, as far as I knew. No reason for a Sourcerer to be out there at all, let alone rejecting Sources. And why hadn't they brought Spiceweed to help them throw up the Sources again?

The earth shook beneath us. It was violent enough that Square Jaw pitched into the mud and let out a shrill cry as Hook Nose tried to help her up.

"Was that you?" Juyi asked.

I shook my head. My innate Geomancy was weak at the best of times, certainly not capable of shaking the earth like that.

Tolster inched towards the scar, craning his neck to peer into the abyss. "There's something down there," he said, drawing his sword.

A fleshy tentacle snaked up over the side of the scar and whipped about in the air for a moment before slapping onto the silty ground where it thrashed, spraying syrupy muck everywhere. The creature was an unhealthy greyish-pink colour and wrinkled like a shaved pig. Every few inches was a knot in the flesh and a cluster of wiry black hairs erupted from the skin. A second tentacle whipped out of the scar and Tolster ducked beneath it. A third and then a fourth crawled out of the hole and dug into the ground. Damn my slowness, but it took me too long to realise what was happening.

I shoved Juyi aside and shouted at Tolster to get back. He turned to stare at me, confused. A moment later, the hideous bulk of the Abomination hauled itself out of the scar.

CHAPTER SIX

"DON'T LET IT TOUCH YOU!" IT WAS ALREADY too late when the words screamed out of me.

The Abomination was a massive mound of rubbery flesh the size of a small house, hairy tentacles springing from its skin, flailing, crawling, reaching. It pulled itself out of the scar and flopped onto the earth with a spray of mud that spattered us all. Tolster stumbled away, spitting muck and desperately trying to wipe it from his eyes. The Abomination rolled over him and he was gone. Just gone. Already absorbed into its mass. Whether he was devoured or if his flesh was pulled from his bones, I don't know. No one knows how the Abominations work, only that it is madness to summon one.

Hook Nose was the first to react, I have to give that to him, even if he did the most stupid thing imaginable. He rushed the Abomination, sword swinging. As more of its flesh hauled itself from the scar, tentacles whipped in every direction. Hook Nose severed one with his sword, a spray of grey ichor striking his chest. The tentacle dropped to the mud, still writhing, quickly absorbed back into the mass. Another tentacle wormed its way out of the central body, hairs bristling as it swiped through the air. Hook Nose tried to dodge, but the tentacle slapped him across the face. He screamed, a raw, wet sound, and was flung away by the force. He rolled in the mud and when he stopped, we could all see the ruin that simple touch had left of his face. White bone showed through his cheek, the skin and muscle not torn but just scooped away like liquid through a straw. His eye was missing, the socket also bare bone.

Juyi rushed toward Hook Nose, squelching through the muck with Shine a step behind, shield and spear raised and ready to defend.

"What do we do?" Marshal Araknar squealed like a child who had kicked over a hornet's nest and was running to his parents rather than face the consequences.

"Burn it, you idiot!" I snapped.

As the marshal fumbled for his Source, I found my own little bag and reached inside. I had just two Sources with me; Pyromancy and Kinemancy. Neither of which I wanted anyone to know I was attuned to. Unfortunately, my innate Necromancy wouldn't help me here and my innate Geomancy was too weak.

The marshal popped his grape-sized Source in his mouth and swallowed hard. The three remaining soldiers were crowded together, weapons held at the ready and entirely useless against such a monster. The Polasian woman stood behind me, mouth open in shock. I think it's fair to say when she signed on to the expedition, she hadn't been expecting to face literal nightmares. She was ill-prepared. Arex crowded close to me, shield up and sword ready. Of them all, he was the one I wanted to protect. He was next to useless and smelled like garlic all the time, but he was from Wrysom. He was one of my people.

Marshal Araknar raised his hands and shouted. A plume of fire erupted from him, scorching the air as it struck the Abomination. The mound of flesh shuddered as the skin turned black and blistered before sloughing away. Most of the flames skidded off the rubbery flesh, and the central mass of the monster shied away from them, tentacles whipping out at the marshal. He let the fires go out, leapt away just before one of those tentacles could get him.

The Abomination recovered from the flames quickly, reabsorbing the flesh that had been burned from it, and growing new rubbery skin. The fire had worked to a degree, but we would need more if we hoped to beat it.

As far as I was aware, only one person in the history of both worlds had been stupid enough to summon an Abomination. Me. I was twelve years old at the time and had no idea what I was doing. Unfortunately, the tutors had rushed me away before killing the damned thing, so I had no idea what tactics they used. What I do know is that two of my tutors were killed and six more seriously injured, and that one incident caused the Abomination to be banned by every Sourcerer with a drop of sense to them.

I fingered my Sources and considered our options. If I swallowed the Pyromancy Source and joined my flames to the marshal's, we might have enough firepower to beat it back. But we'd need the others to protect us, to survive long enough to protect us.

The Abomination lurched forward, bulbous mass

flopping and squelching in the mud as it rolled further out of the scar toward us all. The marshal let loose another ball of fire at the monster and the flames scorched its skin. A tentacle thrust out at him. Arex ran to the marshal and held his shield high. The tentacle punched through the wooden shield. Arex pulled his arm from the straps just as the tentacle wrenched away, dragging the shield with it. Both tentacle and shield disappeared into the amorphous mass.

Hook Nose was still screaming, Juyi desperately tending him. A true healer, doing all she could regardless of the danger around her. The other three New Picarr guards turned as one and fled down streets, disappearing into the drowned city. I never saw any of them again and a savage part of me hopes the other monsters in the city got them. Fucking cowards! Leaving us there to die like that.

The Abomination rolled towards Hook Nose and Juyi, tentacles questing across the ground. Shine slammed the rim of her shield on one of the tentacles that got too close. The fleshy thing pulled away quickly, but another shot out at the woman. She swung with her shield, batting it away, then darted in, stabbed her spear into the quivering mass of flesh. The point sunk deep, grey ichor spurting from the wound and running in the mud.

A new tentacle formed next to the spear, coiling its way around the haft in an instant. It tugged on the wood, pulling it further into itself and dragging Shine with it. She wasn't quick enough to let go and her hand disappeared into the mass. She screamed in agony, but it was cut short as the Abomination rolled forward again and absorbed her head, shoulders, and chest. Her legs kicked for a few seconds, then went still. The mass convulsed, sucking the rest of Shine into itself inch by inch like a snake swallowing its prey.

Juyi stood, eyes wide and mouth agape. Hook Nose forgotten at her feet. She took a step forward and stumbled over him, falling to her hands and knees in the mud. The Polasian woman rushed to her, hauling Juyi to her feet and dragging her away. The Abomination rolled forward again, tentacles slithering around, eventually finding Hook Nose. He never stopped screaming, even as it pulled him towards its mass, rolled over his body, smothered him in its putrid flesh. Devoured and absorbed.

Everybody was helping but me. The marshal was pelting the Abomination with fire while Arex protected him with rusted steel. Juyi had tried to help Hook Nose. The Polasian woman was dragging Juyi to safety. Shine died protecting them. Even Hook Nose had tried to kill the damned thing. And there I was, standing still, doing nothing but watching. I was as useless as the guards who ran away. No. I was worse. At least they were gone, no longer a burden to the others, someone to protect. I was useless and all because I was too scared to reveal my Source attunements lest the others realise my identity.

Well, enough was enough. Too many had died already because of my cowardice. I would not stand by and do nothing while others fought and died to protect me. I would protect my people, even old garlic breath, Arex.

I snatched the Kinemancy Source from my pouch and popped it into my mouth. It was the size of a pea, small for a Source, and all rough edges. It caught in my throat as I swallowed it down, and I thumped my fist against my chest to help it pass. Power flowed through me. A connection to energy, to movement, sang in my veins. It had been so long since I felt Kinemancy at my control. Too long. Oh, I had missed it. The rightness of it. The power of it.

My power.

I stepped forward and threw a kinetic blast at the
Abomination, the purple rush of energy pummelled it.
The flesh rippled like a slapped beer belly and the monster
rolled on. Of course, my kinetic attack had so little effect,
the Abomination probably weighed as much as a small herd
of abbans. Kinemancy is the magic of kinetic energy and
will always be constrained by the weight and strength of
the Sourcerer as much as the power they can draw from the
Source. Of course, kinetic blasts were also the most basic of
things one can do with Kinemancy and I was far beyond the
basics. I could create weapons of any kind, shields as large as
houses, protective bubbles all but impervious to harm.

A tentacle wormed its way toward me, slithering
through the mud like an eel. It erupted from the muck a few
feet away, darting out to grab me. Arex was there before I
could react, sword swinging. The tentacle fell to the silt and
writhed, already worming its way back to the main mass. I
knew then we couldn't kill this thing by inches. We needed
to finish it in one strike. Marshal Araknar threw another
fireball at the Abomination. The flames burst apart against
its skin, burning it black but then dissipating, the heat
escaping into the air. And suddenly I knew what we had to
do. What I had to do.

I raised my hand and imagined the shape I needed to
create. A spherical bubble around the Abomination, hollow
inside, with a single hole. Then I pushed my Kinemancy into
the shape. The purple haze of energy flowed from me, filling
my creation. A fluted vase of kinetic energy with a writhing
monster at its centre. The Abomination's tentacles slapped
against the walls of its prison, trying to shatter it, and I felt
each blow through my arm like a hammer strike. I could see

the Abomination, through the haze of my kinetic prison. It rolled forward, its bulk leaning against the wall, and my feet slipped in the muck as it pushed me back. I couldn't hold it, couldn't move it. All I had done was restrict its tentacles, but that would last only as long as my strength held out.

I waved my stump at the fluted opening I had created to the prison and growled at the marshal. "Cook it!"

Realisation dawned on the marshal's face, and it looked like that most insidious, hateful of all emotions: hope. He rushed to the fluted opening just as one of the tentacles found it, the whipping, rubbery flesh coiling and slapping about as it explored a possible way out. Too late. Marshal Araknar extended both hands towards the opening and let his fires rage.

The flames rushed into the kinetic prison, turning it into an oven. The Abomination screamed. I hadn't known it could. It didn't seem to have any mouths, but the noise was high, and its panic was unmistakable. It thrashed inside the oven, tentacles battering against the walls even as flames melted its flesh and it cooked in the heat. Still, the marshal funnelled his fires into the oven, and with nowhere to go, the heat flared. I felt pressure build inside the kinetic construct. Even as the Abomination's struggles ceased, fire threatened to explode outward, shattering the oven and taking us all with it.

Marshal Araknar groaned and collapsed, his flames guttering out. He spasmed, muscles twitching, and I saw blood leaking from his nose. Source rejection. He'd drawn too much energy from the Source and it was killing him. He pulled a clump of brown weed from a pouch and shoved it in his mouth. The retching started even as Arex dragged him away through the mud.

Fire still raged inside the oven I had created. Flames spurted through the opening, but the pressure was building. I clutched my fingers, trying to hold on, but I could feel cracks spreading along the surface as the pressure of the heat threatened to shatter my construct. It was going to happen, I couldn't hold it, and when it did, it would explode. The others were safe, Juyi and the Polasian woman hiding inside a nearby building, Arex dragging the retching marshal to join them. Only I would be caught in the blast.

It has not escaped my notice that I always seem to be in the midst of danger. Some say I court it, others that I create it. I think it finds me, is drawn to me. Danger is a pack animal; it seeks more of its kind and refuses to hunt alone.

I raised my withered stump of an arm and forced Kinemancy along it, bolstering the strength of my construct. That hurt! I had never tried to use Kinemancy through my stump before. The muscles were weak, and it felt like being torn apart. A thousand little daggers ripping into my flesh and bone from the inside. With my right hand, I reached inside my robes once more and tore my Source pouch open, grabbing my Pyromancy Source and shoving it in my mouth. A moment later, the oven exploded, and a twisting vortex of fire engulfed me.

CHAPTER
SEVEN

I WAS SIX YEARS OLD WHEN THE TUTORS OF
the Academy of Magic forced Sources down my throat to
test my attunements. I have said it before, and I hold to the
statement now: It was torture. The tutors I should have been
able to trust with my safety, tortured me to learn my limits. I
was just a child. Sirileth was younger.

She wasn't even five years old, yet Sirileth understood
so much about the world. Things I had never taught her
seemed almost second nature to her. She once watched me
preside over a meeting between two merchants. A dispute
had arisen. The first merchant had paid for a stock of rare
spices. The second merchant's caravan had been attacked
by raiders from a neighbouring province at the moment of
exchanging ownership. The raiders had been driven off, but
not before they set fire to the caravan rather than lose their
prize. The first merchant wanted her money back, the second

refused, saying the goods had changed hands.

I hated mediations like this. I was the Corpse Queen, destroyer of empires, and the most feared, reviled, and celebrated woman in all Isha. Yet there I was, forced to decide which idiot merchant got to keep a few worthless hunks of metal.

I ground my teeth and was about to order both merchants to get the hell out of my sight. I was intending to reimburse them the lost coin from my coffers. It seemed fair, I had the money to spare, and what good was it doing sitting down in a vault? Sirileth stepped forward. A young girl who still had trouble pronouncing certain words, wearing a dress stained with mud at the knees. She announced quite clearly that the money would be taken, both merchants suffering the loss, and we would put it towards funding an invasion into the nearby province to wipe out the raiders so such an attack would never happen again. The merchants both looked at me, dumbstruck. I nodded at them, equally dumbstruck. My little four-and-a-half-year-old daughter had just solved a crisis I was too bored to think through.

But that is not the point of this aside. I want to talk about Sourcery. About Sirileth's Sourcery. She followed me everywhere, except for the times she was gone. At first, I took those absences for necessities. Perhaps she needed a nap as children did often and knew her body well enough to take herself off when such exhaustion called. But no.

She had been watching my foster children Tris and Vi. They were wonderful children, trying at times, but full of energy and the will to enjoy life. They were also Sourcerers and, like me, the Iron Legion had experimented on them. He changed them and now they had innate Sourcery running through their veins. I was training them as best I could, the only way I knew how. I tested them with Sources to learn their attunements. I tortured them just as I had been tortured because damn me, but I knew no other way. When the Source rejection started and the cramps and bleeding and pain hit, I used Spiceweed to make them retch up the Sources. I held them in my loving arm until the pain passed, whispered words meant to be comforting. It was the only way I knew how to test them, terrible though it was. Sirileth watched it all.

So, at first, when my daughter started disappearing for longer periods, I took note of her absence but thought nothing of it. Until one day Tamura came to find me. There has always been a very easy tell of Tamura's when something is serious. He doesn't smile. He pulled me aside and said, A fawn running before it walks. Ships with no rudder at the mercy of unscrupulous currents. Then he jogged off, waving at me to follow. I did, of course, I had long since learned that ignoring Tamura was unwise. Partly because to do so was to ignore wisdom, and partly because he had a habit of hitting me with spoons whenever I tried. Don't ask why it was always spoons, nor why the old Aspect always seemed to have at least one on hand.

He led me down into the depths of my palace and I soon realised we were heading to the vault where I kept my Sources. I had amassed a fortune's worth of them and kept them under constant guard. The soldiers nodded at me and stepped aside, and I pulled the door open. Sirileth lay on the floor amidst a pool of bile, groaning softly and clutching her belly. Her darklight eyes met mine and she started crying. I rushed to her side and scooped her up, holding her trembling body to my chest.

My brave, stupid daughter was testing herself.

Torturing herself to learn her attunements. She didn't even know which Sources she was testing herself with, not fully understanding the process. She took Sources at random, swallowed them, then used Spiceweed to throw them back up once the pain started. All on her own. Stupid, stupid, brave, wonderful little girl! She'd learned the guard routines perfectly so she could sneak in as shifts changed. I didn't even know if she was a Sourcerer. To manifest, it needs two bloodlines with Aspects in the ancestry to cross. I didn't know her father, not really. I knew nothing of him, but his name was Reo, he was a bard, he seemed to have more teeth than was normal, and he had been adequate in bed at a time when I needed to feel wanted.

I held Sirileth until her shaking stopped and she dried her eyes on my tunic. My own tears were still fresh when she pulled away and stood before me, her darklight eyes wide and inscrutable. She said, I need to know you'll love me, too. I sobbed. How could she think I didn't love her? That I loved Tris and Vi more because I was training them and not her.

Sirileth was just four and a half years old when I started training her with Sourcery. I hated myself for the torture I put her through, but it was the only way I knew. And I thought it better she went through it with me by her side than on her own. Of course, I was mistaken. I had not the knowledge nor the context to realise that I had misunderstood her words. That came much later.

It had been a long time since I swallowed a Pyromancy Source and felt that fire inside, warming and empowering me. I had no time to revel in the ecstasy of it. I pushed Pyromancy into every bit of me, let it seep from my skin, stoked the fire inside to burn hotter than the flames outside. It protected me, stopped me from burning to ash, kept the heat and rage of the inferno at bay. Of course, it could do nothing about the fire gobbling up the air like a starving hound over a fresh kill. I held my breath and watched the vortex, lit by flashes of lightning from the scar, twist above me. The ground was scorched dry in an instant, burned black and cracked by heat. Flames twisted into the sky and then blew themselves out, their energy spent.

I stumbled from the fiery wreckage and gasped in boiling air. It would have ruined my lungs if not for the Pyromancy coursing through my veins. Patches of the ground still burned. The Abomination, charred beyond anything that could ever resemble living, collapsed in on itself, and became ash blowing on the breeze. No bones to speak of. Nothing left of the towering monster that had almost killed us all, or of the people — our people — it had murdered.

Arex, the marshal, Juyi, and the Polasian woman stared at me from the doorway of the building they had taken refuge in. It was fair to say my secret was out. At least, one of them. They all knew now I was attuned to Kinemancy and Pyromancy.

A gemstone glinted in the baked mud, the light of an Arcmancy strike making it shine blue for a moment. I bent down, wincing at the pain in my knees, and pried it free from the earth. Most gemstones would have cracked under such intense heat, but this was a Source, and they were all but indestructible.

"You dropped this," I said as I hobbled close to the others. My hip ached and my legs were sore from all the walking. I was in terrible shape. I threw the Source through the air and the marshal snatched at it, hissing as it burned his hand. "Sorry about that."

"How?" the Polasian woman asked.

Arex chuckled. "That's our Silva." He broke cover
and walked toward me but pulled up short, holding a hand
before his face to ward it from the heat. "Always full of
surprises. Denma is going to squeal when she hears about
this."

I laughed with him. He was right. Denma loved to
hear stories like this and was always needling me for them. I
will admit, most of the stories I told her over the years I stole
from Tamura.

Drawing on my Pyromancy Source once again, I
pushed away as much excess heat as I could and staggered
forward, wrapping my arm around Arex. He hugged me
back and I was grateful of the contact, regardless of the garlic
smell. He supported me the rest of the way to the building.
I am not too proud to admit I needed it. Even with two
Sources resting in my stomach, I was drained. I hadn't used
power like that since my fight against the Iron Legion twenty
years prior. I was unused to it and, though I hate to admit, a
hell of a lot weaker than I had been then.

"Wow!" Juyi said, shaking her head. "That was...
Thank you." She smiled, but her eyes were shadowed and
red. Whatever Shine had been to her, it was obvious Juyi lost
more than just a guard. Maybe even more than just a friend.

"You were holding out on us," Marshal Araknar
said. "Kinemancy, though like none I've ever seen, and I'm
guessing Pyromancy to survive that." He narrowed his eyes.
"That's five attunements by my count."

Even at the height of the Orran-Terrelan war,
with recruiters from both sides searching out powerful
Sourcerers, it was rare to find one of us with more than two

or three attunements. He knew that, and I wondered if he'd already put the pieces together. I hoped he never would. But then, fuck hope. If there is any more hateful and insidious emotion, I don't know it. Hope crawls inside and nestles deep, a tumour growing inside a person's heart. It convinces you to trust to that most inane concept: luck. Hope is the denial of reason, the willingness to blind oneself to the truth no matter how obvious. I have hoped for too many things in my life and that hope betrays me every time. Apparently, I am unwilling to learn my lesson.

The marshal smiled and extended a trembling hand smeared with his own blood. "We make a good team, Silva of Wrysom." His words were warm enough, but his voice was glacial.

I took his hand. Friendship, given freely and honestly, is something you should never turn down.

Thirteen of us entered the drowned city of Lorn, and only five of us walked out. We made better time, striking out to the closest side of the city and climbing up the muddy banks to the shore where we had left the abbans. I used my innate Geomancy to help us, firming the ground beneath our feet. We reached the bank just as the sun dipped over the horizon and night gripped hold of Isha. The city came alive once more, perhaps even more vibrantly now that its most dangerous predator was dead. We did not close the scar, I'm not even certain such a thing was possible, nor did we deal with all the monsters that had crossed over from the Other World. But we had solved part of the mystery. We knew what had killed the villagers, and we also knew that we would need an army to hunt the monsters down and wipe them out. Better to warn the villagers and let them protect themselves.

The journey home was a much more sombre affair, though I admit I found it more comfortable. We had three abbans between five of us, so had space and rations to spare. Talk was rare, and Arex did most of it for all of us. The marshal was quiet and contemplative, both Juyi and the Polasian woman were thick with grief. I was comfortable enough inside my own head.

I have never liked being alone, I still don't. It is a unique torture. Left alone, my thoughts assail me, my doubts and fears, my guilt and grief. I replay my memories, both old and new, in my head and analyse them, critiquing my actions and seeing better ways I could have acted if I had just not been so... me. It was better since leaving my old life behind and settling in Wrysom. I was better. I had gotten used to being alone and coping with my traitorous thoughts. Somewhat. Better and good are two wildly different states of mind.

When we reached New Picarr, the marshal offered us the chance to stay in the tavern again, but Arex and I declined. We were both eager to get home. I wanted my own space, my own little yurt. I wanted the option to be myself again, even if it was only briefly and in private. I struggled with being someone else. The mask I wore was ill-fitting and came with too many sharp edges. The marshal smiled and said he understood, and he would follow in a day or two to bring back the abban.

When Wrysom appeared on the horizon, the tents jutting out from the earth in colourful swirls, I felt my heart lurch and my shoulders slump. Relief washed over me, and I could not keep the smile from my wrinkled face. I had been gone less than ten days, but it felt like an age.

Denma and her cadre of little savages were the

first to spot us and the girl charged us, shouting a myriad of questions. I cupped my hand to my ear and claimed I couldn't hear her, causing her to shout even louder. When I pulled the same trick a second time, she leapt onto one of the abban's legs and started climbing its fur. The beast sighed dramatically and plodded on, resigned to the annoyance.

By the time we stopped the abban to let the poor beast graze and slid from its back, the rest of the village was there to greet us. We were welcomed like heroes even before we told them our story. Tsera flung her arms around me and hugged me tight. She wrinkled her nose when she pulled away and complained about the smell, but I couldn't exactly blame her for that. Besides, I wouldn't have the woman any other way. Arex and I walked into Wrysom amidst a crowd of excited chatter, wild questions, and claims of a celebration to be thrown in our honour.

My face ached from smiling by the time we reached our little village square where the communal campfire cooked stew all day. It was there my smile died when I saw who was waiting for me.

CHAPTER EIGHT

"I FORGOT TO TELL YOU," TSERA SAID AS SHE guided little Denma out of the way, leading me to a seat at the campfire. "A couple days after you left, your daughter turned up. We put her in your yurt, I hope you don't mind."

"Heya!" Imiko waved at me from across the campfire. Her grin was wide and wild. The low flames bounced off her burning ember hair and made the rash of freckles across her nose and cheeks stand out. She was wearing loose brown trousers and a tunic to match, a dark jacket over the top, and a black cloak hanging from her shoulders.

I ignored the press of the crowd and stalked around the fire, picked out a chair next to Imiko and flopped down onto it. Tsera opened her mouth to say something, but Cona the cook pulled her away with some questions. For a few moments, Imiko and I were alone in a crowd.

"Daughter?" I asked quietly.

Imiko shrugged. "You got old." She paused and smiled again. "I didn't think sister would sound truthful."

"Bah!" I was glad to see her, yes, but at the same time an ill feeling filled my stomach. It was like drinking curdled milk. "What are you doing here?"

Before she could answer, Grek slid onto the bench beside Imiko. His shirt was already off, of course, and his dark skin glistened with sweat. He grinned at Imiko. "Silva, you never told me you had such a beautiful daughter." He said, his gaze locked on her.

"Oh, stop it, Grek," Imiko said, rolling her eyes playfully. She placed a hand on his bare chest and gave him a light push that he leaned into. "I keep telling you, I'm happily married."

Grek finally tore his eyes away from her and threw his hands up. "All the good ones are."

Imiko glanced at me, and I mouthed married? at her. She pulled an incredulous face and snorted. Of course, she wasn't. This was all a game to her, an act. She turned up at my new home, and was playing a part, disrupting everything I had built for myself. Besides, Imiko was many things, but she wasn't the settling down type. When I left Yenheim, she had been the head of a criminal organisation that spread into four of the neighbouring provinces. Over a few bottles of wine, she once said to me Sex is wonderful, but who has time for relationships? They're all mess and misunderstanding and changing yourself to fit into someone else's space. Or changing yourself so someone fits into your space. And let's not forget the tears when you tell them it's time they looked for someone else's life to clutter up. No, fuck relationships. A bit of slap and squelch occasionally is all I have time for, what with keeping your empire afloat.

She made a good show of it, too, but I always thought she was hiding rather than risk the pain. But that was Imiko, always guarded, always on the run, and just when you needed her most, she'd vanish.

My celebrated return was muted after that. The village made a show of it with whiskey and wine and food, a small fortune for our little settlement. I took part where I could, but I struggled to enjoy it. Imiko had found me, and I doubted anything good would come of it. I had left Yenheim for a good reason. I left behind my name for a good reason too. I couldn't shake the feeling it was all about to come crashing down around me, and she'd be the cause. And yet, I wanted to pull her aside and talk to her so badly. I wanted to know why she was there, yes, but I also wanted to know how things were back in Yenheim. How were Hardt and Tamura? How was Josef? Was the little queendom I started still thriving? And, of course, how were my children? Sirileth would be nearing twenty years old now. Perhaps she even had a family of her own. Questions burned inside of me and every moment I spent grinding my teeth in that celebration was an eternity.

The sun had set, and the children herded off to bed by the time I managed to make my excuses and pull my daughter away for a private chat. We each took a clay cup of whiskey and sauntered off into the night. Grass flattened beneath our feet and the wind whispered in our ears, but Imiko and I were silent until we were far enough away from Wrysom that our voices wouldn't carry no matter how loudly we screamed at each other. The tension that built between us was so dense I could have beaten the thief with it.

"What are you doing here, Imiko?" I snapped. It was

not how I'd wanted to start this conversation, but it was
damned sure the most pressing question on my mind.

Imiko chuckled drunkenly, shaking her head, tousled
red hair flying like embers. She'd had twice as much to drink
as me and I wasn't entirely sober. "It's good to see you too,
Eska. Sorry. Sorry. Silva." She stared at me, eyes sharp as
daggers. "You know how messed up that is, right? Naming
yourself after your dead lover who you murdered! It's really
fucked up, Eska."

I scoffed. "Yes, thank you. I'm well aware how fucked
up it is. Why are you here? How did you find me?"

"Oh, you think the great Eskara Helsene is a master
of deception? There's no way simple Imiko could ever find
her." Imiko kicked at the grass, hit a small mound, stumbled,
and made a show of steadying her drink. "I had people out
looking for you the moment you ran away. I've known you
were here for over a year."

"And you didn't come and see me before. Which
brings me back to the question of why now? What are you
doing here, Imiko?"

She raised her eyes and glared at me, an anger I had
never seen from her before. Fury and resentment and grief
all rolled into a heady concoction and left to stew for most
of a decade. "Why did you leave, Eska? Why run away and
leave me holding the reins of your queendom?" She shook
her head. "Why the fuck did you leave me to raise your
daughter?"

And suddenly I knew what the visit was about.
"What did Sirileth do?" I asked.

Imiko deflated. "Believe it or not, this wasn't how I
wanted this to go." She shook her arms out one at a time,
bounced in place a couple of times, and then looked at me

with a grin on her lips and eyes that sparkled with mischief. So easily she wiped away the past, dusted all our dirt under the rug then set fire to the house for good measure.

"Let's start again," she said cheerfully. "I really did miss you, Eska. Despite, you know, everything."

The change in subject rankled me. This visit was about Sirileth, and now that I knew that, all other matters fell away. I needed to know what she had done, or maybe what had happened to her. You may have noticed this, but patience is not one of my strongest traits. It's barely one of my traits at all, in truth. My entire life, friends have called me impulsive, lovers have insisted I'm over eager, and enemies have happily showered me with evil laughter for walking brashly into their traps. Patience can fuck off. More often than not, it's just an excuse to painfully draw things out. Still, I was old now, and all my life I was reliably informed that age brings wisdom and patience and a bunch of other useless things we tend to ignore in the fires of our youth. Maybe it was supposed to be the trade-off for all the aches, pains, and shrinking bladders that age bestows upon us. I decided to practice some of that vaunted patience, assuming Imiko wouldn't be wasting time if matters were as urgent as I feared.

"I missed you too, Imiko." We started walking, a pleasant evening stroll of two old friends. Our moons, Lokar and Lursa, stared down at us. I could plainly see the faults and cracks on their surfaces as the two moons ground into each other. Neither was dominant today and they shone with blue and red light that mixed to an ethereal violet haze.

"How is everyone?" I sipped on my whiskey, finished it, wished I had more.

Imiko shrugged as she skipped along beside me.

"Much the same. Much different. Hardt got married." She glanced at me out of the corner of her eye, but I refused to show the surprise I felt.

"It's probably about time."

"Oh, too right there." Imiko snorted. "The moment he stopped chasing you around, he realised every woman in Yenheim got a bit moist whenever he walked past. A year later, he was married. Beff is an annoying bitch, make no mistake. I hate her. I really hate her. Far more than I ever hated you. She walks about the palace like she bloody well owns it and gives orders to everyone. Even me. Even Siri." That stare out of the corner of her eye again, a smile that graced her lips but reached no further. Imiko was enjoying drawing this out. "He has a couple of kids now. Two boys, Tam and Sen, run around terrorising the place just like Vi and Tris used to."

The thought of Hardt with kids made me smile. He had always been so good with my children. We had only known my first daughter, Kento, for a few days, but Hardt had loved her so fiercely. He was Tris and Vi's fun uncle who taught them how to fish the ponds and throw punches. And he had the patience of a boulder with Sirileth. Perhaps that was why she allowed Hardt — and no one else — to brush her hair. He kept trying when everyone else gave up on her. "What about Tamura?"

"Happy as a garn in a mud pool," Imiko said. She quaffed the last mouthful of her whiskey and made to throw the clay cup away. I took it from her and pocketed it with my own. There was no sense in wasting a perfectly serviceable cup. "He quit as advisor to the crown a few years back and took up with a troop. They tour all the taverns in Yenheim and our neighbours. Bards sing, Tamura tells stories, some

The pieces fell into place and my stomach turned so violently bile rose in my throat. Lake Lorn. The scar caused by a Sourcerer going through catastrophic rejection. Sirileth. The ground shifted beneath me, and I fell on my arse. Imiko wasn't fast enough to catch me, but she was on her knees in the grass a moment later, a steadying hand on my shoulder. I'll skip ahead with the story, as I admit I may have babbled quite a bit, but I got the story of Lake Lorn across, and my suspicion of what, and now who, had caused the scar.

Imiko shook her head, looking oddly guilty. "It wasn't Sirileth," she said once I'd finished my story and laid out my suspicion. "Well, that's not entirely true. I don't doubt she did it, but it wasn't her."

"What?"

Imiko lay back in the grass and threw an arm across her face. "You're not going to like this, Eska."

"I like the suspense less, I assure you."

"About a year ago, a Polasian prince by the name of Jamad al Rahal came calling. Apparently, he'd been sent by his mother because Sirileth was still unmarried."

The idea of anyone, much less a prince of a foreign land, courting my daughter made me feel strange. Pride mostly, I think. Also, shame. I had never discussed the matters of love or lust with Sirileth, and now I had to hope she hadn't fallen as foul of both as I had.

"Jamad wasn't like most Polasian men," Imiko continued, her arm still covering her eyes. "For a start, he could talk without asking permission from a woman. Still wore one of those veils over his mouth though. Makes you wonder if there's something wrong with their teeth."

"Imiko," I said, putting as much warning into my voice as possible. "Are you trying to tell me my daughter is married?"

Imiko flung her arms wide and barked out a laugh. "Lursa's Tears no, Eska! The prince definitely tried to get between her sheets and believe me he wasn't the first. But Sirileth isn't like you. She doesn't fall head over heels for every bad choice who bats her eyelids at you. She's got a heart of stone. Never shown the slightest interest in any men like that." Imiko winked at me. "Or women."

"Get to the point, Imiko."

"Right. Well, I'm pretty certain she never dropped her trousers for the prince, but they did spend a lot of time talking. A lot of time. So much, I honestly started to wonder if they were in love. I figured it couldn't hurt, might even mellow Siri out a bit, but I was suspicious so I had some of my people follow them and listen to their conversations. They weren't whispering sweet nothings, Eska. Sirileth was interrogating the prince, dragging out everything he knew about Sourcery."

"What does that have to do with rejection?" I was eager for her to get to part that proved my daughter hadn't detonated herself and died alone in the middle of a lake.

"Well, one of the things the prince told Sirileth was the queen of Polasia's garden. They call it the Penitent Garden."

I'd heard of it, an expansive and lush garden full of trees and flowers and fountains. In a land where sand was plentiful and fresh water was not, it was an extreme extravagance. "It's full of stone statues of people in penitent poses or in pain," I said. I'd been to Polasia a few times, but I'd never seen the gardens. Then again, the queen didn't much like me and was unlikely to invite me to see her fancy project of green foliage and well-placed rocks.

Imiko sat up and shook her head at me, eyes wide. "This is where it gets unpleasant. They're not statues." Her gaze flicked to my stump. The last of the stone had long since fallen away, but we both remembered how I had lost the arm.

"Geomancy rejection," I said immediately. "They're people the queen had turned to stone?"

Imiko nodded, screwing up her face in disgust. "Those who betray the queen of Polasia are made to swallow a Geomancy Source. Once they're turned to stone, the Sources are dug out of their stomachs, and they're left as statues. Warnings to all those who might do the same thing. And probably a pleasant reminder to the queen of their suffering because she's a sick fucker who enjoys that sort of thing."

I raised an eyebrow at that. Imiko caught it and shook her head. "We've had some dealings over the years. That bitch scares me almost as much as you do. Anyway, not long after Jamad told Sirileth about the garden, she sent him away with his cock as dry as his desert. But she started experimenting with Source rejection." Imiko shivered visibly. "She started with criminals we'd normally execute anyway. Murderers and such. But instead of an axe to the neck or a dagger in the heart, the traditional way, she started making them swallow Sources and observing the rejection. She had a little notebook with all sorts of things like type of Source and what it did to a person, how long it took them to die, what was left of them afterwards."

"She made her own penitent garden?" I couldn't keep the anger from my voice. I had left Sirileth in Imiko's care and she let my daughter become a monster.

Imiko shook her head again, frowning and

exasperated. "No. She didn't seem to care once they were gone. It wasn't about torturing them for punishment. She was just curious. Soon, it wasn't enough to wait for criminals to get themselves caught. Sirileth had volunteers, and by now you can do the guessing of what she did to them."

"Volunteers?" I couldn't keep the surprise from my voice. "To die painfully and horrifically of Source rejection?"

Imiko pinched the bridge of her nose and let out an explosive sigh. For just a moment, I saw past the paint and powder to the woman beneath. She looked tired. Then she sniffed, blinked, and her mask was back in place. "She's good at finding people who… Who want to die, I guess. Who want the pain to end."

The call of the void. That insidious voice in my head whispering at me to kill myself and find a final, blissful peace of nothing. Yes, I understood that well.

Imiko shivered. "Sirileth finds them and offers them more than just an end though, she offers to give their end meaning." She shook her head.

"So I'm pretty certain it wasn't Sirileth who detonated and took Lake Lorn with her. However, I'm just as certain she made it happen." Imiko was staring at me hard now. All signs of her usual mischief were gone, and there was a haggard look in their place. The tired eyes and well-worn lines beneath them were back. "She's up to something, Eska, and…" She paused and shook her head. "I love Siri, I do. I love her and I tried my best to raise her after you ran off and left us all. But…"

I sighed. "Too much of her mother in her." The words tasted bitter and all too true on my lips.

Imiko nodded. "Too much of you and not enough restraint. If you can fucking believe that." I couldn't fault her the words. We had both seen what I was capable of when I left restraint behind. We had both lost people we loved because of it.

There didn't seem to be much to say after that. Well, that's not true. We could have chatted the night away and barely scratched the surface, but neither of us wanted it. I knew the real reason why Imiko had come to Wrysom now. She wanted me to take the responsibility off her hands. To track down Sirileth and stop her before she did... whatever it was my daughter had in her mind to do. I didn't want to do it. Imiko wanted to hand the responsibility off, and the truth was it wasn't her responsibility in the first place. It should always have been mine. But I didn't want to leave. I had a life in Wrysom. I was happy for the first time in so long.

We walked back to my yurt in silence and I argued with myself. By the time I fell asleep, I had made my decision. Whatever Sirileth was doing, she was old enough to make her own mistakes. Just as I had when I was her age. It was not my problem, and I was not about to leave my happy little village to spend the last years of my life trying to fix someone else's mess. No, I would leave her to it, whatever it was. Besides, how bad could it be? It wasn't like she was going to destroy the world.

CHAPTER NINE

WHEN I WOKE THE NEXT MORNING, IMIKO WAS gone. The sun shone arrogantly through the front flap of my yurt, and I knew I was alone. There was a comfort in that. Not in being alone. I missed the feel of a body next to me, of the sure knowledge that there would be noise outside of the harping in my own head. It took me a long time to realise that, in truth, it wasn't being alone that I hated, but being alone with myself. The comforting thing was that Imiko had gone without saying a word. Despite all the years and all the trials, despite everything it had carved away from her the world had never taken that from my little sister. She always loved to slip away, vanish without a trace, and she tended to appear in much the same fashion. I have said many times that I hate that about her, but envy and hate are often mistaken.

I threw my poncho over my shoulders and levered

myself back to my feet. My thighs burned. It's always amazed me how a body can endure so much while balanced on the edge of collapse, but the moment you get home and relax, everything you put your aching bones through comes crashing down like a moon shower. I hurt everywhere.

I was most of the way to the tent flap when I paused and looked back. My pouch of Sources was a vague, barely noticeable bump from underneath my pillow. I spent a few long seconds staring. I had gotten used to leaving my Sources here. While in Wrysom, I got by with using only my innate Geomancy, even as weak as it was. My friends in the village didn't even know I was attuned to anything else. I'm not sure they understood what attunement was. But at Lorn, I had swallowed two of my Sources and felt the power inside, the connection to movement and fire, and it felt good. It felt right. I missed it. I wanted it. And why shouldn't I? Sourcery was part of what made me. To deny it was to deny myself. Which, of course, is exactly what I had been doing for the better part of a decade.

I waddled back to my pillow, kicked it aside, and plucked my Source pouch from the floor. Two Sources, Kinemancy and Pyromancy. My eyes slid sideways to the corner of my yurt, and I glanced about to make sure the tent flap was still down. No one was watching. I hurried to the corner, pulled back the floor mat and dug up a handful of dirt until my fingers found a small stone no larger than a prune. I rubbed my fingers over it, then popped it in my mouth to suck the dirt off. A pleasant tingle touched my tongue, and I felt my heart quicken. The desire to swallow it, to reignite the storm inside of me was overpowering. My Arcmancy Source, buried but never forgotten. If I swallowed it, the storm would rage once more. My eyes would flash with distant lightning, and there would be no denying who I was. I snatched the Source from my mouth, dropped it in the pouch with the other two Sources, and tucked the pouch into my belt. It felt good knowing they were close.

Pushing through the tent flap into the morning sun, I grinned and stretched out my arm. My little adventure was over, and it was time to get back to my life of obscurity.

Oh, how nice it would be to end my tale there. But, of course, we all know that's about as likely as our gods apologising for any of the shit they've pulled over the years. I have long since learned that gods don't apologise for anything. Even when you bring them to their knees and threaten them with annihilation. Obnoxious bastards, one and all.

Imiko had not left. Instead, she was causing quite a stir in my little village. For a start, she was blatantly flirting with Atanial. She had a hand on his chest, threw back her head in that horribly false way of laughing that tousled her hair and exposed her long, pale neck, and then snorted. Most people sound like pigs when they snort, but Imiko has always had this way of doing it that was adorable. It clearly had the desired effect as Atanial grinned like a wolf over a fresh catch. Mira, the young woman who had been all but throwing herself at Atanial daily since they were children, sat beside her wash bucket and glared with enough force that even I was impressed. Meanwhile, Grek had his shirt on, which was never a good sign. He was busy hauling wooden logs for chopping and sending pained glances Imiko's way like a puppy abandoned by its owner in favour of a younger puppy. Unrequited love is like a freshly plucked rose; beautiful to witness from afar, but if you hold it wrong you're likely to get stabbed by a little prick.

I ambled over to the cook pot and sat on a log with a groan. Tsera approached and spooned some leftover stew into a bowl, then handed it to me. "Your daughter is..."

"Turning my life inside out," I growled. I spared Tsera a glance and saw her frowning over toward Imiko. "She's doing it on purpose."

"Why?"

"Because she wants me to leave with her and figures the best way to convince me is to ruin my life here." I closed my eyes and would have buried my head in my hands, but I only had the one and it was currently holding a bowl of stew.

"Silva," Tsera said, her voice calm but firm as worked iron. "Make her stop. I don't enjoy expelling people from the village, but everyone can see she's looking to cause trouble." She paused and sighed. "Everyone but Atanial, anyway. That boy can't think of anything past getting his tip wet."

I opened my eyes and put my bowl of stew down, finally meeting Tsera's cool stare. "She's leaving today," I said. "I'll make sure of it."

I considered a few different approaches to the conversation as I made my way towards Imiko, but in the end, I settled on brusque, angry, and commanding. When in doubt, go with what you know best. "Atanial," I snapped. "That's my daughter you're trying to seduce. Fuck off."

The boy went pale, which was impressive given his dark colouring, then ran away fast as a hare out of a trap. Imiko watched him go, then turned to me with a mocking smile.

"You're not welcome here anymore, Imiko," I said.

Her smile fell and her visage of youth dropped with it. Suddenly, Imiko looked every year of her middle age.

I noticed wrinkles at the corner of her eyes, her neck too. "You're really gonna stay? Going to let me find Sirileth on my own?"

"She's old enough to look after herself, Imiko."

Imiko snorted. Not the adorable type, but the angry one. "Siri didn't run off to have some alone time, nor is she chasing after a wet crotch. Nor, apparently, is she looking for you." She looked around to find most of the village had stopped to stare at us. They probably couldn't hear us, but even so. "She's driven, Silva. I don't know by what, but whatever Siri has planned..." She paused again. "She got worse since you left. A lot worse."

"What's the worst she can do?" I said, desperately trying to wallow in my ignorance.

"Beyond getting herself hurt, you mean?" Imiko asked. She frowned at something behind me. "You might not care about her anymore, Eska, but I do."

"That's not fair." I hissed. I heard heavy boots on the ground behind me. Heard some of my friends start whispering and this time, it wasn't about me.

"Besides," Imiko continued, still staring past me. "You want to know the worst she might do? Ask yourself, what was the worst thing you almost did. I clearly remember an army of monsters and you set on using them to slaughter an entire empire." I remembered that too. I remembered Imiko pulling me from the brink before it was too late. But Imiko wasn't with Sirileth now, so who would pull my daughter back?

"Marshal," I heard Tsera say. "What's going on?"

I turned away from Imiko then, a sinking feeling worming its way through my gut. It felt like the sky darkened, like Lursa's Tears were threatening to rain down upon us and destroy everything I knew, everything I had worked for, everything I had made for myself here. Marshal Araknar had come back to Wrysom, and I already knew he wasn't there to collect his abban. He had a host of soldiers at his back, all armoured, and I could guess the three people at his side were fellow Sourcerers. They had that feel about them. It is a strange thing, but sometimes you can tell just by looking at a person. It's in the way they stand, apart, aloof, and secure in their power. It's in the way they look at you, measuring you up for what you might be capable of, comparing it to what they already knew they could do.

"Shit," I said the word quietly enough only Imiko heard it over the clamour. My suspicions were only confirmed when I went to meet the marshal and his entourage near the centre of Wrysom. I saw the way the soldiers at his back nervously shifted. It was impossible to miss the Sourcerers flexing their fingers, preparing to draw on their power. Beneath my poncho, I found my own Source pouch and gave it a reassuring squeeze.

The marshal stared at me. Gone were the smiles from a few days before. The companionable jokes shared between two people who had relied upon each other to survive the worst situation imaginable. Marshal Araknar stared at me with eyes like steel and his jaw writhed beneath his perfectly groomed beard. He opened his mouth to speak, so I cut him off rather than cede him that power.

"Don't do it, marshal," I said. "Please." I can count on my fingers, and I remind you I only have the one hand, the number of times in my life I have said please. Some people throw it around so much it loses all meaning. But not me. I use it so rarely it retains its weight and power. Please. It is not any mere request; it is a plea. It is begging, and I hate to beg.

"They deserve to know," the marshal said sharply. He tore his gaze from mine and swept it over the villagers like a shepherd over his milling flock, making sure none had strayed. "They all deserve to know the monster they have been harbouring." And then returned that spiteful gaze to me. "And you deserve to pay for your crimes, Eskara Helsene."

His words hit me far harder than any punch and believe me, I have been punched by some very strong men. I staggered from the blow into a silence that sounded as loud as thunder. Tears stung my eyes and I closed them to await the coming storm in darkness.

"Don't be stupid, man. That's Silva." I knew that voice. Po, the village guard I had taught to read and write and nursed back to health when she'd been savaged by a feral cat. I could have kissed her for sticking up for me.

"Aye, it's a load of crap." That was Onaron who had barely been more than a boy when I met him, covered in dirt and proudly declaring he would be a soldier one day. I taught him to read. Now he was a teacher, a lover of books, and dedicated to passing his knowledge on to the village children. "Lots of people only have one arm."

"Who's Eskra?" A child's voice. Yory, who I had helped deliver into the world.

"The Corpse Queen," said Yory's mother, Dory, who might have died giving birth if not for me.

Yory gasped loud enough for me to hear.

"You can't just go around accusing people of that," said Cory, Wrysom's trader. We'd shared many a bottle of whiskey over the years, and shared stories too, though most of mine had been untrue. "You need proof."

"I saw her use fire and other Sourceries. Never seen anything like it." That came from Arex. So quickly do opinions turn. Only a few words exist between freedom and the noose.

"I knew it!" This from little Denma, her voice balanced between victory and fear. "Didn't I say it? Been saying it all along."

"She's always been odd. Remember when she turned up out of nowhere? Dark storm that night." I knew that voice too. Hershan, who I'd treated for the crotch itch more times than I cared to remember. I never told a damned soul about the affliction.

"What about last year when poor Terron died," said Bera, the first person I taught to read when I arrived in Wrysom. "Strange circumstances, that death. She was the last person to see him alive."

"Silva?" Tsera's voice, cutting through all the others.

"Sorry, Eska," Imiko whispered from close behind. I took comfort in that. Despite everything that was about to happen. Despite everything that I had put her through and all the years between us, Imiko stood at my back.

I opened my eyes to the sight of my tribunal. All the villagers of Wrysom gathered around. Some clutched knives, sticks, whatever they could find that might pass as a weapon. Some kissed fingers and pointed towards the moons, barely visible in the morning light, a foolish prayer for protection that had sprung up over the last decade. Marshal Araknar and his entourage were more confident now. I saw it in their posture, the squared shoulders and raised chins, the hands that didn't tremble on the weapons they held. And then there was Tsera. The leader of our little village, one of the most competent people I have ever known, and for the past few years, my closest friend. She stared at me with steely eyes and crossed arms. Closed. Guarded.

"Is it true, Silva?" Tsera asked. It did not escape my notice she still used my assumed name. She was giving me a chance to argue my case, to fight for my innocence. Well, that would be pointless. Even if I could somehow convince her, convince them all, the accusation would follow me the rest of my life. The people of Wrysom, my friends, would never look at me the same. They would always be suspicious. A decade of trust, of friendship, of love and laughter were broken with two words. My name had that power.

There was no fighting what the marshal had started here. There was no innocence to be claimed. The only kindness I could show those I had come to care for, was to make what had to be done easier on them.

All communities are a toxic geyser just waiting to erupt. To spray molten anger and hate over anyone who deviates from the accepted behavioural norm. You might be welcomed into the community, even loved within it, but all it takes is a single misstep to turn you from paragon to pariah. The end goal of any community is enforced conformity. Not by physical coercion, but by social exorcism. They wanted to oust Eskara Helsene. Then I would show them the Corpse Queen they so feared.

I turned around to face Imiko and she gave me a sorry smile that I appreciated. She might have been trying to get me to leave Wrysom and follow her, but I knew she would never betray my secret like this. I worked my hand into my Source pouch and found the one I was looking for, still damp from my saliva. "I hope you're packed." I popped the Source into my mouth and turned back to face the villagers

of Wrysom, my friends, and the idiot who thought he could
arrest me.

I swallowed the Arcmancy Source. How to describe
that feeling? It was as though my arm had been tied behind
my back and finally it was free. Like I had been wandering
the world with my eyes shut, and now they were open.
Dying of thirst and then finding a river. The Arcstorm, so
long dormant, raged to life inside of me. My eyes flashed
like a storm at sea. Lightning ripped free of my body and
coursed burning trails through the ground around me. Dust
particles charged by the shocks rose into the air, floating and
sparking off each other. There was something else too. More
than lightning striking around me and flashing behind my
eyes. More than the power flowing through me, ready to be
thrown forth from my fingertips. Intense anger filled me. A
restless rage like a caged animal just waiting to be set free
and wreak its vengeance upon those who had caged it, and
upon the world for allowing cages to exist.

I do not exaggerate when I say it took an immense
act of will to gain control of that incandescent rage and
the storm that fuelled it. I wanted to destroy everything.
Wrysom, its people, the land, Isha, the world. I wanted it all
to pay for the atrocity of existing. It would all burn by my
hand.

But it wasn't my anger. It was not even terran anger.
It was the anger of a dead god. The Djinn who had died and
become a Source. Its rage threatened to undo me and lay
waste to everything through me, but I would not let it. I have
made a habit of defying our wretched gods, and I wasn't
about to stop now. I intended to spare the people of Wrysom
their guilt for evicting me, not destroy them for it.

My show had the intended effect. The villagers who

had so recently called me friend, sat with me, learned from me, drank with me, and welcomed me now recoiled. I saw fear on their faces, disgust too, maybe some shame. After all, they had been living with the continent's most feared criminal for years. The bogeywoman was right under their noses, next to where they slept and played with their children. They were right to be scared and disgusted. It hurt. Like icy daggers digging into my chest, searching my withered heart, it hurt. It didn't take long for that fear to turn to anger. Well, it was still fear, but anger is an easy mask to wear. That anger quickly led to insults, all thrown from the relative safety of not being the closest person to the monster.

"Still want to arrest me, marshal?" I asked as I approached him. I did not hear Imiko behind me and was fairly certain if I glanced over my shoulder, she would be gone. Disappeared in the midst of a raging crowd had always been a particular skill of hers. Everyone was usually staring at me, which helped.

"I should." He scanned around at the villagers of Wrysom as if realising for the first time he had created a mob that could easily spiral out of control.

"But do you think you could?" I asked, smiling viciously at him. The other two Sourcerers he'd brought stepped back. I have played more games of cards, dice, and chance over the years than I can count, and I have learned to read faces quite well. Those two fools were done. Their own fear betrayed the bluff the marshal had been betting on.

"No further!" the marshal snapped. He raised his hand and fire burst to life in his palm.

I laughed. I was starting to enjoy the theatre of it. "Or what?" Another step closer, lightning arced from my body and tore furrows in the ground between us. The people of Wrysom watched, still screaming their hatred for me. "Funny thing about Arcmancy, Marshal. It can be used to block Sourcery. It's far more efficient to fight fire with fire, but at a pinch, it turns out lightning works pretty fucking well."

The marshal stepped back now. His bravado was broken, his bluff called. I would find no fight here, and that was for the best. "Tell me something. Why now? You must have known who I was back in Lorn. You could have tried to arrest me at New Picarr with a larger force, but you wait until I get back home. Why?"

Marshal Araknar cleared his throat and glanced around as if searching for help and knowing it wouldn't come. We stood on a knife's edge with bloody violence on either side and neither of us wanted to fall. "I had suspicions. But it wasn't until I got back to my office that I found the reports I needed. You were spotted in Old Picarr not twenty days ago, poking around the scar there."

My heart beat a little faster. "Was I?"

"I dismissed it at first." He swallowed hard and took another step back. I followed, claiming the ground he surrendered. "Reports of Corpse Queen sightings aren't unusual. But three people said they spotted you around the scar. It's the eyes, they recognised. Weird eyes."

"Weird?"

"Lit from within."

"Fuck!" Imiko was right. I knew of just two people in the world who had eyes lit from within and I was one of them. The other was Sirileth. She had been here. Poking around the scar in Old Picarr where the Iron Legion had detonated so long ago. Why?

"My scout was waiting for me back in New Picarr

too," the marshal continued. Now that his tongue had loosened there was no stopping it. I love it when people give up their information so easily. So much more pleasant than torturing it out of them. "He saw you leave the crater."

"Did he?"

"That's why I hadn't heard from him for almost a week. He followed you North on the road to Lanfall."

Perhaps I was in better shape than I realised, if I had done all that while also dozing my life away in my sleepy little village. "I see. And I assume I laid siege to the city when I arrived," I said. "And then somehow reappeared here to wait for you. Wherein I agreed to help you investigate the same scar I apparently created. Tell me something, Marshal. Do you have to work hard to be such an idiot, or does it come naturally? I imagine stupidity like yours takes years of training."

Speaking of idiocy, I'm a little guilty there myself. Take it from me, when someone is willingly spilling everything they know, don't belittle them. Just let them go. At my insults, the marshal promptly shut his mouth and I had a feeling I wouldn't get more from him. But I had enough. Sirileth had been here. She had come to Old Picarr and whatever her reason, it had something to do with the scar. She had been the one to drain Lake Lorn and open a new scar in the world. And then she had gone north to Lanfall. But if that was weeks ago, then she could be anywhere by now.

"Thank you, Marshal Araknar," I said with a mocking bow that I immediately regretted thanks to my aching back. "As you can now see, you have the wrong culprit, but at least you successfully identified the Corpse Queen. Thank for you for ruining my pleasant little life here, I shall be sure

to remember you." The marshal blanched at that. I didn't
care. I was done with the fool. I was done with all of them
now, I supposed. My chest ached at the thought, and for a
moment I wished I could turn it all back and continue my
quiet life. But time never flows backwards.

I could have made a dramatic exit. Threatened
them all to ensure they felt justified in their eviction of me.
Maybe even showered them with a traditionally evil laugh.
I could have played the part of the villain most of the world
believed me to be. But what would be the point? I was
suddenly tired of it all. I retreated to my yurt, my home
for the better part of a decade and packed up my meagre
belongings, surprised at how little I had gathered that I truly
cared to keep. Then I set fire to the yurt and walked away, all
to the jeers of those who had once welcomed me.

I didn't know where I was going. I had no destination
or direction in mind. I couldn't even see the path ahead for
the tears in my eyes. Imiko soon joined me though, suddenly
walking by my side as though she had always been there.
Once we were out of sight of Wrysom, she put an arm across
my shoulders, and I finally let my tears fall.

It had all come crashing down around me again.
Everything I touched withered and died. Everything I loved
I corrupted with anger and hate.

I've heard it said there is a power in names that goes
beyond the letters that form them. It goes beyond even
the meaning. I never really understood it until that day. I
built a life for myself in Wrysom. Years of friendships and
memories. All destroyed with two simple words: Eskara
Helsene. Therein lies my power. It is not used to build or
protect, but to destroy.

CHAPTER

TEN

IT IS POSSIBLE TO LOOK AT YOUR CHILD WITH both unfathomable love and also inexplicable fear at what you have created. Sirileth was never a normal girl. Normal is another terrible word that has very little meaning. What is normal? The absence of abnormality? The deviation from expectation? Uniqueness? I have always celebrated uniqueness both in myself and in others. And so, when it became clear that Sirileth was unique, well, I was proud. My daughter was something special in the world. She was strong in both spirit and will, not to mention Sourcery, and had a passion for learning. She was also calculating in a way I had never seen in a child.

I trained my children together. A few hours each day away from the toil of running a kingdom was the perfect time to dedicate to Tris, Vi, and of course, Sirileth. She was younger than them by five years, and so much smaller too. Sirileth had a way of approaching a situation, a problem, a puzzle all her own that I couldn't help but admire.

Often, I would present all three children with a way to use Sourcery they had never seen before, had never considered. We shared a few attunements, one of which being Kinemancy. Early on, I taught them how to make kinetic arms. I started with those I considered less dangerous. Shields were perhaps the easiest with no working parts, movement, or sharp edges. I had discovered the technique to form kinetic arms quite by accident, and Tamura had played his own part in helping me develop it. It's quite amazing the sheer number of things that can be done with Kinemancy once you understand the technique. Sourceblades were always a favourite of mine, given my love of stabbing things, but almost any tool could be made with Kinemancy if the workings of that tool are understood. Shields, swords, hammers, pliers, spoons, carts, even ovens, though the fire needed to be supplied separately.

Tris and Vi leapt to the task with their usual boundless enthusiasm. It was wonderful to see. Whenever he and Vi encountered a new challenge, it was always Tris who strode into it headfirst, leading the way. Offering his own advice and trying to get others to use his methods. Vi, on the other hand, was more prone to following and doing what she was told in the hope of pleasing others. Often, I think she would have learned quicker and easier if she had just explored the problems in her own way instead of trying to mimic her brother. She also rarely shut up for more than a minute, which probably slowed her down a little.

The children tried again and again to form the basic shape from the Sourcery and then fill it with their energy. Again and again, they failed, often knocking themselves and each other over in the practice. Laughter filled the training hall. They were just eleven years old, and Sirileth only six.

For a few hours, Tris and Vi attempted to figure out the technique I'd used. I gave them pointers here and there and let them experiment. Sirileth watched. She had her own Source. She could have joined in, played with the other children and tried to learn. Instead, she just watched, an adorable little frown creasing her brow.

Eventually, I knelt before Sirileth and asked her if she wanted to give it a try. I thought she was reluctant to attempt it, maybe for fear of failure or perhaps hurting herself. I took her thoughtfulness for timidity. I couldn't have been more wrong. Sirileth was many things, but timid was never one of them.

She looked at me with a curious expression in her darklight eyes and said quite simply she didn't know how to do it. I explained the technique again, just for her. I did not think her simple, but she was young. I didn't learn it until I was eighteen in a twenty-eight-year-old body. Age has long been a fluctuating scale for me thanks to the damned Chronomancy.

Sirileth listened patiently to my explanation again and nodded. Then went back to watching Tris and Vi play about with the technique. She did not attempt it herself. Not that time, nor the following three. I started to wonder about my daughter. She had been so adamant that she wanted to learn Sourcery. She had been experimenting with it herself in secret. But here I was trying to teach her, and she refused to try.

I thought perhaps I was teaching too fast. Tris and Vi had been using Kinemancy for two years already, they knew all the basics. So, while they trained, still trying to form kinetic arms, I took Sirileth aside and showed her the most basic of Kinemancy techniques.

Throwing a blast of kinetic energy is as simple as drawing on the Source and letting go. She watched me do it with that same frown. Then when I told her to try. She looked at me and said simply and clearly that she wasn't stupid. Then she turned away from me and went back to watching Tris and Vi.

On the fifth session of teaching them, Tris managed to create and hold a kinetic shield for ten seconds before it popped. I thought that quite impressive. It takes time and training to build up the strength required to hold a kinetic arm, even one as simple as a shield. He was young and had many years to train, but it was promising. More than promising, really. It was amazing. He had quickly grasped a complex technique I had taken months to learn as an adult. I set him the task of creating that same shield and holding it for longer, and helped Vi with some pointers. She didn't manage it that time, but her failure didn't quash her spirits and she took our private sessions as an opportunity to tell me about a wonderful little lizard she had found crawling around a stone outside the palace.

Vi was not slow or lazy, yet she was not as naturally talented as Tris. Regardless, our next training session had her creating her own shield and she held it for longer than ten seconds. I'm not sure how long she might have held that first shield for as I got a little overexcited by her success and wrapped Vi up in a crushing hug making her giggle and popping her shield.

With my adopted children training their new technique, I turned my attention back to Sirileth. I found her holding a Source-blade. Well, not a true Sourceblade. It had no edge, so it was more like a Source-stick. Regardless, it was more advanced than a shield. And she had no problem keeping it formed, waving it about with no effort at all.

That was when I realised how different my daughter

was from the other children. She did not practice by failing. She watched, she considered, she learned. And when she was certain of how a thing was done, she did it. She was calculating and deliberate, always understanding a thing before attempting it. So, you can imagine, when she started creating scars in our world, it was not by accident. Sirileth had a reason, even if neither I nor Imiko understood it.

I let Imiko lead the way that first day while I wallowed in my grief. You may remember I've never dealt with grief particularly well. Unlike Hardt, I was never able to come to terms with loss easily. I either wallow in it, or run from it, and I was not in any shape for running, so I spent some time wallowing instead. You may also remember that I've always hated wallowers. Well, one more reason to hate myself.

We trudged along in companionable silence. That quiet was probably the most comfortable thing that has ever existed between Imiko and I.

On the second day out from Wrysom, we joined a well-travelled road. A winding line of packed dirt, stripped of greenery amidst a sea of swaying grass, hidden rocks, and grazing beasts. Isha had once been a single empire and governed with a tight grasp. Since I had brought that empire crashing down, it had become more peaceful while also being in state of constant turmoil. The disparate provinces were always scrapping over land or rights or resources, but out here in the space between civilisations, there was peace to be had that one could never have found before.

I clawed my way out of my grief, tripped it up, turned tail and ran from it. I couldn't deal with it and wallowing in it wasn't helping, so I left it behind and busied myself with more important things. We were heading north. I didn't know why yet, but Imiko was always the flighty type who blew from one place to another in an effort to avoid her past. I may run from my grief, but I always faced my demons head on. But not everyone liked a good fight as much as I. We were chasing after Sirileth. Now that I had nothing else to do and nowhere else to be, finding her suddenly seemed important. Besides, if Sirileth was playing around with scars, there had to be a reason. Nothing good came from poking holes in the world. There was also the other thing. I wanted to see her again. I wanted to see my little girl and the woman she had become. It had been seven years since I last saw her, and I knew better than most just how much could change in seven years.

We were sauntering along. Well, Imiko was sauntering. I was almost keeping up with her longer, easier strides. "I need you to push me," I said.

"Okay," Imiko's hand shot out and she gave me a solid shove. I stumbled, tripped over my own feet, and crashed to the dusty road in a heap.

"What the fuck?" I cried from the dust.

"You told me to push you," Imiko grinned. Then she extended a hand to pull me up. My old bones ached, and I'm not too proud to admit I took her hand. There's a good life lesson for you. If you're down on your luck and someone offers you a hand, take it. Especially if it's an enemy. That's an opportune time to stick them with a knife.

"I didn't mean..." I stopped and brushed some dust off my legs. "Actually, keep at it. The odd attack out of nowhere might help. But I meant don't go slowly on my account. I've gotten soft."

"And wrinkly," Imiko said with a grin. "Like one of those grapes left in the sun until it's all skin, then left a bit longer until it's covered in fuzzy mould, then a bit longer still until it starts smelling like old shoes."

I glared at her and let the flashing storm in my eyes do their job. No one could ever hold my stare for long, especially not when the Arcstorm was raging.

"Oh, don't try the scary eye thing on me, Eska." Imiko chuckled. "I spent the past decade raising your daughter. You remember how she likes to stare at things, working it all out in her head. You think your eyes are unnerving? Siri's are worse."

I conceded that point. When she was a babe, I thought Sirileth's darklight stare was beautiful. I gazed into her eyes for hours, watching the light play around the edges of her iris, so bright it was almost blinding if you looked at it just right. But the older she got, the more that stare became something else. Still beautiful, but in that terrifying way. Like a tsunami is beautiful before it drowns you. Or a moon shower, trailing fire as the rocks fall, and then it hits you and you're pulp.

I started walking again. There was a caravan headed towards us, three carts each pulled by a giant humanoid figure plodding along step by relentless step. Golems. When I was training at the Academy of Magic, Golemancy was a school of magic the Polasians guarded jealously. Since the fall of Terrelan, trade had opened Isha like never before. Still, it took a rich merchant to afford a trio of golems. Well worth the cost, though. They needed little rest, were strong as an abban, and only a foolish bandit would try to rob a caravan with even a single golem protecting it. I'd seen them squash people into bloody pancakes.

"I mean it, Imiko," I said. "Don't spare the pace because I'm old and slow. I've lost too much of my fitness, and if we're going to be running after Sirileth, I'm going to need to be faster. I wonder if I can remember how to fight. Ishtar used to say, scrapping was just like fucking. Moist, noisy, over far too quickly, and you never forget the steps."

We passed the caravan, and the lead driver gave us a friendly wave. Right up to the point he could see my eyes. Then he startled and mumbled a curse — I think it was something to do with Lokar's sagging arse — and barked an order at his golems. All three of them quit pulling their wagons and formed a threatening line before me. It might have been more defensive, but honestly when a twelve-foot-tall creature made of rock shuffles towards you, it's tough not to take it as aggression. Even more so when three of them start herding you backwards.

"Stay back, Corpse Queen!" the lead wagon driver shouted. "I'll not have you taking my boys."

That was one of the worst things to come out of the whole Corpse Queen thing. Fair enough that the entire continent of Isha decided to band together in their hatred and fear of me. I have no problem being the terran bogeywoman. I also accept that the fall of the Terrelan empire and the destruction of its capital city, Juntorrow, are laid at my feet. I may not have set out to destroy the city, and I'm certainly sorry that so many people died in the chaos, it's a weighted burden I will never shed, but I cannot deny I caused it. I wasn't exactly thinking straight at the time. Considering I'd just suffered a few months of daily torture by the emperor, including taking my arm off at the elbow. I certainly can't argue with being called the mother of the Cursed, though it's not exactly a pleasant moniker, given that I had actual children who are not cursed. But of the mindless souls who exist only to destroy the living... Yes. Yes, I did that. Again, I lay at least part of the blame at the Emperor of Terrelan for driving me mad with torture. My point is, there are a great many atrocities that can, and rightly have been, laid at my feet. However, I honestly have no idea where the stealing people's children myth came from. That one should have belonged to the Iron Legion, evil fucker that he was. Instead, he gets to be remembered as a hero while I am vilified despite being the one to stop him. Life is unfair at the best of times.

"I don't want your boys." I leaned a little to the side to peer past one of the golems and caught sight of one of the driver's boys. He was man grown with full beard, a once-broken nose, and a slack jaw.

"I said stay back!" the driver shouted over the golems. The three of them took another step forward in perfect unison, their giant footfalls shaking the ground and crushing the grass flat.

"Can't you do something?" Imiko said. She was standing behind me. Hiding behind me, really.

I shrugged. "I could probably paint their fists red." Golemancy was not a school I was overly familiar with, but I did know that the golems tended to be oddly resistant to Sourcery. I might be able to chip chunks off the things with some kinetic blasts, but if I tried to use my innate Geomancy to harm them, I'd get nothing but a headache.

The lead wagon driver shouted something else, but I was done with listening. The golems would follow his orders without hesitation or question. He hadn't yet ordered them to attack so I very much doubted he was going to. The truth is, if someone is going to throw a punch your way, they're unlikely to tell you about it first. If they do, they are probably looking for a reason to avoid the violence. Admittedly, we weren't talking about a fist fight here, but the sentiment scales up to almost all levels of conflict. The best way to de-escalate a situation is often just to walk away. So that's what I did. Let the fool wagon driver have his little victory.

"Go on," the driver shouted. "Off with you."

Let him tell all his friends he scared off the Corpse Queen. It's not like any of them would believe him. No doubt a fanciful tale told over a few cups.

"You did it, da'. She's running!" shouted one of the driver's boys.

Yes, that would be a good tale to tell in the local tavern. How he met the Corpse Queen on the road, all flashing eyes and one arm, a bedraggled old lady. No one would believe him.

I rejoined the road, the wagons behind me and Imiko at my side, still staring over her shoulder at the golems as they swaggered back to their carts.

The fool would crow about how he had scared off the bogeywoman with his golems, probably framing it as some epic battle. Even with his sons backing him up, none would take that seriously. Surely.

Then again, he was on the road heading towards New Picarr. They knew I was nearby. Perhaps people would believe the fool. No doubt the marshal would already have returned to tell the story of how he evicted the Corpse Queen from Wrysom. And just a few days later, a dumb as rock merchant rolls into town and tells everyone who will listen how he defeated the Corpse Queen on the road and sent her running.

I stopped walking. I didn't really mean to, but my feet refused to move. That's my excuse and I'll stick to it. I was rooted in place listening to wagon driver and his boys congratulating each other as if they had won a battle rather than forced an old woman off the road. I felt the golems plodding along as they settled back into place and took up their loads, the vibrations of their steps thrumming through the earth and into me. My innate Geomancy felt where they were, how they were moving.

It was possible people would believe the driver and his stories. Another blow to the Corpse Queen's reputation. My absence had only made the legend grow, but my reappearance might soon bring that reputation low. How long before people no longer feared me for what I had become? How long before I became a joke instead of a horror story?

Oh, I met the Corpse Queen on the road. Flicked her the finger and sent her on her way. She looked a beggar, but if you give her a coin, she'll beg for another.

Was that how my reputation would end? Not as a dark queen feared by all, but as a cautionary tale of feeding beggars on the side of the road?

Fuck that!

I had not gone through all the pain and turmoil of my life just to be forgotten. To become a joke to be shared in taverns rather than a name to be feared. My body might have become frail, soft, and old. But I was still me. And no backwater merchant with more teeth than brains would get the better of me.

I should point out that it was entirely possible I had gone a bit Source mad. It can happen. I hadn't swallowed a Source in a long time and was no longer used to the feeling of power they give. I would not be the first Sourcerer to abstain for a prolonged period only to find themselves believing they were some sort of god when they finally swallowed a Source once more.

Yes, I'll blame Source madness for this one. It's slightly more excusable than Eska got pissed off because some old arsehole of a merchant disrespected her. Truth is all about perspective really, and well, this is mine. So, fuck it. Source madness.

I had a Source in my mouth before I realised it and had swallowed before Imiko could let loose the sigh she had readied for such a moment. Now, I have said my innate Geomancy is weak, and that's true. However, I know more about Sourcery than most. I also know that combining Sourceries is a good way to exponentially increase the power. So, with that in mind, I swallowed my Kinemancy Source, set my sight on the caravan. I let the bastards feel the rage of the Corpse Queen.

I stomped on the ground and sent pulse of kinetic Geomancy trembling through the packed dirt. It cracked the earth beneath one of the golems, opening a fissure just large enough to sink the damned thing up to its neck. The screaming started as I caused a pillar of rock to rise and topple the rearmost wagon, spilling both its driver and its cargo of yellow and green fruit all over the road.

The lead driver clearly had a good idea of what was happening and ordered his two standing golems to charge me. A smart move. If just one of them got close enough to grab me, I was done for. Of course, that wasn't going to happen if I had my way.

The sigh finally ripped from Imiko and it was a pointed thing, aimed with unerring accuracy. I glanced over my shoulder and found her shaking her head. Well, fuck her! I wasn't about to apologise for teaching some dumb shit bully of a merchant a lesson in respect.

Rock golems were slow to get moving, but once they started they held the power of a stampeding avalanche. The first had just about gotten up to a flattening everything in its path speed, when I tore a rock the size of the cart it had been pulling from the earth and flung it at the bloody thing. Rock met rock golem with a mighty crash, and golem met ground with a similar impact, skidding to a halt and tearing up the earth. I sank the ground beneath it half a dozen feet for good measure.

I was dripping sweat when I stepped forward to meet the final golem. I was unused to drawing so much power from a Source. Unused to combining Sourceries to make them stronger. Unused to the strain it put on my body. My limbs ached, none more so than my stump, and my mind was fuzzy either from rage or exertion. Possibly both. However, there was still one golem left and I needed to put on a show. The waggoners were watching, shouting, baying for my blood.

The last golem was a dozen paces away, charging ahead and arms held wide to grab and crush me. I drew on my Kinemancy Source, mixed it with the power of the Arcstorm inside, and hurled a bolt of raw kinetic energy at the thing. The force of it threw me backwards, feet skidding in the dirt. Lightning-laced purple haze ripped from my outstretched hand and struck the rock golem full in the chest with the sound of an earthquake. The golem staggered from the force; its momentum arrested. Bits of it flew to scatter in the grass at the side of the road as it went down on one knee.

But it wasn't done yet and neither was I.

I threw another blast at it. And another, and another. Each one was powerful enough to level a house and seethed with lightning. Kinemancy has many uses, some of which are delicate and require precision. But sometimes you just want to hit a big rock hard enough to fucking shatter it. I blew its left arm off, then its right. My final blast cracked its core and blew a hole in its chest large enough to fit a full-grown adult. The thing slumped, the Sourcery leaving it, the rock falling still and dead once more. That shut the stupid bloody merchant and his boys up. All the jeering and the insults stopped. Even from a distance, I could see the wide eyes and the slack jaws gone slacker. Fuck them, fuck their mockery, and fuck their inexplicable hatred of an old woman who just wanted to pass by unmolested.

I could have destroyed their other golems, their wagons too. I could have left a ruin of their entire lives, but I didn't. My point was made. I had turned a tale about how they had found a beggared Corpse Queen on the road and scared her off, into a story of how the Corpse Queen had come again, ambushed them on the road with a storm in her eyes and Sourcery at her fingertips. With that done, I turned and walked away. I still had no idea how to get to Lanfall but hanging around the scene of the crime was unlikely to help matters.

"Can I expect this to happen again?" Imiko said as she matched my stride with ease. I was sweating some and struggled to keep going. Exhaustion was setting in quick. My legs ached, my hip kept twinging in a way that I thought might pitch me onto the ground, and I couldn't catch my breath.

"Expect people to recognise me? Or me to teach stupid arseholes a lesson?"

Imiko dragged a hand down her face in frustration. "Both."

"Well, I'd say people are going to recognise me anywhere we go," I said. "It's the eyes. Mostly. Perhaps I could get one of those insufferably floppy hats to hide my face."

Imiko clapped. "A wonderful idea, Eska. Maybe you could keep quiet at the same time. Let me do the talking so we get in slightly less trouble. Do you think you could manage that?"

I glanced at her. Imiko glanced back. We shared a chuckle then, though it may have been a little more bitter than I remember. We both knew I could no more be the quiet, demure one, than she could be the angry, half-insane one.

"And the other thing?" Imiko said once the laughs had turned into that horrible awkward silence. You know the type. Like someone had laughed a bit too hard and shit themselves, and it wasn't funny anymore, and no one wanted to talk about it.

"The idiot wagon driver started it," I said sulkily.

"Mhm." Imiko kicked a stone from the path. "And you couldn't help but finish it." She sighed. "Why did you leave, Eska? At first, I thought it was because you were tired of it all. Of being the Corpse Queen. But, well, you clearly still enjoy it. Don't try to tell me you didn't have fun wrecking that golem. So, why leave? Why did you run away and abandon me with a kingdom to run and a child to raise?"

I didn't answer her. I didn't want to lie and I sure as Lursa's Tears couldn't tell her the truth.

CHAPTER ELEVEN

LANFALL HAD ALWAYS BEEN THE LARGEST
city in western Isha, the lands once known as Orran. It had
been the seat of the Orran empire and the last holdout of our
people before the Terrelans finally crushed our resistance
and made everything Terrelan.

Lanfall was a sprawling, chaotic mass of terran
life. Haphazard buildings of a thousand different designs
shouldered up against each other. Streets that twisted,
turned sharply, dead ended in inexplicable walls. It had
been built, rebuilt, built on, built over so many times that
there was no rhyme or reason to its layout. And at the
centre of that unfathomable chaos, stood Fort Vernan. Five
giant towers rising from the seething mess to lord over the
madness. The city had no walls to protect it from the outside,
but Fort Vernan did. High walls, high towers, all built with
a defending force of Sourcerers in mind. Fat lot of good

that did us. Walls or no, towers or no, we still bloody well lost. Lanfall was sacked. Fort Vernan was taken. The Orran Emperor was killed. And I was captured and sent to the fucking Pit.

That is my memory of the city of Lanfall and why I had never been back there since. I remembered it in the midst of the greatest battle Isha has ever seen. Tens of thousands of soldiers on each side, all clashing down in the streets, a furious melee with burning buildings, and screaming children all around. Winged monsters from the Other World claiming the skies. Their clawed brethren hunting through the streets and alleyways, heedless of who was considered friend or foe. Iridescent Sourceries clashing behind ashen clouds. Explosions rocking the earth, slaughtering hundreds at a time, painting the nearby fields red. And, of course, me at the centre of it all. The last hope of the Orran empire. The last failure of that doomed empire.

Even three decades past, I remember it all so damned clearly. The sense of rightness as I rained death and hell on the soldiers below, as I did just what I have been raised to do. Trained to do. Conditioned to do. The furious struggle up on the tallest tower as the Terrelans sent in their own Sourcerers to stop us. The betrayal. Josef staying my hand, knocking me senseless even as our flags fell, and our surrender was sounded. The memory stokes the fires of anger in me even now. I have long since come to terms with the fact that Josef's betrayal saved my life, both our lives. And yet it still hurts.

So, the fact that Sirileth had made her way to Lanfall was a bitter pill to swallow. I had to follow her so I could find her. I had to see my daughter again and stop her from opening scars in the world. I didn't know why she was doing it, but it was dangerous, both to her and to everyone around her. But Lursa's Tears, why did she have to go to Lanfall?

It took us thirteen days travelling northwest to reach Lanfall from Wrysom. We made good time, all things considered, though a part of that was because we came across a caravan heading that way. This particular train of wagons was hitched to trei birds, not golems, and I consented to letting Imiko do all the talking while I tried my very best not to let anyone see my eyes. I failed, but in the end I needn't have bothered. The lead driver was a savvy old merchant with a scarred lip that made him look like he was always smiling at a joke no one else would ever understand. He remembered me. Apparently, I'd saved his life a good fifteen years back. I'd been on one of my adventures, digging up ruins and secrets better left forgotten, and had come across him being attacked by wild ghouls. I'd run them off, and Hardt and I had spent a night drinking and sharing stories with the caravaner and his family. Once he told me that story, I remembered it well enough. Not for the man himself, and not for the attack I saved him from, but for his daughter. She was really quite pretty, and we talked long into the night, and then we retreated to her tent and didn't talk for even longer. Unfortunately, his daughter wasn't with him on this run. Though in truth that was probably for the best. I had aged a lot in fifteen years thanks to the Chronomancy, and I didn't want to imagine what that pretty woman would think of me now.

Imiko and I spent much of the time getting re-acquainted. I'm not saying it wasn't tense at times, there was a gulf of resentment between us a few fathoms deep, but there is a comfort in old friends that is undeniable. When someone knows you, has stood by you through your worst and has revealed their own to you in turn, it breeds a level of trust. It's like coming home only without the home. We fell into familiar rhythms. We chatted, we laughed, we shared jokes from long ago that no one else thought was funny at the time, let alone decades after the fact. We reminisced about times long gone. Shared drinks and tears over friends gone too. The years apart fell away between us, and by the time we reached Lanfall, we were sisters again. And just like any siblings, we hated each other as much as loved each other.

Lanfall was not much changed from the last time I saw it. Well, that's both true and not. The city itself had not changed much. Still a haphazard mess of varying architectural styles, new buildings and old, a gyrating mob of terran life and ingenuity all thrown together in a pot and left to boil over. But the armies were gone, so that was different.

We joined the road and the traffic heading to and fro and lost ourselves in the noise of it. It was dizzying to be surrounded by all that life and energy and noise after so many years in Wrysom. Here, a man and woman walked hand in hand, their voices snatched by the press. There a giant of a man shouted about some bread he had for sale to weary travellers. A merchant with a cart told another, fatter merchant, to get out of his way, and then both started slinging insults. A young girl bumped into Imiko and found the hand she put on my sister's purse suddenly caught and twisted. Imiko sent the girl off with a push and a smile aimed in my direction. We had met in similar circumstances a long time ago. The smile she shot me grew shadowed, and Imiko quickly looked away. I was missing something there,

but I had not the wisdom, despite my advancing years, to
see it. I thought, just like me, Imiko probably sometimes
ruminated about all age and time had done to make war
on our bodies, and how life had been both simpler and less
painful when we were young.

Buildings rose around us and Imiko funnelled us
away from the press of bodies. This was her world, not
mine, and I was wise enough to follow in her wake. She led
us through alleys, somehow choosing ones that didn't dead
end, and cut across busy streets. The smells of a hundred
different industries assaulted me on all sides. Spices from
Polasia and salts from Itexia, tanning leather and fires stoked
hot enough to forge, sweat from ten thousand different
terrans and waste from beasts shitting in the streets.

It was mid-afternoon before Imiko pulled us to a
stop outside a tavern. I'd be lying if I didn't admit that I half
collapsed before we even made it through the door. I had
ordered Imiko to push my endurance, and she certainly was
doing that. I was exhausted, but I could feel some of my old
energy returning. Age may make a mockery of how sturdy
our bodies once were, but it is disuse that saps our strength.

The tavern was a dingy little space with no windows,
casting the place in a permanent gloom. Perfect for skulking
thieves and crownless queens in hiding. Well, I wasn't really
doing any hiding. As soon as I looked at the owner behind
the bar, my eyes decide to flash. I'd say it was pretty obvious
who I was and any attempts at hiding went right out the
window. A poor choice of phrase, I know, but sometimes it's
best to stick with what's comfortable.

"No no no," the owner said. He made a sign with
his hands, touching his chest and then reaching for the sky.
Another moon worshipper then. I could not fathom why

people did it when they heard my name or, in this case, saw me. Was there some new tale I hadn't heard where Lokar or Lursa would protect people from me? I decided it sounded a good story and I'd have to ask around. "You can't be here."

I glanced at Imiko. She shrugged. "Do you want to deal with this one, or should I?" I asked.

Imiko stuck her hands in her pockets and sighed. "That depends. Are you going to kill anyone?"

"No."

"Promise?"

I treated her to my very best fuck you stare. She laughed and dipped into a dramatic bow, gesturing towards the owner. He hadn't shifted from behind the bar but was wiping it down with a cloth quite furiously. I ambled towards him, my legs aching with each step. I needed to sit down. Or lie down. Or sit down and drink until lying down became a necessity instead of a possibility. I heard at least one half-drunk patron mutter something, push out a chair, and flee through the front door once I had passed, but most of them just went silent as the air before a storm. My legend was a terrible thing, and it was full of stories of pain and death and worse, but tales of my exploits were also old enough now that people were often as curious as they were scared.

"We need a room," I started. "A bath, if you do that here. Food and drink. Preferably water."

"And wine," Imiko said loudly and cheerfully.

The owner, a fat man who probably outweighed me three times over, stared with a look on his face like a shark had just sauntered in and asked for a bite of his arm. "You... You can't be here."

I sighed. "I am here."

"You're the Corpse Queen."

Another sigh. I really hoped he wasn't as ignorant as he seemed. There is a level of stupidity that is entirely acceptable, even wonderful to deal with. It's a gullibility sweet spot. The really intelligent people question everything and come up with their own opinions on matters based upon observable criteria. They are a pain in the arse to deal with because they have a habit of not believing you when you lie. The really stupid people don't question a damned thing because they already have their opinion and nothing you do, say, or threaten them with will change it. Their opinion forms early in life, quickly settles into stone, and, like stone, is dense and senseless. They are also a pain in the arse to deal with. But there's this wonderful level between intelligent and stupid where people think they are smart but aren't. What they are, is gullible. Gullible people are fantastic because they are so easy to manipulate.

"I am Eskara Helsene." I cannot accurately describe to you it felt to say my real name and claim my true identity instead of hiding behind a persona. I had been different as Silva; I could be different as Silva. But it wasn't me. I was hiding, pretending to be someone else, something else. Admitting my true name, claiming it, saying it out loud and to others... It felt right. It felt like I could finally stop lying.

I leaned on the bar and smiled, and the owner leaned away. "This encounter can go one of two ways," I said. "Either you continue to refuse to serve me and suffer a catastrophic loss of property in the ensuing fire. Or you can make a lot of money." I grinned at him, and my eyes flashed, a fork of lightning arcing behind my gaze. "Just think, put the word out that your tavern has the one and only Corpse Queen as a patron. People will flock from all over Lanfall to come and see."

"Or people will curse me and call it bad luck," the owner said.

"Bah," I spat. "Luck is nothing but abban shit. Opportunities are like orgasms. Better to take matters into your own hands, than rely on the competence of others. This right here is an opportunity. If you're willing to make it one."

The owner glanced about his gloomy tavern. There were maybe a dozen other patrons seated in the space and most of them looked a poor, sorry lot. He wasn't going to get rich slowly drowning those sods, and he knew it.

"If it helps," I said, cracking a wrinkled smile at him. "I won't burn down the city while I'm staying here." That was a promise I mostly kept.

CHAPTER
TWELVE

WE HAD A MISSION, BUT THAT FIRST NIGHT IN Lanfall both Imiko and I were too tired and road weary to go about it. We ate, bathed, and slept. Well, I slept. Imiko drank deep into the night and, judging by the repetitive thumps coming through the wall, did not retreat to her room alone. I buried my head in my pillow and tried my best to ignore the sounds. Wonderful things, pillows. Useful for resting your weary head, covering your ears, and smothering people when the need arises. They were noisy enough, I was tempted.

The next day I woke with a mind to go about finding my wayward daughter. If Sirileth was in Lanfall, I would find her and... I wasn't sure what I'd do then. Spank her bottom and call her a naughty girl? She was probably a bit old for that and I'd never taken to beating my children anyway. Maybe some harsh words and an order to get back to her queendom. I didn't really have a leg to stand on there, considering I'd run off and left the whole thing to her. I honestly had no idea what I'd say when I found Sirileth. All I knew was that I had to find her. I had to stop her from ripping scars into the world before something worse than an Abomination made its way through. And believe me, there are worse things.

I found Imiko in the common room, nursing a plate of cooling eggs. Her eyes were bleary, and she yawned wide enough to swallow the moons when I sat down.

"Had fun entertaining a local last night, did you?" I grinned and stole her fork, snatching up some of the cold egg. It was not pleasant, but at least it was edible. I quickly discovered I was ravenous.

"Don't be such a nag, Eska," Imiko said, grinning. "Sex doesn't always have to be about love. Sometimes it can just be about need." She wriggled in her chair in a way that made me uncomfortable. I understood both love and need far better than she realised. In my life I have taken some lovers because the sight of them made my heart flutter, and others because I felt an ache deep inside and they were the most convenient person able to satisfy it. But both those feelings came less often now that I was older, and better able to resist the urges when they did. In my later years, I contented myself with fond memories instead of warm beds. Well, I suppose I tortured myself with fond memories would be more accurate. I still remembered Silva; the smell of her, the feel of her, the taste of her. The weight of her body as she bled out in my arms.

There were more patrons in the inn that morning than the night before. More sets of eyes pointed my way. I tried my best to ignore them all.

"It won't be long before the whole city knows I'm here," I said as I speared another bit of egg off Imiko's plate. There was still plenty to steal. Perhaps I should have noticed how little she was eating.

"Use it. Sirileth isn't as famous as you, but she has her own following these days. Plenty of folk might be happy to tell you where she is if they know who you are."

"Any idea where to start looking?"

Imiko shrugged. "I've got some contacts that might talk to me, depending on if Siri got to them first. You go do your thing, and I'll do mine."

I headed out into the city after breakfast, and I made no attempts to disguise myself. I became a walking tourist attraction. Everywhere I went, people stopped to stare, gossiping behind their hands. That wouldn't have been so bad, but I secured an escort. Before long, a trio of burly soldiers started following me about. At least they had the good graces to keep their distance. No one was willing to talk to me once they saw the mean looks shot their way by big folk with sharp swords. I considered knocking the guards senseless with a kinetic blast, then running off down into the labyrinth of alleyways. But my legs ached, and I didn't feel like running. Besides, I saw the runes etched onto the silver armour they wore beneath their tabards, and I knew the type well. Armour enchanted by an Augmancer to absorb Sourcery. Their weapons held similar runes, and at least one of the soldiers, the biggest one with arms wider than my waist, was a Sourcerer. I noticed the pouch at her belt and saw the way her hand brushed it regularly to make sure it was still there. We Sourcerers have some distinctive tells when you know to look for them, and Source addiction is one of them. We feel the hunger all the time and no

amount of food can satisfy it. It is the hunger for power,
to feel a Source inside. To be one with the connection it
provides. I had spent many years denying that hunger but
no more. I swallowed my Sources every day and suffered the
Spiceweed I needed to retch them up each day too. It was
painful, but worth it. I felt the lightning inside, the storm, the
fire, the nervous energy begging for movement. I felt it all. I
revelled in it. I was a fool to have denied myself for so long.

It's important to remember that I was in the seat of
what was once Orran. The war was decades over, but there
were still plenty who remembered it and remembered who
they were before the war and subsequent occupation. Not
everyone was happy when the Terrelans slaughtered the
Orran royal family and claimed the whole continent as
their own. In the same way that not everyone was unhappy
when I slaughtered the Terrelan royal family and brought
their empire to a violent end. That was why the reactions
to my presence were so mixed. Some people stared after
me with awe, others with fear. Some slunk away, into the
shadows, others came to me with their thanks. Many made
signs with their hands and reached towards the sky. Others
still, gave me that wary look a deer gives to a lion when
it's unsure if it's about to have to run for its life. I ignored
as many of all of them as I could. Fame is a shitty reward
when you're remembered for all your mistakes rather than
your accomplishments. No one knew that I saved the world
from the Iron Legion's plans to resurrect our idiot gods, but
they all knew I unleashed a plague of undeath upon the
continent.

I found no sign of my missing daughter. No one had
heard that the queen of Yenheim was visiting. That seemed
a bad sign. If Sirileth's presence in Lanfall was common

knowledge, surely it would be as momentous as my own.

After a day spent trudging through the streets of Lanfall, thoroughly losing myself in the winding alleyways and haphazard architecture, I found myself in a small garden. An oasis of nature amidst the bustling hive of terran industry. It was nestled between three buildings that reached into the sky, one of which leaned at a worrying angle. Much of Lanfall was in disrepair, and much else was in a constant state of repair.

I honestly cannot say how I found that garden, and if I wandered the streets for another ten days, I probably couldn't find it again. It was my first real time alone since leaving Wrysom. I stayed there until a shadow crept its way across the garden and engulfed me. When I looked up, I realised the tallest tower of Fort Vernan was the only thing I could see above the buildings. Then it dawned on me. I had an idea about where I might find my daughter.

When I finally found my way back to our little tavern, I had an audience waiting for me. It seemed the owner had taken my suggestion to heart, and there was now a sign outside that read Offshal Drinkin Hole of the Copse Quen. Illiteracy aside, it was good marketing, and I couldn't fault him for that. He greeted me with a smile and shoved a couple of patrons off a table to make space for me. I ground my teeth at the charade. It exposed the very worst truth terran kind has to offer. No one cares past the colour of your coin, and enough of it will smooth over even the worst atrocity.

I just finished a bowl of something that might have passed as sausage stew when Imiko squeezed through the growing crowd. If my passage was marked by every eye in the place, hers was invisible. Just the way she preferred.

I've always liked to say her ability to vanish and reappear is somewhat magical, but that's a load of crap. Imiko is no Sourcerer and has no powers past the ability to take advantage of a good distraction when it presents itself. She deposited a couple of bags at the foot of our table and waved at the owner.

"Wine," Imiko said to the beaming fool as he sauntered over. "Two bottles."

I held up a hand. "None for me." It's not that I don't like a drink. I do. Getting arse over tits drunk is one of my favourite pastimes, but I have learned not to do it with a Source in my stomach. Relaxing inhibitions is not wise when you have the power to flatten a building with a wave of a hand. I learned that one the hard way.

The owner looked to Imiko. She shrugged. "My order stands, man. On with it." She shook her head and rolled her eyes at me. "Damn, but I'm thirsty."

"Who owns Fort Vernan these days?" I've never been good at pleasantries. When I have something to say, I say it.

Imiko leaned back in her chair and frowned at me. "Merchant Union. Bigger bunch of crooks than my lot. Some of them were old nobility back in the Orran days. They paid off the Terrelan authorities to let them stay in their big houses, then moved into the fort when the Terrelan empire fell apart. Now they control the Lanfall militia. And half the bloody trade on Isha."

The owner arrived with a couple of bottles of wine and Imiko grinned at him. "Some food would be lovely too. Nothing too salty." She sent him away with a wink and waited until he was gone before continuing. She needn't have bothered. The tavern was so full of bodies and noise, I could barely hear myself think.

"They also brokered a deal with Ro'shan," Imiko continued. "Sole trading rights for all of Isha. You don't think it's an accident that Lanfall remains the biggest and most profitable city on the continent? Nor that it boasts the largest area of influence. Ro'shan stops here and only here, and anyone who wants to trade in goods the flying city brings in, must do so here. To trade Ro'shan bartered goods, you need to be an associate of the Merchant Union." She smiled viciously as she poured a cup of wine. "Membership fees are something else."

"That's where she'll be," I said, knowing it for the truth. "Not skulking around back alleys like some thief."

Imiko gasped. "I do not skulk. I stalk, flit, and occasionally tumble. All very elegantly."

"Well, Sirileth is a queen."

"That's more your department than mine, Eska. I'd say you used to stride, but now you're more of a hobble." Imiko sipped at her wine, then grinned at me. I really did miss her during my years in Wrysom. People like Imiko have a breeziness about them that makes them impossible not to like. Trust me, I really tried.

"So, she's either staying at the fort while she does... whatever she's doing or someone in the fort knows where she is."

"A wonderful plan," Imiko agreed. She plucked up one of the bags she had brought with her and dumped it on the table in front of me. "You'll need this."

I had the sinking feeling I had just walked into a trap, and Imiko was far too happy to spring it. The bag contained clothes. Actually, the bag contained a dress. It was made of many folds of black cloth, exquisitely cut and just my size. It was a dress fit for a fucking queen.

CHAPTER THIRTEEN

SIRILETH WAS ALWAYS SUCH A CURIOUS LITTLE thing. She loved puzzles, even from an early age. When my other children would have played with wooden horses or toy soldiers, Sirileth found childish joy with puzzle boxes and riddles. Tamura used to make them for her. The puzzles, I mean, though he also made riddles every time he spoke. He was handy with a carving knife and had knowledge of the inner workings of most things. He'd present Sirileth with a wooden cube built of various shapes that had to be taken apart in just such a way, or box with a dozen different moving parts that all had to be twisted, pulled, pushed in the correct order or whatever mechanism was hidden inside would reset. He'd tell Sirileth that it was considered easy, or hard, or one time he claimed a puzzle was impossible. Then he'd step back and watch as she went at the conundrum with ruthless examination. Perhaps I should have apprenticed her to the puzzologists down in Ark Naren. It might have saved the world a lot of pain.

We were so similar in many ways, my daughter and I, and yet so different in others. We both loved puzzles, but I hadn't the patience for the practical kind, and never met one I couldn't smash to get to what was inside. Sirileth was driven to understand them, the mechanics, the whys and the hows.

By the time she was eight, her room was filled with puzzles she had long since mastered. They weren't forgotten though. She didn't keep them as trophies to sit and gather dust until they became nothing but scenery. To Sirileth, they were lessons. Lessons she had learned and would never forget.

Maybe it was her love of puzzles and riddles that made Sirileth crave Tamura's company. She never missed a chance to sit at his feet and listen to him talk. I think she understood more of what he said than anyone, and I considered myself quite adept at deciphering him. But it wasn't just his puzzles that Sirileth liked. She was mesmerised by his stories too, and that was something we did share. Tamura has always had a way of telling a tale, of drawing you in, knowing when to pause and when to rush forward. Deepening his voice to add gravitas or speaking in a whisper to pull you close. The telling of stories is an art form in itself, and it is one Tamura has got nailed down. Of course, he's immortal and has been alive for centuries, so it's maybe not that surprising.

Sirileth loved every story he chose to tell, always listening with such fierce attention, her darklight eyes wide and blinding. She loved stories about me most of all. Unfortunately for us all, Tamura had a habit of embellishing them.

I think she was eight years old when he told her the story of how I freed Do'shan, and the god who called it home, from its bondage. He made such a hash of it. Well, that's not entirely true. Tamura just emphasised the wrong points.

"Your mother saw the suffering of the people of Do'shan and knew a way to help." Tamura said in his sing song story teller's voice. It was shit, of course. Any suffering the people of Do'shan were in was because I had heaped it upon them by slaughtering half of them. He left that bit out though.

"So, she went to the Djinn and made her second deal with him." I should point out that he calls this tale Eska and the Three Deals with the Djinn. It's a play on our centuries old saying that states quite clearly and emphatically, Never make a deal with a Djinn. It's a lesson that holds true; only fools ignore it. What does that say about the bitch who ignored three times?

"The Djinn came before your mother in the guise of a great storm," Tamura said in that overly dramatic voice. "All fury and bluster." Then he lowered his voice to draw Sirileth in. She leaned close, her darklight eyes shining so bright, flicking between Tamura and me. "Of course, we all know that Eskara Helsene doesn't fear the storm." Tamura let a slow smile creep across his face. "She stood in the face of godly rage and told the Djinn I don't fear you!" Another lie. I actually accused the god of having a bloated ego and told him to stop trying to impress me.

I'll skip ahead. You know the truth of the tale, and by now you can probably see where I'm going with it. Tamura twisted events here, blatantly lied there, and painted me in a heroic light. Well, I am not a fucking hero. And I should never be considered one. Heroes are something people look up to and emulate. I wonder how much suffering Tamura is inadvertently to blame for? All because he tried to make me a mother and not a monster in my daughter's blinding eyes.

Sirileth listened to the whole thing without a word, a wide smile plastered on her impish face. She so rarely smiled. Most children cannot seem to stop themselves. Joy is felt so strongly and so easily by them, that it can strike like lightning and eclipse even the darkest thoughts. Adults are the other side of the coin, I think. Joy and love and wonder are fleeting, but hate and anger and fear are like a houseguest you invited over for an afternoon drink, and they just won't fucking leave.

When Tamura was done with his tale, Sirileth was quiet for a few minutes. I think she liked to absorb them fully, revisiting them in her own mind. Her eyes darted about as she considered. Then she looked up at me, her face a picture of innocence and asked, What about Ssserakis?

I floundered, unsure how to respond. I looked to Tamura for help but saw only a frown of confusion. I could not understand how my daughter knew that name. I had carried Ssserakis inside of me, coiled around my soul for years. But I had sent the horror home before Sirileth was old enough to speak. I had never shared the horror's name with anyone, never even told my friends that I carried the ancient being inside. Ssserakis was mine. My horror, my burden, my passenger. My comfort and my strength. My fear and my anxiety. My friends knew something was wrong with me, perhaps even that I was possessed, but not the horror's name. Yet my daughter knew it. She had not misspoken. There was no doubt in her. She knew about Ssserakis.

I did not answer Sirileth. I was not ready to share my
ancient horror with anyone, even years after I had let it go. I
did not answer her the next time she asked either, or the time
after that. And Sirileth, little puzzle solver that she was, did
not ask again. But that doesn't mean she forgot. When my
daughter met a puzzle no one could solve, she created her
own solutions.

The first time I went to Fort Vernan, I arrived with
Josef at my side, and a small unit of soldiers at my back. I
stared at the looming towers and knew a great battle was
to come. It thrilled me. I was full of nervous energy, eager
to throw my power against the oncoming army, ready
and willing to murder hundreds, thousands for the Orran
Emperor. I was righteous. Fuelled by indoctrination. The
Terrelans were savage beasts and we, the Orrans, were
valiant defenders. And we would win because we had right
and justice on our side.

We left that tower in chains, surrounded by our
enemies, stripped of our powers. I was exhausted by
betrayal, twisted by rage, fooling myself with the belief that
the Orran Emperor I was so willing to kill for would come
and rescue me. Unaware that he was already dead and
would not have come even if he weren't.

This time, I approached Fort Vernan with Imiko at
my side, and a gawking mob of citizens at my back. I was
nervous again, but for an entirely different reason.

Imiko had gone a little overboard with the dress, but
at least she had stopped short of making me wear a crown.
Besides, I wasn't going to argue with her. It was a lovely
dress and it made me look damn good. The very picture
of a dark queen. I may not have had my youth anymore,

but I stood straighter in that dress. Proud, revelling in my reputation. The goggling citizens followed and grew and chattered like crows atop a battlefield, waiting for the spoils. I considered giving them a show. What would be fitting of the Corpse Queen? Probably burning the city to the ground or unleashing a plague of Cursed. I decided they were already getting all the show I intended to give them.

The guards at the gates of Fort Vernan didn't stop me. You don't stop a queen, no matter how small her entourage, or how removed from her lands she might be. A simpering servant ran from the doorway of the first tower to meet me. He bowed low three times, almost kissing his feet, before stammering out an apology because no one had expected me, which was the point, to be honest.

Politics is much like war. Many sides clashing, tugging at each other, feints and charges, flanks and outmanoeuvres. Alliances made in a moment of need, then shattered once the usefulness is over. There can be benefits to pulling back, consolidating one's power, considering options. But at the same time, there is something to be said for bulling forwards and catching your enemy with their pants down. If I had let the merchants who called Fort Vernan home know I was coming, they might have prepared lies or traps. In truth, even with that in mind, I might still have been walking into a noose with my head held high. But I had to believe Sirileth was there somewhere. I had to find my daughter before she did something she couldn't take back. Sinking Lake Lorn was one thing, but if she opened a scar in a city like Lanfall, the devastation would be on a scale she might never recover from. I knew that from experience. I have the death of more than one city attributed to me, and the people of Isha will never forget it. I will never forget it.

The servant led us through pristine halls, decorated with grand paintings of merchant lord Arsechin the first, or lady No Chance Her Tits Are That Big. I didn't really pay much attention to the plaques beneath each painting, but if I had learned one thing about the so called terran nobility, it's that no painting ever gets hung on a wall without being a massive fucking lie. The servant, a pinch-faced man with oily hair, deposited us in an antechamber, apologised another dozen times, and ran off to fetch his masters. I turned to Imiko and fixed her with a stare even as she skulked towards the nearest window.

"Don't you dare leave me here alone."

Imiko gave the window a push, found it locked with bars on the outside. Well, that was no surprise. The place was originally intended to be a fort, hence the bloody name. What they had done to it since the Fall of Orran was a travesty in my mind. Plush carpets, warm wall hangings, a table with a pitcher of wine waiting on it. I had to wonder if they just kept wine waiting around in chambers like this on the off chance an evil queen sauntered up to the gates unannounced.

"I'm better sneaking around on my own, Eska," Imiko said. She gave up at the window and decided to try the wine instead. "You know the way this works. You cause a big distraction by being you. Maybe kill a few people, start a war. You know, Eska things. I'll sneak around and do what actually needs to be done."

I gave her the flat stare she was so very good at ignoring.

"If Siri is here and wants to be found, she'll have heard you're here and will find you. If she doesn't come to you, then she doesn't want to be found. That's why I need to sneak away and find her."

"We find her together, Imiko. You wanted me along to help stop her if she's planning something stupid. Well, I can't do that if I'm not there."

Imiko poured the wine and narrowed her eyes at me. I couldn't tell what she was thinking. "Fine," she said, downed the glass, poured another.

How long did we wait in that antechamber? Long enough for Imiko to polish off three glasses of wine. I paced. For lack of anything else to do, and because I've never been good at sitting still. It seemed every bit of patience I had learned at Wrysom fell away along with my dead lover's name.

Eventually the greasy servant reappeared and begged us to follow him. We walked through halls that had once bristled with soldiers. Instead of arrows stacked in alcoves, they were filled with statues or potted flowers. Murder holes were filled in or covered up with decadent wall hangings. I saw a few soldiers standing about here and there, but most looked bored rather than attentive.

The servant led us into the bowels of the fort. The towers were massive, looming things, built high to allow Sourcerers like myself to stand atop them and rain down death. But the most secure place in the fort was actually below ground in huge rooms that could be filled with soldiers and barricaded against incursion. Fat lot of good that did the old emperor of Orran when the Terrelans came for him.

I had never seen the throne room of Fort Vernan before. Last time I was there, I had been rushed to the tallest tower to await the enemy. The emperor had come to see us, to wish us well, and deliver his rousing speech about how

Josef and I were the last, greatest defence of our mighty kingdom. Then he ran away and hid down here in the dark. Such a courageous leader he was, though I will admit at the time I thought him mighty. But then, that is how I had been trained to think of him.

The thrones had been done away with, though there was still a stone dais at the far end of the room where they had clearly once sat. Instead, the large hall was dominated by a massive horseshoe-shaped table in the centre. It had three dozen seats arrayed around it, some with hideously plush cushions. There were four doorways leading from the hall, each one guarded by soldiers wearing enchanted armour. I knew they were enchanted because I could see the runes glowing on the breastplates and vambraces. The merchants of Lanfall were taking no risks, it seemed. Enchanted armour is useful for only one thing: defending against Sourcerers. Unless there were a couple of other Sourcerers hiding under the table, the soldiers were there for me.

The whole thing was a display of power meant to impress. Well, I wasn't impressed. I have stood in the face of howling gods, stared into the ancient darkness, raised a city from the earth, and brought an empire crashing down on top the still twitching corpse of its ruler. It would take more than a big room, a fancy table, and some halfwit guards to impress me.

I sauntered to the table, found one of the chairs with a nice plush cushion, and lowered my old, bony arse into its gelatinous embrace. Nothing says disrespect quite like taking the chair meant for another. Imiko sighed and rubbed a hand over her face. She looked tired. But I expected that after seeing the amount she drank the night before, not to

mention hearing just how little sleep she got. I was a little
worried about her, I will admit, but I had so little time to
dwell on it with thoughts of Sirileth dominating my mind.

A few minutes later, one of the doors at the side of
the hall opened. Three more guards entered the great room,
a man in robes strode behind them. He had bearing, that
fellow. He wore it in the way he stood straight backed and
stiff, in the way he glanced about the room but not at me. He
was in his middle years, though his grey hair was thinning
on top. He held one hand inside a fold of his robes, while
the other hung limp by his thigh, the fingers dancing against
his leg. I took him for a Sourcerer and wondered what his
attunements were. I'd find out soon enough. He stepped
aside after surveying the room and made way for the real
power to enter.

It was the man from the painting I had seen earlier.
There was no mistaking the cleft chin, the steely eyes,
and the perfectly coiffed hair short and artfully thrusting
forwards from his head to hang above his eyes, probably
the fashion of the day. He wore plain black trousers that
matched his skin, a frilly white blouse buttoned all the way
up to make him appear taller than he was, and his eyes were
dark enough to put the night sky to shame. All this is to say,
he was utterly gorgeous. Had I been twenty years younger,
I'd have happily tested the waters. I was tempted to have a
go despite my wrinkles and aches.

The man glanced at Imiko, dismissed her
immediately, and settled his gaze on me. I warmed a little
under the intense scrutiny and sat a little straighter in the
chair I had assumed. There was something about the man
that made me want to appear strong. Some people have that
effect on us. They project such an image of themselves unto

a room, that we feel the need to match it. Those types of people can make their allies around them seem stronger by their mere presence, or their enemies seem like weak, pitiful things under their scrutiny.

"Eskara Helsene, is it?" the man asked. Lursa's Tears, but even his voice was mesmerising. An anvil struck just right so it rang pure, resonating for hours and letting you know how strong and solid it was.

Imiko coughed. "Queen Eskara Helsene," she said. She affected a bow like she was a servant rather than criminal mastermind and took the opportunity to send a pointed glare my way.

"From what I gather, you abdicated your throne many years ago," the man said, his voice the purr of a contented cat.

I recovered enough of my wits to stop acting like a fool. "How do you get your hair to stick up like that?" I asked. I'm afraid starting off important conversations with inane questions is a habit I've never quite grown out of.

We stared at each other across the room. It did not escape my notice that he had not approached the table. Nor that his guards and pet Sourcerer remained so close to him. Was he that afraid of me? Well, he had good reason to be.

The man smiled, the slightest tug at the corner of his mouth. I recognised this meeting for what it was. The opening salvo of a negotiation. My old lover, Silva would have loved it. She was never quite so alive as when duelling over a deal to be had. I always loved that about her, though I never had the patience to match her wits. That was always a desire she had to satisfy with others. I always caved too easily and gave her whatever she wanted in my feverish desire to please her. I have gained some perspective over the years, but when I look back, I know I would have done nothing differently. I was always so utterly powerless before her.

"I've seen you before," the man said. He began pacing, three steps to the left, turn on his shiny heel, and back to the right, his shoes clicking on the stone floor. "At the fall of Orran, Terrelans on our doorstep. We Orrans of power and wealth, those of us who hadn't fled, were ushered inside the fort to keep safe from the marauding army."

I scoffed. "Power and wealth. You mean the rich hid behind the walls and let the poor buggers outside get stabbed and burned."

He stopped pacing for a moment and glanced at me, one eyebrow arching so fucking elegantly he had to have practiced the manoeuvre in a mirror for years. "And how many of those poor buggers did you burn while indiscriminately attacking the Terrelans?" Oh, the purr had left his voice alright. He said those words to the tune of thrusting steel.

I had no answer. No witty retort. I had rained fire down on our enemy, but our own people were hiding in their homes. Some of them, no doubt, were caught in the crossfire. In my fires. I am the weapon. My little mantra the Orran academy beat into me reared its head. It occasionally did, even years after, but it no longer held the same power over me. Now I knew it for the lie it was. But then, knowing the shackles aren't locked is very different from removing them.

"You were much younger then," the man continued, his voice ringing around the hall like he had been trained to project. I still didn't know his name. Should have looked at the damned plaque beneath the painting. "So was I, of course, but you were much younger. I thought we were about the same age. I saw you stride past in the very halls above us now, a wild grin on your face. I remember it clearly. I thought, there goes a woman of power and the will to use it. Was I wrong?"

I have said I don't have a head for negotiation. Well, I was already tiring of this one. "I did use my power. For Orran."

"Yes," the man smiled, a wistful ghost of a thing gone before it ever truly formed. "For all the good it did our kingdom and its people."

"That battle was lost before it began." No truer statement, but still an excuse.

"I agree," he said, pacing again. "And yet you fought it anyway."

"The emperor ordered me to." I didn't know game we were playing, but I had a feeling I was losing.

"He would have kept fighting, you know," he paused. "Until you were dead. Until his army was crushed. Until every person under his rule was gone. The Orran Emperor had no give in him."

"Good job the Terrelans didn't give him a chance then," I said sulkily. I will not lie, despite everything I now know, it has always been a matter of damaged pride to me that I lost at the Fall of Orran. The tutors told me I could win. The emperor told me I had to win. I believed them both.

The man smiled again, this time wide and predatory. "All that power and will to use it. Useless in the end. You couldn't beat the Terrelans. You couldn't save the emperor."

"What's your point?" I growled. My eyes flashed and my Arcstorm grew restless inside. A bolt of lightning leapt from my fingers and scored the cherry wood of the table black, smoke rising in the air before me stinking of burnt polish.

He stopped pacing and met my flashy gaze with the fathomless dark of his own. "Just this: The Orran emperor would have sacrificed everything and still lost. You couldn't save him, nor beat his enemies, nor save the Orran people of Lanfall. But one young man with no Sourcery did, armed with nothing but a key and his will to end a pointless war. He opened the door, let the Terrelans in, and brought the war to an end."

"Shit," Imiko groaned, looked like she was deflating.

I stood slowly, ignoring the protest of my aching knees. I balled my hand into a fist and knuckled the table. "You," I ground the word out between my teeth. "You let the Terrelans in. You killed the Orran Emperor."

The man stared at me. Straight as a spear and solid as rock. "I did. I ended the war when you could not."

I would like to say it didn't matter to me. That I had long since put it all behind me and realised the emperor was a fool, and the Orrans were never any better than the Terrelans were. I would like to say I didn't still harbour a grudge against all those who had a hand in ending the war. That would be a lie. Part of me still wonders if we could have won. Could I have won if we had just kept fighting? Could we have beaten the Terrelans back if the emperor hadn't been killed and the signal to surrender hadn't come? I will never know the answer. And now I knew why. Because this man had taken it upon his young shoulders to end the war himself. We would have been of an age, just fifteen years or so, and yet he saw the way the infection was spreading and had the wit and will to cut off the arm before losing the body.

"Thank you." The words hissed from between my teeth. And I meant it, though probably not how he believed. Nursing grudges is one thing, something I'm quite practiced at, but I realised something else. If not for him ending the war, I might never have been sent to the Pit. Never met Hardt or Tamura or Ssserakis. I would never have had my daughters, nor met and fallen in love with Silva. This man was responsible for one of the most momentous events of my life, something that shaped everything that happened after. If I was to blame him for the bad, then I had no option than to also thank him for all the good. Besides, I doubted killing him would help me find Sirileth, but thanking him might. So, I chose diplomacy over the other option. I know, it's a rare thing.

The man stared at me a few moments longer, that same almost smile playing across his lips. Then he nodded. "Good."

He sketched a small bow that was nothing more than a sweep of his arms and a dip of his coiffed head. "My name is Jamis per Suano." He stood from his bow and a new, radiant smile beamed at me. "And now we can begin negotiations. Tell me, Eskara Helsene, what is you want?"

CHAPTER FOURTEEN

YOU MIGHT THINK, FROM THE STORIES I HAVE shared so far, that my children were always little angels who never did anything wrong. Of course, that's a pile of abban shit. They were children and getting into trouble is at least three quarters of the reason for their existence. I simply have not shared any of the more troublesome stories until now.

It is my own failing. I look back on that time, my children, and my friends in my fledgeling queendom. It was a time of peace and comfort. I think that was the happiest I had ever truly been. More so than my infancy in the forest village of Keshin, before the recruiters stole me from my parents and brother and gave me to the Orrans. More so than my early years at the Academy of Magic when Josef and I forged a bond stronger than blood, before the tutors started conditioning us to be the weapons they needed us to be. More even than my time with Silva, up on the flying city of Ro'shan, tangled in her limbs each night, feeling her hot, rushed breath on my skin as we explored each other, and the unfathomable completeness of lying sweaty and exhausted in her arms afterwards. No. It was the early years of ruling Yenheim, of raising my children that are my happiest memories.

I hoped to put some joy back into the world. My life has ever been complicated and painful and destructive. In raising my children, in trying to teach them better than I had been taught, in trying to instil within them a respect for life and love that had always been denied me. I thought that would be my legacy. I hoped they would improve the world. But then, we never raise our children hoping that they will destroy it instead.

I remember Tris. He'd gathered his usual group of child adventurers and they had set off to investigate a new area of the catacombs. I have already said I had cleared them out of monsters and Damned a while back, but that was true only so far as I could make it. The lower levels were unstable. I had ripped the palace from the earth, after all, and things below were not always safe. A wall had collapsed, and new passageways opened. I didn't know about it, but Tris had discovered it before anyone else, and of course he meant to explore it.

I thought they were going on one of their usual expeditions, chasing shadows and using their imaginations to conjure the adventure around them as children are prone to do. I watched them set off, Tris in the lead his Sourcestick held high. Vi a step behind him, chalk in hand, already making marks on the walls. Three other children, all around the same age, friends from the growing town outside the palace. And last, Sirileth, trailing behind but determined to take part.

I set about my day, mediating and declaring and generally signing things; tedious as those tasks were, but every queendom needs a bit of ruling now and then. Imiko had returned from one of her visits to a nearby town in the neighbouring kingdom of Kottlelan. She informed me the people of that town, I forget its name, had made the decision to leave Kottlelan and join Yenheim. My little queendom was growing, all thanks to Imiko and her recruitment. I never asked how she managed to convince so many to join us and thus extended our borders, and she never offered to explain. I assumed promises were made on my behalf and trusted her to keep them. I didn't know the truth. Didn't want to know.

Imiko and I were standing in the centre of my throne room, discussing possible repercussions from Kottlelan, when I heard the familiar paper ripping noise of a portal tearing open behind me. A couple of Tris' friends staggered through, children bawling their eyes out and screaming for their parents. Sirileth fell through after them. Blood streamed from her nose, and she clutched her stomach. I knew the signs right away, Source rejection. My daughter had found a Portamancy Source somewhere. It was the only explanation I could think of as to how she had opened a portal. But Sirileth was not attuned to that school of Sourcery. Just swallowing a Portamancy Source would kill her in mere minutes, faster if she was trying to use it, which she clearly was. Worse still, to have opened a portal with such accuracy and to keep it open, I knew already this was not the first time she had done it. It took me years of practice to open portals large and stable enough for people to cross through. Sirileth, just eight years old, already knew more about a school of Sourcery she wasn't even attuned to than I had at thirteen. How could such a smart girl be so damned stupid?

Sirileth collapsed to her knees, blood running down her face, dripping from her lips and chin, hands fumbling for her Spiceweed pouch, just where I had taught her to keep it. I let the other two children careen past me and surged toward Sirileth. Imiko beat me there, sliding to her knees, heedless of the rough stone floor. She gathered Sirileth into her arms, tore the pouch from her belt and shoved Spiceweed at her. Sirileth shied away, pointed a trembling finger toward the portal and managed to say one word: hurt. Then she coughed, spraying blood over Imiko's jacket.

I was torn in two. On one hand, my idiot daughter was playing with Sourceries she couldn't handle. She needed tending to, reprimanding, looking after. On the other, she was holding the portal open for a reason, and neither Tris nor Vi nor the third village child had come through yet. I could extrapolate my daughter's meaning well enough. Someone was hurt on the other side of the portal.

Imiko clutched Sirileth's spasming body tight and nodded toward the portal, telling me to go. It should have been me; I knew I should have been the one looking after Sirileth, but I was also the one who had to go check on the others. Sirileth whimpered in pain, blood leaking from her eyes as well as her nose. She couldn't hold the portal open much longer without it killing her.

I strode towards the portal, and it flickered. For just a moment, it showed that other place. A darkness so vast it was everything and nothing. And in the distance, somehow both far away and near all at once, the eye of the thing that existed beyond the portals. The same eye that stared through the great rift in the Polasian desert. Then the portal flickered again and showed a decrepit corridor of rock and carved statues. Portals hadn't worked right around me for many years, but right then I didn't have a choice. My children were hurt. I leapt through.

On the other side I found a dimly lit hallway that had been twisted and warped, probably many years ago when I raised the city. The corridor ended rather abruptly in a wall of fallen rock. I could already guess what had happened. Tris' band of adventurers had come down here exploring, not accounting for the instability in the tunnel. It had collapsed.

Tris was on his hands and knees, scrabbling at the fallen rocks, picking up small boulders and throwing them behind him. The portal snapped shut, Sirileth's strength having given out. I could only hope Imiko had given her Spiceweed before any of the more serious symptoms of rejection set in. Tris heard the sound of the portal shutting and turned to me. His hands were bloody, fingernails torn, his eyes wide. Another child might have run to me crying, begged me for forgiveness or claimed it was not their fault. But not Tris. He turned back to the cave in, pulled another rock away, and told me in a voice rushed with panic that the tunnel had collapsed on Vi and their other friend, but he could hear Vi's voice beyond the fallen rocks. Such a succinct report from a twelve-year-old boy in the midst of a panic, but then that was Tris. Panic is a focus for some.

I pulled him out of the way and used Geomancy infused with Kinemancy to grind the fallen rocks to dust. It was perhaps not the smartest of ways to deal with a cave in, but I, too, was in something of a panic. Vi was hurt, but not too seriously. A broken leg and a handful of cuts and bruises. She detailed every injury to me clearly in a high, pain-filled voice. The other child was not so lucky. He had been crushed by the falling rocks and did not survive.

I carried the dead boy's body out of the catacombs while Tris helped Vi hobble along. Vi filled the trip with noise, but far from her usual energetic nonsense, it was a subdued chatter. She told me everything that had happened until the cave in, and all the things she had seen, and about some of the other adventures the dead boy had been on. I maintained a brooding silence throughout.

Fury pumped in my veins like hot fire. I couldn't remember ever having been so angry. And anger, you may remember, has always been a passion of mine. My children had put themselves in such danger, had put others in danger, had gotten a young boy killed. I wanted to scream at them. To yell until my throat hurt and their ears bled. To make them see... To make them bloody well understand what they had done. But, of course, they already did understand. Tris was twelve years old, easily old enough to understand death. He could see the body I carried and he knew it was his fault.

When we got back to the throne room, I found Imiko tending to Sirileth. My daughter was alive at least, and she had been mostly cleaned up. She seemed quite calm about the whole thing, but I could see Imiko had been crying. Her eyes were red, the paint she always wore about them had run in charcoal streaks. I kept my seething silence and Imiko saw to Tris and Vi too. Instead, I summoned the boy's mother.

What can you say to the parents of a dead child? I'm sorry? I'm sorry my children were reckless idiots. I'm sorry they're still alive while your child is not. I'm sorry I wasn't watching them. I'm sorry I am secretly relieved because it was your child and not mine. What the fuck can you say? There are no words that can make it better. No words that can bring the dead back. Believe me, I know.

I apologised to the woman and took responsibility. Weathered her storm of tears and scorn. Promised her... Fuck, I don't know what I promised. It is all a blur to me now.

When finally, she was gone, taking her child's body with her, I turned on my own children. My eyes flashed, such fury behind them. Imiko was with them still, shielding them from... from me. As if I might turn that fury to violence.

I sent them away without punishment or reprimand, or even condemnation. Sometimes silence is worse than any scream. Imiko led them to their rooms, called the Biomancer for Vi, washed the blood from Sirileth's face. She played the part of understanding aunt, while I... I seethed.

Perspective has put things right over time. Now I realise it was not the children I was most angry at. Oh, believe me, I was still angry at them. But I place most of the blame at my feet, where it always belongs. I gave them no boundaries, taught them that power could overcome all obstacles and lied to them with promises that they owned such power. I made them feel invincible, so of course they didn't fear the danger all around them.

I found the dead boy wondering my palace halls that night. Not his body, of course, but his ghost. One of mine. Raised by my guilt. The world is full of ghosts. I ignore most of them but this was one I had created. I had given him form too. And it always feels right to take that form from them, to give them peace and send them on their way. To allow them to be reborn, or simply a final end from the torment of a half existence. It's the least I can do.

Never trust a merchant. As a rule, they'll happily sell
you a bucket while claiming it's a hat. When you get it home,
you'll realise the bucket has holes in it, smells like week-old
corpse, and is already home to a particular vicious slime
that keeps trying to jump into your eye. Also, don't trust
a stunningly beautiful merchant because you can bet your
bucket, they know just how pretty they are, and just how to
use it to squeeze you for coins.

Not that I'd have minded being squeezed a little by
Jamis per Suano. Trust me on this, you might eventually
reach the heady heights of age where you can no longer act
on your lusty thoughts. Doesn't stop you having them.

"I'm looking for my daughter," I said quickly before
the merchant could somehow twist my thoughts into
wanting to buy a goat instead.

Imiko groaned.

"Really?" Jamis said. He left the safety of his guards
and pet Sourcerer and approached the table, skirting it and
perching on the inside rim. "How refreshingly honest."

I matched Jamis, hobbling around the table with far
less grace and perched opposite him. I say I perched, but
it was more of a lean and then gritting my teeth against a
twinge in my back. "Would you prefer I lie?" I asked.

"Yes!" Imiko snapped. She stepped closer too, but
not up to the table. "Reach for the moons, be happy with the
sky."

I rolled my eyes at her. "Fine. I'm looking for a Djinn
in a bottle."

Jamis swept his midnight gaze from me to Imiko. I
hate to say it, but I felt a little stab of jealousy. "You must
be Imiko. Master thief, true power behind the throne of

Yenheim. You know, a few of my fellows have put a bounty on you." He delivered the hanging threat with such a deadpan voice, I couldn't tell if he was trying to make a joke. But then, that was the point.

Imiko shrugged as though the idea that someone might try to arrest her was too boring to consider. "Never heard of this Imiko," she said. "My name is Okimi, aide to queen Eskara Helsene in her dotage." I shot her a savage glare. She ignored me, of course.

"Well, Imiko or Okimi, or whatever you might decide to call yourself. It's a pleasure to finally meet you." Jamis gave that little half bow again, somewhere between mocking and respect. "So, the queen of Yenheim is missing?"

Imiko flicked an impatient gaze my way. "Something like that."

"And you're looking for her to..." Jamis swept his stare from Imiko to me, then back again. "Take her back to Yenheim? Against her will?"

Imiko crossed her arms. "Right now, we're just looking for her. Queen Eskara here hasn't seen her daughter in years. They have plenty of catching up to do."

"And you think she's in Lanfall," Jamis said, his voice flat as a newly minted coin. "Perhaps staying with one of my fellows?"

"We had that thought in mind, sure." Imiko took a couple steps closer to the merchant and I noticed the man's guard step forward, hands on weapons. Imiko stopped and held up her hands, smiling. "I guess we're not quite trusted enough."

Jamis sighed and waved a hand over his shoulder. The guards stepped back. "Your queen, the one in this room, has quite a fearsome reputation."

Imiko crossed the last of the distance between them and perched on the table next to Jamis. They looked so striking next to each other. One dark and beautiful, with a presence that drew the eye. The other pale, hair the colour of a dying forge.

"It's mostly bluster, I promise," Imiko said.

"She didn't burn down a city and kill an emperor?" Jamis asked, smiling.

"I said mostly bluster," Imiko grinned back. "A bit of truth, where we planted it."

You may have noticed, I do not enjoy being talked over, around, or ignored. I especially do not like being talked about while I'm in the bloody room. And though I really hate to admit it, Imiko looked like she was flirting with Jamis, and it made me unreasonably jealous. I blamed the Chronomancy. My body was somewhere in its sixth decade, but in reality I was still young enough to consider myself in my prime.

I have spoken at length on the differences and perils of both love and lust. Lust in the young is an unleashed flame that burns everything it touches. Lust in the elderly is a scent on a breeze that stirs something deep inside long thought forgotten, but fleeting all the same, lost as quickly as the memory of a dream. But what of those ages between the young and old? Well, then lust is a flower waiting to bloom. If fed and watered, it can blossom into something new and beautiful, opening a world of possibilities. If left to wither and die, it rots and leaves a smell like old sweat and regret.

What was I? Young? Old? Something in between? Confused, I think. Both in body and mind. Well, confusion and lust are regular bedfellows. All I really knew at the time was that Imiko was flirting with Jamis and the jealousy I felt stabbed deep. I wanted Jamis to look at me that way, smile at me that way. Even if it was all fake.

My head was swimming, thick with thoughts and emotions I was sure I'd long ago left behind. It wasn't lust, it couldn't be lust. Rather, it felt like desire. Desire is something entirely different. I wanted his attention, to be the subject of his focus. I wanted him to look at me and see me as his equal.

"Three times," I said loudly enough to draw the attention of both Jamis and Imiko. "I killed the emperor three times."

"Now that is impressive. How does one go about killing a man three times?"

I grinned at Jamis. Mystique can do wonders when trying to spark interest. Of course, when trying to flirt with a man, there are better ways to go about it than talking about the men you have murdered.

His smile vanished, wiped away like dust before a storm. "I'm afraid I don't know where you daughter is," Jamis said, his voice losing the playful edge. It felt like loss. The sun disappearing over the horizon and shrouding the beauty of the world in shadow. I wanted it back. I wanted the sun to return. I wanted Jamis to smile at me again. By Lursa's Tears, I didn't understand what was happening to me. Why was I so desperate for this man's attention?

"But that doesn't mean I can't help," Jamis continued. "If Sirileth Helsene is in Lanfall, or has passed through, someone will know. Most likely, one of the other members of the union."

Imiko chuckled and leaned back on her perch, arching her back. "And now we come to it. The price."

Jamis turned to look at Imiko and spread his hands

apologetically. "This is Lanfall, ladies. If someone gives you information without pay, either the information is false and your believing it leads to their profit, or there is a favour to be cashed in later."

"So, which is it?" I asked, desperate to inject myself into the conversation. "Pay now or pay later?"

Jamis glanced at me, his gaze flicking up and down in a way that I did not enjoy. There was hunger in the way he looked at me, but not the type I wanted. His gaze was frank and appraising, like he was inspecting an abban and deciding whether to breed it or slaughter it for steak.

"I think a favour would be best, don't you?" His eyebrow arched again, the same half-smile ghosting his lips. My heart quickened in my chest from the sight. Yes, of course he would request payment in the form of an unspecified favour at some later date. One glance at me and he could tell I had nothing but the clothes on my back and a dark reputation to my name. In retrospect, I should have traded him the clothes. Any favour relying on my reputation was one not worth considering, but I had no other choice. I agreed before Imiko could point out it was a bad idea. That doesn't mean she didn't berate me for it later.

"Wonderful." Jamis all but leapt from his perch on the table and strode towards me, dark eyes sparkling. He held out a hand for me to shake and I took it greedily. I'm not sure which of us held on to the other for a bit longer than was necessary, but I found myself staring into his eyes and struggled to form a coherent thought past so damn pretty.

My eyes flashed at him. "They really are as striking as the stories say," Jamis said, his voice husky. He licked his lips, then let go of my hand and turned, already making for the same door he had entered through.

"There is a function tonight." His voice trailed over his shoulder. "Nothing too big. We hold one once a week for Merchant Union members and clients. The representative from Ro'shan will be there. She arrived just this morning by flyer." I had heard the flying city was only a few days away. I will admit, I hoped to be gone before it arrived. I was fairly certain Mezula wanted me dead. The feeling was mutual.

Jamis flicked a hand at the oily servant who led us to the hall. "Deniel will lead you to your quarters until the auction starts. I suggest you stay there. I will make some subtle inquiries on your behalf." He breezed out of the hall without waiting for a reply, his pet Sourcerer scurrying after him, hand still tapping against his leg.

Deniel cleared his throat, making me want to smear his oily hair all over the floor. He opened the door and gestured at it impatiently. I ignored him. Now Jamis was gone, I found I could breathe again, think again. Like waking up after a week-long drunk and wondering what the fuck have I done?

Imiko stood from her perch on the table and strode over, sitting down next to me. "Idiot," she said, nudging her shoulder against mine. There was no real venom to her words.

"I got us what we wanted, didn't I?" The last vestiges of my fuzzy intoxication were fading away like the memories of a nightmare. I saw Jamis now for what he was. A pretty man, to be certain, but not so handsome I should have been as flustered as I was. There was something about his presence though, about being in his presence. It was maddening. Like a lover's breath tickling your lips as they hold a kiss just out of reach. I feared it, what his presence did to me. I craved it, too. Now it was gone, I wanted it back.

She frowned at me. "Never promise the sun when you can get away with a lamp."

"You sound like Tamura."

"Good." Imiko pushed off the table onto her feet and held out a hand to me, pulling me up. "You actually listened to him."

"Sometimes," I grumbled, determined to have the last word.

"Sometimes," Imiko agreed.

CHAPTER FIFTEEN

SIRILETH WAS NINE WHEN WAR CAME to Yenheim. I should clarify. Sirileth was nine when I inadvertently started a war that almost consumed the little queendom.

With no empire ruling over everyone, imposing their own form of law, the rules on Isha became somewhat more flexible than they had been. Yenheim had land, much of it arable. It had an extensive underground city, the part I hadn't raised out of the earth, with connections to what had once been the Pit. This gave us access to water and to rock, as much as we could ever need. I find it somewhat fitting that half of Yenheim is built from the rock I helped dig out of the Pit. We even had the Forest of Ten nearby, giving us a near unlimited source of lumber. What we didn't have were animals.

Abban, despite being large and tasty, are not the

easiest of beasts to raise, and my little queendom had not yet managed anything but a fledgling cacophony. That's what we call a group of abban, a cacophony. If you've ever heard them gather and howl at the moons, you'd probably know why.

There is no part of an abban that isn't useful. Their horns make excellent tools or jewellery. Their shaggy hair once sheared and cleaned — never forget to clean it — can be made into winter clothing. They produce milk that is wonderfully nutritious, even if it does taste like sweaty crotch. And if you have a particularly successful cacophony, you can butcher one up for abban steak, which I assure you, is just about the most wonderful meat you could ever want. It melts on your tongue and has a flavour that goes on for days. Excellent with a pinch of salt, and some nice gravy. Abbans are also the premier beasts of burden in Isha. All in all, really bloody useful animals. And in Yenheim we were struggling to get our cacophony howling.

Another thing Yenheim did not have access to was ore. We had rock a plenty, but I think the Pit had been chosen by the Terrelans because it was worthless ground. There was no ore or coal down there, just rock. It was also currently flooded and home to aquatic creatures who happily fed off decaying terran flesh. Not a nice place to take a dip.

But back to focusing on abban. We didn't have any, or not enough to get a good cacophony howling. Our neighbours to the south, Tor, had many cacophonies. They were rich enough in abban that many of their taverns served abban steak. I should probably point out that Tor was named after the remnants of old Juntorrow. The city I burned down after unleashing a plague of unliving death. The same city whose populace had named me the Corpse Queen in the first place, who had once dragged me through their streets in chains, throwing rocks and rotten vegetables and shit at me. They had begged Aras Terrelan to gut me and display my body. It's safe to say, despite our relative proximity, the people of Tor and my queendom had a complicated relationship.

I chose the target. I led the raid. We stole across the border into Tor, knocked a few shepherds senseless, then made off with a couple of dozen abban, mostly females. No one died. I made sure of it, not that it mattered.

Tor was run by a council not a monarch, a wise system of rule if you ask me, and a few days later we received their reply. I don't know how they managed to sneak past my guards, nor Imiko's spies. I was in our practice cavern with my children, teaching them. Well, I was teaching Tris the basics of Necromancy while Josef, in one of his more lucid states, was teaching Vi something about Biomancy, though I have no idea what. Sirileth watched on as Sirileth often did. When I asked her if she wanted to learn something specific, she just shook her head and continued to watch, figuring it out before moving on.

A quarrel flew from the darkness. It was almost on target too, but the caverns in Yenheim had strange wind currents. The damned bolt was low and sank into the meat of my thigh, knocking me down and tearing a pain-filled scream from me. I just about managed to raise my arm and form a kinetic shield to stop the next one I'm certain would have found my skull. It was rendered harmless against my barrier and fell to the ground.

I screamed at my children to run. None of them did. Brave fools. Why didn't they just fucking run? I suppose that's my fault too. I taught them to fight. I remember struggling back to my feet, hearing shouts, the sounds of steel clashing against steel in the darkness. Half a dozen black-clad warriors with straight swords running at me. Tris and Vi erected their own kinetic shields as another volley of quarrels hurtled out of the darkness beyond our lantern light.

Vi didn't even scream. She didn't have chance. My adopted daughter had always struggled with kinetic arms. Her shield was weak. The crossbow bolt shattered it, and buried itself in her chest, flinging her to the floor. She didn't move. Blood shone in the lantern light. Tris screamed. Not the cry of pain, but of horror, of something so unfathomable it couldn't be allowed.

My rage has ever been a terrible thing. There are times when it grips me so thoroughly that all sense is blasted away, leaving only a red-hot haze through which no thought can penetrate other than a relentless desire to inflict my pain on someone else. Not one of the attackers made it out of that cavern, and I was painted with their blood by the time I was finished. It wasn't enough. It would never be enough. Not for what they took from me.

When I turned from the slaughter, I found I had missed one of the attackers. Too caught up in the rage, in the red dance, I didn't notice him slinking around in the gloom. He was tall and broad as a bear, wielding a big axe I might have struggled to lift. He slunk from the darkness and ran at Sirileth. I saw him charging my daughter, axe raised to strike. He was too far away, Sirileth between us. There was nothing I could do but raise my hand, scream at him, beg him not to do it. Of course, he was deaf to my words. He had just seen me slaughter his comrades and had committed himself to murdering a nine-year-old girl. People like that don't listen to words. People like that, willing to kill children, do it not for queen or country or any other supposedly noble cause. They do it because they want to. Because they enjoy the killing. Because they are fucking monsters who are willing to murder children.

Sirileth turned at the last moment, saw her death coming. Another child might have cried out, tried to run, begged for her life. Not my daughter. She faced the man head on, raised her hand, and crushed him.

I haven't seen anyone with that level of Kinemancy control since the Iron Legion. She gripped the man in the centre of a kinetic storm that pressed in on him from all sides. He must have outweighed her by four times, and yet Sirileth didn't move. She stopped his charge and lifted him from the ground with her Sourcery. As I have stated, there are forces at play. Kinetic forces. His momentum from his charge did not disappear, Sirileth absorbed it. She lifted him from the ground, something she should not have been able to do unless she was not just using Kinemancy to crush the man, but also to strengthen herself and brace herself against his weight. On any other day, I might have stopped and stared in wonder at this act of control and power that dwarfed my own.

But my daughter was still in peril.

I rushed to her side even as I watched her tighten her grip. The man screamed as his arm snapped like kindling, a sound so sickening I will always remember it. Yes, I have broken arms before, both others and my own. This was different because it was my daughter doing the breaking. She was killing a man. Blood sprayed from his cracking limbs, bones pushed through skin, muscle, and flesh. I couldn't let it happen. Sirileth was not me, shouldn't have to be me. She was too young to be a killer. I reached her side, a Sourceblade already in my hand, and swung, decapitating the man, ending his torment. Sirileth held him in her kinetic grip a moment longer, then simply let his body drop. She looked at me then and said I didn't need your help, Mother. Well, that was a too much. My daughter of nine years old claiming she could easily have killed a man without my help. I struggled to sort through the tumult of emotions, but at least one of them was relief. I put my arm around her and pulled her close. Of course, I was still covered in the blood of others, those I had killed. I got a lot of that blood on Sirileth. Yes, I'm sure you can all see the metaphor there. It's not exactly subtle.

My people started filling the cavern, bringing noise and questions with them, but over them all, I heard Tris crying. Sirileth looked up at me, blood smeared across her pale face, and said Vi is hurt, Mother.

It was too late. I was too late. From the moment that quarrel left the bow, it was too late.

Vi died.

The little girl I had rescued from the Iron Legion, brought into my home, sworn to protect was dead. She was always so chatty, asking questions, filling the air with her noise. Silent now. She loved to chase animals, cats, dogs, lizards, chicken, not to torment them but because she loved watching them. Never again.

Vi died... was murdered over a few stolen abban.

Tris wailed. He had been with Vi since before I knew them. They were as close as Josef and I had ever been. He screamed and he sobbed, and he begged her to wake. I don't think he meant to do it, but he brought her back, of a sort. His own innate Necromancy, so much like my own, caught

Vi's soul as it left her body and tethered it to our world.

Vi's ghost watched on as Tris cried over her body, pleaded her to open her eyes and say something, anything. She watched as he slumped, his exhaustion and grief reaching a point where he could take no more and Tris just stopped. He wasn't unconscious; he just wasn't there anymore. I had some of my people take him away, sent for Hardt to watch over him. Then I went to Vi.

She was so brave. Even as a ghost, she understood what I had to do, and she smiled at me and nodded. I embraced her, what was left of her. I felt her grip tighten on me, my Necromancy making her ethereal form corporeal for just a moment. Then I unravelled her. It was all I could do to save her the eternal torment of life as a ghost. A damning half-existence. I saved Tris the torment of being haunted by his sister.

I have always absorbed memories of those I unravel. I have hundreds of them, thousands, maybe. Memories that are not mine, yet they feel like they are. Vi gave me a memory of herself and Tris and I seated around a campfire. We were younger. It was just days after I rescued them from the Iron Legion. We sat at that campfire, staring into the flames, and I hugged them both. Vi's relief at her rescue, her love for Tris and for me, flooded into me. That was what she gave me, her last gift. Her happiest memory.

CHAPTER SIXTEEN

I STARTED TO REALISE HOW WELL I HAD BEEN played the moment a seamstress turned up at the quarters we had been all but confined to. She carried a silken suit fit for a queen and indicated she was there on Jamis' behalf. After half an hour of poking and prodding, she made some quick alterations to the suit and left it with me. Along with a painful girdle, and a selection of jewellery. Imiko laughed at my grumpiness but helped me get into the girdle all the same. That was when it slipped into place. Not the girdle. They don't slip into place so much as are secured by enough rigging to confuse a sailor.

I had agreed to providing Jamis with a favour down the line. And he would collect, I had no doubt about that. But, of course, he was getting a more immediate payment as well. He was bringing Eskara Helsene to his little party. Trussed up in a costume of his making. He was showing off

to his fellow merchants by saying, Look here, I've dressed
the great and terrible Corpse Queen up like a doll. Now
watch while I make her dance.

I will admit, I was angry. Furious even. I was
moments from the tearing the suit to pieces and stalking
through the halls of Fort Vernan with murder on my mind
for a second time in my life. Then Imiko reminded me why
we were there. That I could suffer a little indignity if it meant
finding Sirileth. Fuck! But she was right.

So, I turned up to that bloody ball wearing Jamis'
clothes and jewellery and looking every bit the dark queen
he intended me to. Besides, the suit did make me look good,
and the earrings and necklace somehow managed to make
the flashing of my eyes more striking. Bloody man knew his
stuff, and that was the point. He might try to dress me up as
a jester and show me off, but that would hurt my reputation
more than bolster his. If he dressed me up as the monster
I was feared to be and showed his peers he had me under
control. Well, that only made him more powerful in their
eyes. It was all a show, and I was the gruesome centrepiece.

Deniel reappeared when it was time and led us
back into the heart of the fort. I noticed more guards than
earlier, standing in watchful silence. Most weren't wearing
enchanted armour though, so I contented myself with
knowing I could kill them with ease in case things went
badly and some fool decided to try to arrest the old queen
of Yenheim. There were more servants too, running about
with trays of food or bottles of wine. Imiko watched a few
of those go with thirsty eyes. Deniel led us to a lift, and
suddenly I knew where I was. I recognised the tower even
as we ascended it. I settled into the back of that lift, as much
as my bloody girdle would allow, crossed my arms, and

brooded. Of course, they would hold the ball here. What better place to show off the Corpse Queen than where she had first been defeated? How fucking fitting. Jamis had thought of everything.

We stepped off that lift into the great arming chamber at the top of the tallest tower of Fort Vernan. Not quite the rooftop, though it was accessible. This was where Sourcerers were supposed to gather in case of attack. Organise defences and prepare to shoot magical death out of each window. This was the grand chamber where Josef and I stood while the Orran Emperor delivered his rousing speech about loyalty and power, and all the bollocks that got me fired up and ready to fight the last fucking battle of a losing war.

It had changed in thirty years. Gone were soldiers in plate, all standing in line for inspection. Gone were armour racks and barrels holding nothing but arrows. The barricades that were in place before the stairs to the roof were no longer there either. The merchants had taken a place dedicated to battle and defence and turned it into a display of unreasonable wealth.

Decadent woven tapestries covered the walls, each one depicting a lord or lady, or the crest of a merchant house. I imagined there was probably one for each of the fools there, or at least each one who counted among the Merchant Union members. There were two long wooden tables at one side of the hall that held plate upon plate of food. Servants stood guard behind, ever watchful in case a plate ran empty. Or possibly in case a guest tried to poison the chicken. I've always wondered about those places that allow people to serve themselves in such a fashion. Seems a recipe for a lot dead guests. I wondered if they'd even allow me to approach the food without a chaperone. I saw Jamis' pet Sourcerer perusing the plates, picking at skinned fruits with one hand, the other still buried in the folds of his robe.

At the far end of the chamber, just before the stairs leading to the roof, a band of bards were playing. One had a lute, another a lyre, and one plucked away at a stringed instrument I had never seen before. It was the size of a horse and produced a wonderfully low sound that seemed to travel throughout the hall but didn't dominate the space. The bards were on a small wooden platform, barely large enough to stand all three of them. Apparently, there's a reason for having them stand on wood instead of stone, something about acoustics. Barrow Laney used to go on and on about it back at the Orran Academy of Magic. Before the Iron Legion drove him insane, of course.

Merchants infested the hall. They clustered in groups like flies on an open wound. Yes, I use the gruesome analogy on purpose. I have an unflatteringly low opinion of merchants, despite calling one the love of my life. I will not begin to argue that Silva was different. If anything, she embodied all the worst traits of the mercantile class; greed and the will to manipulate chief among them. She wasn't different. She was just Silva. And I would forgive her every party she ever attended, and every shady deal she ever made, because I loved her. No other reason was needed. That is what love is. It's easy to love a person for who they are, but much more difficult to love them despite what they are. I did not love any of these merchants, and so I let my scorn grow wild.

Here a cluster of three women, two wearing lavish dresses of colours I couldn't name, one wearing a fine red suit of silk. The woman in the suit had a notebook and pencil in hand and was jotting down details. In the middle of some sort of deal, no doubt. Probably determining the price of salt for the next few months, driving them high enough that some poor sods who relied on the damned stuff would suffer and go hungry all because these rich fucks wanted an extra coin in their pockets.

Over there, a fat man in a blue sash, his flabby right breast uncovered. He possessed more jowls than I did wrinkles, despite my age. The fat bastard waved a cup in the air as he cavorted and laughed. The other three men clustered around him, laughing like good little sycophants, hanging on his every word as though he were spitting gold at them rather than wine.

A dozen smaller groups dotted the chamber. All wearing gaudy colours and more jewellery than I had seen during my time as queen. That much is only partly due to my own austerity. Yenheim was never a rich little queendom. Though what we lacked in affluence, we made up for in reputation.

Terrans were not the only peoples in attendance, I noticed. Three pahht mingled with them, all wearing the same colours. Angry orange with deep black trim. One was greying around the muzzle, no doubt the eldest of the three, and moved with more care than abandon, clutching a cane with one clawed hand.

There were Polasians too. I spotted at least one large woman wearing a purple dress that barely constrained her. She laughed and joked with a terran man half her size, often putting a hand on his arm. A Polasian man stood behind them both, mouth covered by a lilac sash, and eyes watchful.

I did not see Jamis in the crowd, though there were enough people, I could have missed him. What I did notice, was that the party was in full function already. I had been delivered late. It wouldn't do to have the Corpse Queen arrive with only a few people to witness it. My entrance needed to be a spectacle. Damn, but Jamis really had planned it so perfectly. I should have hated him for that, but I was too bloody impressed by the theatre he had set in motion.

Deniel cleared his throat. Lursa's Tears, I hate it when people do that. He stood just past the lift, waiting. I stepped off the lift, Imiko melding into the shadows behind me. She'd do what she needed to do. That probably meant slink off at the first opportunity and leave me to face this hell alone. I swear to you, I have faced down monsters with a desire to swallow my soul, I stood before gods and screamed my name into the howling void, I have suffered time and again under the torturers' knives, and I have watched my friends and family and loved ones fall to battles we had no hope of winning. I would take every one of those situations over the false pretences and insufferable politeness of this court of crows I found myself attending.

"Your honourable merchant lords," Deniel said so loudly I thought he might be a Vibromancer. "Jamis per Suano presents Eskara Helsene."

Gods save me from pageantry. It was all so calculated. Jamis had written the script, placed his players, and pulled open the curtain. We danced to his merry little tune.

The gathered merchants fell silent. The hush sweeping over the chamber so quickly only the lingering notes of the bards' instruments echoed from the walls. I stepped from the lift, and a large man with a harelip gasped, a pudgy hand flying to his open mouth. They got a good look of the monster in their midst. Damn me, but it felt good. I had been hiding for so long, trying to convince the world,

by my absence, that Eskara Helsene was dead. Well, I wasn't
fucking dead. And I wasn't hiding any more. Let them look
at me. Let them witness my triumphant return. There was
something yet left for all these fat parasites to fear in the
world.

The whispers started. Whispers amidst a crowd
spread faster than fire. First one, a hushed murmur like
crinkling paper in a library. Then another joined and another
and another. Within moments, half the people in that hall
were whispering to each other, the noise growing louder by
the second. As the volume grew, those whispers turned to
shouts.

"Quite the stir," Imiko said quietly. She was hiding
behind me, all but unnoticed.

"Do your thing," I said other my shoulder.

She chuckled. "Give me a few minutes to do a round.
Then create a distraction."

"This isn't enough of a distraction?" I got no reply.
Imiko was already gone. I looked about and found her
striding towards the food tables. No one else took notice of
her.

Alone in a room full of hungry leeches — sorry,
merchants — I strode forwards, ignoring the voices saying
my name, the pointing fingers, the accusations. Jamis was
still nowhere to be seen, but I guessed that was by design.
This was clearly my part to play in his production.

The bards struck up a new tune. I knew it. I knew
it because I knew the man who had written it. Sirileth's
father. The bard Wyn, as he later came to be known, though
I knew him by his first name. We met in a tavern between
old Juntorrow and Yenheim. I was a broken woman, recently
maimed by the Terrelan emperor. I had just destroyed

Juntorrow, released a plague of undeath upon the world, and secured my title of the Corpse Queen. I hated myself. He called me beautiful, listened to my woes and got me very very drunk. We spent a single night together, and it was… fine, as far as pleasure goes. Certainly nothing compared to my nights spent under Silva's considerable attentions. I got some small measure of confidence back from his feverish attention. But far more importantly, I got Sirileth. His name was Reo, and his eyes were so dark they looked like pupil and iris merged into an inky void. Though he may never know of the daughter he fathered, he got something from the exchange. He listened to my story and turned it into a song that made him famous. The name of that song is The Fury of the Storm. It was played everywhere on Isha for a few years, known by every bard worth their notes. Some still play it, though not many. Most know only what is left after so many years: the chorus that was adapted into a child's rhyme.

> Night shall fall and the dead will rise.
> The Corpse Queen comes. The Corpse Queen comes.
> Hide under your bed and hold your breath.
> The Corpse Queen comes. The Corpse Queen comes.
> Pray to the moons, pray for the sun.
> The Corpse Queen Comes. The Corpse Queen comes.

That is but the chorus, the most well-known part of the song. I will not embarrass myself by trying to sing the rest of it. Suffice it to say, it was no accident that the bards at that gathering of merchants knew the full version of The Fury of the Storm.

Some of the attendees backed away from me as I walked further into the centre of that ball, as though my mere presence offended them. Others flocked closer, sensing within the moment a way to advance their own agendas.

The fat merchant in the blue sash was the first to reach me, his right breast flopping about as he hurried to get in my way. He stank of some flower so aggressively I couldn't help but wonder what he was trying to hide. He towered over me, a good head taller, and as fat as a pig preparing for the winter months. His jowls wobbled as he spoke, and his wine-soaked breath somehow managed to out-stink his perfume.

"Oh, the Corpse Queen," he all but shouted. "I thought you'd be younger. More intimidating." His sycophants waited nearby, watching eagerly. Other eyes turned our way too, everyone in the room paying attention to the encounter. "You did a great service for us when you killed the Terrelan emperor. I must applaud you." He clapped his hands so daintily his palms barely touched.

The loudest person in any room is usually also the least important. It did not escape my notice that this fat merchant was speaking loud enough, his voice carried to everyone in the room, nor that he was claiming I murdered the emperor for him. The best way to take away someone's power, is to claim it as your own.

Between the bards banging out their rendition of my crimes, and the choir of noise from the merchants watching and waiting to see what I would do, there was no way I could answer this fat bastard without screaming, but actions speak louder than words. I leaned forward, sniffed dramatically, wrinkled my nose, then recoiled and walked past the gawking fat man. I'd like to imagine his reputation suffered some after that, but honestly, I didn't stick around to find out.

I searched for Jamis. Not because I was looking for
a friendly face. I found myself the centre of attention of
everyone there, and yet his was the only attention I wanted.
My head felt fuzzy again, my palms sweaty, my emotions a
roar within my veins. Something wasn't right with me, but I
couldn't think clearly enough to reason it out.

A woman stepped in front of me, blocking my path.
She was dark skinned with hair the colour of the sea on
a summer's day. I doubted it was her natural colour. She
bowed ever so slightly to me and smiled as she straightened.
"Lady Es'kara." She had an accent I couldn't place, though
it was certainly not one from Isha or Polasia. Still, terrans
had spread all over the world, unlike the garn or tahren who
liked to stay on their home continents. "We have a friend in
common, I think. The Queen of Ice and Fire would no doubt
like to see you again."

That certainly made me take notice. Without thinking
of the consequences, I backed up a step, quickly checking the
woman's hands for knives. The Queen of Ice and Fire was
also known as Lesray Alderson. Or, as I have always liked
to call her, the Bitch-whore. She is the one who helped make
my life at the academy so miserable. Lesray is the one who
planted the seed of suicide in my mind with her damned
Empamancy. I couldn't imagine any reason she'd want to see
me again, other than to finish the job she started thirty years
ago.

My backstep provided every other merchant in the
place the opportunity they were waiting for. It showed
weakness and every predator loves weakness. They closed
in around me from every direction, a dozen voices all
demanding something of me.

"Oh, do show us your living shadow."

"I heard you were dead."

"Your filthy Cursed children killed my father."

I couldn't keep track of them all. Enemies on every side. No way out. Closing in on me like darkness on a guttering flame. My head spun. I couldn't find Jamis. My emotions didn't fit. My thoughts were mired in desire. I wanted Jamis. I wanted him to see me, to know me. I couldn't think. Didn't understand. Fuck it. Fuck them. Fuck Jamis for putting me in the position. At least I would give Imiko her distraction.

I unleashed my Arcstorm.

Anger has always been a catalyst for my storm, but fear has as well. It reacts differently to those emotions though. With fear, instead of striking out as a targeted fork of lightning, it crackled chaotically around me. Lightning ripped from my skin, arcing out to score searing lines across the floor. My eyes flashed like they hadn't in years. The storm grew in intensity, surrounding me with a wild shield of sparking lightning. The merchants learned their place then, backing away, gasping, falling over each other in their attempts to get away from the monster. I flexed my hand and lightning played across my fingers. It ached to be free, energy building to an uncomfortable throb that demanded violent release.

Then Jamis per Suano was slinking out from the crowd in front of me, a coy smile curling his lips. My head swam, my vision tunnelled, and suddenly I found I could think of nothing but him. I could feel nothing but the desire to be close to him, to feel his attentions on me and only me. I wanted to hate it, to hate him, but I couldn't. He walked through my storm, almost daring it to strike him. And for a wonder, it didn't. My lightning crackled, striking the floor

around him, setting the carpet alight. But it didn't touch
him. I'm not sure if that was my doing or his. Probably
mine, though almost certainly his will. He was gorgeous.
Beyond beautiful. He wore a bleached bone suit and a deep
green waistcoat too tight around the arms to show off his
muscle. His hair was longer than before, with thick, dark
braids trailing down his back. His fathomless eyes caught
my lightning and reflected it back at me. I found myself
breathing hard, my knees weak. Lursa's Tears, but this man
did something to me. Unmade me. I could not fathom how.
It wasn't right, but he brought me to heel as easily as Silva
had once done. I hated him for that, and yet... I wanted to be
close to him.

Jamis stopped close enough to me that I had to look
up to meet his gaze. He smelled sweet, like freshly picked
fruit. He licked his lips and smiled at me. I almost collapsed
from the rush of desire that swept over me. Then he leaned
down and, damn me, I thought he was going to kiss me. I
wanted it. I wanted it so much I rose onto my shrivelled old
toes to meet him. He made my pulse race, my head fuzz, my
legs tremble, and my stomach flutter. Or at least, I thought
he did.

But Jamis did not kiss me. He leaned to the side just
slightly, heedless of my lightning. It calmed before him, the
crackling turning to energetic trails racing along my skin.
His face brushed mine as he leaned down. I heard him gasp
a little as one of my trails of lightning touched his cheek.
Pleasure or pain, I don't know.

His lips brushed my ear and he whispered for me and
me alone. "I know where your daughter is. Come with me."

And I did. For a reason I couldn't fathom, without
question or hesitation. My storm died around me. I stood

amidst the most powerful merchants in all Isha, all eyes on me. What a show I gave them. All to Jamis' script. He played me as surely as the bards their instruments. Eskara Helsene, the Corpse Queen, the most feared monster in Isha. Tamed by Jamis per Suano with only a whisper.

CHAPTER SEVENTEEN

JAMIS TOOK ME BY THE HAND, HIS SLENDER
fingers interlocking with my own. His skin was cool and
soft. His thumb rubbed light circles on the back of my hand.
I tingled at his touch. He pulled me from within the crowd of
merchants, and led me towards the rear end of the chamber.
We mounted the stairs slowly, and I lived for the moments
he glanced back over his shoulder and smiled. It felt wrong.
So viciously wrong. It felt like a betrayal. Like I was setting
fire to Silva's memory, even so long dead, by desiring to be
close to this man, a desire I hadn't felt since her. And then
that thought was overwhelmed by a wave of intense longing
for Jamis that weakened my knees and left me gasping. Why
could I not control myself?

We left the whispers behind, rumours already
growing as they did. Rumours are voracious, carnal things.
Breeding like ghouls left unchecked and consuming every

bit of air they can find. I had no doubt that by the time we reached the top of those stairs, there were half a dozen different rumours flitting about that chamber. Breeding with each other in mid-air and spawning yet more of their kind. That, too, was by Jamis' design.

The cool air of the open tower roof knocked some sense back into me. Or perhaps it was because we were finally alone. Out of sight of all the merchants and servants below. With my first breath, I felt some of my wits return. I realised just what a fool I had been. I let those snivelling merchants get to me, almost murdered them, all because I let my fear rule me. Then, I'd gathered up every bit of power I had earned over the past three decades and handed it to Jamis with a bow. I wondered how he had done it? How had he manipulated me so easily? With my head finally clearing, there was only one answer.

"You're an Empamancer!" I spat the accusation with as much venom as I could muster. It wasn't much. I was still reeling. I also couldn't seem to let go of his hand.

I heard footsteps on the stairs behind me, couldn't let anyone see me in such a state of weakness. And then suddenly I didn't care. Didn't care about showing weakness, or who saw me, or anything other the man clutching my hand.

Jamis' fingers squeezed my own and he spun about to face me. His thumb continued its lazy circles on the back of my hand and damn, if that wasn't just the most distracting thing. He stared at me, his smile genuine, and shook his head. "I have no Sourcery, Eskara." I knew it was true.

"Call me Eska," I said. I could have screamed at myself for that. Treating him like he was some old friend. But I didn't want the formality. My full name has always felt more like a formal title. My friends call me Eska. My lovers have always called me Eska. I wanted that intimacy with Jamis. I wanted him. Not to love. Not to fuck. Just him. Just desire. Unbound, unfettered desire.

We stood atop the tallest tower of Fort Vernan, hand in hand. Lanfall spread out below us. The bards had started playing again, their music mixing with the chatter, but all of that was muted. A dull, pointless noise drifting up from the chamber we'd just vacated. The night air was cool. The stars shone. The moons stared down at us, Lokar in dominance, his blue bulk swallowing his lover's red flesh. And I was drowning. Swept up by Jamis' presence, trapped by his magnetic gaze, swallowed whole. It was wonderful and I hated it. I tried to hold on to that hate, but it slipped from my mind like water through fingers.

"Thank you for that, Eska." He raised my hand in his own, gave my fingers one more squeeze, then pressed his lips to the back of my hand, his eyes never leaving mine. "You can consider your debt paid in full."

I didn't want my debt to be paid. In that moment, I wanted a reason, any reason to stay close to Jamis. I would have done anything for one more drawn out, pitiful, tantalising second in his presence.

Do not let him rule you like this. That thought saved me. Like a plank of wood to a woman lost at sea, it gave me something to hold on to. It sounded so much like Ssserakis, my old horror. But Ssserakis was gone. It was just me, alone in my own head. Or at least, I should have been alone in there.

"Stop it," I snarled, breathless. "Whatever you're doing to me. Stop it!"

"Doing to you?" Jamis let go of my hand and took

a step back. His smile faded to a frown that somehow only made him more beautiful. With a flick of my fingers, I could have sent him careening from the tower, ended whatever madness he held over me. His pet Sourcerer was not there to protect him, and... It all made sense. His fucking pet Sourcerer.

I was panting, the fuzzy edges creeping in again, trying to disarm me. But no more. "Tell him to stop," I growled at Jamis.

Jamis met my flashing gaze and I saw fear fill his eyes, there and gone in a blink. He looked over my shoulder and nodded once.

The fuzzy edges disappeared from my mind like smoke blown away on a gust of wind. Finally, I could think clearly again, and I understood just what had happened. What Jamis had done. How he had manipulated me. Rage made everything hot and sharp and damn, but new fuzzy edges crept back in, and these ones, I knew, had nothing to do with an Empamancer. This was all my rage. All me.

I turned slowly to find Jamis' pet Sourcerer standing on the top step, watching me with nervous eyes. His fingers tapped against his leg, and he slowly backed into the tower. Too slowly.

I have said before, more than once, that I fucking hate Empamancy. It is a truly despicable school of magic. It is the ability to manipulate a person from their very core. To swell their emotions, to impose a Sourcerer's emotions onto someone else. It is a violation of heart and spirit, and I will not suffer it.

The desire I felt for Jamis was not mine. It had never been mine. The fear I felt when I'd been surrounded by those simpering merchants was not mine either. Everything I had felt since entering this cursed tower had been by design. Emotions imposed upon me, implanted within me. Not mine! I had been controlled; my strings pulled like a will-less puppet. And I had not the sense to see it happening to me.

The Sourcerer took another step backwards into the tower. Not fast enough. Not for my liking. I threw out my hand and released a blast of kinetic energy that smashed into the Sourcerer and threw him away down the steps. Judging by the musical crash, he hit the bards and possibly broke that massive stringed monstrosity. I didn't care. As far as I was concerned, it was quite an act of mercy that I hadn't melted the man's skin from his bones and kept his damned spirit attached to the charred ashes.

"I'm sorry, Eska," Jamis said. The playfulness in his voice was gone now. Replaced by something wary but hard as iron. "If it helps, you played your part perfectly. I couldn't have asked for a better performance."

"Performance," I spat the word. I turned to face the man who had orchestrated all of this and staggered from the warring emotions within me. The rage was there. Oh, yes, it was there. But so was that fucking insidious desire.

This, more than the initial act of violation, is why I truly hate Empamancy. It changes a person, overwrites their natural instincts, and it does not go away just because the Sourcerer stops using their magic. Just as with Lesray Alderson, all those years ago, convincing me to take my own life by wrapping me up in her own despair magnified a thousandfold; this damned Sourcerer had given me his desire for Jamis. I could not get rid of it. Could not separate myself from it. And I fucking knew it would be with me for all my remaining years. It was not mine. Never mine. And yet, now it was my burden to bear. A part of me I didn't want, that I fucking hated, inflicted upon me by someone else.

I tore my gaze from his and stalked to the edge of the tower. Close enough that I could stare down at Lanfall. The lights in the streets, flickering and dancing. The people moving about like ants through a hive. The noise, a multitude of roars so far away it reached me as only a single echo of its glory. Lesray's legacy called to me, and for a moment I felt like stepping off the edge of the tower and letting it all go. Life was such terrible pain, and only death could end it. Could free me from it.

I heard Jamis shuffle a little closer, but I didn't dare look at him. My mind was all over the place, my emotions a confused jumble I couldn't sort through like a vase smashed into a thousand pieces, I didn't even know how to start putting myself back together. I hated this man. I had every reason to throw him screaming from the tower. And yet, I still wanted him. I was driven by an overpowering need to be close to him, to feel his attention on me. To possess and be possessed by him. It was hideous.

"You never intended to keep your favour for later," I snarled. "This was it. The plan all along."

"Yes," Jamis admitted. "I needed them to see the show, I'm afraid. My fellow merchants are powerful. Money gives them authority. Influence from their many deals. They are, however, terrible at agreeing with one another. The Merchant Union has the combined power to reunite Isha, over time, but not unless it is also unified. A ship without a captain. I have my own allies within the union, but I needed something to help me push through the vote to make me head chair. This was it, Eska. You were it. Thank you." Reasoning a truly hateful crime away with pretty words.

Oh, yes, I may have violated you in the most heinous way imaginable, but it was all for a good cause. As if his uniting Isha was the only way the continent could survive. He just wanted a fucking crown.

"Why not just tell me the plan?" I've never liked being kept in the dark.

"Ah." Jamis sighed. "Imiko said you do not follow plans particularly well. She said if you knew what would happen, you would probably find some way to derail it. But if you have no idea of the plan, you usually follow them quite well with a little direction."

Imiko had done this to me? My chest hurt. My eyes felt raw, my cheeks swollen like I had been weeping. How could she? She might not know everything I had been through, what I had suffered at the hands of Lesray Alderson, but she knew I hated Empamancers for a reason. And even if she didn't, how could she have helped plan such a vicious violation?

"The trick, Imiko told me, was to make you think it was your plan all along really. Or at least, like you were defying everyone."

I seethed. I raged. I despaired. My vision tunnelled to a pin prick that was somehow still too bright. My breath echoed in my ears, too damned loud. How could Imiko have done this to me? I trusted her. I thought I could trust her. But then, had she ever really been worth that trust? The first time I met her, she tried to steal my Sources. She convinced us into a suicidal climb up the great chain to Ro'shan. She was never there when I needed her, always disappearing when times got tough.

My hand spasmed, fingers clutching into a claw and then released. I wanted to kill Jamis. I wanted to slaughter

every merchant who had witnessed my disgrace. I wanted
to bring the entire fucking fort crashing down onto the city
of Lanfall and leave another ruin in my wake. And I wanted
to be buried there among it. But most of all... most of all, I
wanted to hurt Imiko for betraying me.

It was unfortunate, therefore, that she chose that very
moment to make her appearance.

"Quite a mess you made down here," she said, her
tone light, flippant. "I hope everyone's decent. Eska, if I see
your naked arse, I'm going to scream." She reached the top
of the stairs, a glass of wine in hand, grinning. It slipped
away the moment she saw me. "Oh shit."

I was not in my right mind. That is the only excuse I
can give. I have never reacted to well to betrayal, no matter
how many times it is visited upon me by those closest to me.
I was struggling for control, and I lost.

Sourcery sang within me, ever a comforting embrace
to fall back to. I extended my hand and reached out with
a claw of Kinemancy and Arcmancy infused into one.
I grabbed Imiko in a sparking, amethyst vice of kinetic
energy. She squeaked in alarm and pain as I crushed her
arms against her chest and my storm ran along her skin.
Not strong to burn, not yet, but more than enough to hurt.
Her glass slipped from her fingers and shattered on the
flagstones, shards and wine spilling everywhere. I moved
her away from the steps, towards the edge of the tower,
holding her over the drop. It would be so easy to let her go.
My lightning danced over her arms and chest and skin; my
kinetic fist pinned her in place. And I advanced upon my
little sister.

She stared at me. One part fear, one anger. And
something else too. Fuck. I think it was relief.

"Do it, Eska. Do it. End it. Please." Her chin raised. Tears streaked her cheeks. My storm arced, tracing red lines over her face.

Something shifted inside. My rage fell away in the face of... something I both understood and could never hope to all at once. I recognised something inside of Imiko then, that urge for self-destruction, but I never thought to see it in her. Not in Imiko. Always so cheerful and carefree. Not in her.

I pulled her back, away from the drop and onto the tower top. Let my storm fade and released the kinetic claw. Imiko stood on her own, trembling, sniffing, staring at me with... was it fear? Not fear I would harm her, kill her. She wanted that. It was the fear of having shown someone else, even someone you loved and trusted, that most hideous part of yourself. That deepest, darkest core that you've always kept hidden. I saw her. For the first time, I saw the call of the void within Imiko, perhaps the most real, raw, vulnerable thing she had ever showed me. And she was waiting. Waiting on what I would do now I had seen it.

I heard footsteps behind me, on the stairs leading from below. Someone had come to find us. Imiko watched me, eyes darting about my face, searching for something. For what? Judgement? Hatred? Acceptance? Compassion? Her breath came short and sharp, on the edge of panic. I wanted to run to her, cross the immeasurable distance between us, pull her away from the drop and into my embrace and help her. Even if I didn't know how.

Jamis gasped, I had almost forgotten he was there. A moment later, I understood why.

"Hello, mother."

CHAPTER EIGHTEEN

AFTER VI'S DEATH AT THE HANDS OF TOR assassins, I went wild. I know, it's not a surprise to anyone at this point. When Silva was killed... When I killed Silva, I blamed Aerolis. I threw every bit of myself at the Djinn. My storm, my swords, my Sourcery, and my horror. Everything I had. When Vi was murdered, I had my queendom behind me and I threw it at Tor.

In polite civilisation, it is prudent to extend a declaration of war prior to serious hostilities. The Orrans and Terrelans may have raided each other's borders for years, but before the war started, an envoy was sent to Terrelan with an official declaration including terms of surrender. That was the historical start of the war. That the Terrelans sent the envoy back to Orran minus his tongue is often forgotten. When I took Yenheim to war against Tor, I sent no formal declaration. I marshalled my army, drawn

mostly from the soldiers who had once policed the Pit,
and the survivors who had once inhabited it. I ignored my
calmer councillors, telling Hardt to go diddle a goat when he
wouldn't leave it alone. Then I marched my army across the
border, striding at the head of a thousand eager killers.

Sirileth came with me. She demanded it. I should
have said no, she was just nine years old, far too young to
see the horrors of war. But she wanted to go, and I wanted
her next to me. I wouldn't allow her out of my sight, not
after the assassins had snuck into my palace so easily. I was
plagued with thoughts of returning from war to find my last
remaining daughter dead. I could not... would not let that
happen.

I can't remember the name of the first village we
sacked. I was so caught up in my need for vengeance, I
ordered my forces to attack without a second thought.
People died. A lot of people. Innocent people. I don't
remember the name of that village, but I remember burning
houses, smoke thick in the air, the smell of loosened bowels
and roasting flesh, the screams of the dying. The screams
of the survivors. Most of all, I remember the way Sirileth
watched it all with dispassionate darklight eyes. We turned
a village into a grave and marched on. The ghosts of that
village marched with us. With me.

For five days we struck out into Tor. Villages were
sacked, towns ransacked, people murdered. At the time, it
seemed so righteous. Now... Now, it's the other thing. We
met little resistance, only a few scattered soldiers here and
there, farmers with rusted blades, not a single Sourcerer. If I
had been thinking more clearly, that might have been all the
warning I needed.

We had just sacked a town; more houses burned,

and people of Tor put to the sword. Night fell and we made camp. My soldiers broke open the ale they had stolen and drank heartily, singing of victory, of justice for their murdered princess. We didn't see the attack coming until it was too late.

A hail of arrows fell among the tents. A hundred of my soldiers died in that first volley. I woke to their screams. I threw up a kinetic barrier inside my tent, protecting myself and Sirileth even as my daughter struggled to rise, wiping sleep from her eyes. Arrows pierced the cloth roof and scattered harmless against my shield. I heard my soldiers screaming, shouting to get shields, to locate the enemy. Sirileth and I emerged from our tent into the chaos of a battle all around. Soldiers in the black of Tor swarmed into the camp, slaughtering everyone they could find. My own soldiers, wearing the red of Yenheim, were slow to react, still fighting their drunk from a night of celebration. They clustered in small groups, desperately trying to defend against a force that was quickly outnumbering them.

Back in the palace, when we were attacked by assassins, I killed a man to prevent Sirileth from doing it. In that battle, surrounded by darkness and fire and chaos, I could not do the same. We fought together, back-to-back. My daughter, little nine-year-old Sirileth, killed as many as I did. Whether it was Kinemancy or Pyromancy or Geomancy, Sirileth had surgical precision and the raw power to back it up. She flung soldiers aside, sunk them into the earth and crushed them, released arrows of fire that sought their targets with unerring accuracy.

The soldiers of Yenheim fell in their hundreds, but the survivors flocked to us. They found their queen and their princess in the thick of the battle and rallied around us. Even so, we lost. It was the first true battle of the Yenheim-Tor war, and my forces were decimated.

It became clear we had lost when my soldiers gathered and I realised maybe fifty remained. I raised my hand and created a shield around us. I infused it with both Kinemancy and Arcmancy. It was strong enough to repel both sword and arrow and Sourcery. The soldiers and Sourcerers of Tor battered it, and I felt every blow, but I was at the height of my power and weathered it all. Still, I knew it couldn't last. I couldn't hold out forever. We needed to escape, and I knew of only one way.

I carried a Portamancy Source with me. I refused to use it most of the time. The thing that waits beyond the portals, the thing that stares through into our world from the great rift above the Polasian desert, the thing that our gods call God, had long ago taken an interest in me. A portal, however, was our only way out. I swallowed the Source and ripped open a doorway with a sound like tearing paper. It flickered a few times, one moment showing a small hill we had passed half a day back, the next showing utter black and something darker still stirring in that vast nothing. I had to concentrate to stabilise that portal, and even then, I could feel that thing picking at it, trying to find me.

My soldiers charged through, eager to be away from the site of such slaughter. I sent Sirileth through before me, and then finally leapt through myself. Out of almost fifty soldiers who went through, seven never reached the other side, taken by the creature beyond. They weren't alone.

Sirileth was gone.

I searched for her, silently praying to the moons that I'd find her, but none of my soldiers had seen her come through the portal. Eventually, I admitted the truth to myself: it had taken her. The thing beyond had my daughter. Well, fuck that. I am not good at letting go of what's mine. I could not fathom a world without Sirileth in it.

Once before, I had torn open a portal to nowhere. Up on Do'shan, when the creature beyond had taken Ssserakis from me, I ripped open a portal and pulled my horror back to me. It had only worked because Ssserakis and I were bound. I knew it couldn't work the same way for Sirileth, but I had to try.

When I tore open that hole to nowhere, I found the great eye staring at me. It is not a terran eye, nor pahht, not anything like a creature from our world. It is entirely alien. A myriad of shifting colours beyond colour, sparkling lights, pulsing hues. It is an eye that burns, and its attention is heavier than any physical weight. The eye winked out of existence, and Sirileth flew from the portal. I snapped it shut and ran to my daughter. When finally, she opened her eyes, her darklight was more brilliant than it had ever been. She was truly blinding to behold, and yet I couldn't look away. She smiled at me then. Sirileth so rarely smiled. I gathered her in my arm and held her tight as the soldiers of Yenheim cheered for their returned princess.

I thought it luck. I tore open a portal and Sirileth tumbled out, and I considered myself fortunate. It should have occurred to me that only Sirileth came out of that portal. Seven other soldiers had gone missing, and they were forever lost. I should have realised that I did not retrieve my daughter from that other place. The creature beyond had given her back to me.

CHAPTER NINETEEN

I WAS SLOW TO TURN. CAUGHT BETWEEN two needs; to run to Imiko, pull her away from the edge and comfort her; and to see my daughter again. Hesitating through fear and apprehension. I know I was chasing Sirileth, trying to find her. But I was also scared of seeing her again. I realised I had no idea what to say to her. What can you say to a daughter you abandoned seven years ago?

What can you say to a daughter you abandoned for much longer than that?

It was not Sirileth who stood before us. The woman who stood on the tallest tower of Fort Vernan had dark skin, pale blue eyes, hair as black as night cut so short it barely reached her ears. She was tall — taller than me — taking after her father in that. She had Isen's build, tall and broad, his skin, his square jaw. But she had my thin nose, my icy eyes, my smile quirking one side of her lips. It was not

Sirileth I saw. It was a ghost.

"Aspect?" Jamis said. The word sent a jolt of fear coursing through me.

The woman stepped forward. Just a few paces away now. I saw a sword dangling at her hip. It was long and single-edged, a slightly curved blade. It was not the sort one carried unless they knew how to use it. So, she was a warrior then. I found myself smiling at that. It is good to know your children are strong and have become strong even without you. Isen and I created this wonder. We gave her the building blocks, but neither of us had a hand in what she did with them.

"It's good to finally meet you, Eskara." Her voice was beautiful. There was a depth and richness to it. That, too, she got from Isen. This woman who stood before us now was undeniably my first daughter. Kento.

I stepped forward to meet my long-lost daughter but I stumbled and almost fell. I staggered forward another couple of steps and stared up into Kento's face.

"They told me you were dead." The words fell out of my mouth and landed between us, still and unmoving on the floor.

Kento smiled, but only briefly. "I was."

"How? How are you alive?"

Kento shook her head, a bitter smile twisting her lips for a moment. "Of course, of all the questions you could ask, Eskara, your first is the one to absolve you of any blame." She looked away, dismissing me, and staring over my shoulder at Jamis. "We have matters to discuss. They won't wait."

I was drowning all over again, though in a very different sense. I had so many things I wanted to ask her.

How was she alive? Had she grown up on Ro'shan? What was her life like? What did she do there? Who did she love? Did she have a family of her own? How the fuck was she alive?

There is a strange truth about questions. For the intelligent, too many tend to paralyse a person. They realise the enormity of what they don't know, and that they can never know it all. That realisation often brings inaction. It is impossible to understand everything so why try to understand anything? Stupid people do not seem to have this problem. They are more than happy assuming they already know the answers they need and are willing to barrel forwards regardless. I often straddle that line.

"Aspect?" I said slowly. Kento glanced down at me again, a frown creasing her brow. "Jamis called you Aspect."

My daughter did not answer the implied question.

Jamis sighed. "You two have some catching up, perhaps?"

"Yes," I said eagerly.

"No," Kento sounded like the final nail hammering into a coffin.

More people sounded on the steps leading up to the roof. I suddenly wished everyone would just go away. Everyone except Kento. I had known my first daughter for only three days. I gave her up, certain that I was not ready to raise her. That all I would do was pass on the worst parts of myself to her. Months later, I realised what a mistake I had made. I wanted her back, I begged Silva and Mezula to return her to me and they told me she was dead. Another lie. One more time Silva betrayed me.

Jamis' pet Sourcerer, looking more than a little worse for wear and bleeding from a cut on his cheek, stepped gingerly up the stairs onto the tower roof. I hated him still, but the rage found no purchase in me right then. Not while I was staring into the face of my daughter come back from the dead.

I heard Imiko sniff from behind me. Saw her step past me, wiping a hand across her cheeks to chase away the last remnants of her tears. The raw pain had vanished, replaced as if she had donned a mask. "I'm Imiko," she said, far too happily, all things considered. Far too good at hiding herself from others.

Kento's mouth quirked up into that half smile of mine. "Aunt, it's nice to finally meet you. My memories of you are hazy at best." I didn't understand. Kento had only been with us, with me, for three days after she was born. How could she possibly have memories of that time?

"Huh?" Imiko grunted.

"I don't suppose my uncle is with you?" Kento asked.

"Hardt?" Imiko said, then shook her head. "No chance you'll get him to leave home these days."

Kento smiled wistfully. "A shame. I would love to meet him."

"We could go there," I said, words spilling from me before my thoughts could get in the way. "Together." Kento did not answer me.

Jamis glanced past his Sourcerer to the stairs leading below. "Perhaps we should take this conversation somewhere a little more private. I have quarters in my tower that are secure. Polter?"

Jamis' Sourcerer stepped forward. He raised one hand and clicked his fingers. A portal tore open, the image on the other side was of a warm study, flicking hearth light, a plush carpet, a desk stacked with papers. Jamis started towards the portal, but I caught his trailing hand in my own, pulling him to a stop. Then I let go, recoiled, echoes of that desire that wasn't mine flooding through me again. Too much was happening too quickly, I couldn't keep it all straight. I should have let him go, step through and be claimed by the thing stalking me from the other side of the portal.

"I wouldn't risk it," I said, shaking my head. As if to make my point, the portal flickered. The study on the other side vanished. The image transformed to that of a dark void, a distant creature so large it might as well have been formless. One of the creature's eyes snapped to us, staring out through the portal. "I'd close that, if I were you," I snarled at the Sourcerer.

We watched as the thing on the other side drew closer. A thin tendril of purple haze quested out of the portal, snaking toward me. "Close it now," I snapped.

Jamis nodded to his Sourcerer and the man clicked his fingers again. The portal shut, the haze of purple smoke coming apart now it was cut off from that other place. All eyes turned to me.

"You can't use portals around me. They don't work right." I couldn't keep the bitterness from my voice. I missed travelling via portal, it made getting around a lot easier. Unfortunately, it had been dangerous since my time on Do'shan and had only gotten worse over the years. It used to be one in ten portals would attract the attention of the thing on the other side. Now, every portal opened within a hundred feet of me would draw the eye of that monster.

Kento took a small, round, metal device from her pocket and spoke into it. "Pickup. Tallest tower. Roof." She tucked it back into her pocket and shrugged. "Useful device. Limited range and distorts the voice but being able to communicate over distance is invaluable."

"What about Siri?" Imiko asked. "Did you find her?"

Jamis took a deep breath, as if steadying himself. "Sirileth. Yes. She arrived in Lanfall twenty-five days ago. I'm told queen Sirileth has allies, both among the general populace, and the Merchant Union. I might be better off calling them followers though. By all accounts, they worship her as some sort of saviour."

"Worship her?" I asked, still staring at Kento and trying to collect some semblance of cohesive thought.

"There's a prophecy about a cataclysm apparently. I don't know the details at the moment. Unfortunately, I can't just pull the offending merchants aside and torture them for details. Not yet." I saw him smile out of the corner of my eye and couldn't decide if he was being serious or not. "They seem to think that your daughter is the catalyst for this cataclysm. The one who will bring it about."

"And they want that?"

"Oh yes. A cleansing of the world, or some such, I imagine. As long as there are prophecies of the end, there will be fools seeking to make it happen. They probably think they'll rule over whatever is left."

"A cult!" I spat the word. "My daughter is the leader of a bloody cult."

"I'm afraid so."

I ran my hand down my face. One thing you never realise you'll miss about having two hands, is being able to really bury your head in them. "Where is she?"

Something slid into place in my mind. Like Sirileth, I have always enjoyed puzzles, theoretical ones at least. But unlike my daughter, I am not thoughtful enough to reason them out. Leave me alone with a puzzle, and I will worry at it, pull it apart, and solve it by any means necessary, even if I have to destroy it in the process. However, if all the pieces are presented to me, and I have something else to focus my attention on, my mind will continue to connect the dots. I didn't yet have all the pieces, perhaps if I had things would have worked out differently, better. But some things suddenly snapped into place, and I reeled from the truth of what my daughter was doing. Sirileth really was going to kill us all.

"Well," Jamis said. "That's where it gets interesting. She..."

I felt suddenly dizzy and staggered. My head was swimming the way it had with the Empamancer working on my emotions, but now I knew to look for the signs of Empamancy and they weren't there. Jamis rushed forward, steadied me with a hand on my arm. For just a moment, I was grateful. Then I remember what the bastard had done to me and wrenched my arm away.

I was still picking up the puzzle pieces Sirileth had left and slotting them into place in my mind when a Ro'shan flyer rose beside the tower to hover next to us. By then, Jamis' fellow merchants were starting to brave the stairs. One of the other merchants, a rakish woman with long blond hair asked Jamis what was happening. She never got to answer as the flyer took that moment to arrive. They're quite loud when in flight, multiple sets of thin blades spinning about in unison creates quite the racket. Jamis was right though, we needed to take the conversation somewhere else. If any of the merchants were working with Sirileth, we couldn't risk them knowing what we did.

We hustled aboard the flyer with as much haste as we could. Jamis and I, Imiko and the Sourcerer Polter, and

Kento of course. She took over the controls, relieving the
terran man who had been flying the contraption. Then
we were rising into the air above the tower. Power and
perspective are ever at odds, always revealing each other for
what they truly are. Fort Vernan is a wonder, built to be the
tallest structure in all Isha, a defending Sourcerer's dream,
but the flyer rose above it with ease.

Jamis stood beside my daughter and pointed to one
of the other towers. Kento ignored him and the flyer kept
rising. I saw Polter huddle in his robes and Imiko rubbed her
hands together. It was quite chilly so high up, but I didn't
feel it. I had a Pyromancy Source in my stomach, a little
flame keeping me warm. Kento turned the flyer about, and
then we were moving away from Fort Vernan and away
from Lanfall. In the distance, a splotch of darkness on the
horizon hid the night sky, blotting out the stars. I sighed and
finally let my legs give up, sitting on the floor of the flyer,
and settling into a sulk.

"What are you doing?" Jamis demanded of Kento.

My daughter spared the merchant a glance. "We're
not going to your tower. We're going to see my mother."

CHAPTER TWENTY

RO'SHAN QUICKLY GREW LARGER AS WE approached. The noise of the flyer was oppressive enough to make conversation difficult. It was one of the smaller ships, for transporting people over short distances. The cargo hold was limited, but it was faster than its larger cousins.

Imiko paced, pulled out a hip flask and swigged, paced some more. Her eyes were shadowed, her movements sharp and jerky. I wanted to go to her, but she wouldn't meet my gaze. And besides, we had much to discuss, and I didn't think shouting over the racket of the flyer was the best way to go about it. It was a conversation that would have to wait for later.

Jamis consulted with his pet Sourcerer. He did not appear happy and sent many a pointed glare at Kento. It was the first time I had seen him rattled. I liked it. His Sourcerer stood still but for his hand dancing against his leg, fingers tapping at his thigh. I entertained dreams of throwing him from the flyer and watching him plummet, screaming to his death. He, too, would not meet my flashing gaze.

I brooded. I say this mostly because it sounds a lot better than admitting I was sulking. My heart had been tugged in too many directions too quickly, and I was struggling to make sense of everything that had happened. The overwhelming intoxication of someone else's desire for a man who was using me to make a play for a throne that didn't yet exist. Imiko's betrayal. Her begging me to end it. To end her. My long-lost daughter who I believed dead for two and a half decades popping up. Then she calls the most powerful enemy I have her mother — don't think for a moment that escaped my notice. And, of course, there was still the matter of Sirileth. What she was up to and why? And where was she? Jamis had been interrupted before getting to that part, but I still needed to know.

Light was starting to peak over the horizon when we reached Ro'shan. The sun rose behind the flying mountain and made the city into an enormous silhouette. Kento pushed the flyer higher still until we were above Ro'shan, staring down at the city. It looked exactly as I had last seen it. A massive forest on one side, with trees that grew too fast. A lake that sparkled in the dawn light, blue waters only a couple of feet deep.

The city itself, formed of polished white bone and grown into an intricate architecture matched nowhere else in all the world. People were already moving about the streets. I saw pahht mostly, a few garn, even some terrans. What I didn't see were tahren. The little blind caretakers of the world who had once scurried about the city in their blind throngs, polishing the buildings to a shine despite being unable to see them. I dismissed it as a curiosity at the time, but I should have paid attention. It wasn't that there were fewer tahren about, but that there were none.

We knew the moment we passed into the strange, localised atmosphere of Ro'shan because the temperature suddenly increased. Kento flew the flyer not to Craghold where I remembered most of the ships docked, but to the palace. I never knew Mezula had a personal dock at the palace, but I suppose it made sense. As soon as we touched down, Kento shooed us off the flyer. She gave me no time to ask her the throng of questions crowding my mind.

We were all tired, me especially, but Kento did not allow us to rest. She marched us through the palace and into the great throne room of the Rand. I remembered it well. I had given her up in that great hall. Laid her on the floor with the Rand towering over her, and fled with her cries echoing behind me, damning me for my cowardice. I had thought I wasn't ready to be a mother. That I would pass my sins and my scars to her. Excuses. I'm good at those.

Wide bone pillars stretched the length of the great hall. Dark doorways led into parts unknown along the walls. A pile of broad, golden-brown leaves nestled in a corner, as though they had blown in and been raked aside.

In the centre of the room stood a grand table, the surface of which was level with my shoulders. It could have happily seated fifty terrans with space to spare. Beyond that table sat two thrones where there had once been only one.

Mezula already had an audience. She towered above the table, just as I remembered her. Her snakelike tail coiled beneath her, fuzzy brown fur running up her flanks. She had the torso of a pahht, covered in fur and enlarged to grotesque portions. Her head was almost terran, though with no eyes to see there, only flat skin. Her hands, all six of them, were in constant motion. They twisted and turned, long fingers flexing. At the palm of each hand sat a single eye, the pupil slitted like a pahht's. One of those hands flicked our way, and Mezula smiled. Her teeth were sharpened knives, like a tahren's. Mezula is grotesque combination of the people of Ovaeris she helped to create.

Two hulking garn rested at the opposite side of the table to her. The garn are a strange people. They remain unchanged by the Rand, having been sentient since before the Rand and Djinn arrived on our world. The garn are slug-like in appearance, but huge. Each one must weigh as much as an abban. They have fleshy tentacle-like appendages that can form from any part of their skin and can also be reabsorbed. They have huge mouths and wide, fishlike eyes. They also leave a trail of mucus behind them wherever they go, and it smells like foetid swamp. Probably not surprising given their homeland is on the continent of Ferusa, and it's mostly covered in dense jungle and, you guessed it, swamp. I've been there. I lived amongst the garn for a full month many years ago. It was horrendous and took me two months of bathing to wash away the smell.

There were also five pahht nestled around the table, each one standing on a stool so they could comfortably see onto the surface. Whiskers twitched and nostrils flared as we entered the hall. Cat-like pupils narrowed as they glared at us. I had the distinct impression we had just walked in on some sort of war council.

It's easy to forget, when you remove yourself from the world, that it continues without you. Nations rise and fall. Wars are fought, won, lost. People of all the races of Ovaeris are born, live, and die. The world forges on, relentless as time, even when you spend a decade hiding from it.

How best to describe that meeting? I half expected Mezula to snarl as soon as she spotted me, or tear me in two. I didn't doubt she could. For all my power, I was still nothing compared to a god. I know I often make light of our gods, mostly because I hate them, but it cannot be forgotten that they are our gods in the truest sense of the word. Before the Djinn came, our world was very different. They altered it for us, made it hospitable. Before the Rand, terrans didn't exist. We were mindless beasts infesting caves and feeding on each other. The Rand and Djinn are gods. Our gods. They're still arseholes though, and I will take every opportunity to defy them.

Despite it all, I would have welcomed a confrontation. It would have been preferable. Instead, Mezula watched us for a few moments with three of her hands, while still conversing with her council over their oversized table. Then she turned away all but one of her hands. Rather than a confrontation, we were ignored. I cannot abide being ignored.

I took a step forward, ready to demand Mezula face me. I will admit, I was quite angry with the Rand, and I had more than enough reasons to pick from. Where should I start? I had never forgiven her for Silva's death. Yes, I struck the killing blow on my lover, but it was Mezula who sent her daughter to Do'shan to die. Mezula killed Silva as surely as I. I could never forgive her for that. Now, I discover she had also hidden my daughter from me. Oh, I wasn't just angry. I was fucking furious. And, as I'm sure you're aware by now, I do not make the best decisions when enraged.

Kento raised a hand before me, pinned me with a stare so like my own, and shook her head slowly. She wore a grim expression, hard lines around a scowl. "My mother will kill you if you make a scene, Eskara." Damn that word! Yes, it's my name, and I have never hated hearing it until then. Until my own bloody daughter called a monster her mother, and me by name.

And so we waited. I hated every moment of it, but we waited as minutes stretched on and Mezula consulted with garn and pahht, gesturing at the table before them. Eventually, she dismissed them all and we waited while they left the throne room. Once they were gone, my patience was at a limit. I strode past Kento, drew in a deep breath ready to accuse Mezula of... I'm not entirely sure. Killing the woman I loved? Stealing my daughter? I had no idea what I was going to say. A hundred different possibilities raced through my mind, but none of them mattered.

Imiko ran ahead of me, outpacing me easily. She knelt a few paces away, reached inside her jacket, and pulled out a small leather-bound book. She held it in both hands up to the Rand and bowed her head.

"A gift," Imiko said loudly. "Reparations for the past. The queendom of Yenheim, and all its people, apologise, mighty Mezula." My blood boiled at seeing my friend prostrate herself before the Rand like that. Worse. She did it because of me. I didn't know what the book was or why it mattered, but I didn't miss the implications. Imiko was apologising to Mezula on my bloody behalf.

"I know that book," Jamis said quietly. "Hestas is always carrying it about. He's been reading it for years." So that was what Imiko had slunk away to do. She'd stolen a book from a merchant.

The Rand took the book and flicked it open, smiling down at the pages. "Hello Arkanus, my old friend."

The book screamed. A shrill cry that resonated throughout the throne room loud enough that everybody who could covered their ears. I, unfortunately, could not, only having the one hand. But at least I understood what was happening. There was a Djinn trapped inside the book. Just like Vainfold trapped inside his flaming crown. Mezula had collected another of the surviving Djinn.

"Oh, do stop screaming, Arkanus," Mezula said, her voice cutting through the book's cry. "You've lost. No one will ever open you again. You have learned all you ever will."

The book stopped screaming. "You traitorous bitch," the words were soft and crackly like old pages curling before a flame. "We will..."

Mezula snapped the cover shut, cutting Arkanus off before he could get going. Then the Rand reached up with another of her slender hands and plucked free a strand of her hair. She wrapped it around the book twice, then spoke a word I'd never heard before and couldn't repeat if I tried. It sounded something like Kermugerplunck. The strand of hair glowed golden.

"Now you'll join our brothers, Arkanus." Mezula chuckled and slithered back to the table, placing the book on the bone surface.

The Rand turned to Imiko then, focusing on her with three waving hands, another pointed my way. "A gift of such worth requires payment," Mezula said.

Imiko was still on her knees, head bowed. "No, it doesn't. It's an apology, reparations." She glanced over her shoulder at me. Mezula's head jerked, another of her hands waved my way, the eye focusing on me.

As if I needed to apologise to the Rand. I took a step

forward, balling my fist, and sucking in enough breath to
scream Mezula out of existence. The sheer arrogance of her,
of all our gods, to believe they are so much better than us
that they can step on us and expect an apology for dirtying
their boots with our blood. How dare they!

Kento stopped me from venting my rage. She held up
a hand before me. My daughter met my eyes and shook her
head once slowly. I recognized the steel in her blue gaze. If I
attacked Mezula, Kento would be the one to defend her. That
took a lot of the fight out of me. It's probably for the best. I
blamed Mezula for Silva's death, yes. But Mezula blamed
me for the same thing. That is the nature of perspective, it
is formed from our experience inside and out. Silva was
dead. Twenty years dead, but not forgotten. I saw her death
one way, Mezula saw it another. Neither were the truth.
The truth, as ever, lies somewhere in the middle. We were
both to blame. Just as we both grieved for the loss. Perhaps
we should have been united in that. I had been through
this argument with Coby, and it led nowhere but pain. So, I
decided to let it go. That didn't mean I let all my grievances
go.

"You told me Kento was dead," I shouted at Mezula.

The Rand's lip curled, revealing rows of dagger-like
teeth. "In fact, I did not, terran," the god said calmly. "I told
you she was beyond my power to give back to you. It was
the truth. At the time."

I shook my head, felt my storm rising once again.
"You took her from me."

Mezula slithered forward to tower over me. "At your
request."

"After all I did for you."

All of Mezula's hands darted forward to stare down

at me. The god loomed above. "Did for me? You killed two of my daughters. I took one of yours. I would call that more than fair."

I ground my teeth. This thing didn't understand. Family, to it, was nothing but a resource to be exploited. The Rand might look like all the people of Ovaeris mashed together, might take on some of the appearances of a terran, but she did not understand. She could not. She wasn't capable to love like we love. She could not need another person in her life so powerfully that the mere concept of them not being around is like knives slicing her on the inside. She could not know what it was like to break down in tears at the sight of someone for the sheer joy or being near them. Mezula would never know the simple rightness of being entangled in a lover's limbs, nor the exploding joy of staring down into a newborn's face. It is not beyond my notice that the Rand make their Aspects a part of themselves. All they care about is themselves. Mezula never loved Silva, she simply loved the part of herself that lived within the woman. And she did not love Kento either.

"What did you do, Mezula?" I snarled, staring up at the god. My lightning crackled to life around me, racing along my skin.

Mezula cocked her eyeless head at me. "Such brash behaviour you terrans are capable of. An oversight on our part, but not beyond our power to fix." She reached for me, hands clutching, eyes staring. I realised what she meant and I knew the danger I was in. Mezula was talking about changing us.

The Rand had taken the Damned and turned them into terrans. Could she really do it again? Could she reach into my mind, into my heart, into everything that made me me, and... alter me? Make me different, make me passive, docile. Of course, she could. An Empamancer could do it given enough time, and she was so far beyond any Sourcerer. It was horrifying to think. I would not let it happen. I could not let anyone, not even a god, violate me like that. I was still reeling from what Jamis' Sourcerer had done to me. I drew on all my Sources at once and formed a blazing Sourceblade in hand that crackled with fire and lightning both.

"Enough, both of you," Kento said sharply. My daughter stepped between us, heedless of the god I faced, or the lightning arcing from me. My storm struck her, but she didn't seem to notice. "Mother," she said reproachfully.

Mezula stared down at Kento for a few seconds with all her hands, then chuckled, turned, and slithered away.

Kento turned to me next, her face a wall of stone. "Eskara. Stop this now!"

Faced by the admonition of my daughter, I let my anger go. I dropped the Sourceblade, and it puffed out of existence in a rush of kinetic energy, lightning, and fire. Kento stared at me, her disappointment clear, then turned and strode to Mezula's side. I think I hated her a little for that. She was my daughter. My flesh and blood. I had yet to realise the truth, that blood means nothing in the grander scope of things.

Jamis stepped beside me just as the last of my energy fled. He was graceful enough to take my arm before I slumped. "That was quite something, facing down the Rand like that. You must have a spine of steel." He smiled at me. "Perhaps the stories about you are true."

"You mean the ones that say she's a fucking idiot?" Imiko asked as she strode up to meet us. "They are. All of them."

I dragged my arm away from Jamis, fighting the rising desire all over again. I would not let this man support me. I'd rather die. I turned such a glare his way, he took a step back.

"Why are you here, little terran?" Mezula asked. Sure, I wasn't the only terran in the room, but I knew the question was directed at me and not just because I was the shortest.

"My younger daughter, Sirileth..." I paused and looked at Kento. "You have a sister."

Kento treated me to an impassive stare. "I know."

"She's gone missing," Imiko said, impatience in her voice. "Took a few of her closest followers and fled her own queendom in the middle of the night. I tracked her all the way to New Picarr, then to Lanfall. Still trying to figure where she went from there."

"Karataan," Jamis said. "I was trying to tell you before all this happened. Queen Sirileth has some allies in the Merchant Union. I'm yet to ascertain how fervently they believe in her cause. Sirileth used them to book passage for herself and three others to the tahren's home continent. More specifically, to Karataan."

Though I had never been there, I knew of Karataan. Everyone with a drop of learning knew of the place. It was an island of sorts, sitting just off the coast of Teshta, the continent the tahren called home. Outwardly, it was a port city that thrived on piracy. You might think it odd that a people who stand just three feet tall at a stretch, are covered in fur, and have no eyes might take to piracy of the high seas, but apparently, they're very good at it. Regardless, pirates of all races flocked to Karataan as a home port. It was perhaps even more cosmopolitan than Ro'shan. But even that is not what makes Karataan so interesting. The island boasts a mighty forest with trees that grow taller than anywhere else in the world. The tahren have built themselves a vast city amidst them. Not a village on the ground, scavenging from the forest like my home of Keshin, but a city that clung to the treetops. And it was in those trees, hidden from view both above and below, that the Library of Ever can be found. That's what they call it, and I must admit, it's a catchy name. It is a collection of written works like no other. The tahren have long claimed it holds a copy of every book that has ever existed, and they do not easily allow others access to check on the claim.

"Why?" I asked Jamis. "What's in Karataan for Sirileth?"

Jamis shrugged and gave me such an apologetic smile I felt my traitorous heart race. "I don't know. But she left almost fifteen days ago. Tahren ships are speedy. We have long since theorised that they each carry an Aeromancer to help fill their sails with unnatural wind. Sirileth should be reaching Karataan about now."

"Fifteen days behind her still," I snarled.

"We're catching her up, at least," Imiko said. She sounded worried. Perhaps no one else detected it, but I knew her. Or I once had, at least. I looked at my old friend and saw nothing of the vulnerability she had shown earlier. Nothing but the mask, the face she wanted everyone to see.

Mezula's hands twitched, eyes swivelling in her palms to stare at each of us. "None of this explains why you terrans are here." She sounded bored.

"I think I can explain that. And I can also explain why you're going to help us." I said, offering a savage grin to the god. She wasn't going to like it. "Sirileth has been creating scars in the world."

The pile of leaves in the corner of the throne room rustled.

"Scars?" Mezula asked, suddenly interested.

"Like the one the Iron Legion created when he broke down. Places where the barriers between worlds are thinner. I don't fully understand them, but I think they're smaller versions of the rift you and the Djinn created above the Polasian desert."

The pile of leaves rustled again. Then they moved, shifting and falling into place until a shambling mound in a myriad of colours lurched into motion. It didn't walk, so much as roll towards the thrones. We stared at the thing as it trundled past and settled into a mound beside Mezula.

It was another Rand. The one Josef had brought back to life. I dredged my memory for the Rand's name. "Elorame."

The shambling mass of leaves shuddered, and I had a feeling it was staring at me. Whether from within the leaves, or if eyes were a mortal construct it had no need of, I don't know. "I remember you." Her voice was the creaking trees of a forest given words. "The terran who brought Terthis back."

Well, that was not entirely accurate. I would argue the Iron Legion more guilty than I, though he used Josef and myself as vessels for the resurrection.

Mezula shook her massive head, two of her hands focusing on me, and another two on her sister. "I should have known you would be at the centre of it, terran."

"Not by choice," I hissed.

I will admit, I wondered if Mezula would kill me then. Only Josef and I still knew the secret of bringing the dead Rand and Djinn back to life, restoring them from Sources, their crystal coffins. Mezula would not want that knowledge getting out. She had orchestrated her sisters' deaths after all. She didn't know it, but she had nothing to fear there. I'd die a hundred times over before I ever let that secret slip.

"What do you know of the scars?" Elorame shambled closer to me. I quickly realised how massive she truly was. A rustling patch of leaves large enough to swallow a dozen terrans. Jamis stepped back. I felt like joining him but refused to show fear in the face of our gods.

"Not much," I said. "They are places where Sourceries clash against each, especially when caused by the catastrophic rejection of a Sourcerer. The boundaries are thinner. Portals can be opened to the Other World. For a time, at least."

"What is this about, sister?" Mezula asked.

The mound of leaves rustled before me. "The Second Cataclysm. Raither predicted it, Mezula."

Raither was Tamura's mother, the Rand who had been driven insane by the futures she saw, and had passed on her knowledge, immortality, and insanity to Tamura. Only, Tamura didn't have the vast capacity of a god, so all that knowledge and all those visions of possible futures had broken him. It had shattered his mind like a mirror, and now each shard was separate and reflected something different.

"Oh shit," Imiko said. She snorted out a manic giggle that had no humour to it. "I didn't think this was important before, but, um..." She shot me a sorry glance. "Last year, Sirileth was quite interested in that. The Second Cataclysm, I mean. I had no idea what it was about, still don't, but she kept asking Tamura questions about it. Getting him to tell one of his stories over and again."

More pieces fell into place. The puzzle revealing itself

before my eyes. My legs grew weak, trembled. I locked my knees and refused to let myself fall.

Mezula hissed at Elorame. Elorame rustled back. Kento frowned, tilting her head as if she understood whatever noises passed for speech between the two gods.

"I would dearly love to know what is happening, Eska," Jamis said quietly. "What cataclysm?"

"The First Cataclysm happened when our moons collided. Lokar and Lursa split open, and the Rand and Djinn spilled out. Huge chunks of the moons rained down on Ovaeris. Seas boiled, forests burned, the sun was blotted out by dust. It was the end of the world."

Jamis raised a perfectly sculptured eyebrow. "As we're all standing here now, I'm going to assume it didn't stick?"

I glared at him. "Figured that out, did you? The Rand and Djinn worked together and remade the world and the people in it." I paused and considered lying about the rest, but what was the point? Though the truth was far from pleasant, and possibly dangerous in the wrong hands, I was too tired to lie. "Terrans were once quite different creatures. We call them the Damned."

"Those savage beasts that hide in caves?" Jamis asked.

I nodded gravely. "It's where we come from. Where we'd still be if the Rand hadn't changed us into what we are now through their Sourcery."

Jamis turned his dark stare upon the two Rand rustling and hissing at each other by the thrones. I stared past them to my daughter who stood with them. "They truly are gods then."

I scoffed. "Yes. A real fucking pity, that. One of the

Rand predicted a Second Cataclysm. A time when the creature staring into our world from the great rift above the Polasian desert would pick the rift open large enough for it to pass through. The general understanding is that none of us will survive it."

Jamis considered the Rand for a few more moments, then closed his eyes and shook his head. When he opened his eyes again and looked at me, they were wide with wonder. "Why?"

"Why what?" I snapped.

"Why does the thing above the desert want to come through? Why does it want to destroy Ovaeris?"

I chuckled bitterly and pointed at the Rand. "Them," I said. "The Rand and Djinn. It created them. Imprisoned them in the moons. I don't think it's happy they're free."

Mezula scoffed, turning her head towards us, her hands dancing about, staring at everything all at once. "Terran understanding is so limited. We should have made you smarter." She was talking to us now. "Happy, sad, angry. Those are your emotions. The Maker is beyond such things. What it wants is to understand."

"Understand what?" I asked.

"Everything," Elorame rustled. "What we are. What we have become. Why we are free. What happened to our sisters? We are part of it as Aspects are part of us. It is trying to understand itself." She rustled again, but if there were words, I did not understand them.

Imiko shuffled closer to me, lowered her voice. She was never comfortable in the presence of Gods. "What does Siri have to do with this, Eska?"

This was the part I didn't want to admit. Not to her, or anyone. This was how it was all my fault. "It took her." The words fell from my mouth, landed between us. "The thing beyond the rift, beyond the portals, it's been interested in me ever since..." Ssserakis. I had never told anyone of the horror I once carried inside, and I wasn't about to now, especially not in the presence of the Rand. "Ever since Do'shan. It has watched for me through portals. That's why they don't work around me.

"I took Sirileth through one once, to escape a Tor ambush. She didn't make it through. Minutes later, I opened another portal and it spat her out. I thought nothing of it at the time. I'd refused to think about it."

"Idiot terran!" Mezula snapped. "Your daughter is being controlled by the Maker, and you blinded yourself to the truth rather than face it. How many times must you try to damn us all?" A fair question. I really didn't have an answer.

"Sirileth is trying to find a way to free the thing above the desert?" Imiko asked, clearly sceptical.

I didn't want it to be true, but the pieces were all there and the puzzle was already solved. Years ago, the thing had taken my daughter. Sirileth had not come out of the portals unharmed. It had changed her somehow. Remade her, maybe, just as the Rand had once done to we terrans. Now Sirileth was grown, powerful in her own right. She had followers, those she had convinced to join her apocalyptic cult. Now she was bent on fulfilling her master's desire. The experimentations on rejection, the study of the prophecy around the Second Cataclysm, the creation of new scars in the world. It all led to one thing. Sirileth was planning to open the great portal fully and allow the creature beyond into our world. My daughter was going to destroy us all.

"Change course, sister," Elorame rustled. She was

talking about Ro'shan. It and Do'shan orbited each other around our world, but Mezula could make slight changes to the flying mountain's course.

"It will take too long, sister," Mezula said.

"Why not just fly to Polasia?" Jamis asked. "Await Sirileth there, at the great scar above the desert."

Mezula turned all her hands towards the merchant. "Ro'shan cannot approach the scar. The Maker would tear us from the sky."

"What if this terran puppet does not need to be with the Maker to open its rift?" Elorame asked. I considered pointing out the terran puppet had a name, but the gods were arguing and for once I held my tongue rather than get involved.

"We send a flyer to Karataan," Mezula said. "The strongest of my children will end this cataclysm before it begins." A sinking feeling spread through my gut. A moment later, Mezula turned to Kento.

"I'll go, Mother," Kento said. She wasn't talking to me. "My sister cannot be allowed to bring the Maker to Ovaeris."

"She must be stopped," Mezula said, her voice sharp.

"I will stop her," Kento said.

"No matter the cost."

Kento nodded.

And that was that. One daughter sent by the gods to kill the other. Of course, I didn't let Kento go alone.

CHAPTER
TWENTY ONE

THE WAR AGAINST TOR LASTED FOR YEARS. WE traded lives and land back and forth in what time has made meaningless encounters. I considered myself righteous, fighting to bring the murderers to heel for what they did to Vi. I signed orders to raid villages. I led war bands in the largest skirmishes Isha had seen since the fall of the Terrelan empire. I waged my war with passion and passed that same passion on to those who should have known peace.

Tris was enraged by the death of his sister. They were always close, an intimacy once forced upon them by the Iron Legion became something true and wonderful. But it was gone just like Vi was, and Tris could not contain his grief. He was a wallower. But unlike some, he did not wallow in sadness and despair, but in rage. I never meant to make him into that, but I was too blind to see it as a bad thing. I, too, was grieving. That is no excuse. There can be no excusing what I did to him. Tris became a terror the people of Tor feared even more than I.

Sirileth did not care for the war one bit. I couldn't figure out why. A part of me thought that maybe she never cared for Vi, so the war meant nothing to her. The rest of us were fighting for a murdered princess, but whenever the subject of war came up, and it came up often, Sirileth buried herself in a book. Perhaps I should have seen then that she had been affected by outside influence.

After three years of war against the people of Tor, I grew tired of it. They killed us, and we killed them. This town swore fealty to the Corpse Queen, that one raised the flag of Tor. Lines on the map moved like waves rippling across canvas. What did it all amount to? I made the call for peace, sent a message to the Tor council to send an ambassador who I would meet at the border of our lands. It was a risk, but I had to believe they wanted peace too. This war would consume both nations unless we ended it.

The Tor ambassador never reached me. That's not to say they didn't send one. Tris got word of what I was doing and slipped away with a force of my most ruthless soldiers. They met the ambassador on the road, inside Tor territory. Tris slaughtered them in their camp. Then my adopted son had the temerity to approach my camp flying the flag of the ambassador he had just butchered.

We argued then. That's putting it mildly, of course. There was shouting, screaming, insults thrown on both sides. Tris was no longer the young child to be cowed by my flashing eyes and parental tone. I suppose it helped that he was now a good head taller than me and filling out by the day. He was seventeen years old, training daily in combat as he was fighting for his life, and he had a grasp of Sourcery

a decade in the Orran Academy of Magic hadn't been able
to teach me. He knew what only I could teach him. Worst of
all, he had the blind arrogance of youth backing up his self-
righteous anger.

Tris argued there should be no peace, that the people
of Tor had sent assassins and murdered his sister. True
enough, but how many had to die to pay for that loss? How
many soldiers? How many civilians? What was the price
in blood of a single life? Of course, that wasn't enough to
sway my grieving son. He insisted there was no sufficient
price. That war must continue until Tor was ground to dust
beneath the boots of Yenheim. I asked him what that meant.
Should we should keep fighting until Tor surrendered and
became Yenheim's vassal? Or perhaps until every single
person who called the lands of Tor home was dead? When
would it end? When would it be enough to stop fighting?

Tris didn't balk at my words. I saw his jaw clamp, his
resolve harden into steel. We stood in the centre of my camp,
surrounded by his soldiers and mine, all watching queen
and prince argue. I was still foolish enough to think we were
debating whether the war should continue. I was too blind
to see what my son really meant. He made it very clear with
his next words.

Tris told me it would never be enough. It would never
end. Vi was dead and nothing could bring her back. All
the world could burn, and it still wouldn't be enough. He
shouted at me, screamed that I knew nothing of grief or the
pain he felt. He accused me of never having loved Vi. I came
so close to knocking him on his arse for that. We should
have been united in our grief, but of course, we couldn't be.
There can be no union in grief because it is a sundering. It is
something we all experience alone. Vi was dead. There was a

hole in the world, and its jagged edges cut us all differently.

His next words hammered his knife into my back. He demanded I abdicate, step down from the Corpse Throne and let someone younger and stronger do what needed to be done. Of course, he meant himself.

For the first time since we started shouting at each other, Sirileth put down her book, and gave us her full attention. I saw her darklight eyes shining through the night. I wondered then, if I did step down, would she sit by and let him ascend the throne? I honestly didn't know my daughter's mind well enough to say, and that frightened me. Would Sirileth fight Tris for the right to rule my queendom? Would Tris stand a chance against the furnace of power that my youngest daughter had become? The idea of them fighting, killing each other drove the air from my lungs. I had done all of this, caused all of it. I had ruined our happy little family. The assassins were my fault. Vi's death was my doing. The war? I waged it. Me. I caused Tris' rebellion too. And unless I stopped it, I knew his death would lie at my feet as surely as it would Sirileth's.

I refused to abdicate. Tris expected that though. He smiled and challenged me. Matters of rule are not often decided on the outcome of a duel, but I looked around and realised he had as many men in the camp as I. If I refused him, he might order his troops to attack, and we would all probably kill each other right there on the Yenheim-Tor border. I couldn't risk that. Couldn't risk Sirileth's life, or the future of my queendom. So, I accepted my son's challenge.

He came at me fast, ducking into a sprint and forming a Sourceblade in his hands. Tris preferred a massive two-handed scythe as his weapon of choice. I have no idea who had taught him to fight with it, but he was a terror on the

battlefield and there is little like a scythe to strike fear into
the hearts of those who are about to die. Lursa's Tears, but
he was quick.

I let my storm out and it thrashed around me, wild
with my anger. The air lit with my lightning; the ground
sizzled at its touch. I formed a Sourceblade and leapt to meet
my son in a clash of sword and Sourcery.

Tris did not hold back. Despite the love between us,
he truly meant to kill me. His scythe lashed out time and
time again as he twirled it about in certain hands. Horrible
things, scythes, you can't really block the blades, and if you
try to block the haft then you're already dead. He blasted
me with Kinemancy, scorched me with fire, opened the earth
beneath my feet. I weathered his storm even as he waded
through mine. We were so evenly matched. Almost. He was
quicker than me, youth lending him a swiftness I could not
hope to match. Stronger, too. But he did not have my raw
power.

I don't know how long we fought. Time is strange
like that. It felt like hours, but it could have been moments.
It ended when I ducked beneath a swing of his scythe. Time
seemed to slow, and I saw everything clearly. I leapt inside
his guard and drove a knee into my son's crotch. I could
have killed him then. Perhaps I should have. But I had
already lost one child to that stupid war against Tor, I would
not lose another.

That's not true. I lost both my adopted children the
day Vi died.

I dropped my Sourceblade, snatched a clump of
Spiceweed from my belt pouch, and shoved it in Tris' mouth
as he cried out in pain. Then I leapt at him, wrapped my legs
around his arms, my arm around his head to keep his mouth

shut, and bore him down to the ground. It didn't take long for the Spiceweed to take effect, and I let him go to wretch up his Sources onto the ground. With his magic stripped from him, his bid for my throne was over.

Tris did not accept defeat gracefully. He raged at me with words for a while, made angrier by my refusal to engage with him. I should have exiled him myself, made the choice before he did. But part of me hoped he would vent his rage, then be my son again. He had always been the brooding sort, but only at times. Most of the time he was so happy, jovial, quick to laugh, to make others laugh with rude jokes or wild antics. But no. He had not been that person for a while now. He had become this angry young man who stood before me, challenging me. Hating me. He did not come back. He left and he took most of the soldiers loyal to him. Most of them.

There was too much of myself in Tris. Too much of the raging youth I had once been. The self-righteous determination I possessed. The casual cruelty and callousness that had helped form my reputation. He learned those traits from me. And though I never purposefully trained him to be the weapon they forged me into, he became one all the same. Tris' reputation is as bloody as my own, as dark as Sirileth's came to be. And he earned every bit of it.

We passed a single day up on Ro'shan while the flying city drifted closer to Lanfall. Kento was busy preparing for an extended period away, and I was not privy to what that entailed. I found myself left to my own devices with nothing to do but wait. I am not good at waiting. During my years in Wrysom, I came to relish those lazy days. Staring at the sky, contemplating the world. In Wrysom, I found a strange ability to silence the little voice in my head that drives me to action and nags me with fears and doubt and guilt until I can no longer sit still. That quiet calm was gone once more. The voice returned. And so, every minute spent languishing with nothing to do drove me to distraction.

Jamis and his pet Sourcerer were gone, flown back down to the city by a flyer. That was good, mostly for my sanity. Every moment I looked at the man, I felt echoes of the forced desire reverberating through me. Along with the burning rage of need to tear his fucking face off and burn everything he ever loved to ash. Yes, it was good he and his Sourcerer were gone.

Imiko vanished, as she was wont to do. It was a shame. We needed to talk. I needed to make her drop her mask once again. But I had a feeling she was avoiding me to prevent just that, and I have never known anyone as good at hiding as Imiko.

With nothing else to do, I spent some time indulging in nostalgia. I visited my old house. It still stood, and I still owned the damn thing, despite two decades of neglect. It was dusty, but other than that, just as I remembered it.

The kitchen where Hardt cooked, and we gathered as a bizarre family to eat. The spare room where I had given birth to Kento. I had laid in that bed and screamed and growled and pushed. An exhausting labour to give my perfect little daughter to the world. My bedroom where I first lay with Silva. The nights we spent sitting on the windowsill, sharing fruit wine and talking about everything. The nights we spent pressed so close I couldn't tell where I ended, and she began. I tortured myself with those memories, purposefully forgetting the sharp edges and betrayals. In that jaded recollection, Silva was perfect, beautiful, and mine. But that is what we do with memories. We shave off all the sharp edges until all that is left is a lie or we focus in on the smallest, damning details until everything around them becomes a blur, and they lose all context past the emotion experienced in the moment.

I could no longer take the torture I inflicted upon myself, so I fled my house, and left the memories behind.

The next day we assembled at the palace docks, and boarded Ro'shan's swiftest flyer. What had taken Sirileth fifteen days would take us just five. We would soon catch up with my wayward daughter.

Kento said goodbye to the people she was leaving behind. They came to the docks to see her off. A young man with the olive skin of a Polasian showed up. He was tall as she and had an easy smile that looked well-used. I think he was the first Polasian man I had ever seen without a veil covering his face. He kissed my daughter goodbye. Then Kento knelt before the girl at his side, and gathered her up into her arms, hugging her tight. The girl was no more than three or four years old, skin almost as dark as her mother's. She held a cloth doll of a garn in one hand, gripping it by the tail, and clutched at Kento with her other. When they finally separated, the man had to pick the girl up and hold her to keep her from crying. Kento wiped away her own tears and boarded the flyer without a word, taking up the controls. I stared after the little family as the flyer slipped away. They watched, not me, of course, but Kento. The little girl shouted something, the words lost before the racket of the flyer's blades.

In my defence, I waited until Ro'shan was out of

sight, and that took almost an hour, but I could not hold my questions in any longer. I strode across the deck to the wheel where Kento controlled the thing and blurted out, "Am I a grandmother?"

Kento stared at me for a few seconds, then turned her attention back to the endless sky ahead of us. "No." She pulled her warm, woollen coat a little closer. It was chilly so high, and both Kento and Imiko had dressed for it. I relied on the Pyromancy Source in my stomach to keep myself warm. The terran pilot, who was currently below decks while Kento was flying us, had wrapped himself in so many layers he looked half an abban.

"That wasn't your daughter?" I asked, unwilling to let it go. "She certainly looked like you."

Kento didn't even look at me this time. "She's mine." I waited for more, but Kento volunteered nothing.

"I guess that's fair," I said. I did not miss her meaning. Kento did not consider me her mother, and so she did not consider me her daughter's grandmother. But I was. "What's her name?"

"Esem."

"She's beautiful."

"Yes."

It was like drawing salt from the ocean, but we had time. Nothing but time, really. Five days cooped up on the flyer. Imiko had already retreated to the hold to sleep, so for now it was just me and Kento.

"You're named after your grandmother," I said.

Kento tore her eyes from the sky to stare at me a moment, and something passed across her face. I thought it looked a lot like curiosity. She quashed it quickly enough and went back to contemplating the horizon.

"I could tell you about her," I said. "Or your father."
I didn't know much about Isen, not really, and what I did
know painted him in a less than favourable light, but I
thought Kento deserved to know whatever information I
could offer.

"No," Kento said.

And that was how we made the trip to Karataan. I
tried to talk to Kento, but she was cold as winter. She would
answer my questions as vaguely as she could, and often with
single words. She asked for nothing from me. I heard her
in conversation with Imiko a few times, and they laughed,
swapped stories, shared a drink. But as soon as I made my
way up onto the deck, Kento fell silent and stony.

I don't blame her for it. Kento owed me nothing. I
had abandoned her as a babe. Besides, she was raised by the
Rand, considered Mezula her mother. No doubt, the mother
had passed on her own anger to her daughter. There was no
doubt in my mind Mezula was angry with me for my part in
Silva's death, and Coby's disappearance.

I tell you this to impress upon you how painful and
lonely those five days aboard the flyer were, and how bloody
glad I was when Karataan rose from the ocean below us.

CHAPTER TWENTY TWO

GIVEN THE STONY SILENCE MY DAUGHTER treated me to each of the five days aboard that flyer, I was more than glad when we touched down in the waters surrounding Karataan. Let me tell you, whatever you might have heard about that city does not do it justice. An island off the coast, it might be, but it was a bloody big island.

The port itself was a dizzying miasma of varied peoples, atrocious smells, bawdy sights, and more types of ships than I could name. I think Hardt would have liked Karataan. He'd always loved boats. I counted two dozen ships in the harbour of varying sizes and shapes, but it also seemed that each building in the port city was made from a boat, the hull turned upside down and four walls slotted beneath it.

I saw a group of pahht corsairs lounging about outside a tavern on one side of the nearest street. They wore black leather like a uniform and had salty fur. Each one carried a long, curved sabre, and a brace of knives strapped to their dark tunics. On the other side of the street, outside an entirely different tavern, a group of terran pirates made a pretence at games of dice. They were dressed in a motley of garish colours and carried anything from rusty cutlasses to wood hatchets to sharp sticks. Both groups were not-so-subtly keeping an eye on each other.

The city stretched up the beach and the street ended at yet a third tavern further back. I had thought Lanfall a dizzying labyrinth of haphazardly built structures, but the port city of Karataan was worse. Buildings were clearly erected wherever they could be with no regard for whether it was in the middle of a street or not. The street, therefore, veered left around the building. That building, when I looked, was quite clearly a brothel. The first storey windows had balconies, and men and women both lounged on those balconies showing off their wares, which is about as polite a way of putting it as I can manage.

Above it all, the forest reached for the sky, looming over the port city. It was beyond massive. I had spent my first five years in a forest, and was used to trees. But the trees I grew up with were but children compared to the ancients on Karataan. Each one towered hundreds of feet into the sky, was wide enough it would take five minutes to walk around, and they crowded together like new lovers. When I squinted, I could just about make out wooden platforms ringing the trees at various levels, structures built upon those platforms. Up there, in the forest, was where the real city lorded above the dregs of the port. Up there was where the tahren lived. And I was certain it was where we'd find Sirileth. I couldn't imagine my calculating daughter, lover of books and puzzles and being clean, would find the port city appealing. In that we differed.

Imiko squeaked in alarm as a tentacled grey mass of slightly larger than terran proportions, attached itself to the flyer, hauled itself out of the water and up onto the railing. I will admit, I was also alarmed, but I hid it slightly better than Imiko.

The tentacled creature seemed to be surveying the deck of the flyer before it turned to us. Its bottom half was a writhing mass of flailing limbs and suckers. The top was an amorphous blob, but as I watched, it took on the shape of terran. A torso, two arms, a head. A mouth split the skin in the centre of that head. No eyes though. It was my first time meeting a mur. I had heard stories of them, from Isen and Hardt mostly, but they are an aquatic people and stick to the oceans, though they can leave it for short periods of time. I, on the other hand, did not enjoy the water other than for a bath or a brief swim, and only then when it was shallow.

The mur drew in a deep breath through its newly formed mouth, inflating its rubbery torso. It had no features; I think that is what I find most disconcerting about mur. When dealing with us, they tend to take the form of terrans, at least the top half, but their skin remains grey and rubbery and entirely featureless. It's bloody weird.

The mur drew in another breath. "Cargo?" It had a strange voice, the word drawn out and distorted as if half spoken through water.

"Just passengers," Jed, the pilot of the flyer said. I had spent some time chatting with him during our flight and discovered he was a fan of dice games. We didn't have enough players for a good game of Trust, but he showed me a wonderful game involving dice, cups, and lying. "These three terrans."

The mur waved a tentacle my way and I had the strange compulsion to wave back. Then it waved another at Imiko, and she squeaked, stepping back and standing behind me. Finally it waved a tentacle at Kento, who stood with her arms crossed and face impassive.

"What is it, Eska?" Imiko asked.

"It's a mur," I said as though it was as commonplace to me as it clearly was to Kento. I might have been surprised by Imiko's reaction, but the truth was she was terrelan born and raised. The terrelan empire was quite xenophobic and had impressed those beliefs upon its citizens from birth. Normal was terran. Anything else was different and different was bad. Imiko, despite being one of the most well-travelled terrans in the world, and despite having spent a lot of time with the pahht, could not easily escape the lessons drilled into her as a child. We all suffer from the same malady.

"Length of stay," the mur gurgled lethargically.

"Unsure," Kento said. "Hopefully no more than a few days."

"Payment?"

Kento smiled at the mur. "Ro'shan bone."

The mur was silent for a few seconds, its torso inflating and deflating. I took it for struggling to breathe out of the water, but I think it was greed. I must admit, I was ignorant to the value of the bone that grew out of the monster Aspect at Ro'shan's heart. It was stronger than steel, yet lighter than bread. A wondrous material that could be created at Mezula's whim.

The mur extended one of its arms toward Kento, the end morphing into something approaching a hand, though with only three fingers. Kento fished in the bag at her hip and brought out two lengths of bleached bone, each as long as my hand. She placed one in the waiting appendage of the mur.

"That's for the berth," Kento said. She held up the second bone. "This is for if you provide some information. We're looking for another terran. She would have arrived recently from Lanfall, aboard a tahren ship. Her name is Sirileth, and she is..."

The mur released the flyer from its tentacled grip and dove into the clear depths of the bay, disappearing in a flash of motion.

"Well, I'd say we're on the right track." I turned back to the bustling pirate city, and the forest looming above it.

Kento stared after the mur, frowning into the waters. "I've never seen the mere mention of a name cause such fear in a mur."

Imiko snorted. "You've never met Siri."

"But they're normally such reasonable people," Kento said.

There would be no convincing her. She'd probably understand when they met. I suppose I should have included myself in that thought. It had been seven years since I had last seen my daughter. By all accounts, she had changed quite a bit, though maybe not for the better.

"Stay on the flyer," Kento said to the pilot. "Be ready if I call for you."

Jed nodded. "Yes, Aspect."

I threaded my arm through Imiko's, and we stepped off the dock and into Karataan together. I was grateful of the support. Too long aboard the flyer had my legs wobbling and my knees aching. Imiko glanced at me out of the corner of her eye.

"What?" I snapped.

"Believe it or not, you look younger, Eska." Imiko grinned as I frowned. "I'm being serious. I think moving about has been good for you, got the muscles working. You're standing taller again. Still wrinkled like a sack of balls though."

"You might be right there." I conceded her point.

Imiko sighed. "I guess meeting Jamis probably helped, too. Got the old juices flowing."

I whisked my arm away and gave Imiko a solid push. She staggered a step, laughing. As if she didn't realise what she had done. But of course, she didn't. Not being a Sourcerer, she didn't understand Sourcery. No doubt she thought the Empamancer had stoked a bit of lust in me. She thought nothing of the insipid violation of having your emotions supplanted, your thoughts toyed with. It is ever the way that those who have not been hurt, can consider the brutality a trivial thing. A younger me might have wished the same pain on Imiko, so she might experience what I had been through and know the hurt I suffered. But no, I would not wish that on her. Despite everything, I would do anything in my power to protect her from it.

I fixed her with a flashing glare. One thing I have long since noticed about my Arcstorm is that it will flash behind my eyes whenever it will, often at inopportune times. However, with a bit of effort, I can also make my eyes flash for dramatic effect. I will admit, I have often used to it to cow enemies or entice lovers. Imiko was neither, so she just laughed at me.

As we walked through those streets, I was assaulted by music bellowing out of taverns, the sounds of crowds within singing along a merry accompaniment regardless of ability. The smells were something else entirely. Salt and fish were a pungent background, but there were spices in the air I couldn't name, from places I had never heard of. Hulking garn slithered through the streets. Tahren scuttled across the rooftops. Pahht and terrans filled the taverns and brothels. All the peoples of our world mingled together, they spoke, sang, ate, and fought together.

I was shocked when we sauntered past one busy tavern in time to see a terran thrown through an open window to sprawl in the sandy street. A moment later, the tavern door slammed open and a couple of pahht backed out, fists raised. Then a garn followed them, slithering across the wooden decking. The terran picked himself up and moved to stand next to the two pahht, then all three leapt at the garn, fists flying. Fleshy whips formed from the giant slug's skin, and it battered two of its assailants. The pahht brawler it missed leapt onto the garn's back and thumped it. A green, slimy hook formed from the garn's skin, high on its back, and wrapped around the pahht brawler's waist. It then flung the pahht across the street into a stall that was selling roast fish. The remaining pahht and the terran roared and charged the garn again. All the while, we stood in the middle of the street and watched. We weren't alone. It appeared the spectacle was drawing quite the crowd. A second garn waited in the tavern doorway, a terran standing by its side, and more terrans and pahht crowding the windows. They were all cheering. I realised this wasn't some battle to the death between warring races, but a tavern brawl probably over something as irrelevant as a spilled drink.

The garn won the fight handily, as I expected everyone watching knew it would. A piece of advice I give

freely: never fight a garn. You will lose. They might look
like slow, overgrown slugs, but they are ferocious in battle.
Their entire culture has formed around constant internal
warring. Killing each other in such vast numbers is the only
way they keep their population from exploding. Suffice to
say, even without weapons they are dangerous. Stick a few
blades in those flailing tentacles and they become deadly.
After taking a solid beating for a few minutes, the terran
and two pahht picked each other up, and made their way
back into the tavern. The garn followed them in, as if they
hadn't all been beating ten shades of shit out of each other.
As soon as it stopped, the music started flowing from within
again, followed by cheers and laughter. The crowd around
us moved on, the fight forgotten. Only the owner of the fish
stall seemed at all put out by the entire event.

It was fair to say, I liked Karataan.

"We should find an inn," Kento said as we slogged up
the sandy streets. We were aiming toward the forest above,
but that was as far as a destination as I had in mind. Sirileth
would be up there, but Karataan was a big place, and if
the mur's reaction to her name was anything to go by, we
wouldn't get far simply by asking around.

Imiko shook her head. "What if Siri is here? We
should look for her." She strode on, quickening her pace.

Kento grabbed Imiko by the wrist and dragged her to
a halt. "You believe my sister is here?"

"Yes."

"In this..." Kento looked around at the pirate-infested
town we had come to. "This part of town? Or up there with
the tahren?"

Imiko tugged her hand free of Kento's. "She'll be up
there."

"Then we should find an inn," Kento repeated. "One where we can bathe. Tahren care little for appearances, but they do not appreciate people who smell. We have spent five days without a bath." She smiled warmly. "All of us smell."

I certainly couldn't argue with Kento over that. Of course, she had never spent a year of her life in an underground prison. She had no idea what level of stench a terran body could reach. I did. We smelled downright pleasant compared to my time in the Pit.

Karataan did a wonderful job of reminding me how large the world was. For all my travels, my time up on Ro'shan and Do'shan, my conflicts against the gods. I had never dreamed this place could exist. The peoples of our world interacting so freely. I, too, am a product of my upbringing. I was raised in the lands we once called Orran. We were not truly any different to the Terrelans, though. I did not hate the other peoples of our world simply because they were different, but neither had I gone out of my way to interact with them. I had a pahht midwife for my pregnancy with Kento, a pahht companion and sword instructor in Ishtar, but that was as far as my involvement in the other races of our world went. That needed to change, I decided. Perhaps Karataan, despite all its debauchery, crime, and brazen piracy, was actually the ideal settlement. A place where we could all mingle without prejudice.

We found a suitable inn, one with very little evidence of bar brawls, and Imiko paid with coin. Ro'shan bone was far too valuable to pay for a couple of rooms and a bath. We settled in to eat as night fell around us, and shared a few drinks too, Imiko more than Kento and myself combined. I noticed a few of the terrans in the common room take notice of me. It was the eyes, no doubt. My reputation has spread much farther than Isha. One of the terrans did that thing I noticed people doing around me in Lanfall, pressing one hand to their chest, and reaching the other to the sky. I still had no idea why people were doing that when they saw me. Well, I was about to find out. It turns out Karataan was located where it was for a good reason.

CHAPTER TWENTY THREE

I WOKE TO A RESOUNDING CRASH FOLLOWED by screaming. In my younger days, I would have been on my feet in moments, Sourceblade already in hand, but youth was behind me. So, I woke slowly, my first thought to bang on the wall and tell Imiko to keep her exploits down. But it wasn't her. Imiko wasn't a screamer.

We had secured rooms on the first floor of the inn, a nice little place situated in what was roughly known as the good part of town. In truth, my room was little more than a cupboard with a rickety bed, and an itchy old mattress. I was glad to get up.

I heard a whistle so loud it sounded as if it came from everywhere at once. Then another crash. Screams; some anguish, some excitement. A frantic banging on my door.

As I moved to open the door, I heard another high-pitched whistle. The roof of my little room exploded inwards. The bed I had so recently been sleeping in was gone, swallowed by the new, rather expansive, hole in the floor. I unlocked and pulled open the door in something of a daze. I had no idea what was going on, but if not for the knocking I would likely be dead.

Kento was on the in the hallway. She grabbed hold of my wrist and wrenched me from the room as soon as the door was open. I barely managed a confused what? before she dragged me down the stairs and into the common room of the inn. People were everywhere, in various states of undress or injury. One pahht man was lying on a table, screaming for all he was worth. One of his legs ended in a ragged stump of torn flesh and singed fur that was pissing blood all over the floor.

A burly Polasian woman with enough dark hair on her lip to count as a moustache was wrestling with a slight terrelan man with bone-white skin. The man appeared to be clutching at something and snarling at the woman. Gone, was the common joviality of the night before. This was no bar brawl over a spilled drink. The way the two of them were thumping at each other, I thought it likely to end in death.

Kento shouted for Imiko. The common room was in a state of aggravated chaos, and I couldn't see her anywhere. It did not escape my notice that Kento had not yet let go of my hand.

"Are we under attack?" I asked. My daughter did not bother to answer.

I heard another whistle, close and followed by a resounding thump I felt in my feet. Another whistle further away, then another. The screams outside were getting louder, more voices added to the din. The Polasian woman had the pale-skinned man on the floor now, thumping her meaty fists into his face. He was still clutching at something, refusing to let it go even as she beat him to death.

Imiko rushed down the stairs. Her dark green jerkin was only partially buttoned, and she had one leather boot on her foot and the other in her hands. A half-naked terrelan man with a bald head and blatant erection followed her down the stairs. Imiko immediately ran towards Kento and I, but the terrelan looked around with a wild grin, spotted the Polasian woman prying open the unconscious man's hands, then leapt at her.

More whistles, more crashes, more screams. An orange glow outside of one of the windows was so fierce it had to be a substantial fire. Kento tugged on my hand again, dragging me towards the door of the inn. There was a panicked look on my daughter's face, and I wandered if she understood what was happening because sure as the night sky, I didn't.

Kento dragged me from the inn, Imiko close on our heels. I thought it was chaos inside. It was worse out in the streets. Buildings burned, people of all races lay dying or dead in the sandy muck, others were fighting each other with tooth and claw like mortal enemies. Some were clutching things in their smoking hands, apparently heedless of whatever it was burning their skin. And above us, Lursa's Tears rained down.

I understood then what was happening. It was a thing I had heard stories of since I was a child, yet I had never experienced. It was a moonshower. Rocks from our twin moons, broken free as they crashed into one another, falling onto our world. In Isha, it was common knowledge that if one of Lokar's or Lursa's tears hit you, you were lucky. It meant you owned the rock. Chances are, you were dead, but the rock then passed to your family who could sell it for a fortune that would keep them fed their whole lives. In Karataan, ownership of falling moon rocks appeared to be less defined. As we stood in that street, surrounded by falling rocks and men and women of all peoples fighting each other, killing each other, I saw greed. Greed in its most basic, hateful form and I saw the unity of it.

Whether we are terran or pahht or garn or Rand or Djinn, whether we are male or female or anything else, whether we are Sourcerers of immense power or farmers with nothing to their name but a rake and a seed, we are all united in our greed. A trait common to all sentience.

A rock whistled through the sky, so close I saw it trailing fire. It hit the ground no more than a dozen feet away, spraying dirt and sand into the air. Imiko crept towards the sizzling crater it left, peering down at the small pebble at its heart.

"It's mine. Get away!" a pahht woman screamed at Imiko. She had black fur with dazzling white stripes and brandished a scimitar in her hand as she ran at my friend.

I tore my hand free from Kento and drew on my Kinemancy Source. With a wave of my hand, I hit the pahht with a wave of kinetic energy that shattered her arm and sent her careening away into the wall of a nearby butcher shop.

"This is madness," Kento said. She stared around the street in horrified confusion. I wondered then how sheltered a life my daughter had lived up on Ro'shan. Yes, she no doubt had travelled down to the world below on occasion, but only to visit. She probably had no idea of the atrocities we people of Ovaeris committed on each other.

Imiko crept closer to the crater. I recognised the gleam in her eyes. "I've never actually seen one of Lursa's Tears," she said dreamily.

I pulled her away even as a garn slithered towards us from up the street. I did not doubt I could kill the thing. With my Sourcery, I could have squashed it, but I didn't relish killing. I hadn't for a long time.

We weathered that storm of falling rocks just like the port city of Karataan did. By clinging to each other and hoping nothing falling from the sky hit us. No shield I could have formed with either Kinemancy or Arcmancy would save us. The rocks came from the moons, they had that hateful bloody ore running through them. I don't know its true properties, but it fucks with Sourcery. Absorbs it, counters it somehow. That was why the Rand and Djinn were imprisoned inside the moons: it rendered their magic moot. If one of those rocks fell on us, it would pass straight through any barrier I created. And that was when I realised why people were making that sign, reaching for the moon whenever they saw me.

My reputation had spread far and wide. The bogeywoman of Isha. The Corpse Queen. A Sourcerer of terrible appetites and power to match. It turns out, people thought moon rocks would protect them from me. One of Lokar or Lursa's tears was immensely valuable for the ore it contained, but somewhere in the last two decades a rumour had started that claimed if you kept a moon rock in your home it would ward away the Corpse Queen. No more worrying about the evil Sourcerer stealing into your home in the middle of the night and devouring your children, or whatever they fuck they thought I might do to their kids.

I had so easily passed into folklore, and like any

monster from myth and legend, there were ways to protect yourself. Scared of a blood-sucking leechure rising from the swamp to drain your cattle dry? Nail a sprig of thyme to your fences every ten feet to scare the monster away. Heard a tale of an unleashed hellion swooping down and carting off young virgins? A piece of chalk clenched between the arsecheeks will protect said virgin from the beast's dark wings and grasping claws. Corpse Queen bothering your children in their cots? Buy yourself a hideously expensive rock that will have her skulking over to your neighbour's house instead. Bloody ridiculous. I swear half these tales, and the wards, and probably invented by unscrupulous merchants who are trying to unload some useless junk.

Karataan was built precisely where it was because there was no place in the world more prone to moonshowers. It's greed again, that universal trait common to all people. It drives us to colonise the most inhospitable places on Ovaeris for a chance at profit. It probably started as people sailing to the island and collecting the moon's tears after every moonshower. Then some bright sod with little regard for personal safety realised if they settled on the island, they'd have first chance at picking up the rocks, assuming they weren't killed first. However it started, here they were now, an entire city built on an island regularly peppered by deadly, unpredictable fortunes.

The shower stopped just before sunrise. The injured were taken in and seen to, the dead were shoved onto carts and wheeled away. By then, all the rocks had been claimed, even those that had fallen into buildings. The damaged homes and businesses were already well on their way to being repaired, new planks hammered onto roofs to cover the holes. Despite the chaos of the night before, Karataan picked itself up and went about its business. People who just a few hours earlier had been trying to kill each other over a stone, were now working alongside each other to rebuild. At least one ship down in the port had been sunk, a hole the size of a horse ripped into its hull. Luckily, Kento's flyer had come through unscathed.

So it was that come the morning, we headed up the last stretch of town toward the forest where the tahren city sat above the pirates and fishers, and all the other races. We were not alone in our trek. We were also not the first in line. Dozens of people were waiting to pass into the forest and ascend the trees, and a small army of tahren soldiers were blocking the way. Some of those tahren carried spears twice as long as they were tall, and others carried flat bows. The idea of a blind creature shooting a bow at anything had me a little scared, but the truth is that tahren can see just fine, possibly better than us terrans, they just see with their other senses.

We joined the line behind a massive pahht with furry arms as wide as my waist. He clutched one of Lursa's tears in his clawed hand and growled low and threatening when we got too close. The line continued to form behind us as more people made their way to the tahren, almost all of them carrying a moon rock.

"The tahren are buying the ore," I said as it dawned on me what was happening.

"Mhm," Kento murmured. "My mother has often wondered why. Karataan experiences more moonshowers than anywhere. There is a standing order that the tahren will buy any rock that has come from our moons, but they don't trade to anyone else. They hoard it, and my mother has never been able to ascertain why." I swear, I died a little inside every time Kento called Mezula her mother. Of all the things the gods have done to me over the years, that may be the worst.

"Must be a reason they keep it," Imiko said, shadowed eyes glancing first up the line to where the tahren guards were inspecting the rocks before letting the owners through, then back towards the docks where the line continued to grow behind us. "It can be made into weapons, right? Like that big hammer Horralain used to cart around everywhere."

She sounded tired. No, that's not quite right. None of us had slept well all things considered, and we were all a little tired. Imiko sounded... weary. Thin. Now and then I saw her close her eyes and let her mask drop, and it seemed to me she was in pain. I had not forgotten what she had said up on Fort Vernan. She had begged me to kill her. I do not think it was a ruse or joke. At that moment, she had been raw and real and in so much pain. I had not forgotten, but neither had I had time to approach her about it. And besides, Imiko was very good at disappearing when she didn't want to talk about a thing.

"You're talking about Shatter?" Kento asked. "You know who has it?"

Shatter was one of the fabled Weapons of Ten. It was named thus because it could literally shatter anything. I had no doubt Mezula would love to get her greedy hands on it. "No," I said quickly, before Imiko could answer with the truth. "It's missing again."

We stood in that line for another thirty minutes before reaching the tahren guarding the entrance to their treetop city. I noticed to either side of us, every fifty paces or so, bodies were staked out. They were in various stages of decomposition from fresh enough to ooze, to pile of bones held together by regret. Some were clearly terran. There were pahht too, even a garn though that corpse was mostly leathery skin and wasted arrows now. The message was very clear. The forest belonged to the tahren, and no one but the invited would be suffered entry.

The first guard stepped forward to meet us and yawned around a mouthful of sharp teeth. They were wearing an elongated helm and light grey armour over their chest and groin, where their vitals were located, or at least what I assumed were likely their most vital parts, I have no actual knowledge on tahren physiology. The tahren came up to my waist and had fuzzy yellowish fur, losing its colour in places, and patchy in others. I assumed they were an older representative, as some of the others had much more vibrant colours.

"Show rock," the tahren said, holding out a clawed paw. They carry weapons, as do the pahht, but unlike terrans, the tahren and pahht have natural weapons. They were both clearly created from more predatory creatures and possessed both claws and teeth that would be deadly if they chose to use them. They don't, for the most part. Long ago, I once asked Ishtar why she didn't fight with her claws and teeth. She gave me the oddest look and said, Idiot student. Fine, you attack me, open hand, try to slap me. I'll have my sword. We'll see how close you get. Besides, flesh is horrible to clean from claws, and blood tastes... She gagged at the mere thought.

Kento bowed, a form of respect I thought might be lost on the tahren considering they were blind. "We have no rock. My name is Kento. I am the representative..."

The tahren snarled and waved their spear in the air.

"Next."

The terran fellow behind us, a swarthy man with an eyepatch and not a single hair anywhere on his head, started forward. I sent a flashing glare his way and shook my head. He got back in line quick.

"I am the representative from Ro'shan. I am here on the business of the Rand."

The tahren did not look impressed. Or maybe they did. I am worse at deducing tahren facial expressions than I am the pahht. I am fairly certain a baring of the teeth is the pahht form of a smile. Either that, or Ishtar was regularly on the verge of gutting me. But the tahren have no visual clues, which makes a lot of sense, really.

The tahren thumped the butt of their spear on the ground. "No Rand. Ro'shan not come here. Next."

"What about foreign dignitaries?" I asked, stepping up to stand next to Kento. "I am Eskara Helsene, queen of Yenheim."

"Not heard of it," the tahren growled. "Next."

"What about my daughter, have you heard of her? Have you heard of Sirileth?"

I have loved to gamble for most of my life. It's something I picked up in the Pit. Down there, it was just about the only thing to do, but I found a joy in the act of gambling. For me, it's not about the stakes, nor the act of putting something on the line. For me, the joy comes from the people opposite me. I love winning, beating them by skill, or strategy, or luck. I have become something of an expert in reading people during a game. The way they look at their cards or dice. The way they don't look at them. The bets they make and those they fold. How quickly they are to throw their money in the pot. I say this, because it is through that love of gambling that I picked up on the guard's slightest hesitation. It only lasted half a second, maybe less, but it told me what I needed to know.

"Not heard of her too. Next." That was a lie.

I stared into the gloomy forest above. I could just about make out platforms hammered into the trunks. They ringed the trees, stretched between them. From below, it looked like vast webbing bridging between the giants, casting the forest floor in a permanent shade. One tree, just a hundred feet in front of us, had steps driven into the trunk. They looped up and around the trunk, leading up to the first platform a good distance higher. No rope to hold on to. Anyone who fell likely died. I saw a pahht woman laboriously making her way up those steps. She had been in front of us in line, a rock fallen from our moons clutched in her hands.

"We have other things to trade," Kento tried. "Bone from Ro'shan. More valuable even than moon rocks."

"No rock. No entry. Next," the tahren growled. A couple of their fellow guards stepped forward now, and I noticed bows pointed at us from above. Little platforms hammered into nearby trees, just large enough for a tahren to perch. Claw marks lined the bark leading up to those platforms. The tahren had no need of the stairs. With their claws, they could scramble up the bark like blind, tailless squirrels.

It was no good. We weren't getting in like this. But we needed to be up there. The guard had heard of Sirileth. My daughter was in the forest somewhere. We clearly could not trade on our names, nor our connections. We might fight our way past these guards, but there was an entire city of tahren beyond, and I did not like the idea of fighting them all. For a start, we'd lose. Besides, if Imiko was right and they were making weapons with the ore they mined from the moon rocks, then a single arrow could pierce any shield I could erect. That would put a swift end to our incursion.

We traipsed back to the inn, defeated. Imiko purchased a few bottles of wine, two of which appeared to be for her alone. She had always been one for dabbling in her vices, perhaps even more so than I, but rarely a day went by when she didn't drink enough that I'd have been passed out in my own vomit. Wherever we stopped, she found company for the night. Imiko was not sleeping, and the powder she applied to her face each morning was no longer covering up the proof. There was a weariness to her. A stretched out, worn, thin quality I'd never seen before.

I suggested we take Kento's flyer and find a way into the tahren city from above. Kento shook her head, claiming we couldn't risk being shot down long before we landed. The tahren apparently were quite adept at building Source weaponry. I had experienced a few of those in the past and I had no wish to do so again. Somewhere into her second bottle, Imiko suggested I cause one of my distractions so she could sneak in alone and find Sirileth. I did not think it a good idea. Distractions only really worked on those susceptible to shock and awe. I had a feeling the tahren would stick a dozen bolts in me the moment I tried to use my Sourcery to get us in. Given that they relied so heavily on their hearing and smell, I also did not like Imiko's chances of getting past the guards. Especially not in the state she was in.

It all boiled down to one inescapable fact: we had nothing the tahren wanted. If we were to get into their damned treetop city, that needed to change. And we only knew of one thing that they desired. Luckily, Karataan had just been peppered by moon rock, so all we needed to do was to find one. Or rob some poor fool who hadn't been swift enough to turn theirs in. Greed takes many forms, and none of us are truly above it.

CHAPTER TWENTY FOUR

THE YENHEIM-TOR WAR DID NOT END AS I HAD wanted it to. The council of fools who ruled over Tor did not accept my excuse that I had not killed their ambassador. Apparently, the slaughter being perpetrated by my son was close enough. Maybe they would have relented if I had given them Tris' head as proof of my desire for peace, but fuck that. I would have burned down both nations before even contemplating it.

I banished Tris, and though he left, many of his secret supporters stayed. He also didn't go far. He and his followers set up a refuge in the Forest of Ten and made regular raids into Tor territory. Worse still, he did it all in my name. Those he let live, he left with rumours of a major attack coming from the Corpse Queen's larger force. Damn the bastard, but he was forcing my hand.

Sirileth started taking a greater interest in the war.

She was just eleven years old, but she had seen things no child should. She had done things even I had not at that age. She took to martial training with passion, though she hated getting dirty or sweaty. As soon as training sessions were over, Sirileth ran for a bath and scrubbed herself raw. I taught her all I could, but I've never been the best teacher. Tamura taught her more, and I hired a proper sword tutor to help. He was a thickset man by the name of Kareem, with a torso the shape of an upside-down gourd, but damn, he knew how swing a blade. I often dozed off watching him and Sirileth trade blows. Well, she mostly tried to hit him, but he was twice her height, four times her weight, and skilled enough to defeat twenty Sirileths without taking a hit.

I found myself growing tired often. I put it down to the stress of the war, of my son's continued part in it, of trying to raise Sirileth to be above it all. But it was not only that. Hardt was the first to mention it, though likely not the first to notice. He said those words we all fear to hear. You're looking old, Eska. He wasn't wrong, though fuck him for pointing it out. I was starting to feel old too. There was already grey in my once pitch-black hair. My skin had passed the stage of having a few extra wrinkles and was sagging in places. I found myself short of breath far more easily than I once had, and my eyes were not as sharp, either. I had been denying it to myself, but when Hardt spoke those damn words, it made it real. Age was catching up to me. Fucking Chronomancy! I was just thirty-two years old, but I had the body of someone in their late fifties. The magic had wrecked me, just as it had the Iron Legion, but unlike him, I was not willing to pay any price to get my youth back.

Whenever conflict with the armies of Tor was about,

Sirileth was beside me. I stopped taking part in the battles, but I directed our forces. Sirileth watched, listened, and eventually started giving her own orders. At just eleven-years-old, she was ordering about bloodied veterans, and none doubted her right. But she did not always make the decisions I would have. Far too often, I thought she made the aggressive choice where a more patient and peaceful option existed. And always, my generals would bow first to Sirileth, and then to me, with a hearty As the Corpse Queen wills. That was when it dawned on me I was not Eskara Helsene to them. I was the Corpse Queen. How strange it was to realise I could not live up to my own legend.

I tried for peace again. I promise you, I tried. I sent secret messengers to the Tor council. I did not tell my closest advisors, nor even Sirileth that I was sending them. They came back in pieces, a note scrawled in ink and clutched in their severed hands. It read You will not fool us a second time, Corpse Queen.

So rarely in my life have I felt so lost and out of control. I could not stop this horrible war I had started. Every time I tried, my people got in the way, or my reputation got in the way and all the blame fell on my shoulders. It was a terrible weight to carry, this war I did not want. The lives it cost both sides. The brutal hunger it seemed to ignite within my people. I had no one I could turn to. Imiko was away much of the time, running her criminal empire. Hardt wanted no part of governing Yenheim and refused to let me speak of it in his presence. Tamura only giggled and said Only a fool fills their own pack with rocks. Of my closest friends, that left only Josef. On his lucid days, I could not bring myself to burden him with my woes. Those days of lucidity were few and far between, and he did not need my worries. He had his own.

Eventually, I left the battlefields completely. I thought
to detach myself from them. I thought if I removed myself,
removed the bloody Corpse Queen, then perhaps my people
could find another way. Sirileth took my place, accepting
the weight of command without question or complaint. I
wish she hadn't. If only I had been more assertive maybe,
less reticent. I thought I was doing the right thing, but the
reality is I forced command of Yenheim's armies during a
time of war onto the shoulders of an eleven-year-old girl.
And Sirileth, my wonderful, brave, dutiful little daughter,
raised on stories of her mother's ruthlessness, didn't show
her enemies any mercy.

We each had different ideas of how to secure
ourselves one of Lursa's Tears. Though thinking about it, we
never call them Lokar's Tears. Our male moon is thought
to be the aggressive one, callously chasing his wayward
love across the sky, crushing himself into her with a violent
embrace. Lursa cries, Lokar rages. I do not know why. I have
certainly seen men cry just as often as women, Hardt was
never too shy to shed tears. And I know without a shadow of
a doubt, women can rage as surely as men. I've never met a
man who can match me with anger.

I suggested the most direct route. We find someone
with a rock and take it from them by force. I didn't hesitate
to call myself the most powerful terran Sourcerer alive —
though I will admit now, I was wrong about that — and
Kento carried that curved sword at her hip. As I have said,
it's not a weapon you carry, unless you know how to use it.

Imiko, of course, had a different method in mind. She
suggested we steal a rock through guile rather than force.

Unfortunately, she was already quite drunk and seemed more interested in the man at the table next to us than our conversation. I was far from certain she was nimble enough to do the deed in her current state. Stealing the rock, that is. It's fairly easy to do the other thing, no matter how drunk you are, though doing it and doing it well are two different matters. As soon as we finished our conversation, she dragged the terran man to her room and proved she was nimble enough for that deed. I worried about my little sister. She had always been carefree, a whirlwind of motion and words and sticky fingers, but... There was something self-destructive about her now.

Kento took the stance I already knew she would. It was the same thing Silva would have suggested. Kento surmised that if Lursa's Tears fell upon the land, then they would also have fallen into the sea. And she had enough Ro'shan bone in her possession to buy a cart full of rocks from the mur. It was the peaceful approach. The best approach. So, as Imiko slunk from her chair and drunkenly deposited herself in the lap of the man next to us, Kento and I made our way down to the docks.

Damn, but it was awkward. A passive silence emanated from my daughter like a Vibromancer blotting out all sound. The town was lively and then some. People were about the work of repairing their homes and businesses. Pirates, or those sailors I assumed were pirates, were helping wherever they could. Not for pay, but just because that was what the people of Karataan did. They drank and laughed and brawled. When the moonshowers came, they killed each other over rocks. The next day, they went back to being friends, helping each other out. Oddest damned place I've ever been.

We saw an undertaker flush in the middle of business. Bodies lined the street in front of his store, and he was busy measuring them while his assistants carried the corpse of a grey-haired pahht into a coffin. I thought, perhaps, there was no better business to run in a place like Karataan.

"Such a waste of life," Kento said as we passed. I agreed, but I didn't say as much. It was the first morsel of conversation my daughter had offered, and I was scared that if I said anything we would shift back to silence. "They risk their lives every day just for a chance at a rock falling from the sky. It serves no purpose but the coin it can fetch. Greed leads to such folly."

"That's a simplistic view," I said before I could think better.

Kento rounded on me in the middle of the street, her hands balled into fists. "You think it is simplistic to say those people didn't need to die last night?" She pointed to where the undertaker was busy at work, to the corpses laid out in the sandy street before him. At least one of those corpses was a bloody, pulpy mess about the face, and no falling rock had done that. The poor sod had been beaten to death.

There was anger on my daughter's face, but I don't think it was aimed at me. We stood there in the street while the people of Karataan moved around us on their business. I heard music floating out from a nearby tavern and recognised the song. It was the Fury of the Storm. I took my time answering, considering my words, my eyes never leaving my daughter's pale gaze. Truth and lies live so close to one another, and reading them is an art. A slight pause might indicate a lie, but a lengthy one, that usually indicates a truth worth knowing.

"No," I said. "You are right, Kento. Those people

didn't need to die last night. But to say they are fools for risking their lives for money... that is simplistic."

Kento's teeth clenched, and her gaze was pale fury. I realised then, though she shared many of Silva's traits, my daughter was quite different. I had certainly never seen such anger on Silva's face, not even when we fought. There was also a youthful simplicity to Kento's understanding of the situation. It is easy for the young to be righteous, they have not yet seen morality twisted, turned inside out into a sinister mockery of itself. I was older, and I like to think, a little wiser. I had seen first-hand how righteousness was a matter of perspective. I was righteous once, and many innocent people paid the price. Emperor Aras Terrelan was righteous once, and I felt the bite of his righteous knives. Even the Iron Legion was righteous, though he sought to bring back our dead gods and reignite a war that would have consumed our world a second time. Righteousness, just like right, is a matter of perspective.

"People risk their lives every day for the money to live. They die every day, too, when luck is against them." I sighed into the face of my daughter's anger. Her mouth formed a snarl I knew well. She got it from me. "A blacksmith slips, falls into the forge. A soldier thrusts when she should parry. A sailor doesn't quite tie a knot tight enough. A woodcutter disturbs a bear. Every day those people takes risks to do their jobs, to earn some coin. They risk their lives to live. This is no different, really."

"They don't need to die for it," Kento said, her voice tight.

"You don't get to decide that," I said. "It's their choice to be here, to risk their lives at the chance for coin." I could see she was struggling with it. I understood. The anger that drives a person to fight every battle becomes as much an addiction as alcohol. It can consume you. The need to fight. Some of us are never truly happy unless we have a war to wage. The trick is to learn that not all wars have to end in death. "You have to pick your fights, Kento, or you'll never know a moment's peace. That said, thank you for saving me last night."

That brought her up short. I don't think she'd realised what she had done. It warmed my heart that during the chaos, my daughter's first thought had been to pull me close and protect me. She stared at me for a few seconds, her rage draining into confusion, then turned and started striding towards the docks once more. I had to hurry to keep up.

Securing a moon rock was not difficult. The port was abuzz with activity. One of the ships had sunk, and many of the pirates were busy hauling what little cargo was salvageable out of the water with the help of the mur. Other sailors were looking for work, hoping to jump on board one of the surviving ships. Our little flyer had an audience. No one had dared set foot on it yet, but many were staring at it in wonder. I can't blame them; the things are a marvel when you see them flying about in the sky. Less spectacular when you're aboard one and have to shout just to hear your own thoughts. Our pilot, Jed, looked nervous. He had slept on the flyer, keeping guard, and was now warning all the gathering sailors to keep their distance.

Kento caught the attention of one of the mur and set up the deal. A handful of bone later, and we had two dripping wet rocks that the mur assured us had fallen just last night. They were dark, pitted things, with silver lines running through them, each one the size of my head. They also weighed a hell of a lot, but Kento carried them in her arms and didn't seem to struggle at all.

We made our way back to the tavern to collect Imiko. Hungry eyes loitered on our prize, but none attempted to take them. They would have failed. Unless they had a Sourcerer with them, they would have stood no chance, but apparently that was not how things were done in Karataan. The night of the moonshower, the rocks were up for grabs. Having one in your hands did not mean you'd keep it. Come the morning, ownership was established. It was a serious breach of etiquette to steal another's rock once the sun had risen.

We had to wake Imiko. And kick the man from her room. They were both sprawled naked on the itchy mattress, him grinning to himself like a cat in a fish market, her snoring loud enough to rattle the windows. And she was drooling. It's not important, but I still feel the need to tell you that. The man scurried off with his clothes in one hand. Imiko took some waking, and when she did, she quickly pulled the bedsheet over herself when she realised who was doing the waking.

"Don't you knock?"

"Repeatedly," I said, grinning. It felt good to make Imiko squirm a little after she had set me up with Jamis. That being said, passed out drunk with a stranger in her bed during the middle of the day was odd for Imiko. Or at least, for the Imiko I remembered.

She pulled her clothes on and we made our way back towards the forest and the tahren city. Imiko stumbled once or twice, squinting against the light of the day. The line had lessened now, only eight other people standing, waiting to be seen. We saw one woman turned away with a bloody nose, the butt of the tahren guard's spear cracked across her

face. The tahren told her not to come back and threw the
rock she had been carrying. Apparently, they did not take
well to people trying to fool them. I glanced down at the
rocks in Kento's arms and hoped the mur hadn't taken us for
fools.

The tahren sniffed as we approached. "Back with
rocks." They held out one clawed hand. Kento deposited the
first rock in the tahren's hands, and they sniffed it. Despite
their short stature, they didn't seem to struggle with the
weight at all. The tahren handed the rock back and took
the other, giving it the same treatment, then nodded. "Two
rocks, two go." They stepped aside and waved their spear
for us to continue.

Kento glanced at me. I glanced at Imiko. Imiko shook
her head drunkenly. "Fuck no, Eska. You're not leaving me
behind. If Siri is up there, I'm going."

"I'm her mo..."

"Don't you dare," Imiko slurred at me. She gave me
push on my shoulder hard enough that it almost unbalanced
both of us. "You don't get to play that card after the shit you
pulled, Eska." She was a dangerous level of drunk. Drink a
little, and you're as likely to lie as tell the truth. Drink a lot,
and you'll say everything that passes through your head
with little regard to the truth. Drink the amount Imiko had,
and your tongue becomes unstuck, and truths you've been
guarding with good purpose come tumbling out like flies
from a bloated corpse.

"You fucking left us, Eska," Imiko slurred. "I did as
much raising of that girl as you ever did, and a better job of
it too."

Kento said nothing, the tahren said nothing, the
people behind us in the line said nothing. Everybody loves a

bit of fucking drama when it isn't aimed at them. "This isn't the time, Imiko."

"No?" Imiko let loose a wild, vicious laugh. "So, when is the time, Queen I-Have-To-Be-In-Charge?" She made to push me again, but I stepped aside and Imiko sprawled on the leaf-strewn sand.

I stared down at her, unsure what to think. Imiko was angry. Well, I understood that. She also wasn't wrong. I had left her. Left them all. I left Sirileth in Imiko's hands, knowing that she loved the girl and would raise her in my place. But this was not the time, nor the place, to discuss it, and Imiko was too damn drunk to make sense of my excuses anyway.

"Go back to the tavern, Imiko. Sleep it off," I said, my voice low and dangerous.

Imiko snorted and got back to her feet unsteadily. She staggered towards me and for a moment, I thought she'd take a swing. Instead, she lurched to my side and stopped, staring hard. I refused to meet her gaze. "You don't get to have the high ground, Eska," she slurred. "You abandoned her, just like all your kids. Siri is my daughter. Not yours." With that, she staggered past me and past the tahren, toward the tree with the steps hammered into the trunk. Kento hurried after her, taking her arm before Imiko reached the steps. Imiko tried to pull free, but Kento held onto her, and I was grateful for that. I doubted Imiko was seeing straight and hated the thought of her attempting those steps without support.

I drew in a deep breath and let it out, surprised to find tears in my eyes. Everyone was watching me, or in the tahrens' case, listening. I felt heat rising to my cheeks. It had been a while since I had been embarrassed like that. I turned and started following Imiko and Kento.

"Two rocks, two go," the tahren said, levelling their spear in front of me to block my passage.

My storm surged inside, flashing behind my eyes, crackling along my skin. Arcs of lightning ripped loose from my fingers and turned nearby leaves into smoking pyres, paying tribute to the family drama we had just spewed over everyone nearby. It's fair to say I wasn't just embarrassed; I was angry too. I thought that rage was directed at Imiko, but the truth rarely earns such anger. Truth only draws it out and acts as a lightning rod. No, I was angry at myself, because I was guilty of everything Imiko had accused me of.

I stared at the tahren, my storm crackling around me. "We are all going. Get out of my way, or I will burn your city to the ground."

It is a rare thing for anyone to make good decisions when angry. But it did get me what I wanted. The tahren removed their spear from my path, and I stalked after Imiko and Kento.

Part of me wishes I had not stopped that conversation with Imiko then. She was drunk enough that the full truth might have come out, and that would have saved us all a lot of suffering.

CHAPTER TWENTY FIVE

THE STAIRS WOULD HAVE BEEN A DAUNTING prospect to some, but I had once climbed the chain up to Ro'shan, a few steps hammered into a tree were not beyond me. It was quite taxing though, and I found myself breathing hard by the time I reached the top. And by top, I mean the first and lowest platform of the tahren city. It spread out from there, reaching across the forest to a hundred other trees, maybe more. Most platforms were higher up and sturdy wooden bridges spanned the gaps. Some trees had multiple platforms at varying heights, more wooden steps hammered into the trunk between each platform.

I call them platforms, and it may sound as if they were small things, but they were not. They were significant constructions that stretched between the trees, at times almost cutting off all sight of the floor below. This was no mere treehouse for children to play in. The tahren had constructed a legitimate city amid the canopy, with a population in the tens of thousands, maybe more.

We saw the tahren everywhere, scurrying about their business. They probably don't like that word, scurrying, but to my terran eyes that is exactly what it looked like. They could certainly walk upright like a terran, but they could also run about on all fours like a beast, and it made them significantly faster and more stable. I saw goods being carted about on backs, smoke rising from an open building, the fires of a forge within. The sound coming from a nearby behemoth of a building reminded me of a tavern, and there were two older tahren with greying fur and missing teeth sitting outside at a table playing some sort of game involving carved wooden pieces. They placed bets before each move, trading stakes back and forth in a pattern I didn't recognise. I ached to saunter over and spend some time watching, learning the rules, maybe even trying my own hand at it. I love a good game, especially when there's betting to be done.

A particularly small tahren in a green robe waited for us at the top of the steps. They were a good hand shorter than most of their kind I had encountered and smiled as they saw us. I say smile, because I'm certain it was a close approximation of what we terrans call a smile. I believe it is an unnatural thing for a tahren face to do. Remember, they do not have eyes, so have no need to communicate with facial expressions at all. This little tahren was probably trying to put visitors at ease with a welcoming smile, but to a terran eye, it looked like they were baring their teeth in a threatening display of Here are my fucking weapons, they're pointier than yours. The Rand may have made us all, but they did not make us alike.

"You have rocks? Come." And that was all the greeting we got. Not even a welcome to our wondrous city. To be fair to the tahren, they're not big fans of visitors. I always thought the terrelans were xenophobic, but the tahren are worse. They allowed the port city of Karataan to exist because it served their purpose, but despite its proximity, we saw no other terrans, nor any pahht, nor garn up in those treetops. It did not escape my notice, that I hadn't seen any of the people who entered with rocks leave again. Terran children grow up on stories of pahht taking them as slaves, and tahren cooking and eating them. Back in my day, those were often the stories told to children to get them to behave. Obviously, stories of myself replaced them.

Our passage through the city was marked. No eyes turned our way, of course, but I could tell we were marked by the way ears twitched as we passed. Stillness falling over a previously bustling storefront is as good a sign as wary stares, believe me.

Kento had supported Imiko all the way up the stairs, but now we were in the city and footing was a little more stable, Imiko pushed away from my daughter and walked alone. She wasn't exactly steady, but neither did she look fit to career over the side at any moment. I considered that a good sign. Perhaps the climb had sobered her a little. I couldn't shake the feeling that we were surrounded by enemies here, and I didn't want to be fighting Imiko at the same time as a whole city of blind, bitey teddy bears. That is unfair of me to say, some of my Orran xenophobia showing. The tahren are no more teddy bears than the pahht are cats, and neither like being called such any more than us terrans like being called moles. That is what many of them call us in private though. Moles. We are not moles, but I will admit the

Damned do bear a slight resemblance and we terrans did all come from the Damned, so I guess the comparison is about as fair as it is insulting.

The little tahren led us across three separate platforms filled with others going about their daily business, then up another set of steps to a higher platform. This one was less populated and housed a grand building that clung to the tree trunk and had that indefinable official air about it. The tahren led us into a waiting room with benches along all the walls, and a table laid out with cups and jugs of water. Then, the tahren ordered us to wait and scurried away far quicker than before.

We waited. Then we waited some more. Imiko slept, her head lolling to rest on Kento's shoulder, her mouth open and drooling. The drunk care little for where they sleep or who they sleep on. I know. In my wilder days, I occasionally woke up in random bushes on the roadside, or at a tavern table filled with people I didn't know. Back then it all seemed a bit embarrassing but survivable. These days I hate the idea of losing control like that. I still enjoy a drink, but never so much that I lose my senses.

Eventually, an older tahren waddled into the waiting room from further inside the building. They clutched a small, wooden cane in one hand, and walked as though one of their legs pained them with each step. They sniffed as soon as they entered the room and stopped. "You not Karataan."

I sent a glance at Kento, and she caught it, already gently shaking Imiko awake. "We're from Ro'shan."

A significant silence followed. "Rand not welcome," the tahren said eventually. I thought I saw their claw tighten on the cane just a little.

"Yes, I know," Kento said as she stood, leaving Imiko to blearily flounder back to wakefulness. "And my mother has no wish to upset the balance." The words sounded so much like Silva's, all diplomatic and reasonable, but there was a tightness to Kento's voice that Silva had never possessed. It made the words a lie and exposed the raw impatience underneath. "As an apology for the intrusion, I gift these rocks to you for no price." Kento held out the two rocks she had purchased from the mur.

The tahren sniffed again, then tapped their cane on the floor twice. Two other tahren scuttled into the room quickly, and all but snatched the rocks from Kento, then disappeared again. I had the distinct feeling we were balancing on a razor's edge. The tahren didn't fear the Rand, I'm not entirely sure they respected her either, and I thought perhaps the reason for them buying up all the rock from our moons suddenly made sense. That metal they could mine from the rocks was the bane of our gods. What better way to protect themselves?

"We're looking for someone," Kento continued quickly. "Sirileth Helsene."

Again, a slight pause before answering. It gave the tahren away. "Not here."

"But she was," I cut in before the tahren could end the conversation.

One claw scraped along the wooden head of their cane. "Yes," the tahren said eventually. "Your daughter came purchase something. After leave, we find steal too."

"How do you know she's my daughter?"

The tahren scoffed. Strange how, despite how different we may be, all the peoples of Ovaeris share certain mannerisms. "Smell same. Come. Show you." The tahren turned back towards the rear of the building but stopped before the doorway. "Know this. Already suffered theft. Not another. Aspect die easy as terran." I glanced at Kento, and she shrugged. Imiko let out a groan, staggered upright, and was the first to follow the tahren.

"What did Siri steal?" Imiko asked. The only answer she received was another double tap of the cane on the floor.

There were no lights inside the buildings. Why would there be? Even on the sunniest of days, light penetrating into the depths of a forest was considered gloomy at best. Little of it penetrated the confines of the buildings, and I will admit I struggled to see more than a few feet ahead as we were led down twisting corridors. Oh, how I missed that odd dark sight Ssserakis had gifted me while we were together. When the tahren led us to a stairwell carved directly into the trunk of a tree, I refused to go in blind. I have spent long enough in darkness deep underground in my life, I will not suffer to be trapped in darkness when hundreds of feet above the earth too. I drew on my Pyromancy Source and created a ball of fire in my hand.

The tahren paused, one clawed foot on the first step. They sniffed. "Pyromancer," they growled. "Surrounded by wood."

"Which burns, yes, I'm well aware," I said. "The thing about Pyromancy, though, is I can snuff flames out too. Your trees are safe from my fire."

The tahren grunted, tapped their cane on the steps a couple of times, continued up the tree in silence bar the flickering of my flames and the scuffing of our boots. It felt like we climbed those steps forever, and with the walls so close around me, memories of the Pit nipped at me like starving wolves. Prig had chased me down a winding staircase just like this one, screaming for my blood, determined to kill me for the injury I had dealt him. I felt an echo of that panic, my breath quickening in my chest, the scar on my cheek aching like it hadn't in years. I tried to push the memory away, but it hung about in the back of my mind, reminding me of how fucking stupid I had been, and how close to death I had come.

We emerged from the winding staircase, into a well-lit auditorium. The wooden roof had holes cut into it here and there, and the sun shone through them in beams of light that showed dust floating in the air.

"This Library of Ever," the tahren said as they made their way on towards a set of large double doors. The library the tahren kept was said to hold a copy of every book ever written. I wondered at the purpose of it, though. The tahren liked to portray themselves as the caretakers of our world, preserving history wherever they could, but what use was a book to a person with no sight?

Kento was the first to follow the tahren. "I didn't think you allowed outsiders to visit the library," she said. "You have refused my mother's requests many times."

I saw half a dozen robed tahren scurrying about, some carrying books, others brushes. A few were set cleaning the floors and walls, while some sat in secluded alcoves, bent over a desk, pens scribbling furiously at a page.

"What purpose does it all serve?" I asked.

The tahren leading us snorted, but neither turned nor stopped walking towards the doors. "Destruction easy, Corpse Queen, yes? Harder preserve. You walk low, we high."

Wonderful, my reputation preceded me, and was a load of shit. Well, mostly shit. I was known for destroying things. But one thing the rumours never said was that I loved books and libraries. I had quite a collection back in Yenheim, a large library with hundreds of books. Well, I suppose it was Sirileth's library now. All I owned was what I carried.

"I meant why books, when you can't read?"

"Ignorant!" the tahren snapped. "Daughter came learn, not insult."

I rolled my eyes, safe in the knowledge the gesture wouldn't be seen. "You also said she stole from you."

A moment's silence. "Yes." Oh, I was missing something. Or, more accurately, this tahren was hiding something.

The tahren stopped before the double doors and rapped on them twice with their cane. A moment later, the doors split, swinging inwards away from each other. As I stared in at the sight before me, I felt my jaw loosen. The stories I had heard of the library did not capture the grandeur of it. Most libraries I have seen are built in a single straight line, bookshelves lining the walls. The Library of Ever is a twisting maze of a thing stretching between a dozen different trees. It contains multiple levels — five of them that I saw — with staircases leading up and down at regularly intervals. The bookshelves are built around the tree trunks. Thousands, maybe tens of thousands of books crowded around each trunk, their spines facing outwards. Tahren were everywhere, all wearing robes of varying colours, scurrying about cleaning or resetting books or carrying them to alcoves to read, or whatever it was they were doing with them.

The sheer scale of that library dazzled me. The amount of knowledge that must be contained within the pages. Not all of it true. Lies were just as easily committed to the page as the truth, but knowledge can be gained from lies if you see them for what they are. A copy of every book ever written. I had thought it foolish fancy, but looking upon the shelves now, I wondered, what if it was true? What a treasure trove this place was. A person could spend their entire lives here, a hundred lives maybe, and never read a tenth of the collected works.

"Eskara," Kento snapped me out of my daze with a gentle touch to my arm. I blinked a few times before I came to my senses and saw my daughter smile and shake her head at me.

"No fire," the tahren said. I got the feeling it wasn't the first time.

I snuffed the flames without question. I wouldn't need them, the library was well lit, as though the tahren expected others to need the light. Perhaps the books themselves fared better with sunlight streaming through from above, I don't know.

The tahren started walking away, cane tapping on the floor with every step. Kento led me into the library, hand still on my arm, like a senile old woman. Apparently, no matter how old I get, a good bit of awe is enough to shock the senses right out of me. Imiko stumbled, tripped over her own feet, caught herself on a nearby bookshelf. Three tahren hissed at her and she quickly staggered away, blinking blearily. The three tahren set about resetting the shelf Imiko had disturbed.

"Not touch," the tahren leading us said. They tapped their cane on the floor three times.

"What did Sirileth come here to trade?" Kento asked. Of course, the merchant in her had remembered that detail, while Imiko only cared about what Sirileth had stolen. Personally, I just wanted to know where my wayward daughter had gone.

"Make study of ore from moons," the tahren said as they walked. "Lokar and Lursa's tears fall here more. Pay high for rocks. Unique properties in rocks?"

"It negates Sourcery," Imiko slurred.

"Crude and mistake," the tahren said. I would have bristled at the chastisement, but Imiko just pulled a face at the tahren and kept walking. "Absorb Sourcery. Dissipates as harmless. If prepared properly, can focus Sourcery instead. Two of many properties."

"The Weapons of Ten," I said, suddenly certain. "You are trying to figure out how to recreate them."

The tahren stopped, forcing us to stop with them. They turned a little. If they had eyes, they'd be glancing over their shoulder at me. "One potential, yes. Idea start there. Metal absorb Sourcery such render useless. Prepared right way instead focus Sourcery. New power. Devastating power. "

I remembered Shatter, the great hammer that could supposedly break anything. It was the only thing in existence we knew about that could destroy a Source. I remembered, too, when the Iron Legion had formed a manacle from the ore and pressed it around my wrist. It had effectively cut me off from my power, silencing the Arcstorm, gagging Ssserakis, and blocking me from accessing my Sources. With that manacle cutting into my skin, every bit of magic I tried to summon was absorbed before I could grab it. But now I thought about it, the Iron Legion used his own Sourcery to reshape the metal at will. Damn that bastard, but even now, two decades after his death, after I fucking killed him, I see that I am still no match for him.

I was lost in my thoughts again. I could see Kento and the tahren talking, but I was following my own thread. I always assumed everything the Iron Legion had learned about Sourcery and how to wield it had come from the Djinn. He spent time with Aerolis up on Do'shan, they had hammered out a deal I had never discovered the intricacies of. But the Djinn did not know how to manipulate the metal that ran through the moons. If they had, it would never have kept them prisoner. That meant either the Iron Legion figured it out himself, or he had been taught by someone else.

The Weapons of Ten were where the tahren said they had got the idea for preparing the ore in different ways to give it the properties they were boasting of. But at the end of the Orran-Terrelan war, Emperor Aras Terrelan boasted that he had collected all ten of the weapons. He had gifted them one each to his most powerful warriors, the Knights of Ten. I had only ever seen three of them.

"The Iron Legion," I said, almost in a daze as the last of the pieces of the puzzle fell into place in my mind. The tahren stopped mid conversation with Kento and I saw their clawed fingers scrape along the wood of their cane. Oh yes, they had met the man. Only people who had met Prince Loran Tow Orran reacted like that to his name. "He was one of the Knights of Ten. The Terrelan Emperor gifted him one of the Weapons of Ten, and he gave it to you. In return, you taught him how to manipulate the ore with Sourcery. Something even the Djinn never learned."

Kento stared at me, a disbelieving look on her face. Imiko groaned. "Can't we ever escape that fucker?"

"And that's what Sirileth stole," I continued. "Whatever weapon it was the Iron Legion gave you." I had figured it out finally.

Pride is like staring into a fire at night. It's comforting in the dark, but it blinds you to everything but the flames.

"Observant," the tahren said and turned sharply before walking onwards, tapping their cane two times on the floor. We passed one of the tree trunks serving as a bookshelf. I glanced at the books to see the writing on the spines was in a language I had never seen. A series of raised dots and dashes. Some sort of code, I was sure.

Kento fell in beside me. "How did you figure that out, Eska?"

I smiled at my daughter and felt a warmth in my chest when she smiled back. "All the pieces were there, just waiting to be put together. When you live with Tamura as long as I did, you learn to solve puzzles as a matter of conversation."

"Too bloody right," Imiko said sulkily from behind us.

"I missed what our guide was talking about before though," I admitted, prompting Kento to explain. Oddly, I was happy when she did.

"They have discovered the ore has a number of properties when made into an alloy with other metals," Kento said. "For instance, it can be used to absorb Sourcery, but it can also be used to channel it, allowing even untrained Sourcerers to perform complex uses. It can be used to stave off Source rejection when prepared correctly and piercing the skin. In sufficient quantity, it can be used to both repel or attract other bits of the ore." I laughed at that as I realised the truth behind Karataan. It had seemed a little odd to me that while the dock was peppered by moon rocks during the shower, the forest seemed untouched. But of course, it was designed that way. Karataan was the most frequent location for moonshowers in the world, because the tahren had enough of the ore prepared correctly to attract it. Loose rocks breaking free of the moons would fall on Karataan if they could, drawn by the ore kept here. At the same time, they used the ore to repel the ore, so the rocks fell around their treetop city, but not on it directly. It was fucking ingenious. It even accounted for the arduous task of transporting the ore. Due to its innate properties, it was a pain to move as you couldn't use a portal to do it. Try to move the ore through a portal and it disrupted the Sourcery, resetting the portal to lead nowhere.

"What did Sirileth buy?" I asked.

"Ore prepared in a way to stave off rejection," Kento said. "But she stole something and ran before anyone realised what had happened. Our guide says a ship was sent after her, Aeromancers on board to speed its passage, but has not returned."

"This," the tahren said. They stopped before a large wooden display case, the top open. There was nothing inside, but it was big enough to serve as a coffin for someone of my height. The tahren gestured at the empty case. I had seen a few others scattered about the library but had been too distracted to think of what they might hold.

"My skin is tingling," Imiko said, hugging herself. "You feel that, Eska?"

I did. A raw tickle against my skin. "There's Sourcery here," I said. "A trap." I stared daggers at the tahren.

"No trap," the tahren said. They reached out and tapped one claw against nothing. The lid of the display case was invisible.

"Sourcery?" Kento asked. She stepped forward and placed a hand against the invisible surface.

"Kinemancy," the tahren said.

That was all the invitation I needed. I surged forward and placed my hand on the invisible case. It was like touching solid stone, only it was neither warm nor cold, and contact made my skin tickle like fingers gently tracing across my palm. It was detached from Source and Sourcerer. A free-standing, invisible kinetic shield.

"And you could feel it even from over there?" Kento asked Imiko. "Are you a Sourcerer too, aunt?"

"Huh?" Imiko shook her head vigorously enough she almost fell over. She wasn't sober quite yet. "No. I just feel it." It was another thing I have never quite understood. I can feel magical wards and traps as a tingle across my skin. So can Imiko, but she is no Sourcerer. At the same time, I have known plenty of Sourcerers who could not feel wards. It is a strange sense that seems to be completely divorced from any attunement.

I ran my hand around the invisible barrier, searching out its shape, corners and surfaces all. It appeared to be complete with no way inside, and when I pushed at it, there was no give. Like most kinetic barriers, it simply absorbed and dissipated any physical force.

"How did Siri get through it?" Imiko asked.

A slight pause. "Don't know," the tahren said. They tapped their cane on the floor a few times.

"Eska?" Imiko asked.

I shook my head, dumbfounded. "I don't even know how it's done, let alone how to break it."

"See, not broken," the tahren said.

A free-standing kinetic barrier detached from Source and Sourcerer and invisible rather than a purple shimmer. I didn't think such a thing was possible. I could not fathom how the tahren had managed it.

"Can you teach me how to do this?" I asked.

"No," the tahren said.

"Eska," Imiko said again, still slurring but more insistently than before.

I almost rounded on the little tahren and demanded it, for all the good that would have done. The possibilities it presented were amazing. Invisible barriers would be only the most obvious use. I could create a dagger I could throw, completely invisible, impossible to block. More complex structures would make the need for resources a thing of the past. Sourceblades that didn't burst apart when I let go of them. Chairs without any need for wood or stone. Unbreakable doors and windows. The possibilities were endless.

"How long does a barrier like this last?" I asked. "Does it degrade over time? Is it entirely detached from the Sourcerer who created it, or do they need to remain nearby?"

The tahren answered none of my questions. "Not know how daughter broke, stole staff."

"A staff?" Kento asked, focusing back on what really mattered. I still wanted to know everything about the kinetic barrier though. "One of the Weapons of Ten?"

The tahren clutched their cane and tapped it against the floor three times. "Yes," they said through a clenched jaw. "Prince call staff Surge. Metal, metal vines along length. At head, moulded into claw, hold Augmancy Source."

"Eska," Imiko said once more. She was squinting into the gloom of the library. "Something is wrong." I ignored her, assuming she had probably reached the stage of sobriety that made a person feel ill. She certainly looked ill.

I knew only a little about Augmancy. On its own, it was considered a mostly pointless attunement with no applicable uses, yet it was also one of the most common. Augmancy was the magic of augmenting pre-existing materials. An Augmancer could create enchanted items such as magic-resistant armour if they also possessed Ingomancy. They could create magical traps, such as a wall of flame triggered to release upon certain external factors if they also possessed Pyromancy as an attunement.

"What could the staff do?" I asked. Each of the Weapons of Ten had specific properties. Shatter could break anything it hit. Neverthere could pass through metal as though it was not there. Undertow was a bow whose arrows could summon monsters where they struck. I have seen it once. A single arrow loosed from aboard a ship landed in the water between four other vessels. The thrashing beast it summoned from the depths pulled all four ships into the deep in mere moments. But I had never heard of the staff Surge before.

The tahren tapped their cane on the wooden ground again before answering. For a moment, I thought I felt something, a tingle on the back of my neck. There and then gone. I saw Imiko squirm, uncomfortable, but put it down to her blossoming hangover. "Amplifier," the tahren said. "Enhance Sourcery when hold."

Another puzzle, one I thought I did not yet hold all the pieces to. Why would Sirileth want a staff that enhanced her Sourcery? What did that have to do with creating scars in the world? And how did it all lead back to the great eye above the Polasian desert, the thing living in the space between portals? Portamancy was not one of Sirileth's attunements. I knew because I had tested her myself. It is so fucking maddening seeing a puzzle and not being smart enough to solve it. Somewhat ironically, Sirileth was always better at puzzles than me. I had no doubt she would have already solved it, but then, it was her puzzle.

The tahren tapped their cane on the floor again. The sound echoed throughout the library. Kento frowned at me. She mouthed a word but didn't give it voice. Too late. We walked right into the bloody noose that day, and too late did any of us realise the trap before it closed around us.

CHAPTER
TWENTY SIX

IT HAPPENED SO SUDDENLY. IMIKO WAS
caught somewhere between sober and staggeringly drunk,
but she was also a lifelong thief and had the instincts to go
with it. She lurched forward and leapt across the display
cabinet, rolling over the invisible barrier toward Kento.
My daughter drew her sword with such speed the blade
shimmered in an ethereal blur. She turned about, parried an
invisible strike, the sword clashing with the sound of metal
on metal, and then struck out at nothing. A tahren appeared
behind her, bleeding from a gash across their face, to sprawl
on the floor.

I had neither Imiko's reactions, nor Kento's raw
speed. My old body couldn't keep up like it used to. Of
course, that didn't mean I was defenceless. I quickly created
a kinetic shield around me and hoped our assassins weren't
using blades forged of moon ore or it would likely pass

straight through and end me. Luck appeared to be on my
side for once. The blade hit me in my back and would have
skewered one of my kidneys if not my shield. The purple
haze surrounding me played havoc with whatever ability
the tahren was using to cloak themselves. They appeared out
of thin air behind me, knife in hand and ready for another
strike. I turned and gave them a withering look I now realise
was entirely wasted on the blind arsehole. I reach out and
drew on my Kinemancy Source again, gripped the assassin
with a kinetic fist, then flung them into the depths of the
library. When I turned back to the others, I found Kento
and Imiko edging towards me. Kento's single-edged sword
dripped crimson, and death was stamped on her face.

The air shimmered around our tahren guide, and
five more of the fuzzy fuckers appeared around them. They
wore grey robes. Some carried daggers, others did not and
that worried me more. Above them, I saw tahren librarians
scatter, running from the impending conflict, while others
in the same grey robes as our assassins took places on the
balconies above.

"Photomancy," I snarled the word. I had limited
knowledge of the school other than being tortured with it
as a child at the Orran Academy of Magic. They used it to
show me terrible things. To get me accustomed to violence
and death. To desensitise me to it. The tutors used it to
create images out of nothing. Illusions. Of course, it made
sense that it could also be used to make things invisible.
I suddenly understood how part of the invisible kinetic
barrier worked, but it was something I would never be able
to do.

"You're making a mistake," Kento snarled. She was
breathing hard, trembling. Not from fear or exhaustion, I

knew rage when I saw it. "My mother..."

"Irrelevant," our tahren guide said. "No Ro'shan here. Moonshowers protect. Rand gone soon."

Kento's grip tightened on her sword, hands twisting around the leather wrapped hilt. Our assassins spread out before us. The Photomancy was a worry. Fighting things, you couldn't see was a loser's game, but as usual, it's the attunements you don't expect that kill you. What other things could their Sourcerers do?

There was an expansive tree trunk just a few steps behind us, books lining the shelves. I stepped back quickly and grabbed a large red leather-bound tome, holding it before me. Whatever language it was written in was foreign to me. It dawned on me then why the words were written so. A tactile language written for the blind to read. The tahren weren't collecting books to preserve them, they were translating every work in existence into their own form of written language.

I held the book before me, it seemed a pitiful shield. "If you attack us, I'll destroy your book."

A moment's pause. "Don't care," our tahren guide said. They tapped their cane on the floor once.

The assassins surged into action. Two whipped their clawed hands our way and the air shimmered before them. Kento burst into action. She shoved both me and Imiko aside and took the full force of the attack head on. I saw her twist, contort, a blue shimmer surrounding her for a moment. Wind whipped at her clothes and hair as the Aeromancy buffeted her, but my daughter stood strong. Behind us, I heard a couple of thunks, the sound of daggers sinking into wood and leather. I glanced back to see gouges torn out of the bookshelves and their contents. Invisible kinetic daggers propelled with the speed of Aeromancy behind them. And somehow, Kento had not only seen them, but had been fast enough to throw us aside and dodge them.

The assassins closed on us. Three of them shimmered out of existence. The other two whipped their hands forward again, throwing more invisible daggers at Kento. She stepped back, twisted, shimmered blue, and dodged again. Impossibly fast.

Above, the tahren on the balconies staring down at us started moving their hands. Imiko shrieked and clawed at her chest and arms as malformed spiders the size of my fist crawled over her. To my left, a shadow detached itself from the nearby bookshelf and flowed across the floor toward me. It rose before me, inky black and spreading to envelop me. Really, the fools should have known better. They could not scare me with illusions of shadow monsters. I had once harboured the living embodiment of fear inside of me. Ssserakis had taken my shadow for its own and my horror was not some impotent illusion.

Imiko continued screaming, trying to brush the spiders away with no success. I let the shadow roll over me and ignored it. The world went black for a moment, then the darkness faded. I saw Kento struggling against two assailants I couldn't even see.

I couldn't see a way out. With Photomancy, the tahren could weave illusions and have us running in circles. Even if we did escape the library, they could make us see solid ground where there was none. We would step into thin air and plummet to our deaths, or run into an invisible dagger. The truth was we were outmatched. We had no idea of their numbers or abilities. It was a losing battle, and we were so deep within the trap. So deep within the forest.

Another rush of wind and Kento twisted backwards, away from the invisible dagger. She slipped, fell, placed a hand on the ground, flipped herself back onto her feet. An impressive move, but a tahren assassin appeared behind her, dagger in hand and stabbed it into the back of her thigh. My daughter screamed in pain, lashing out with her sword. The tahren leapt away and vanished from sight. Blood ran down Kento's leg, soaking her trousers, and she staggered backwards. Imiko was curled into a ball, her eyes squeezed shut.

Surrender was not an option. They were trying to kill us. I saw no point in making it easier for them. I just didn't understand why they were doing this. Why had they turned on us so suddenly? It didn't matter. We needed a way out and I could think of only one, but the risk was probably as great as trying to fight our way free.

I drew on my Portamancy Source, waved my hand, and ripped open a portal to the docks. Only, of course that's not where the portal went. I will remind you, portals do not work right around me. The creature beyond found me in an instant. The great eye twisted about to stare at me through the opening. Questing limbs of something like smoke twisted through the black space beyond, weaving their way towards the portal. It was hopeless. Stepping through that hole into the void beyond would be suicide, and though that urge had never truly left me, it was about as far from my mind as it could be.

The tahren stopped. All the little buggers stepped back, noses sniffing, ears twitching. They probably had other senses at work too, but I don't know for sure. What I do know, is that they all dropped to their knees and bowed before the portal. Well, bowed before the thing on the other side.

Another piece of Sirileth's puzzle fell into place. "Oh, shit!" I said. I held the portal open. I am not strong in the school of Portamancy and holding portals open has ever been a struggle for me, especially when they lead to the space beyond. The edges of the portal burned, but not with fire. Strange things, portals. They are holes in world, ripped open by magic. Like folding our world in two and poking a hole from one spot to another. Only this portal wasn't to our world, but somewhere else. Somewhere alien. I was holding open a tear in reality. It was challenging. Pain crawled up my arm. It felt like ants were in my veins, biting and stinging. I broke out in a cold sweat from the effort. It only got worse as the great eye on the other side drifted closer, its smoky arms reached the portal and quested out into our world. The tahren bowed in supplication.

"What's going on?" Imiko asked, finally uncurling from her ball.

"Sirileth didn't steal anything from them," I said through teeth clenched at the effort of holding the portal open. "They gave it to her willingly."

Kento stared at me a moment, then back to the tahren. Realisation dawned on her face too. "They're part of the cult," she said. "All of them. That's why all the tahren fled Ro'shan a couple of years ago. That's why they think my mother won't matter soon."

It was too much effort. Too much pain. One of the smoky tendrils touched my outstretched arm and a vision rocked me.

Ovaeris burned. The sky cracked open like an eggshell. Fire and earth and water surged up from the ground towards the open rift, shadow and smoke poured the other way. The creature our gods called God hid within the shadow and smoke. No, not hid. Lurked. Hunted. It descended to our world and death rolled before it in a cloud. Everywhere it touched was rent, warped. The ground bled black beneath it. Water shimmered, turned to glass, shattered into scything shards that sliced those trapped beneath to bloody chum. Forests burned without flames, trees turned black, flaked away like ash. Smoke gathered in great plumes; fire rained from the sky. Terrans gathered, tried to hide before its terrible gaze. It passed over them oblivious. Their flesh melted from their bones, pooled like oil, reformed into a gurgling atrocity. They didn't die, though I could feel their fear and pain and knew they yearned for death. Whatever malformed hideousness they had become, they were still alive, still sentient, still people.

I snapped the portal shut and both the tendril and vision vanished. My legs gave way and I collapsed to the ground, clutching my chest with arm and stump both. I had seen it. Lursa's Tears, I had seen it. The Second Cataclysm. I had seen what my daughter was trying to do. What she was attempting to bring forth. None of us would survive. It was the death of our world. That thing brought nothing but ruination.

The tahren ceased their bowing, climbed to their feet.

"Why?" Kento asked. She held her bloodied sword before her and backed up, standing closer to Imiko and I. "Why would you want to help her?" She was talking to the tahren. "Sirileth is trying to kill us all." It was a good question, but I doubted she'd receive an answer. It simply isn't possible for a sane person to understand the motives of an apocalyptic death cult.

The tahren guide used their cane to regain their feet

and their ears twitched. I couldn't decide if that meant they were considering the question, or if they heard their reinforcements arriving. "Maker cleanse world of false gods. Tahren survive. Prosper."

Faith. Faith is a fucking disease. It spreads from one host to another by way of pestilent words, and there is no way to cut it out without harming the patient. These tahren believed in their fallacy. Believed they would be spared because they worshipped. Had Sirileth bought into the same idiotic notion? Or had she been the one to start it? I don't know. But it was clear that the tahren believed the second cataclysm was a cleansing of the unfaithful. The unfaithful, of course, meant everyone who wasn't tahren. She was unleashing a world-wide genocide and they had bought into it willingly. Fucking idiots!

I climbed unsteadily back to my feet, drew on my Pyromancy Source, and ignited my hand with blazing orange flame. I saw a few noses twitch. "We're leaving," I said, wincing at the pain still knotting inside. I hadn't retched up my Sources in days and the Portamancy had pulled me closer to my limits. Rejection was not far away. "If you try to stop us, I'll set fire to the library."

The tahren guide tapped their cane against the wooden floor. "Fool!" they said. "Pyromancers snuff out flames."

I know I have claimed before never to have burned down a library, and it was only half a lie. I'm sure some of the books survived. But I couldn't read them anyway, and those little cunts were trying to destroy the world. So, fuck it, fuck them, and fuck their library.

I fixed the little shit and their cane with a grin I knew they couldn't see. "Can you snuff out a storm?" I raised my hand and unleashed my Arcstorm. This, I had learned long ago in my battle against the Iron Legion. I could empty myself of the storm and inflict it upon an area. Oh, my Arcstorm was still inside, I could never truly rid myself of it, it was part of me, but I could expel its fury upon the world. So that's what I did, in the middle of the Library of Ever. It raged, arcs of lightning searing across the floor and roof, raking the bookshelves and setting alight everything it touched. The tahren, faced with the destruction of their vaunted library, panicked.

That was our cue to escape, not that I was in any condition to lead it. Unleashing my Arcstorm hastens rejection and I was already getting close. It hit me hard then. Cramps doubled me over like hands clutching at my innards. Blood ran from my nose onto my lips and leaked from my eyes like crimson tears.

Kento ducked under my arm, taking most of my weight, and we were off. The library passed in a blur. I don't know if we fled the way we had come, or further into its depths. I heard tahren shouting. Flames roared behind us, and my Arcstorm screamed its presence to the world.

We kicked open some doors and exited the library and passed into the fading light of day. The tahren's panic had already reached this far, and a trio of them scurried past us into the library, no doubt trying to help. All around, the activity was clear, furry little fuckers running this way and that. The scent of smoke was strong. With their senses, it was probably even stronger.

"We have to get to the ground, make a run for the port," Imiko said, sounding more sober than she had all day.

I gagged on blood, spat it onto the floor. Another spasm of cramps had me crying out.

"No time," Kento said, still clutching me, my arm over her shoulders. "We go up to the canopy."

"And then what?" Imiko asked, her voice high.

Kento raised a hand to her mouth, bit one of her rings, I didn't see which, and spoke into it. "We need to be picked up from the forest canopy. It's urgent." If she received a reply, I didn't hear it. She spoke into her ring, and our pilot heard it through their earring. Some sort of Vibromancy enchantment I would never understand. Bloody useful, though.

Speaking of blood. "Spiceweed," I managed to say through a cough that was wet and tasted like my life seeping out of me.

Of course, Imiko knew me well enough to know where I kept it. She snatched the pouch from my belt and grabbed a handful of the weed, far more than was needed, and shoved it in my mouth. I retched. It was unpleasant. Little more needs to be said than that. I vomited the Sources into Imiko's waiting hands. She was not pleased, but I was bleeding from just about everywhere, so I didn't really care. I may have distracted the tahren, but we all knew it wouldn't be long before they either got the fire under control or gave up and decided to hunt down the bitch responsible.

Kento dragged me with her, and we found the nearest set of steps leading up, ascending to the forest canopy as quickly as we could. The last bit involved a climb. The other two managed it well enough, but it involved Kento pulling on my arm while Imiko pushed my arse. I had once been quite proficient at climbing, but age and injury often make a mockery of our old proficiencies. Suffice to say, we made it up to the forest canopy. We stood on leaves as broad as carts and clung to branches as thick as an abban's leg. Smoke drifted up through inter-lapping leaves, proof of my crime but also a wonderful beacon. It didn't take long before the flyer rose into view, skimming along the surface of the canopy.

It was not a graceful boarding. Kento all but threw me up over the railing and I sprawled on the deck, lost in my pain for a few moments. I was fairly staggered by how strong she was. A moment later, she leapt aboard easily, and Imiko scrambled over the ship's railing. A curt order to the pilot, and the flyer turned away, the propellors spinning faster.

We picked up speed far too slowly for my liking and climbed steadily. But there was something playing on my mind. I used the railing to haul myself back to my feet and stumbled over to Kento. "You said we couldn't approach by air before."

My daughter stared at me. Despite all the danger and the near death, and her wounded thigh, she was smiling. Lursa's Tears but she looked so much like Isen right then. He had always been a handsome one and I feel no regret that my eldest daughter inherited his good looks.

"It's dangerous. They have Source weaponry protecting them," she said. "If we're lucky, they won't have time to use any of it before we get away."

Fuck luck. Trusting to luck is a good way to die. I crossed to the railing and stared down at the forest canopy shrinking below us. I saw our death sparking from within the giant leaves. Yes, they had Source weaponry alright. They an Arc Biter pointed right at us. I spotted it just in time to see it unleash its lightning at us. I had no Source in my stomach to protect us, no time to swallow one, let alone recover from the rejection. Without an Arcmancy Source inside, and without my Arcstorm raging at full strength, I didn't know if I could survive the blast. All I knew was that I had to try. For Imiko and Kento's sake, I had to try.

I had just enough time to scramble up to the railing, clinging to it with my stump. I reached out with my hand and used the last fizzle of my storm to spark from my fingers. The blast from the Arc Biter veered upward and struck me in the chest.

CHAPTER TWENTY SEVEN

Kroto, the Spark rode the tail winds of his brothers, conserving his energy. This was the time. They were finally going to end it. The war against their sisters and their sisters themselves. It had been agreed upon, one final battle to end the war the hateful Rand started. Though Kroto was not without his reservations. He still did not understand how they intended to end the war, when one brother would die for every sister that fell. But Geneus, the Guiding Light, had a plan. Geneus always had a plan.

The waters gave way to land; mild green grass dancing in the breeze and vast jungle reaching for them as though paying tribute. The Rand would be down there somewhere, hiding from view. Kroto saw their creations, the beasts they named terrans, roaming about. It still surprised Kroto to see them standing on two legs. They looked up and saw the mass of gathered Djinn and collapsed to their knees in prayer. It would do them no good. This was the battlefield, and they would be the sacrifices. Kroto did not relish it as some of his kind did. Jagran, the Swift, his brother in lightning, was one of those. Jagran killed the little terrans and the pahht, and any others he could find. He called it justice for what the Rand had done to Sevorai. Kroto found no justice in the deaths of such small, meaningless creatures.

At last, they came to it. The Rand waited for their brothers at the heart of the jungle. Kroto saw forms he recognised. In truth, he missed the time when they weren't at odds. Before the Maker pitted them against each other. Before it sent them to this world and sealed them in their prisons. But those times were gone. The Maker was gone. All they had left was this world, and the fight to own it.

No words were exchanged before the battle began. What could be said that hadn't already? Vainfold, the Eternal, was the first to act. He streaked out of the sky, his flames bursting into roaring life, consuming even the air about him. Their brothers followed in number, tearing down from the sky to join Vainfold in glorious battle.

Kroto felt the urge to join them, to arc downwards and strike. It was fleeting. He wanted no part in the war, but it was so easy to get caught up in his brothers' fervour. He was not alone in holding back. Aerolis, the Changing waited nearby, a torrent of wind whipping in every direction, his chosen form at this time.

Below, Vainfold met their sisters in a furious crash. Flames spewed in every direction, scorching the forest and searing the land. The Rand rose on thrones of water, wings of bone, spears of ironwood, and the battle was met in truth. Kroto watched it unfurl from above.

The earth was torn asunder as Djinn and Rand clashed, each throwing their chosen elements at the other. A storm like none had ever seen formed, great twisting tubes of furious air reaching down to strike the earth, tearing the tops off the nearby mountains and snuffing out the lives of the pitiful terrans cowering in fear. Trees moved, digging their roots in deeper and deeper, branches growing monstrous as they clutched at the Djinn. To be restrained was to be destroyed.

Astera, the Bonded, was the first to die. His chosen form was pure energy, a sizzling haze of purple light. He was always so confident that form made him all but invulnerable to the Rand. They proved him wrong. He struck into their midst, his flailing limbs slicing on all sides and dealing terrible wounds. But Ysla, the Sacrifice, was not easily defeated. She grew in size, taking on the form of a gelatinous creature, and swallowed Astera whole. He thrashed about, but his form could do no lasting damage to Ysla's. More of the Rand leapt into the fray, diving into Ysla's gelatinous form. The sisters wrapped themselves about Astera and sucked away his energy. Smaller and smaller Astera grew until all that was left of him was a softly glowing haze, and the scream of his anguish as he was snuffed out. A crystal coffin formed in his place. Above that conflict, Tern, the Blissful, flew on wings of bone, clashing against Vainfold. At the moment of Astera's death, Tern screamed as well. Her flesh blackened and decayed, soon all that was left of her was her crystal coffin.

Aerolis hissed in dismay, and Kroto turned to his brother. They both knew this war was folly. They would all die. And yet, it was too far gone to stop. Neither side could reign in their hatred anymore.

The storm grew ever more violent as his brothers continued to feed it. Multiple twisting currents of air stretched down to touch the ground. Lightning raged all about, much of it attracted to Kroto's form. It struck him and he absorbed it but felt little of the usual thrill. Below, his brothers and sisters were dying.

A massive wave of water approached, drowning the land and everything on it. The Rand had somehow drawn such *a monstrous body of water from the sea so far away. Tentacles thrashed within the wave, hundreds of them lashing out. Opus, the Ending, stood in its path. His earthen body grew and grew, fed by his power and the element beneath him, until he met the wave head on. It crashed over him and he shouted with joy, his voice reaching over the howling of the great storm. The tentacled monster that rode the waves attached itself to Opus, tearing at him. He struck back, pulling limbs from the creature, leaving great gouts of oily blood. Two behemoths locked in battle. The tentacled monster's beak dug deeper and deeper into Opus, searching for his core, even as his rock speared into its mass. They died together, monster and Djinn, locked in an eternal embrace. Urista, the Life, died with Opus. Half a battlefield away but linked by the rules of their existence.*

Perestes, the Edge, detached from the battle and flew up to Kroto and Aerolis. Perestes took the form of shifting metal, all edges scraping against each other, his voice, the squeal of a rasping blade. "Come brothers," Perestes said. "Geneus says to end this. One final strike, all our power combined, with me as the focus."

But of course, proud Perestes would be the focal for their combined powers. No other had such confidence in their abilities to withstand the pressure. Aerolis sighed, not trying to hide his displeasure, but infused Perestes with his power anyway. Kroto followed. How could he not? It was Geneus' plan, and the Guiding Light never steered them wrong.

With a joyous whoop, Perestes turned and dove towards the battle. He weaved through the storm, their brothers flying behind him, lending him their power. He glowed, then shone, then pulsed with such power as Kroto had never seen focused through one being. Bright as the sun.

The Rand saw what was happening and replied in kind. Sera, the Wings of Reason, took the mantle of their sisters' power.

*She rose from the remains of the forest, the Rand surging behind
her, lending her their strength. Time fractured around Perestes.
Life bloomed about Sera. Rand and Djinn met with an explosion
of power. The earth shattered for leagues upon leagues in every
direction, then shattered again, and again, and again. What just a
moment before had been land and trees and rock became grains of
sand. The sky torn asunder, the storm guttered out, and a vast hole
ripped itself open above them all.*

*Kroto stared down at the devastation. A land reduced to
barren nothing in an instant. Hundreds of Djinn dead, hundreds
of Rand too. Perestes and Sera had borne the brunt, but such power
as was released could not be contained. So many of them lying
dead in their crystal coffins. But while Kroto stared down at the
devastation, Aerolis was the first to look up. His brother let out a
cry of fear, and Kroto dragged his attention to the sky.*

*Above them, at the edge of the world's atmosphere, reality
had been torn open. The space beyond was black, infinite, but not a
void. And then the eye of the Maker opened. It shone down on them
like a star. The eye of the Maker was staring, hungry. Tendrils
reached forth, questing into the world, plucking at the edges of the
scar.*

*Aerolis fled. Kroto waited staring up at the Maker. At
God. The eye focused on him. With a cry of terror, he followed his
brother, fear lending him speed.*

CHAPTER TWENTY EIGHT

I WOKE GROGGY. IT IS A SPECIAL KIND OF travesty waking up tired, almost like it makes a lie of the time you spent unconscious. It had been a long time since I last absorbed someone's memories, and it was always so much more unnerving when those memories belonged to a god. I have quite a few of those rattling around in my head, though nothing compared to the number of terran memories I possess. I sometimes wonder how much of me is still me. Surely who we are is shaped by our memories and if that is true, then what of the memories I possess that are not originally mine? Every ghost I have ever unmade has left a part of themselves with me. Every Arcmancy blast I have ever absorbed came with memories of the Sourcerer who unleashed it, or the Djinn whose power created it. I even have some of Josef's memories. So, what am I? Who am I? How much of who I am now is borrowed from others?

Bah! Idiotic philosophical ramblings. I am me.
Everything else is just baggage I'm forced to cart around.

It has to be.

I opened my eyes to find Imiko upside down and
staring at me. She startled and pulled back a bit. "Wow!
They haven't flashed like that in a while." I might have
looked for a mirror to see myself, but in truth I didn't need
to. My Arcstorm was roiling violence, recharged by the blast.
My eyes were flashing like the storm at the end of the world,
lightning striking every few moments.

Imiko helped me to sit and propped me against the
railing, then fetched me a water skin. I drank and tried to get
my bearings. It was dark. The moons were high and bright,
both visible in their ceaseless struggle to devour the other,
though Lokar was in decline, just beginning to wane and
Lursa's red bulk on the way to obscuring his blue mass. Stars
twinkled down at me, so many of them. I realized, suddenly,
that there were no stars in that space beyond the portals. No
light at all. Just darkness, and the great eye of the Maker.
Or whatever the fuck it was. I refused to call it by the name
the Rand and Djinn gave it. It might have been their maker,
but it wasn't mine, and I would not give it such a title. Not
when it was trying to claw its way into our world to kill
us all. Not when it had taken my daughter and... changed
her? Conditioned her just as the Orran Academy of Magic
had once done to me? Whatever it had done, I hated it and
I would not call it the Maker. What shall I call it instead?
The lowest of the low. A scab. Yes, I like that. It has a certain
cyclical appeal. The great eye of the scab beyond the rift.
Fuck you, scab!

I was cold enough to shiver and pulled my coat a
little tighter. Part of me wanted to swallow my Pyromancy

Source again, have that flame inside keeping me warm, but I was still too close to rejection. I couldn't risk it, needed more time to recover.

Kento knelt by my side and draped a blanket over my shoulders. "Are you alright, Eska?"

I smiled at my daughter then. She was beautiful, as perfect as she had been as a babe. I will forever be utterly amazed by that. As hateful a creature as I am, and as much an idiot and bigot that Isen was, we somehow came together to create Kento. Proof that two wrongs can make a right. Maybe it was for the best we had no hand in her upbringing. Maybe Isen's cowardice and my rage would have ruined any chance of this wonder she had turned out to be. Maybe. But I'm still not about to thank Mezula for stealing my child.

Kento frowned. "Has she lost her senses?"

I chuckled. "No. But you called me Eska instead of Eskara, and it made me happy."

"Oh," Kento said sharply and stood, turning away from me. Damn me, but I had ruined the moment. My daughter was finally warming to me, right up to the point where I couldn't leave it well enough alone. "I'm glad you're alright."

I struggled to my feet, feeling my legs wobble from the exhaustion, and looked out over the railing. I saw clouds beneath us, white wisps made grey in the dark. Below them, the world looked like obsidian glass. We were above the ocean again.

"I saw it," I said, still staring down at the ocean passing below us. "I saw the Rand and the Djinn, and their battle that ripped open the great rift." I shook my head, still only half believing what I had seen. "They created the Polasian desert. A jungle one moment, a desert the next.

Such power. They tore open the sky too, and the thing they call god found them."

"You saw it?" Kento asked.

I explained my ability to absorb memories. I think it surprised her. Excited her too. She found it fascinating. I told her about my innate Sourcery, how the Iron Legion had changed me. It seems strange to admit, but I wanted to impress my daughter. She was so excited by the things I could do, that she forgot her anger with me, and I threw myself into the space between us. I told her more than I should have, more than I had told anyone. I told Kento of how the Iron Legion had used my innate Sourcery, funnelled souls through me for his own nefarious purpose. I stopped short of telling her why Prince Loran had done that to me. I have Imiko to thank for that, but she did not stop me for my own sake.

Imiko scoffed as I told Kento of the Iron Legion sucking the souls out of so many terrans and pressing them into me, of the memories that had been forced into my mind.

"How do you do it, Eska?" Imiko asked. There was such despair in her voice. Tears she refused to let fall.

I shook my head, not understanding.

"How the fuck do you do it? How do you not care?" She was drinking again, though not yet drunk enough to slur, just enough to loosen her tongue. I thought, perhaps, this was something that had been building between us for a while. Imiko needed to get it out, just like she had started down in Karataan. Well, it wouldn't be the first time I had weathered someone else's storm to make them feel better. Let her throw her accusations at me. I would stand before Imiko's bitter rage if it made her feel better. If it helped her heal whatever wound she was picking at.

That's what I thought. I didn't understand.

"I care," I said firmly. "Damnit, Imiko, I care about them all."

"Yeah? You promise?" She snarled at me. She was sat across the flyer, her back against the railing, staring hatred at me over the wine skin clutched in her hands. "What about everyone else? What about those pahht on Do'shan you slaughtered? What about the soldiers you killed when you unleashed your monsters? What about the people of Juntorrow who died at your hands?" She was working herself up, almost screaming over the propellors. "What about the men and women of Tor? What about Ishtar and Horralain? What about Vi, Eska? You still care about Vi?"

Well, that was too damned far. I could take just about anything she threw at me, but I would not sit by and let her question my love for my dead daughter. "Shut up, Imiko," I shouted at her. "Of course, I care about them all. I remember them all. Vi was my daughter. She died in my arms."

"She died because of you," Imiko shouted. "You killed her. You drove Tris mad with dreams of vengeance. You made Siri think life doesn't matter." She shook her head at me, deflated, her voice pitched on the edge of hysteria. "How do you not care, Eska? Please just tell me how to not care anymore."

It all started making sense, the drinking, the sex, the not sleeping; Imiko was throwing herself into vices to distract herself. I saw it for what it was because I finally recognised it. I had been where she was. I can't count the number of times I have thrust myself into the arms of a stranger, a lover just to not feel alone for a night, to feel wanted for a night. How often did I launch into a fight because I was running from my grief or my guilt, and I could not stop, turn around and face it? How often did I convince myself the fight was necessary and disappear into it? I had been where Imiko was and now. She was in pain, and rather than dealing with it, she was lashing out at me, looking for a fight.

I struggled to my knees, pushing Kento away when she tried to help, and crawled over to Imiko. I tried to meet her gaze, but she wouldn't look at me. There was a deep wound there. Not physical. Something far worse. There was a lifetime of agony, and it had been building for so long. I didn't know what to say to her, how to help.

"Tell me about it," I said. It was all I could do. I couldn't take her pain away, but maybe I could share it.

Imiko gave me such a look then, somewhere between disgust and total incomprehension. "You are so fucking blind, Eska. You really have no idea what I've done, do you?"

I tried desperately to think of what she might be referring to. My little sister had been with me since I escaped the Pit, most of our lives. Except the past few years, I supposed. She was a thief, a damn good one. She ran her own little criminal empire. It was a useful connection for Yenheim to have.

"What have you done?" I asked. "You've never killed anyone, Imiko."

She burst into a bitter laugh. "You believe that?" she asked, incredulous. "You really believe that, don't you?" Her face twisted in disgust.

I nodded. I'd seen Imiko steal things, but never anything worse. She simply wasn't a violent person. In all my struggles over the years, she never took part in the fights.

Except she had. She stabbed a Terrelan soldier up on

Do'shan. To save the rest of us, she had killed a man. She had proven she was capable of it. What else might she have done when I wasn't watching?

Imiko buried her head in her hands and sobbed. "You really have no clue what I did to keep your fucking queendom alive, do you?" Her words hitched and trembling. "Never killed anyone? Oh, I've killed plenty, Eska. Not as many as you, sure, but plenty. Too many." She looked at me, eyes red and bleary. "You never wondered why so many of the villages that joined Yenheim had new mayors? Never wondered what happened to the old ones?"

I shook my head.

"I sent my people to investigate them, Eska. I sent people to ask whether those villages would think of joining Yenheim, and if the mayor said no..." She sniffed. "If the mayor said no, they disappeared, and the new mayor didn't say no. All because you wanted your fucking empire." She heaved another sob.

"Tor sent assassins after you once." Imiko sniffed, tears streaming down her cheeks. "They got through, Eska. Fuck, I'm sorry! I am so sorry, but they got through all the protections I put in place. It's my fault. They killed Vi. It's my fault. They almost killed you. They almost killed Siri." She drew in a hitched breath. "They almost killed Siri!"

She gripped her trousers in her hands, scrunching the fabric between fingers like white claws. "I failed to protect you. So, I made certain their other assassins never got close. I made fucking certain."

I hadn't known Tor had sent others. I assumed they tried once, failed, and learned their lesson. Damn, but she was right. I was blind.

"I never asked you to do that." What a stupid thing

to say. But then, I have never been good at saying the right thing. I have never been good at comforting others.

Imiko shot me a baleful look. "You didn't have to. I just did what I had to do. What I knew you would have me do. I did it to protect you and Hardt and Tamura. And Siri." She sucked in a ragged breath. "I just... How do you live with it? How do you stop seeing all their faces? How do you stop smelling the blood? How..." She buried her head in her heads once more. "How?" The last was a pitiful whine.

The truth was, I didn't have an answer. Not one she could understand. I had killed so many people, and many of them did not deserve it. I could not change that fact, nor make it right. But my innate Necromancy raised the ghosts of those I felt guilt over killing. I had long since learned to unmake those ghosts, to give them a measure of peace. It was not atonement, neither did it absolve me of the part I played in their deaths, but it brought me peace. When I absorbed a part of their memories, it made sure I would never forget them. But that was my way of dealing with what I had done. I did not know how others might deal with the same problem. I thought she might be better off talking to Hardt about it. He, too, had guilt on his conscience. But Imiko had not gone to Hardt with her grief and guilt. Instead, she came to me. She had walked halfway across a continent, upended my little life, and came to me. I wondered, was she looking for someone to help her through her pain, or simply looking for someone to blame? I could be the latter. I was good at that, at least.

"You put it where it belongs," I said. Imiko glanced up at me, eyes wet and wide and fragile as a still lake. "You are the hand that holds the knife, Imiko. The hand does not feel guilt or remorse. The hand does what it is told. You are the hand, but I am the head. You were following my orders."

She shook her head. "You didn't give me the orders."

"But I would have," I said quickly. "You were only ever doing what I would have ordered. Those deaths aren't on you, Imiko. They're on me. All of them are on me. Blame me. Please."

Again, Imiko shook her head, her eyes staring into space. I cannot help it, when I see one of my friends in pain, I try to help them, to relieve that ache. I am not good at comforting others, so I try to fix them instead. It is unfortunate, because more often than not, people don't need fixing. Can't be fixed. Most often, people just want someone beside them, a shoulder to lean on. A friend to not judge them. Imiko didn't need fixing, she just needed to know she wasn't alone.

Silence stretched between us. "Why did you leave, Eska?"

I didn't want to tell her. Didn't want to tell anyone. The excuses felt so solid in my mind, so fucking reasonable. But spoken words often betray thoughts for the lies they are. Other people's ears make the lies we shroud ourselves in brittle things. I have always been covered with brittle lies.

I realised Kento was standing nearby, close enough to listen to every word we said. I didn't want to admit it, but I thought maybe it was what Imiko needed, and I would say anything to spare my friend a moment of pain.

"They were turning me into an idol," I said quietly. I barely heard myself over the sound of the propellors, the blood pounding in my ears. A truth I had held so tight for so long. Loud as a thunderclap in my mind, quiet as final breath out loud. "In the eyes of my people, I stopped being Eskara Helsene and was only the Corpse Queen." Imiko

frowned at me. "People started using it, my name, my...
me as an excuse to do evil. I tried to stop the war with Tor,
Imiko, you know that. I couldn't. My own people sabotaged
my attempts at peace, our enemies stopped believing I
wanted it. As long as I was in charge, sitting on that fucking
throne, there would be no peace until Tor was gone. And
then what? It wouldn't take much for some fool with a few
men to start another war in my name. We had plenty of
neighbours to pick on. I saw it, Imiko. Lursa's Tears, but I
saw it all happening, and I didn't want it. I didn't want it,
and I didn't know how to stop it. Not without embracing
it. Not without truly becoming the Corpse Queen they all
believed me to be."

And there it was. The horrible truth of my legacy.
You see, there is a problem with turning people into idols.
We forget they are people, and people are stupid, greedy,
and make mistakes. Some of the fuckers are downright evil.
When you idolise a person, you make monolithic not only
the good they have done but also the bad. It is far too easy
to excuse the evil by pointing to the good. Do it once, and oh
how simple it is to do it again. And again. And again. Once
you start excusing evil, there is no end. It will take and take
until it seems as normal. And instead of the heroic leader
you sought to elevate, you have a dictator crushing you
under her heel.

"That's why I left," I said. "Because I saw it
happening. And I refused to be the fallen idol. Refused to
let them make me into the excuse they wanted to do evil.
I thought... I thought without me in the way, without my
reputation backing them up, Sirileth could change things.
She could be a different type of leader, one unburdened
by my history. She could give Yenheim and its people a

new direction. And I hoped, and believed, she would steer everyone right."

I expected Imiko to scoff, to throw insults or accusations. I think I wanted her to. It would be a relief to see her turn that self-hate on me. Instead, she went very still and silent, her eyes fixed on something no one else could see.

Eventually, Imiko stood unsteadily, clutching the railing for support. She swayed for a moment. Her eyes were red and puffy. She looked like she was in pain. She opened her mouth as if to say something, then sighed and seemed to shrink in on herself. Then she nodded. "I get it," she said quietly. She started towards the hold without another word.

Imiko could have sent anyone after Sirileth. She could have gone back to Yenheim once she had me on my daughter's trail. She hadn't. Every step of the way, Imiko had never considered turning back. She had no contact with her agents, at least not that I had seen. And finally, I think I realised why.

"You're not going back, are you?" I asked just as Imiko reached the steps leading down into the hold.

Imiko paused for a moment. Then she shook her head and descended into the darkness.

That was Imiko's truth. She would cross the world, through any danger, to find Sirileth. But then she was done. I could understand that all too well. I thought, maybe we could all run away together. None of us had to go back to Yenheim. I certainly couldn't go back to Wrysom, but maybe we could find some other sleepy little village. Imiko, Sirileth, and I could run away and live in peace. A foolish dream. Sirileth was too young and bold to accept a quiet life, her actions had already proven that. And besides, I didn't truly understand Imiko half as well as I thought I did.

CHAPTER TWENTY NINE

THE FLYER WAS A RELENTLESS PIECE OF mechanical ingenuity and Sourcery fused together. It carried us above the waves far faster than a normal ship traversed the sea. We saw a few boats cutting their way through the endless ocean. I wondered if Sirileth was aboard one of them, but there was no way to check. We had decided our best course was to fly with all speed to Polasia, then on to the great rift in the desert. My daughter was trying to tear open reality to let the Scab beyond through into our world, and to do that she would need to be close to the great rift. At least, we hoped so. We just had to reach it first and stop her before she started the second cataclysm and ended the world. Sounds easy when I say it like that.

Imiko slept for a full day, and for a wonder, it seemed mostly restful. I thought, perhaps she had needed to have that argument with me. Perhaps she had turned a corner and moved onto the path of healing. A fool, I am. When finally, she woke and sauntered onto the deck of the flyer, she was sober and seemingly back to her old self. She grinned and cavorted nimbly around the deck, staring at the ocean below, occasionally making lewd comments. Lursa's Tears, but it was good to see her like that again. But, of course, those with the deepest despair are often the best at hiding it. Right up until they're not.

Kento and I talked, and I cannot explain how happy that made me. Such a simple thing, my daughter talking to me. She did not call me mother. I was still Eska to her, Eskara if she felt like driving the point home. I realised then that I would always be Eska to Kento. No matter how I felt about it, Mezula was Kento's mother. The Rand had raised her, not me. At least I could say my old enemy had raised my daughter well.

Kento was a strong woman, both in body and mind. Smart and perceptive, with an infectious laugh, and a love for poems. That was a surprise. I found her staring across the horizon, a notebook in her hands, pages flapping in the wind. For a moment, I was reminded of Silva. She, too, was a daughter of the Rand, and always carried a notebook with her. But while Silva's notebook was filled with favours owed to her, Kento's was filled with her musings. She didn't like her poems to rhyme, but instead used contrast to make obvious the obscure.

I asked Kento about her own child too, and my eldest daughter warmed to me, happy to tell me all about the little girl. Esem was just three years old and curious enough to question everything. Apparently, she drove her father, Samir, to distraction with her questions, and she drove Kento to despair with her fearlessness. Kento happily told me about the time little Esem had gotten bored while Kento was in talks with her mother. Esem had climbed onto Mezula's tail and started scaling her like I had climbed trees back in Keshin. Rather than grow angry, Mezula had picked little Esem up and swung her about from hand to hand while she and Kento talked. What a woman she might one day grow up to be, that she could use a god as a climbing frame with no repercussions.

Of course, that was assuming we survived long enough for Esem to grow up. That particular dark cloud was always hanging overhead. Did Sirileth know about Esem, I wondered? That if she succeeded in tearing open the rift, she would be sacrificing her own niece. Probably not. It dawned on me that Sirileth probably didn't even know she had a sister. Sirileth only knew the stories we had told her, and I had thought her sister died long before she was born.

I thought, perhaps that was how we would stop Sirileth. Not by force, but by showing her the things she would be destroying. Kento might be our greatest weapon against Sirileth. A sister she never knew she had. A family unmarred by my corrupting touch.

We knew we were closing in on Polasia when Imiko shouted from the bow of the flyer. She was perched on the railing, staring down at the sea, and gave a whoop.

Kento gave over control of the flyer to her pilot, Jed, and we joined Imiko. Below, cutting through the waves far too easily, were a dozen angled forms.

"Are those what I think they are?" Imiko said.

Kento nodded. "Demonships," she said. "That's the queen's entire fleet. Where would they be heading?"

Where indeed? That worried me. The queen of Polasia and I were still not on good terms after that whole thing

with the prince. Not the one Sirileth entertained. It dawns
on me I never told you about the other one; well, it's not
important now anyway.

Fine, I can see you champing at the bit to know, so I'll
just tell you in brief.

A few years after Sirileth was born, I sailed to Polasia
on a diplomatic mission. Yenheim was still young, and I
hoped to secure an alliance and trade deals that would put
my fledgling queendom on the map. Well, Imiko hoped to
secure them through me. Really, she should have known
better and sent someone else. Tamura maybe, or Hardt, or
even a rabid fucking cat. No good ever came from ordering
me to make nice. But she made her case and it sounded
sensible, and so I went.

The queen of Polasia was happy to entertain me, and
I thought I was making progress. Unfortunately, my fellow
monarch had something other than trade in mind. Namely,
marriage. Not to her, of course, she already had a harem of
comely men and women ready to service her at a moment's
notice. No, she wanted me to marry her eldest son.

Well, I had no intention of getting married. Honestly,
what did I need a husband for? I already had three children
depending on me, I neither wanted nor needed a fourth.
That being said, the prince was very pretty. It usually
takes more than that to turn my head, but I remembered
Ishtar's stories about the things they teach Polasian men.
So, I thought I'd give the prince a try. Like riding a trei bird
before you commit to buying it. I'll admit, it was a very good
night. But I decided not to buy the bird. As pleasing as he
was between the sheets, his tongue was clearly not made for
talking, and I knew I would tire of him quickly.

How was I to know that deseeding a Polasian man

before marriage was a crime? This is the sort of thing
Imiko really should have told me before sending me off. It
turns out, after I'd had my way with him, Polasian society
considered the prince sullied. This meant the queen would
get only one third of the dowry he would have otherwise
fetched. And I wasn't paying it either way. Honestly, I don't
agree with the whole thing. Feels too much like buying a
person, and I've never liked the idea of slavery.

Regardless, the queen was pissed and I'd fucked up.
I had no idea how to fix the situation beyond buying the
bloody prince — I had left him a little bloody — and I wasn't
buying anyone. Also, I didn't think my usual tactic of laying
waste to everything in sight would help. So, I ran. Or sailed,
I suppose. The queen, in her fury, sent her flagship after me.
The monstrosity was apparently the largest demonship ever
constructed.

I've told you about demonships. They are unique
to Polasia because no one else has the skill to make them.
Also, no one else is evil enough to fucking try. I must stress,
they are not alive, although they make a good impression
of it. They are a monstrous combination of Golemancy and
Necromancy, forged by stretching still-living terran skin
over wood and giving it autonomy. That means to create
a demonship, the evil bastards need to flay a person alive
to feed their skin to the hideous thing. Well, not just one
person. I guess it takes hundreds to cover the hull of a ship.
Even Ssserakis thought them ghastly abominations. You
know you've fucked up when a lord of Sevorai, an ancient
horror, the literal living incarnation of fear, considers you to
be a monster for the thing you have created.

Demonships are all eyes and mouths and grasping
limbs that erupt from the hulls, clawing at the world like

they're trying to drag everyone and everything to hell with them. You can hear them from miles away because they don't stop screaming. They tear apart ships and crew, and anything else they can get their hands on.

So, make no mistake that when I tell you the queen sent her flagship after me... the bitch was pissed! It tore my escorts to driftwood in a thrashing tantrum of screams, broken wood, and waters turned to bloody, pink froth. And then I killed it. But fuck me, did it take some killing. I hit it with enough lightning to turn half the desert to glass.

There we have it. That is why the queen of Polasia hates me. I sullied her son and sank her flagship. By all accounts, she bears a grudge as happily as I do. Which is why I've never been back to Polasia. It's also why I try not to go out on the water if possible. I have this niggling fear that she'll get wind of it and send another demonship to finish the job.

"Has she sent them to war?" Imiko asked as all three of us crowded the bow, watching the demonships. From so far above, they almost looked peaceful, but I could hear the screams. "Oh, Lursa's Tears, has Polasia declared war?"

"On whom?" I said. As far as terrans went, no nation on Ovaeris had an army as large as Polasia's. The idea they might have declared war on anyone was terrifying.

"The demonships are more a deterrent than anything else," Kento said. "They're not well suited for landing troops but make for excellent naval patrols. No pirate would ever be caught in Polasian waters because they know they'd never get away."

"And getting caught is death by being eaten by a demonship," I added. "It's not a pleasant way to go."

We watched them until they were mere specks on

the horizon behind us, though my mind still tricked me into thinking I could hear their screaming even after I could no longer see them. We could speculate their purpose all we wanted, but we had no evidence for one conclusion or another. Still, it was strange.

Half a day passed before we saw the Polasian coastline. Polasia is massive. Though most of its cities and people are crowded around the coast, as much of its territory is the great desert that extends on so far that many a poet has described it as endless. That's a load of crap. It's not endless, it's just really fucking big. And, as I now knew, it was created by the Rand and the Djinn in the same explosion of power that ripped open the sky. As far as I knew, there was only one major city taking up space in the desert, and that was Dharhna on the western border just before the land rose into craggy mountains, then passed into pahht territory of Itexia on the other side. I had never seen Dharhna, but I had been told it was majestic with grand architecture. Bulbous towers and sloping roofs, wide streets, and lots of awnings. Truly, all the stories I had heard about Dharhna went on and on about awnings as if they were the most interesting thing ever conceived. I think it's a tactic the bards use. Bore the audience with tales of awnings and drainage and other architectural bullshit, then dazzle them with a bit of action to make the story seem more exciting than it truly is. One thing I do know for a certainty is that Dharhna is a city that couldn't exist except for the diligent work of Hydromancers wringing moisture from the air. But with any luck, we wouldn't need to visit that desert city.

Our destination was right in the bloody middle of the desert where the great eye stared out of the rift. I had never been to it myself. I didn't need to go there, the eye found me whenever I opened a portal, but I knew there was a strange oasis at the heart of the desert. A place where the water ran red, and the trees grew purple. A bizarre place all but the mad avoided. Well, the mad and trade caravans making the trip between Dharhna and Irad, I guess.

Kento had a word with Jed, and he turned the flyer north, skimming along the coastline. Kento told us we were low on supplies and were visiting the Polasian capital of Irad. I had been there twice before, once with Imiko when I was still working for the Rand. I had discovered the Iron Legion was still alive, and had met Ishtar, my old pahht sword tutor. Then again when... Well, I just told you that story and how it ended so badly. I tried to tell my daughter that visiting Irad was a bad idea, but she simply told me to wear a shawl and claimed no one would recognise me. If only things were that simple.

Irad is a sprawling mess of a port city. It's busier than any port I've ever seen, a true trade hub, but most of the work on the docks is done by slaves. Whippings are a regular sight, and they have some truly barbaric ways of punishing those who try to escape their bonds. Polasia may be beautiful, but the empire is rotten and I would happily see it crumble.

Even as we touched down on the glassy waters of the bay, I could see something was amiss. The port of Irad was always busy. With so many goods funnelling through it, how could it not be? There was something frantic about the activity, though. I was certain I saw more ships being loaded in preparation to leave than being unloaded.

The port official, a sweaty woman who looked easily as old as me, ran along the pier, bare feet slapping the wood. A young, skinny boy trailed after her, the grey veil of a slave covering his mouth, the scars of old wounds latticing his arms.

"We were not expecting an ambassador from..." The old port official looked up at Kento standing on the bow, one foot up on the railing. Damn, but my daughter cut a striking pose when she wanted to. "From Ro'shan. Good meetings to you, Aspect. Ro'shan—"

"Is many months away," Kento said warily.

"A shame," the old port official said. She wiped sweat from her forehead and eyed the flyer greedily, as though sizing up an abban for steaks. "How long are you staying, Aspect?"

"Not long," Kento said as she swept her gaze out over the bustling port. "We're heading into the desert. We'll need fresh water and non-perishable food. What is going on here?"

The old port official wrung her hands together and pulled a sour face. She had six silver hoops pierced through her right ear, and when she turned her head they jingled. "Nothing, Aspect. Just a busy period is all. Lots to do."

"That's a lie," I said, fixing the woman with a stare. She met my gaze only for a moment, her eyes going wide, then shook her head quickly. I chuckled from my spot sitting near the pilot. "And you thought I wouldn't be recognised, Kento."

Kento sighed. "You don't exactly try to hide it, Eskara." She used my full name, and I guessed that meant she wasn't happy.

"You shouldn't be here," the port official said. She looked about, her eyes falling on some Polasian soldiers standing where the port was busiest. Ten women all in white tunics with black painted mail over the top. They each

carried a brace of swords, and I well knew how deadly the
Polasians could be with a sword in each hand.

"Please don't," Kento said. "My companion is not
here and will certainly not be stepping foot onto Polasian
land. Will you, Eskara?"

I held up my hands and grinned at the port official. I
will admit, I enjoy certain aspects of my reputation. I like it
when people treat me as dangerous. "No reason I would."

Kento produced a chip of Ro'shan bone and held it
out. The port official eyed it for a moment, then nodded. The
slave boy rushed forward and collected the bone. "Water
and food?" she asked. "That's it?"

"That's it," Kento said. "And news, if you have any."
She looked around the port. "And I think you do."

It took another chip of Ro'shan bone to loosen the
port official's tongue. Even so, she was not particularly
helpful. All she knew was that the royal family had slipped
out of the palace at night just three days back, had loaded up
the entire fleet of demonships with supplies, and had sailed
off into the night. Kento pressed her for more information,
but she had little to give. The whole royal family was gone.
The shrivelled old bitch of a queen, her two daughters, and
her three sons, those not already married off to some high-
ranking foreigner. Apparently, no one even knew who was in
charge anymore. The palace was locked up tighter than the
Pit, no one in or out, and the palace guards threatened death
to anyone who tried to enter. Anyone of any means was
already making plans to flee the city, fearing the worst was
about to come. That was as much as the sweaty port official
knew, and once she had spilled it, she vanished to make
arrangements for our supplies.

Kento and I needed only a brief conversation about

that. Whatever was happening was strange as fuck, and neither of us were about to bet against Sirileth being at the centre of it all. Perhaps the queen of Polasia got wind of my youngest daughter's plans and was trying to put some distance between herself and the great scar. Distance was as useless as the tahren's idiotic faith that they would be spared if they worshipped hard enough. If Sirileth opened the great rift wide enough for the Scab to pass through, nowhere would be safe and no one would be spared.

You might wonder where Imiko was during all this. Well, so did I. But Imiko will do what she's best at. She slipped off the flyer almost as soon as it touched down, not that anyone noticed. I was watching a trio of Polasian slaves, burly men with sun-scorched skin, load barrels of water and food onto our deck when Imiko sauntered up the pier, calm as a summer breeze. She trailed a hand across the arse of one of the slaves, grinning at him as he turned to her in surprise. Then she leapt aboard the flyer and sank down next to me. I smelled the hint of iced fruit wine on her but didn't say anything. She seemed better after our argument, but she couldn't hide the bags under eyes no matter how much powder she applied. Imiko was tired, and she was in pain, and she was doing her best to hide it. That's how most of us deal with pain as we get older.

As a child, it's easy to experience pain, to explore it and wallow in it. As you get older, you just don't have the time. Pain, like so many other things, gets shoved in the closet until you can't close the door anymore. The moment you step away and let go, the moment you stop trying to close the door, it all comes tumbling out to bury you in things you wanted to hide and still can't face.

"Any word?" I asked. Kento stopped directing the

slaves with the supplies and joined us.

"Oh yes," Imiko said. "I'm guessing by you know that the queen took her family and her demonships and fucked off? Well, there appears to be a bit more to the story. Seems the prince, the same one who came to Yenheim hoping to crawl between Siri's sheets, met with a mysterious stranger just five nights ago."

"Sirileth?" Kento asked.

"Can't say for sure, but whoever it was arrived on a tahren ship and was travelling alone." Imiko leaned against the mast and sighed, feigning relaxation. "This tall, dark stranger with shining eyes, broke into the palace, had a few words with the prince inside his chambers, then disappeared into the desert. Two days later, the queen packs up the entire royal household, boards her creepy fucking ships, and sails off to the horizon. No one even knows if she had a destination in mind. The palace is locked, but I spoke to a servant who managed to sneak out, and they said the second princess, a woman known for her loose lips, among other loose things, was far from certain she was returning."

A queen abandoning her empire did not seem like a good sign. Yes, the irony is not lost to me.

"We're out of time," Kento said. She strode to the railing and hefted the last barrel of water over the side. I marvelled at her strength. Even in my prime, I hadn't been so capable. The slaves who had been about to pick up the barrel watched, shocked as well. At least, I think it was shock. Wide eyes, but I couldn't see their mouths under the grey veils they wore. "Have either of you been out in the desert?" she asked.

Imiko and I both shook our heads.

"Me either," Kento said with Isen's easy smile. "My

guess is it's going to be hot."

We left Irad as swiftly as we arrived. I couldn't help but wonder, would the city still be there even if we were successful? Or would Sirileth's mere presence have caused such a panic, that everyone but the most stubborn fled, leaving it a ghost town? What a legacy my youngest daughter was already leaving. It was about to get worse.

CHAPTER THIRTY

WHAT IS THERE TO SAY ABOUT THE POLASIAN desert? It's very big. It's full of sand, and little else. The days are hot as standing close to a forge, sweltering beyond comparison. The nights are frigid as the cold cold north where the sun never shines, and everything is ice. The desert is a place of extremes, where only the hardiest survive and only the foolish dare to visit.

We skimmed just a few dozen feet from the surface. The dunes rose and fell like beige waves frozen in time. The heat shimmers made everything an illusion. I thought I saw a lone figure, dressed in black, slogging their way up the side of a shifting mountain of sand. I raised my hand to point them out, certain we had finally found my wayward daughter. But it was just a trick. One moment it was a figure in black, the next it was an onyx serpent that shoved its head into the sand and wriggled until it vanished from sight completely.

We flew through the night. Imiko and I huddled together for warmth, a blanket draped over both our shoulders. She shivered throughout. Without my Pyromancy Source, I was probably the colder one, sucking the warmth away from her. But I wouldn't swallow my Sources until I needed them. I couldn't risk rejection striking just when we had to stop Sirileth. The flyer sounded strange that night, the propellors louder than normal, but then I was probably just imagining it. The moons shone on us. Well, Lursa shone on us. She was in full dominance now, her red bulk obscuring Lokar entirely. Two more days and she'd start to wane. Then Lokar would rise and swallow his lover. Their eternal dance, spinning together and grinding each other to dust, occasionally showering us with their lethal tears.

I woke the next day as the sun started to break free of the horizon, its dazzling rays set the sand on fire. Kento stood over me, a severe look in her icy eyes. "Prepare yourself, Eska." She pointed to the front of the ship, and I followed the gesture, feeling my heart hammer. The great scar was there ahead of us, dominating the skyline. And the eye was staring through it. Staring at me.

The scale of the thing is truly hard to impress. We were not close to it. The oasis that lay at the heart of the desert, right beneath the rift, was not yet in sight. Despite this, the rift consumed the sky above us. Ro'shan is a mountain turned upside down, flying through the sky. It is huge, monstrously so, and atop it sits the grandest city in the world along with a forest, a lake, and even land for farming. Ro'shan is not just a city and not just a mountain, it is a nation. Ro'shan is tiny compared to the great rift above the Polasian desert. The creature that stares through that rift, the one our gods call God, was large enough that it could not enter our world unless Sirileth tore the rift even further. We are less than ants on that scale. We are smaller than motes of dust by comparison.

I crowded the bow along with Imiko, Kento standing behind us, and we stared up in wonder. The eye is not terran. It is an eye, unmistakably so, but it boils with fire, freezes into crystalline shards, colours twist into a dizzying kaleidoscope that swallows the mind. It was both formed of colour and somehow beyond colour. Thick tentacles like smoke quested through the rift into our world, plucking, tearing at the edges, trying to open it further. They could only exist in our world for a few moments, before burning away to nothing. Yet the creature did not seem to want for more of them.

There was no sign of Sirileth anywhere.

That was when the flyer decided it had enough. The main propellor ground to a halt, dark smoke rising from the mechanism, the smell of burning oil and wood strong enough to make my eyes water. A moment later, we plummeted from the sky.

I had no time to swallow my Sources and my stomach was already making a play for my mouth as we dropped. With nothing else to do, I clutched at the ship's railing and watched the sand rushing up to meet me. Imiko grabbed me, clinging to my stump. Kento lurched forward, pressed in from behind, wrapped her arms around both of us. Just moments before we hit the sand, a bubble of hazy kinetic energy snapped into being around us. It wasn't my shield.

The ship hit the sand. It flew apart, wood and metal splitting, cracking, flying, bouncing off the kinetic shield. The noise was all hiss and roar and crash. The sand erupted around us, pluming into the air, spraying against the shield. We rolled through it all, suspended in the kinetic bubble.

As the last of the wreckage fell, hitting the scorching sand, the shield vanished in a puff of energy. All three of us tumbled to the sand, gasping for air. Kento was first on her feet. She turned and scanned the wreckage, then ran toward a half-buried lump. The pilot, Jed. She dug him out of the sand and pressed her ear close to his mouth. Even from ten paces away, I could see blood leaking from his head and a shard of wood buried in his chest. He was dead. He was also sitting on a piece of wrecked railing about a dozen paces. His ghost had risen already, hazy and undefined, confused by his new half existence. He was not one of mine. I had not raised him as a ghost. I thought that strange.

Imiko groaned beside me, raised her hand to shield her face from the blowing sand. The wind was unpleasantly warm, picking up coarse grains and throwing them at us. Trust me, if ever you have the opportunity to saunter through a desert, don't. Imiko got unsteadily to her feet, staggered once, then shook herself and ambled over to help Kento. Even my little sister, with all her grace and nimble feet, struggled to find good purchase in the sand. I watched them dig the pilot out, then they moved about the wreckage to scavenge what supplies they could. We ended up with three full water skins and a satchel of dried, cured meat. It did not seem like a lot. Probably not enough for the distance we still had to travel.

I looked toward the great scar above us and found the eye staring down at me.

Kento said a few words for the pilot, a prayer of some sort. He looked so young, barely a wisp of hair on his chin. His ghost watched from nearby, ethereal blue and still trying to speak. It takes a while for ghosts to realise they no longer have a voice in the world. I wonder what happened to his body. Did the rolling dunes swallow it? Or did the wind and sand scourge the flesh from his bones and leave a skeleton to bleach in the relentless sun? Or maybe some scavenging beast came and found him and made a meal of his flesh. I don't know. He'd saved our lives on at least one occasion though, so I countered him well worth remembering. Despite that, we left his body there, and his ghost.

I sat in the sand at the bottom of a dune amidst the wreckage of our flyer and watched as Kento scrounged what she could and made us ready to leave once more. She found some black fabric from somewhere and taught Imiko how to wrap it around her head so only her eyes were visible. Then she advanced upon me with a similar scrap of cloth.

"You're a Sourcerer," I said as my daughter knelt before me.

Kento was silent for a moment, jaw clenched. Then she shuffled forward and started wrapping the cloth around my head. I let her. "I never made any attempts to hide what... To hide who I am from you, Eska." Kento finished with the cloth. It was warm, but then conserving heat in the desert is important, as is conserving moisture. She gripped me under my arm and hauled me to my feet. I let her do that too, though given how strong she was, I doubt I could have stopped her even if I'd wanted to.

"We have to move. I don't know how far we are from the oasis, but the longer we wait here the less likely our water will last." She slung a pack over her shoulder and began climbing the dune. The great eye stared down at us.

"You're a Sourcerer," I said again, more loudly this time. Unwilling to let it go. She hadn't lied, true. She had never told me she wasn't a Sourcerer. That was very Rand of her. Mezula, too, didn't lie, but rather spoke in half-truths, equivocations and omissions. It should have been no surprise to me. If you're raised by a woman who never tells the whole truth, you learn to hide things. We all learn so much from our parents, especially the things we shouldn't.

Kento paused halfway up the dune. She turned and stared down at me, bright blue eyes like mine, dark skin like Isen's. Then she shook her head and turned away, already starting to wrap her own shawl around her face. "I'm an Aspect, Eska."

I struggled up the dune after her, Imiko behind me. Kento set a gruelling pace. We spent hours trudging through the baking sun, up and down endless sandy hills that shifted underfoot and looked identical to the last. Hot wind slapped at us, pulled on our clothing, pelted us with stinging grains of sand. Still, we struggled after Kento. I think she set that pace on purpose, knowing I would struggle to keep up. By now, my daughter knew me well enough to know I would have questions, but it's hard to ask those questions when you're struggling to breathe. Stupid fucking desert and its heat and sand. Before long, Imiko was beside me and we laboured on in silence. Well, almost silence, save for the breathing and the occasional curse muttered under my breath whenever the sand shifted and I all but fell. Imiko was always there to catch me, steady me. I think she, too, was struggling judging by the quiet. Then again, maybe she was still dealing with her own demons.

Kento surged along ahead, a shadow slithering across the dunes. At some point, I realised she was brooding. It is difficult to stay angry, especially through exertion. As we trudged through the sand and the eye stared down at me as relentless as the sun, the horizon shimmered and shifted. My anger waned and I looked upon my daughter's back with new clarity. I knew she was brooding because, well, how often had I done the same? Some people like to think of brooding as sitting in a dark corner and melding with the shadows, but that's a load of crap. The best way to brood is to set your feet on a line and walk until your soles blister, your thighs burn, and sweat runs like a river down your face.

The sun was dipping below the horizon when Kento finally slowed enough that Imiko and I could catch up. The temperature was already dropping and despite the sweltering heat of what seemed like only moments ago, I shivered. We had been walking for hours, maybe more, perhaps the whole day, yet the great eye seemed no larger or smaller. It still dominated the sky above and before us, though its gaze was not on me at that moment. I felt oddly lighter for that lack of attention, as though the weight of its gaze was a stone around my neck driving my feet into the sand.

"Ask," Kento said eventually. "You won't like the answer though, Eska."

That never stopped me before. There have always been questions to which the answers are painful to me or others. Unfortunately, I am a curious bitch and when a puzzle presents itself, just like Sirileth, I must solve it. I must know the truth. I have never been good at leaving things be. It's like finding a burr in your skin and needing to scratch it even if it leaves a bleeding wound behind.

We crested the top of a shifting dune and started the slipping slide down to the bottom. "Sourcerers are rare. They are the descendants of Aspects," I said. "When the bloodlines of two Aspects cross, the children are Sourcerers. It takes both parents to have that lineage." I glanced at Kento, but she was staring ahead, watching the sand shift underneath each footfall. "Isen wasn't a Sourcerer. Your father might have been a descendent of an Aspect, but the chances are low. You weren't a Sourcerer, Kento. But you are now."

Kento grunted an affirmation but said nothing.

"What does that mean?" Imiko asked. I was trying my best to keep pace with Kento now her progress was slowed, but Imiko still trailed a few steps behind.

"It's not just a title, is it?" I asked. "You really are an Aspect of Mezula."

"Yes," Kento said as she reached the bottom of the dune. She paused, took her water skin from her shoulder, drank a couple of sips, then raised her face to the darkening sky.

"How?" I asked.

Kento sighed. "Mezula is a god, Eska."

I scoffed, tugged at my shawl, suddenly desperate to breathe air not filtered through the rough cloth, gasped in a breath of cold air. "She's a Rand."

"The Rand are gods," Kento said. "They made us. My mother literally shaped the course of life on Ovaeris. All life. You wish to debate theology, you will lose, Eskara."

I grumbled, but I couldn't dispute the fact.

"Why?" Imiko asked. "Why make you an Aspect?"

I knew why. Mezula hated me. I killed one of her daughters, and another was living as a hermit because she chose to help me defeat the Iron Legion. Mezula said I had killed Coby just as I had Silva, but that wasn't true. Coby had found me in Prince Loran's laboratory, had come there to kill me for murdering her sister. I convinced her to help me instead, to free me and fight against the Iron Legion. We fought, and we won, but the cost was high. Josef had been infused with wild Sourcery, but Coby had been stripped of her glamour. That was what Silva called it, Coby's gift from their mother, the ability to look like anyone she wanted. Anyone except herself. In all her life, only Silva had ever seen Coby's real face, until then. With her glamour gone, I saw her too. Coby, who could look like anyone, who loved to be pretty, to be stunning, who could be man, woman, or anything she chose. Without that glamour, she was... plain. Not beautiful or ugly, not startling or grotesque. She was forgettable. Coby hated that. It was worse than death, it was embarrassing. To her, there was perhaps no worse injury.

Coby did not return to Ro'shan or to her mother. She is not dead, but I think perhaps she cannot face what she has become. I found her a few years after we defeated the Iron Legion together. Or I heard of her, at least. She fled to the Kinei mountain range on western Isha and lives there now as a hermit and a horror story. The stories tell of a wild woman up in the mountain who stalks those foolish enough to leave the marked out trails. She hunts them, captures them, takes their faces, wears them in place of her own. It could be shit. I know far better than most that rumours are often just that. It might not have even the slightest grain of truth to it. And yet... I believe it.

Of course, Mezula took the opportunity to take revenge on me by turning one of my daughters against me. By turning her into something else, a part of Mezula herself.

Kento opened her eyes, blew out another sigh, and started up the side of the dune. Sand cascaded around her, and I had to fight through it to keep up. "Mezula did it to save me from you, Eska. To save my life from your legacy."

Oh yes, no doubt she laid the blame for it at my feet too. "Which legacy?" I asked bitterly. "I appear to collect them as a beetle does dung." Rolling them into ever greater balls, but no matter how large those legacies might grow it could never be forgotten that they were all nothing but shit.

Kento glanced at me, eyes as hard and fragile as ice. "Your Chronomancy."

"Fuck!" Not the most eloquent of responses, but the truth hit me as hard as Hardt when he was training angry. Back in the Pit, when Josef found us just as we were making our escape, he killed Isen. He was going to kill Hardt, too, then drag me back to our prison. I swallowed a Chronomancy Source, suffered through the rejection. It was a gamble, and my life was the stakes. "I didn't even know I was pregnant when I did it."

"I don't think the Sourcery cared whether you knew or not."

Imiko slogged up the dune and inserted herself between us. "Hi, yeah, not a Sourcerer and don't understand."

"The Chronomancy Source I swallowed to escape the Pit," I said. "It aged me back then, has continued to make me age faster than most people. I was pregnant with Kento at the time."

"It didn't just affect you, Eska," Kento said. "Mezula gave me to a pahht family to raise. But two weeks after you gave me up, they brought me back to her. They didn't know much about terrans, but they knew something was wrong. I was growing wrong. Too fast in some places, too slow in others. Apparently, I wouldn't stop crying. Mezula says it was because I was in constant agony."

"I didn't know," I said.

"Of course, you didn't," Kento snapped, anger boiling to the surface. "You only knew me for three days before you decided to give me away."

I opened my mouth to argue, but what could I say? Actually, I made the decision to give you up about a month before you were born. Yes, I'm sure that would have helped matters.

"I don't blame you for the Sourcery, Eskara," Kento continued. "You didn't know, I understand that." She looked at me again and I found I couldn't hold that gaze. There was too much in it. Too much pain and grief and hope and hate and love and... just too much. "I don't think I even blame you for giving me up. I understand the reasons you did it. I also don't forgive you for it. I don't think I can."

By all the fucking gods, by Lursa's Tears, by the Maker's great shitting eye, and by any and every other thing worth swearing to, all I wanted was to wrap my arm around my daughter and hug her pain away. All I wanted was to be there for her this one fucking time. One time in a whole lifetime of absence. I tried. We were still walking up the dune, but I lurched toward her. Kento fixed me with a baleful glare, staggered away, raised a hand in warning. I wanted to be there for her, but it wasn't about what I wanted. It was about what Kento needed, and she sure as hell didn't need me. She never had.

"Mezula couldn't take the Chronomancy out of me," Kento continued. "So, she remade me into something that could control it. She made me a part of herself."

"She turned you into an Aspect."

"My mother saved my life, Eskara," Kento crested the top of the dune and stopped, squinting into the distance.

"By turning you into a slave," I hissed. I couldn't stop myself. Silva had died... I had killed Silva because her mother had sent her to Do'shan to die. Silva herself said she had no choice but to obey. And now... Now Mezula had done the same thing to Kento. How much free will did she truly have? Was she hunting down her own sister by choice? Or was Mezula pulling her strings all for some twisted revenge on me? I have said it before, but it bears repeating; I hate the gods, our gods. All fucking gods. And I hate Mezula most of all.

"What did she give you?" I asked as I reached the top of the dune beside Kento. "What part of herself did she force on you? I know all about Aspects. What..."

The glare Kento turned on me was so vicious it brought me up short. "You know nothing about Aspects. Now shut up and move. We're almost there." She started slide-walking down the slope, sand tumbling around her.

I almost followed her, pursued her and my line of questioning both. But something stopped me. Perhaps I can claim it to be wisdom. I would like to believe that I have learned that some things need to be left alone. Sometimes people need to be left alone. During an argument the air between two people can become so heated that it leaves no space for thought. But that's a load of abban shit really, isn't it? It's a lesson I always struggled to learn. No, the truth is that Kento scared me. Not just with her words and not just by the darkness lurking behind her glare. I was terrified both by the things she said, and those she had not. I wanted to know the truth, the rest of the truth, but what it might mean was a fear even Ssserakis had never managed to match. What was Kento? Who was she? How much of her was the little girl I had given birth to? Had Mezula altered her just as the Maker had apparently altered Sirileth?

"She's right," Imiko said. She had slipped next to me, as silent in the sand as she was in a crowd. She pointed. "There's something on the horizon. Might be the oasis." She wore a concerned stare, but I do not think it was for me or for Kento. Imiko stared at the horizon and saw Sirileth, I think. She saw what we might have to do to stop my youngest daughter.

CHAPTER THIRTY ONE

A STRANGE THING ABOUT THE POLASIAN desert I realised is that it is never fully dark. Once the sun falls below the horizon, it certainly darkens, but the light from our moons keeps it well lit. There is also the light pouring from the great rift, which is doubly strange given there is nothing in the place beyond the rift. No light, no stars, no land. Nothing but the creature the Rand and Djinn call the Maker. The burning light shines from the eye staring down at us all. During the day, the desert is bright, almost blindingly so, and infinitely beige as only sand can be. But at night, the light paints the sand in shifting violet hues. It was almost as though the dunes were made of powder the likes of which painted women apply to their faces. Very odd. Surreal. Unnerving.

As we drew closer to the oasis, we saw tracks in the sand. Little valleys and ridges winding up and down the dunes. I stared at them as we trudged on, feet dragging in the violet grains, and my mind worked slowly at trying to puzzle out the tracks. What manner of creature made them? What sort of beast could survive in the desert? We had seen no caravans from the air, but then I knew they existed. Trade across the desert was difficult, but necessary. It was the most direct route from Irad to Dharhna and back again, and over the mountains at Dharhna's back was the lush jungle infested land of Itexia, which is the place the pahht call their home. This meant there was a lot of money to be made for merchants willing to risk the desert, bringing goods from Itexia to Polasia.

Lokar and Lursa were high in the sky, at their zenith and all but hidden behind the great rift, but their light made everything bright. Certainly bright enough when we got close to the oasis that I could see for myself how mistaken I had been. I had thought the oasis a small collection of trees surrounding a pool, maybe some horses or trei birds staked out to graze on whatever shrubberies they could rip from the sandy soil. It was not small. It was not some tiny little paradise nestled in the centre of the desert. It was a community, a village, a bustling hub of terrans and pahht. It was also filled with insane people, but what else would you expect of folk who live their lives under the gaze of an alien god?

The trees around the oasis were squat things with broad leaves that grew purple, and produced a yellow, hairy fruit that when split open sometimes contained edible flesh, other times they contained rusty daggers, or spiders, or eyes. I once heard a story from a Polasian merchant who bought a crate of the fruits then opened one to find a terran mouth complete with lips, teeth, and tongue inside. Apparently,

it asked them what time it was, then died, assuming it had
ever actually been alive. It appeared almost anything could
be found inside the bizarre fruits.

The oasis itself was formed around a shallow lake
where the waters ran red as blood. I have it on good
authority that it is just water and is perfectly safe to drink.
Then again, the people who settle at the oasis are quite mad,
so I would not recommend drinking from those waters for
prolonged periods of time. That said, there was apparently
quite an exclusive market for oasis water. Aristocrats around
the world, those with more money than sense, would pay
exorbitant sums to transport a cask of red water as if it were
somehow special. Fools with too much money will always
find idiotic things to do with it. I have long since noticed that
some people would rather burn their money than give it to
someone who has none.

There were dozens of tents dotted around the oasis.
Some sank their foundations deep into the sand, out of the
shelter of the trees, while others preferred the loamy soil.
There seemed to be no real organisation to it. People just
pitched their tents wherever they pleased, caring nothing
for how close they were to others. In some places, you could
walk ten abreast between the cloth homes, and in others
you had to pick your way between the lines of rope that
secured them. It reminded me of Wrysom, and I felt a pang
of sadness for the sleepy little village I had left behind.

The only true organisation I saw within the
community surrounding the oasis were where people staked
out the horses, and where they staked out the snakes. On
the south side, under the shade of the trees, a dozen horses
milled about, ripping up tufts of violet grass and flaring
their nostrils. On the north side, however, out on the sand,

were six huge snakes. I say snakes because I do not know what else to call them. The pahht who rode them called them Cchtktera, but if there was a translation for the word, I never heard it. They curled into reptilian coils at night and lay very still. They almost looked like rocks in the dark, until we got too close, and one started hissing at us. Each one was taller than I, and as long as five abbans in a row. The length of their bodies was all scale, but their heads were short and hairy, with a beak rather than a snout. Apparently up to ten pahht could ride each one, and they could carry a whole caravan's worth of goods. They were also quick as a trei bird across the sand, at least during the day, and needed very little water to survive. They were the perfect beasts of burden for the desert. Though quite how the cat-like pahht managed to tame such beasts I'm not sure I want to know.

By the time we reached the outskirts of the oasis settlement we were all tired, footsore, and thirsty enough to drink our fill of water no matter its colour. I could no longer tell whether I was too hot or too cold, and each plodding step sent waves of agony racing up through my blisters and all the way into my skull which was throbbing like a struck drum. The pain made me testy.

A gummy old terran who looked like he bathed in sand rather than water was the first to greet us. He sat outside a small tent, little more than a pale blanket draped over a few sticks, and had a campfire going. He held a metal pan in a thick glove and waved it over the flames. Whatever was in the pan was spitting and hissing like a caged animal promising painful retribution.

"Takes a special type of fool to walk across the desert," he said with grin, proudly displaying all two of his teeth.

I glared at him, hoping to scare him with the storm in my eyes, but he met my gaze and giggled. There is a way some people giggle that lets you know just how detached from reality they are. They can hold a conversation like any other, but the madness always spills out of their laughter, as though that moment of mirth sheds whatever mask they shield themselves with. This man was cracked, and we would get nothing but crazy from him.

"Our flyer crashed," Kento said. Out of the three of us, she was fairing the best, but she still both limped and dragged her feet all at once, and her shoulders had a weary slump about them.

A mad giggle spilled around the fool's two teeth once more. "Well, of course it did."

I ignored him, started to walk away, but Kento stopped in front of him. "What do you mean?" she asked.

Might as well ask a fish what it feels like to walk for all the sense we'd get. The settlement was busy further in and I could all but smell the water on the air. I wanted nothing so much as to stumble my way through the tents and milling people until I could dip my head in the oasis and drink my scratching throat into submission.

"Flying things," the gummy fool said. "Sourcery, ain't it." He giggled. "Don't work here. Not outside, at the least. Works right inside, but not outside. Nope. Nope. Not outside. Never seen it myself and I been here for..." He paused and looked around, stared at the campfire and his spitting pan, at the sand beneath his feet, and then up at the sky and the great eye staring through the rift at us all.

"He's an idiot," Imiko said. She had already pulled her shawl from her face and was staring into the crowded settlement, eyes darting about as she scanned the faces.

I didn't exactly disagree with her, but he had mentioned Sourcery and that always piqued my interest. I considered myself quite knowledgeable on the subject. Actually, I thought myself the most learned Sourcerer in the world. I was wrong about that.

I limped closer to the terran madman staring up at the eye above us all, stopped next to Kento. She was looking down into the pan the man held over his campfire. The hissing and spitting continued, and I glanced down to find a person in the pan. Or, at least, something that was person-shaped. Two legs, two arms, a bulbous head. Its flesh was a pale green though blackening on one side from the heat, and it was covered head to toe in red thorns. It had no eyes that I could see, and no mouth either, but it writhed and leapt in the pan, and as I listened, I could tell the sounds I took for hisses were actually screams of pain.

Kento kicked the pan out of the man's hands. It hit the sand and the little creature spilled out, rolling to a sizzling stop.

"What?" The crazy terran quit his staring up at the eye and glanced about hurriedly, eyes falling on the little creature. "STOP IT!" he yelled. "Don't let it get away."

The little creature picked itself up and leapt back just as the old terran flopped from his wooden stool onto the sand, reaching for it. The creature spun in a circle and then ran towards the settlement and the oasis. It threw itself to the side as a pahht woman wrapped in green silk slammed a wooden spoon down on the ground next to it. The little creature backed away as the woman slammed her spoon at it again and again. The crazy old man was yelling for others to catch the thing, and more of the settlement's inhabitants were leaving off whatever they were doing to join in the chase. Kento and I watched in silence, occasionally sending each other confused looks. It was nice to know I wasn't the only one entirely lost by what was happening.

They didn't catch the creature. It leapt, dodged, ducked, and bounded away from a dozen people as they tried to catch it. Eventually it turned away from the settlement and streaked past us as we watched. It quickly disappeared into the dark violet of the dunes.

The crazy old terran slunk back to his tent under the reproachful stares and sharp reprimands of all those who had joined in the chase. He picked up his overturned stool and sank onto it. "Lucky they don't roast me over the fire for losing that one. The Red Thorns are the worst, you know?" He nodded at us. "You know."

"Before, you said Sourcery doesn't work right. Why?" Kento asked.

The gummy terran pulled a pack out from inside his tent, flicked away a beetle that was crawling over the hemp, then thrust his hand inside to root around for something. "The Maker says so."

With the rift right above us, I could see almost nothing else but a sliver of Lursa's bulk beyond.

"Enchantments don't work, Source-powered weapons don't work." He grinned at Kento. "Flyers don't work." He pulled his hand from the satchel and was gripping a small, grey, opaque stone no larger than a grape. "Only way to tell you got a Source." He popped the stone in his mouth and swallowed hard. Then he pointed at Kento, and a gust of wind whipped at her, tugging her shawl. The man grinned. "Gotta swallow 'em or they just look like stones."

I turned away from him. He was nothing but a distraction. That's when I realised that Imiko was gone. I was not surprised, of course. Imiko's habit of disappearing had long since stopped shocking me. I was, however, concerned. She was acting strangely of late, and I could already tell that the oasis seemed to bring out the strangeness in people.

Kento and I picked our way between the tents towards the oasis at the centre. The mad old terran was certainly not the only crazy person we spotted. I noticed the tents fell into two categories. Some were brightly coloured, well looked after, the lines dug into the sand. Others were ratty old things bleached pale by the sun, tears patched over with discoloured scraps, the lines old and fraying. The people were different. Those who sat outside the scrappy tents were scrappy themselves, often unwashed and unkempt. Some were pahht, but most appeared to be terran. Those who sat around the newer tents, however, were mostly pahht, and they clearly held themselves apart. They were the caravaners, the merchants, those who crossed the desert rather than lived here at the oasis.

"This place is strange," Kento said as we reached the first trees that marked the edge of the oasis. "It feels..." She shook her head.

"Wrong," I said, also struggling to find the right word. "It's like I can hear a constant buzzing like a mosquito near my ear."

Kento nodded. "And there's an itch I can't find, travelling around my body. Why would people stay here?"

I shuffled aside as a naked man ran past, red water streaming from his skin. He sprinted to the edge of the settlement and leapt into the sand, then rolled around like a puppy experiencing mud for the first time. "The Sources, I would imagine," I said. "Hundreds, maybe thousands, of

Rand and Djinn died here. It was the largest battle of the
War Eternal. There's probably no better place in the world to
search for Sources."

"Yes," Kento said through a clenched jaw. "I imagine
that's why people often come here. I think they stay for
another reason though." She looked up at the great eye.
I realised then that other people occasionally did the
same. The crazy old man had looked up and appeared
mesmerised, lost in the vastness of the alien gaze. Others,
mostly those with the ragged tents, were similarly staring
into the rift.

There is a strange fascination with power that all
sentient peoples share. A draw to it as irresistible as gravity.
I am not beyond the fascination myself; I have spent half
my life seeking power. I have sacrificed so much under the
spell of its allure. I have killed for it. I have died reaching
for it. But when power is a person, it becomes even stranger.
People will travel half a world to see a queen with a
reputation for slaughter. Like a desire to draw close to a
flame even knowing it might burn. The great rift was power.
The Scab staring through it was power. And the people who
lived in the oasis were stuck here, trapped by the Maker's
gravity just like Lokar and Lursa could not escape Ovaeris.

We passed beneath the purple, leafy canopy and
finally came upon the oasis itself. Far larger than I had
originally thought, I could see the other side only as a
hazy blur in the gloom of the night. There were bathers on
this side of the shore, men and women, terran and pahht,
standing in the red water and scooping up handfuls to dump
over each other's' heads in what looked a lot like ritual.
Well, that made a sick sort of sense, I suppose. They lived
underneath a hole in the world where a creature our gods

called God stared through. Of course, some crazy religion
had sprung up around it. Perhaps everyone here, like my
youngest daughter, was brainwashed by the Scab into trying
to bring it across into our world. Let's be fair, religion is just
a word for a cult that's grown too large for its socks.

I detested that place. The insanity of it. The great
eye staring down at us. The discoloured water. The bizarre
trees. The fruit that asked what bloody time it was. The little
thorny creature that escaped the fire. Most of all I hated the
people offering stupid prayers to a creature that wouldn't
even notice when it stepped on them. Do you think ants
pray to terrans? Do you think they worship the boot that
squashes them? No. They're smarter than that, than us. Ants
know the inexorable truth of the situation: big thing from
sky means danger, get the fuck out of the way.

I felt like swallowing down my Sources and laying
waste to everything there. Burn the trees and boil the water,
scour it all back to the desert and chase away the stupid
bastards who were stuck there. Force them to flee back to
civilisation where they might recover some of their senses
away from the monster glaring madness down at them all.

"Eska," Kento said, touching my arm. She gestured
to the left where a lone figure sat at the shore of the oasis,
just beyond the waterline. Imiko was hugging her legs, her
chin resting on her knees, fiery hair loose and stirring in the
slight breeze. She stared out across the water and tears rolled
silently down her face.

I approached slowly and stopped just behind her. I
didn't want to sit or get comfortable next to her. The draw
to this place was subtle and seditious. I think far too many
people got comfortable here and never left. If Imiko was
staring at anything in particular across the water, I couldn't

make it out.

"Imiko," I said warily.

She stiffened a little at my voice but didn't move. "I think I understand this place."

"You might be the first."

"It's a haven," she said, her voice almost beatific. "There are places like this all over the world. Places where people can get lost and be lost. To change into something new and leave themselves behind. Like a butterfly."

"Yes, change into something new," I agreed. "Learn to drink poisoned water out of a shoe." I gestured to a man doing just that a little further down the shore. Imiko didn't look.

"You did it," Imiko said bitterly. "You ran away. You ended up in that shitty little village and changed your name. You became someone else."

"Mhm, right up until my old life found me and dragged me back. Probably fucked up the poor people of Wrysom in the process. I doubt they'll ever trust a stranger again."

"What was it like? Being someone else."

She deserved the truth. "Hard. Might seem like it should be easy, a nice way to escape the consequences of everything you've done. Other folk didn't know about them, about me, but I sure as hell did. I could go days without thinking about the past, sometimes even weeks. But eventually the reality caught up to me. The memories. The pain I caused, and the people I killed. The people I... we lost because of the choices I made. It always came back, Imiko, and when it did, I had no one to share it with. No one who knew about it. I had to suffer through it all alone because no one in that village knew who I was."

Tears stung my eyes and I refused to let them fall. I wiped them away with my shawl. "I have always hated being alone. Feared it more than… anything. I went to Wrysom to escape being me, but all I really found there was me. It was torture, Imiko. Torture I put myself through by staying there because I believe..." I stopped myself, damn near bit my tongue off. That last bit was something I'd never told anyone. Something not even Ssserakis knew about me.

"What?" Imiko stood, turned, stared at me. I might refuse to let my tears fall, but she didn't. They coursed down her cheeks, cutting paths through the crusted sand and old paint to reveal the freckles beneath. She looked so tired. Strung out. Used up. I had thought — hoped — our argument back at Karataan had fixed whatever was broken inside Imiko. But that was such a stupid, simplistic thing to hope for. Imiko felt broken inside, and it would take more than a few heated words, some airing of dirty laundry to put her back together. But she had donned her happy mask once more, and I had accepted it. Depression is a war without end we have no choice but to fight, and the worst afflicted of us wear smiles like armour. "What do you believe, Eska?"

I clenched my jaw until I felt my teeth would grind to dust. But it was no good. What good had hiding it ever done me anyway?

"I tortured myself because I deserve it." The words fell like lead between us. "I have spent so much of my life being tormented by others. My older brother, the tutors at the academy, the Iron Legion, the Terrelans, the foremen in the Pit, the Iron Legion again, the Terrelan Emperor, the Iron Legion a-fucking-gain. There has to be a reason. Can't just be chance all those fuckers have spent so much time and effort torturing me. So, I must deserve it. Even though they're all gone, I do it to myself. I torture myself. And being alone is torture to me. And I thought... I hoped you might live better lives without me."

Imiko shook her head, tears shining red like blood in the water's reflection. "It didn't work," she said softly. "You ran away and still didn't find peace. There really is no escape."

"None but death," said a woman from behind me.

Imiko looked up sharply, a grin splitting her tear-streaked face. Then she lurched into a run and sprinted past me. "Siri!"

CHAPTER THIRTY TWO

DISTANCING MYSELF FROM THE WAR AGAINST Tor didn't work. Tris continued to fight his battles. His forces were small, but he had enough people to raid villages, sneak into cities, set food stores alight, and abduct the children of important Tor council members. That is too generous a way of putting it. He kidnapped children, forced their parents to give themselves up, murdered them. He struck terror into the people of Tor and did it in my name.

Sirileth picked up where I left off. I do not believe she wanted the war, but she viewed it as necessary. Tor would not surrender to us, and Yenheim was hers and its people were hers too. She was a smarter tactician than I, and never led her troops into an ambush. She was also less experienced and made choices I thought were naïve, often choosing to draw back when I would have pushed forward. She was also ruthless and when she saw an opportunity to strike, she

384 ROB J. HAYES

took it no matter the cost. A lot of people died, and yet still the war didn't end. Such a foolish thing, that war, started over a handful of abban. Bah! My mistake, my war. Sirileth inherited it from me and even she couldn't find a way to end it.

Distancing myself from the rule of Yenheim didn't work either. I no longer sat on the corpse throne, no longer held council with advisors and magistrates, no longer made public appearances at all. I became a hermit in my own queendom. A bustling city was spread all around me, and I sat apart from it all in my palace. Alone. Hardt no longer liked to set foot in the palace. Well, he never did. It brought back too many memories of Isen, I think. Tamura had his taverns and schools where he told stories and passed on his insanity to others. Imiko had her criminal empire and I thought she was more content with that than she ever had been with me. Vi was dead. Tris was exiled. Sirileth was... there, in my palace. She sat on my throne and made decisions in my stead. She commanded my armies, passed laws to make Yenheim prosper. I saw her rarely and briefly. Josef was still there, of course, often roaming the lower levels of my rocky palace, his attendants seeing to his every need, listening to his every word. I talked to him sometimes, but other times it was like trying to hold a conversation with a fish. On his lucid days, he was my old friend again and we could reminisce, but those days were few and far between. More often than not, he would gape at me without comprehension, or stare through me as though I wasn't there. Sometimes he'd just turn to stone mid-conversation.

Despite removing myself from the rule of Yenheim and from the public eye, my reputation grew. The stories surrounding me became bigger, grander, more horrible than the truth. One claimed I was stitching together monsters in the palace, taking bodies from the nearby graveyards, and constructing an army to crush Tor. Others that I was in a cocoon and would soon emerge as... I don't know. A moth? Probably not. Probably some new terror with more mouths than arms. Terrans do love to scare themselves with horror stories. It's probably why the Rand plucked so many of Sevorai's creatures from our imaginations. The people of Yenheim leaned into my legend. Raised statues of me in courtyards. Murdered, and justified it with a hearty Corpse Queen always needs new bodies. I had seen it happening, had tried to stop it by removing myself but my absence only made it worse.

I formed a new plan. Well, I told myself it was a new plan to stop my people from turning me into the demagogue they wanted. I decided to run away.

I told Josef and no one else. I don't think he understood me, but then he was ice at the time. I don't mean encased in ice; he was literally made of ice. I don't even know if he heard me, but I told him all the same.

Then I went to see Sirileth. She was asleep. Curled up in her bed, clutching her sheets between her legs. Just thirteen years old. A girl just starting to turn into a young woman. I watched her flail in her bed a few times, caught in some dream. She didn't wake. I almost broke then, my resolve so close to shattering. I knew what I was giving up, what I would not get to see. I knew I would miss watching her growing into the woman she would become. I didn't want to miss that. I wanted to be there, to see it, to help her through it. But I was poison. I corrupted everything I touched. Vi was dead because of me. Tris was exiled, a terror in the making because of me. Sirileth was already following

in my footsteps. And every time I tried to stop any of it, I just
pushed her closer to being a monster. It was all my fault, and
I did not know how to stop it.

I turned and fled from her room with tears in my
eyes and hate in my heart. Yes, I hated myself, even as I
convinced myself it was the only choice I had. The only
chance she had. I knew Imiko would look after my daughter,
and I honestly believed she'd do a better job than I ever did.

I snuck out of my palace and out of Yenheim in the
middle of the night and fled west. I disappeared, hoped
people would think me dead. I wanted the Corpse Queen to
die. Of course, she didn't.

I can't say I didn't look back. I did. Every day I was
gone I looked back. Despite the miles of travel and years of
distance between us, and despite the comfort of the peace
that I found in Wrysom, I never stopped looking back. I
never stopped wanting to see Sirileth again.

"I'm so happy you made it, Auntie," Sirileth said.
Her voice was a deeper than I remembered, but then, I
still thought of her as a child. A little girl with pale skin,
dark hair, blinding eyes, following me about and mostly
quiet save for when she had questions. But time made my
memory a lie, as it did all things. I turned around then to
look on the woman my daughter had grown into.

She was taller than me, a good head at least, though
I will admit age had shrunken me slightly. She looked
strong, healthy. Her skin was no longer the ghastly pale of
a girl who spent most of her time underground. Now it had
some colour to it. The wear of outdoor life, sun and weather
darkening her complexion some. Her hair was almost raven
black, longer than she had ever worn it as a child, tied into

a single thick braid that dangled past her shoulder. Her left ear was pierced with six silver rings dangling from the outside edge. And her eyes still shone brightly with her own special darklight, the glare of an eclipse. She wore black, just as I usually did. Loose trousers, a matching blouse, and a jacket over the top. My youngest daughter had grown into a woman who had travelled. And, perhaps strangest of all, she was smiling. I had so rarely in my life seen Sirileth smile, but here she was, grinning like a starving woman at a feast.

Sirileth dropped the satchel she was carrying and met Imiko in a tight embrace. They clung to each other like braided rope. I saw Sirileth bury her face in Imiko's shoulder, saw Imiko shaking with either tears or laughter. It was a touching reunion, a private one most looked away from. Not me though, I stared at them and felt... Damn me, but I was jealous. This was the reunion with Sirileth I had wanted, hoped for. I knew it would never happen, but that traitorous little part of me that liked to hope had dreamt of it. Fuck hope. Hope only leads to disappointment. They held onto each other for a long time, a crushing embrace to match our moons. And when finally, they separated, they pressed their foreheads together. I saw tears in my daughter's eyes, the water casting her darklight into a kaleidoscope of colours. I was embarrassed to find myself watching so intently, so eagerly, but I couldn't look away. I knew I would never experience that reunion with Sirileth myself, so I imagined it. I imagined being Imiko for a moment.

"You found me," Sirileth said, still clutching Imiko.

They separated and Imiko gave Sirileth a solid push in the chest. She staggered back from it, but Sirileth didn't budge. "Stupid girl!" Imiko snarled. "You left me behind."

Sirileth grinned again and looked abashed. "Sorry,

Auntie. I had to. I couldn't figure out who I was, who I needed to be, without being alone." She looked uncertain. "Does that make sense?"

"No!" Imiko sighed. "Yes. But you were hardly alone, Siri. We've been following you. The tahren..."

"You went to Karataan?" Sirileth asked, wincing. She still had the same lurching way of speaking I remembered from her childhood. Rushing out a few words, then the slightest of pauses, before hurrying through a few more.

Imiko nodded. "They tried to kill us."

Sirileth rubbed her left arm, and I heard the jingle of metal against metal. "Yeah, they're a little, uh, zealous."

I heard footsteps and found Kento beside me, her eyes locked on Sirileth. No one else at the oasis paid us the slightest bit of attention, they were all too absorbed in their own lives, bathing or collecting red water, or one fool of a pahht who was licking a tree. No one else had time or reason to watch my little family reunion. I noticed Kento had a hand on her sword hilt, ready to draw. I had known this confrontation was coming, I suppose. Didn't make it any less appealing. I had to stop it somehow. I had to stop Sirileth somehow. Some way that didn't involve killing her. I put my hand on Kento's arm and she flinched away from me, tight and coiled like a snake about to strike.

Sirileth looked past Imiko then, met my stare. Her darklight was still so blinding, so hard to meet head on, but I refused to look away. "You brought her," Sirileth said quietly, her voice neutral. Was she happy I was here? Angry? Scared? She gave me nothing to guess at.

Imiko turned to look at me and nodded. She opened her mouth to say something, then shut it again. By Lursa's Tears she looked tired. Not just the exhaustion of our trek through the desert, but something more, something deeper. It was as though the search for Sirileth had been the only thing keeping her going. Now that we had found my daughter, Imiko was coming apart. Her shoulders slumped, her skin sagged around her eyes, her firebrand hair dulled to dying embers its usual lustre gone. Imiko was only as old as I should have been, middle aged, sure, but now she looked every year of it and more.

Sirileth took a single step forward. She was tugging on her hair, just like she used to as a child. She stopped, clenched her hand into a fist and purposefully pulled it away from her braid. "Hello, Mother."

We faced each other on the shores of that oasis. The few paces separating us might as well have been leagues. But there was more than just distance between us, there was time. A handful of steps, and seven years. I could feel the weight of Sirileth's darklight stare, and the pressure of the Maker's burning gaze too. It was all too much. I had no idea what to say.

First words are always the hardest. They are weighted like no others. One wrong — or right — word spoken too harshly or too softly can set the course of an entire conversation. We balanced on a knife's edge, reunion and reconciliation on one side, violence and pain on the other. And my first words could tip the balance. What could I say to that? What fucking words were right? I had to know how to steer us away from destruction. But I didn't. Of course, I didn't. I am not a force for good, for comfort, or safety. I have never been that. I am the whirlwind, all chaos and devastation. I am the sunset, all darkness and death. I am the weapon, all sharp edges meant to wound.

I said nothing for too long. The silence between us

grew pregnant, gave birth, and reared its children. Sirileth reached a hand towards her braid, then clenched it again and dropped the hand back to her side. I opened my mouth to speak, still found no words. I heard Kento shuffle beside me and rushed for something, anything to say before my elder daughter started trying to kill my younger one.

"Did you cross the desert on a snake?" I said. It is a strange habit of mine to start off conversations with an inane question, but amazingly it often works wonders with breaking the ice.

Sirileth narrowed her eyes a little, her darklight flaring like the corona of an eclipse. "On a cchtktera?" She said the word with such ease, as though she had been speaking pahht her entire life. "No. The pahht wouldn't let a terran ride one. Horses. I... I crossed on horses. A horse." She fell silent, still staring at me. Nervous as a mouse watching a hawk's shadow, hungry as the hawk waiting for the mouse to move. "You?"

"A flyer," I said.

Her eyes flicked to Kento beside me for a moment. "Did it crash?"

I nodded.

"They'll do that. Flyers. They, uh, crash."

In the quiet that followed, I heard someone splashing in the water of the oasis. Far off, a horse whinnied, a man was humming a song. Damn me, but that conversation was awkward. No matter how hard I tried, I couldn't seem to find a way into it.

"I missed you," I said eventually.

Sirileth reached up, wrapped a hand around the end of her braid, started rubbing the hair between her fingers. She had always hated others touching her hair but couldn't seem to stop fiddling with it herself. "Not enough apparently. I mean, you didn't miss me enough to come back. You could have come back. You didn't have to stay in that little village. It looked nice. Cosy, I suppose."

She had seen Wrysom. That shocked me, but I should have known better. Of course, she had. She had been to Picarr. Imiko had known I was in Wrysom, so it was likely Sirileth did too. Had she stood at the outskirts and watched the villagers go about their day? Had she watched me chasing the children, cavorting with them as I never had her?

"I'm sorry." The only words I could think of. So flat, so worthless. Is there any word more meaningless than sorry? People throw it around as if it can make up for all the ills they visit upon others. I kicked your cat, I'm sorry. I stole a loaf of bread, I'm sorry. I murdered half a city, I'm sorry. What a useless fucking word. It's not even a promise not to do it again. Sorry isn't an apology, it's just begging to be forgiven without doing the work to warrant it. Fuck it! I don't deserve to be forgiven, but I'll damned well try to be better. Let my apology be my actions because no useless words will make up for the things I have done. Or for not being there when I was needed.

"You're here now," Sirileth said, fiddling with her hair again. "That's something, I guess. You being here."

"What are you doing, Eskara?" Kento asked.

I turned to glare at her. "Trying to stop something before it begins." I turned back to my younger daughter. "Sirileth, this is Kento." I stopped myself just before the next words, waited to see if she would figure it out.

Sirileth stared at Kento a moment, smiled, then grinned. "You're alive? Mother said you were dead. I mean, she said you died as a child. Before I was born."

"Eska wasn't lying." Kento spoke slowly, steadily, entirely opposite from the way Sirileth spoke. She took a step forward, hand still resting on the hilt of her sword. "She thought I was dead. I did die."

Sirileth tugged on her braid, turned her smile on Imiko, back to me, then frowned. "It's been a long time since I had a sister. I mean, I had a sister, another one. Vi, she died too. But she's still, uh, dead. Shame we can't swap stories about how crappy a mother we had. Me and you, I mean. M-maybe you had a good mother, or someone who raised you, at least. It's nice to meet you, sister."

Kento frowned. I saw her jaw working like Isen's used to when he spoke to Yorin. Barely restrained anger.

"You have a niece, too," I said quickly. "She's called Esem."

"She lives on Ro'shan," Kento said. Another step forward.

Sirileth let go of her braid, balled her hand into a fist, dropped it to her side. She turned a blindingly dark stare my way, all smiles gone. I could almost see her figuring it out. "My sister is an Aspect of Mezula." It wasn't a question. As I have said, Sirileth loved puzzles, and she was always good at solving them. She saw round corners I didn't even notice. She could solve puzzles even missing half the pieces.

"Oh. You didn't come here to help me. I mean, that's not why you're here. You were sent by the Rand to stop me." Sirileth glanced at Imiko, but the thief wouldn't meet her eyes.

"Yes," Kento took another step forward and drew her sword. The blade slid from its sheath without a sound.

Sirileth stepped back, crouched, reached into her

satchel, and pulled out a metal staff almost as tall as I was. It had a dull Source clutched at its head, and intricate vines carved all along its length. Surge, one of the Weapons of Ten, a staff that could amplify Sourcery. She held it across her body as if to defend herself from attack. "Why? I don't... understand why," Sirileth said.

"Because you're going to destroy Ovaeris," Kento snarled.

"Am I?" Sirileth asked. "Hmm. I don't... Tell me something, sister. Who told you that? I mean, that I'm going to destroy the world."

Kento paused her advance, her hands twisting around the hilt of her sword. "You've been toying with rifts."

Sirileth shrugged. "I, um, call it experimenting." She stared to one side for a moment, then nodded. "Studying maybe. Collecting data. Researching. The things I've learned already are—"

"Killing people."

"Only those who chose it. I mean, I only killed people who were willing. They understood the need. The... the need for the research. They wanted to... I mean they needed to end it. End themselves, I suppose. And only when it was necessary. I didn't... It... it was never murder." Sirileth looked at me. "It wasn't. I promise."

"You convinced the tahren to give you that," Kento nodded at the staff in Sirileth's hands.

"I convinced the tahren many things," Sirileth said. She took a small step back, glanced upwards towards the rift above. "I'm out of time. I mean, it's almost time. I have to do this now or I won't get another chance for twenty-two days. The moons, they need to align. It has to be now."

Something about that struck me as odd. Why would

there be a time frame to opening the rift? I had that annoying feeling, like an itch I couldn't scratch. I was missing something.

"I won't let you bring that monster into our world," Kento said slowly as if speaking to a naughty child.

Again, Sirileth looked at me, then back to Kento. She grimaced. "Hmm. You think you can stop me, sister?" I heard the waver in her voice. Sirileth was not nearly as confident as she claimed.

"Yes," Kento growled and rushed forward. Her first strike clanged against Sirileth's staff. Kento tried to twist her blade to stab down over the haft, but Sirileth spun away, putting more distance between them.

"STOP IT!" I roared, running toward them. For a wonder, neither of them moved. I couldn't allow them to do it. I couldn't let my two daughters fight each other, kill each other.

None of this made any sense.

"Sirileth," I said as I reached Kento's side. "What are you doing here?"

"You don't know? I thought you knew, Mother. You and my sister and auntie Imiko all came here to stop me. Because, of course, I must have no idea what I'm doing. I mean, it wasn't the great Eskara Helsene's plan, after all, so it must be wrong. Right?"

"Damnit, girl, I'm trying to save your life."

Sirileth's smile was a crack splitting the earth just moments before it swallowed a continent whole. She took a step back, her bare feet sinking into the muddy water at the edge of the oasis. "Oh, I see. Years of neglect, of abandonment. I mean, you ran away and left me, but now you want to be a parent? Now that it's convenient for you.

No. That's not the way it works. You don't get to walk back into my life and be in charge. I'm not a kid. I'm not... You want to be my mother for once? Then trust me. Believe me. Believe in me."

"Enough!" Kento inched forwards, sword held ready to strike again. "We don't have time, Eskara. She's already said she needs to do it now. We cannot risk her bringing the Maker into our world. It will destroy everything."

"I know that fucking thing abducted you as a child, Sirileth," I said.

She nodded, eyes wide. "It did. It took me."

"I don't know what it told you. What it did to you. But opening the rift and letting it into this world will destroy everything. You, me, Yenheim, Hardt, Imiko, Esem. Everything."

Sirileth nodded. "I'm sure it will." She didn't look happy though, nor scared. I thought she looked hurt.

"Please, Sirileth." I rushed forward again, standing on the shore of the oasis. "Tell me what you're doing?"

Sirileth shook her head savagely, braid swinging. "That would make it easy, wouldn't it? For you, I mean. Then the great Eskara Helsene gets to judge what's right and what's wrong. No! No. No. I will not beg for your approval, Mother. I will tell you this: I am doing the right thing. I am! Now you decide, do you believe me? Do you believe in me? You either stand behind me or before me, but you do not get to the be the grand arbiter of what is right and wrong here. Not this time." She shook her head. "Not this time."

How is it possible to be so proud and so fucking infuriated by someone all at the same time? Here was my little daughter, my quiet, timid Sirileth standing up for what she believed, what she thought was right. Defying everyone else, even me, to plant her feet in the ground and do what needed to be done. But she had chosen the wrong side. I respected her, loved her more than anything or anyone, but I could not support her while she tried to destroy the world. And yet, I was still missing something.

Damn, it was frustrating. It was a puzzle with half the pieces missing. I couldn't solve it. No matter how many times I tried, or looked at it from a different angle or rummaged through the pieces for the one I needed, I couldn't make it fit together.

She was asking me to have faith. Not in an institution or religion or god. Sirileth was asking me to have faith in her. To take my hand off the reins and let her steer the horse. The girl I had raised for thirteen years, who had followed me about and looked up to me was asking for my trust. Could I trust anyone who had used me as a role model? My life consists of one mistake after another. But then, who can claim to have never made a mistake? No one can claim a perfect life.

Faith. Fucking faith. Faith is like herpes. You might think you're rid of it, but it's always there, just waiting to rise and fuck you all over again.

I was out of time. We were all out of time. I had to choose a side.

My eldest daughter who I had never known, a daughter of the Rand as much, if not more, than my own. A woman with a family to protect, with everything to lose. I had never known her, but I was beginning to. She was strong, and proud, and moral.

My youngest daughter who I had raised, who I had tried to steer right but had too much of me in her. Who had always wanted to follow in my footsteps and stamp her name on the world. Who had been taken by the Maker and had never been the same afterwards. She was odd, and headstrong, and ruthless.

I was out of time.

I reached into my Source pouch and pulled out my Sources, popped them in my mouth and started swallowing even as I ran forward, sloshing my way into the waters of the oasis.

Kento surged forward, sword swinging. I threw out my hand and hit her with a kinetic blast that sent her flying away across the water. She hit the shore, rolling to a stop at the base of a large tree heavy with the bizarre fruit. She was stunned, blinking away confusion and... hurt. Not wounded but staring at me with such pain. I realised then Kento had believed I would choose her side and I had just proven her wrong. I had betrayed her.

Sirileth stared at me, darklight eyes shining, lips curved into the briefest smile. "Thank you, Mother," she said. Damn me, but my chest gave a flutter at those words. It is a strange thing having children, for as much as a child wishes their parent to be proud of them, parents wish the same thing. I had chosen Sirileth over Kento, and my youngest daughter beamed with pride, and it made me feel... good, happy. It made me feel right.

"What do you need?" I asked. Sirileth was sloshing out further into the waters of the oasis, up to her knees now. She stared at the great eye above, and it stared back.

"Keep her away," Sirileth said. "From me, I mean. I need you to protect me." She waved her staff to the shore where Kento was on her knees, knuckles white around her sword hilt, face twisted into a snarl of rage. "I need time and... oh, this is going to hurt."

"You're still not going to tell me what you're doing?"
I asked.

"No."

"Fuck!"

Sirileth shrugged out of her jacket and let it fall
into the water. Her blouse was cut off at the shoulders and
revealed strong arms, tight with muscle. Along the outside
of each arm were thick silver hoops pierced through her
skin. Ten on each arm all the way from her shoulder down
to her wrists. Sirileth reached into her own Source pouch,
and popped three Sources into her mouth, each the size of a
marble.

She saw me watching. A trickle of blood leaked from
her nose. "Geomancy, Ingomancy, and Kinemancy," she said.
I knew my daughter's attunements because I had been the
one to test her. Ingomancy, the magic of manipulating metal,
was not among them.

"What are you doing, Sirileth? You'll reject the Source.
You already are."

Sirileth wiped the blood from her top lip, spat a small
gobbet into the water. "That's what these are for. The rings,
I mean." She shook her arms, jingling her metal hoops.
"The tahren know how to treat the metal from the moons to
stave off rejection." She grimaced at some pain. "Now stop
distracting me, Mother. Please. I don't have long." Already I
could see one of the hoops pierced through her left arm was
glowing as though just out of the forge.

Useful stuff, that ore. If I had had some of it, I might
never have lost my arm to Geomancy. If I had chosen right
and Sirileth didn't destroy the world, I decided it was not
too late to get my ears pierced.

Kento was back on her feet, hands twisting around

her sword hilt so tight the blade was trembling. She screamed. No words, just anger. Then she thrust a hand toward me. A ripple sped along the water. I raised my hand and erected a kinetic shield just as Kento's kinetic blast hit. She was strong. The blast shattered my shield, threw me onto my back in the red water. I thrashed for a second and then got to my feet, already struggling to erect a new shield. Her blast had been invisible. She had learned that from the tahren at the library, figured the technique out so quickly. It also meant she had a Photomancy Source as well as a Kinemancy Source in her stomach. An unfortunate annoyance about Aspects is that they do not have attunements. They can use any Source they wish and do not suffer rejection. Kento was limited only by the number of Sources she could hold in her stomach, and I had no idea what she was capable of.

Kento stepped out onto the waters of the oasis, and it froze beneath her feet, each step spreading the ice further. Pyromancy then. That explained why she never seemed to feel the heat or the cold, even in the desert. It was also going to make fighting her awkward. I could only hope she didn't have an Arcmancy Source too, or I was well and truly fucked.

"Why, Eskara?" Kento asked through clenched teeth. Another step forward, the ice creaking beneath her. The water was getting cold around my shins, and I honestly wondered if she had the power to freeze the entire oasis.

Why, was a good question. Why choose one daughter over the other? Why choose a gamble over a sure thing? Why choose Sirileth?

I sloshed forward a couple of steps, putting some distance between myself and my younger daughter. If I was going to fight Kento, I needed to do it away from Sirileth, give her the time she needed to do... whatever the fuck she was doing. Lursa's Tears, but I hoped I had picked correctly.

"Because I know her," I said. It was the truth, as cold and bare as I could make it. I knew Sirileth. I had raised her, watched her grow from a quiet little girl full of unasked questions, to a young woman with a desire for purpose and meaning. And no, I hadn't been there for the past seven years, hadn't seen her grow into the woman she was now, but Imiko had been there for her all this time. Imiko had been Sirileth's mother in my absence and I knew she wouldn't steer my daughter wrong. "I know her, and I trust she is doing the right thing."

"Because she said she was?" Kento spat.

I nodded. "Because I trust her."

Kento took another step forward. Her jaw writhed just like Isen's. But her eyes were so like mine and full of cold rage. My eyes were never quite like that and not because they flashed. My anger was never cold. I didn't do cold. "Are you really willing to risk everything? Your life, mine, my daughter's life on her?" Kento growled, pointing her sword at Sirileth. "Even after everything she has done, all the people she has killed?"

I sloshed another step forward, let my Arcstorm loose so bolts of lightning crackled around me. "Yes!"

Kento stopped just ten paces away and stared down at me with all that anger. I knew then, even if we somehow all survived what Sirileth had set in motion, I would never be Kento's mother. She would never call me by that name, never think of me as her family. One more bridge burned. One more relationship I screwed up.

"You still want to know what part of herself my

mother gave to me, Eskara?" Kento ground the words to dust between her teeth. "She gave me her rage." She was breathing hard, heavy, fast. "So, let's see how your famous anger compares to a god's!"

CHAPTER THIRTY THREE

I AM THE WEAPON. FOR OVER A DECADE, THE Orran Academy beat that into me. Tortured me and told me time and time again I was nothing but a weapon. I believed them. I became the weapon. I fought for the Orrans. I killed for the Orrans. And long after the Orrans were gone, I tortured myself with that same phrase, repeated in my head and out loud daily. I used it to convince myself that I could do horrific, impossible things. Despite my attempts, despite Silva's gentle insistence, I never quite managed to free myself of the mantra. Even now, so many years later, I still find myself uttering it. I was raised to be a weapon. I became the weapon. And sometimes I think I've never been anything else. But not this time. This one fucking time I would not be the weapon.

I would be the shield.

Kento threw another kinetic blast my way, but I was

ready. I formed a hazy purple buckler and infused it with
Arcmancy. I flung my arm out, connected with the kinetic
blast, deflected it to splash harmlessly in the red waters of
the oasis. Kento ran at me, water freezing beneath her every
step, sword held ready. I could already feel the water around
my shins getting cold. I hate it when Sourcerers use ice. I
drew on my own Pyromancy Source and spat flames at my
eldest daughter. Kento leapt through the flames, scattering
them around her harmlessly, but they served their purpose.
The ice beneath her feet melted enough that when she
landed, it cracked beneath her, and she fell to her hands and
knees in the water.

Kento screamed with raw fury. The water around
her rippled, then burst upwards in a flurry of geysers. One
of those geysers hit me in the chest, knocking the wind out
of me, throwing me backwards. I thrashed for a moment,
on my back, trying to get my feet beneath me. Kento was
already moving, sloshing onwards, reaching for Sirileth. I
did the only thing I could think of. I erected a hasty kinetic
shield and grabbed Kento by the ankle. She turned, snarling,
swung her sword at me. It hit me in the head, my crappy
shield shattered, the blade skittered off and cut a bloody
slash down my cheek, bisecting the old scar Prig had given
me so long ago.

Kento gasped, her eyes wide and opened her mouth
as if to apologise. Then she snarled, kicked my hand away,
turned back to Sirileth, sword raised to strike again. I thrust
my hand forward and hit her with a kinetic blast that sent
her tumbling away.

I got shakily back to my feet, staggered, almost threw
up from the exertion. I really wasn't used to all this anymore.
Too old, too soft, too weak, too tired. Only my body's

refusal to give up the Sources I swallowed stopped me from retching them into the oasis there and then. I glanced at the rift. The eye of the Maker stared back at me, blazing and unblinking.

"How long is this going to take, Sirileth?" I asked, wading forward to put myself between my two daughters once more.

Sirileth was sweating, blood dripped from her ears and nose. Her knuckles clutching the staff, Surge, were white. The Source at the top of the staff glowed pink. Her other arm was thrust upwards, reaching like a claw towards the great rift. One of the metal hoops through her arm was already slag, the liquid metal having seared a bloody, smoking track down her skin, the hoop beneath it was glowing orange. I smelled burning flesh. My daughter's burning flesh, sharp and nauseating.

"Stop. Distracting. Me," Sirileth growled, her eyes fixed on the rift. She clutched her hand a little tighter, dragged it back a bit as if pulling on something.

Kento was up, standing in water up to her thighs. She was trembling, shaking, and the oasis shook with her. The lake danced, ripples forming everywhere. The trees swayed, leaves waving, fruit dropping onto the loamy soil. Fear settled deep in my gut. I had never seen power like this from a person before. Only Aerolis up on Do'shan, only a god had ever shown me such raw power. I raised a new shield on my arm, and planted my feet, waiting for Kento's next attack.

My eldest daughter stared past me, past Sirileth, squinted, grimaced. I had a feeling I wasn't going to like whatever came next. This is the problem when a fighting a Sourcerer without knowing their attainments, you never know what they will throw at you. I, on the other hand, had far less nuance than most people gave me credit for. Fire, lightning, and kinetic force were pretty much all I could use.

I heard a low hiss from behind me, quiet but getting louder. I turned to see one of the pahht's giant snakes slither out from between the trees and slide into the water, beaked mouth open and aiming right for Sirileth. Impomancy is not just the magic of contacting the Other World, it is the magic of command. A well-trained Impomancer, someone with greater skill than I have ever managed, can use the Sourcery to order lesser-minded creatures to their purpose. I realised Kento had reached across the oasis to where the snakes rested, commanded one of them to seek out and kill her sister.

I switched stances, turned, let go of my shield, and stretched my hand towards the oncoming snake. At the same time, I raised my stump and forced a new kinetic shield to bloom outwards from it, hoping it would be enough to stop any attack Kento might throw at Sirileth. I had to grind my teeth against the pain. Then I unleashed a storm of lightning from my fingers. A hundred bolts of sizzling electricity arced out, slammed into the snake. It spasmed, curled, rolled, screamed. Its flesh blackened, smoked, cooked. The water around it became a seething mass of white rapids beneath its thrashing.

Lursa's Tears, but the struggle was taking it out of me. I was so exhausted. I just wanted to collapse into the water and float away, but I couldn't. I didn't have time. I turned away from the snake just in time to see a blue blur skirting my shield and rushing in to strike at Sirileth. Kento was using Chronomancy.

Kento slipped around my kinetic shield, rushed in to drive home the final strike against Sirileth. My youngest daughter was unaware, her entire attention focused on the great rift above. Only I could stop Kento, but I wasn't fast enough.

I have said I only use fire and lightning and kinetic force, but that is not altogether true. I also had Geomancy at my command, though it was weak. I tapped my foot and sent a pulse through the earth beneath the oasis waters. The ground shifted just slightly beneath Kento's feet. She slipped, stumbled. The blue blur of Chronomancy did not vanish from her, and she recovered in an instant. Not quite fast enough to beat me. I turned, felt my old bones creak, muscles strain. Something in my chest felt like it snapped. I dashed underneath Sirileth's outstretched hand. The water sloshing away from me so slowly and I realised I, too, was glowing with hazy blue light. I was also somehow using Chronomancy. Innate Chronomancy. Kento recovered her footing and our gazes met. Hers went wide with shock or fear or maybe something else. I didn't give her time to ask the question already forming on her lips. I swung my arm about and used the last of my strength to create a wave of force strong enough to flatten a building. It smashed against Kento and flung her out across the water and onto the shore. She hit the sand hard, rolled to a stop against a tree, didn't move.

Time resumed its normal course. I dropped to my knees in the red waters. Done. Spent. Exhausted. I felt... Fuck, but I felt old. Tired, drawn out, stretched thin like a bubble blown too large about to pop into nothing.

The ground shook once more. I felt it through the mud cushioning me, saw the water leaping into miniature waves. I raised my head to see Kento clutching the tree I had thrown her against, staggering back to her feet. Blood ran dark and red from a wound hidden in the tangle of her hair. It coursed down her cheek, dripped from her chin. Her eyes were wide, full of icy rage. Her lips drew back into a snarl. The air seemed to shimmer around her. I knew then, it was over. I had done everything I could, but this fight was beyond me. My daughter was stronger than I had ever been, and I was weaker than I had ever been. I slumped amidst the sloshing waves, unable to even summon the effort to get back to my feet and waited for Kento to finish it.

Behind me, Sirileth laughed. "Do you remember me, god?" she shouted. I almost turned to look at her, but then I saw Imiko slipping through the trees, unnoticed.

I raised my hand, surged back to my feet, almost shouted out to warn Kento, caught myself a moment before it was too late. Imiko dashed around the tree Kento was leaning against, stabbed a dagger into my daughter's leg.

Kento screamed. Imiko let go the dagger, left it sticking in Kento's thigh, and stepped back. Kento swung her sword, but her leg gave way and she fell to one knee. She dropped her sword and clutched at the dagger in her leg, growling past the pain.

"You too?" Kento said, voice trembling as anger and pain mixed into a brutal agony I knew all too well. She clutched the hilt of the dagger, screamed again as she tried to pull it out. Then Kento looked up straight at me.

"Please, Eska." I know all too well how much those words must have hurt her. My eldest daughter, a vessel for a god's anger, the mirror of my own. I knew how hard it was to say those words, but she choked on her pride and said them anyway. "Please stop her. She'll kill everyone. She will kill Esem. Your granddaughter. Stop her."

Again, I was struck by the doubt. Had I done the

SINS OF THE MOTHER

wrong thing? Had I sided with the wrong daughter? Kento only wanted to protect her family, and yes, she was willing to kill her own sister to do it. But Sirileth was the sister she had never known. Would I kill a stranger to save my daughters? Well, if I need to answer that question, you really don't know me.

"Do you remember me now, god?" Sirileth shouted. I turned to find her staring up at the portal, hand reaching, pulling. Blood streamed from her eyes. Her right arm was a mess of sores, molten metal, glowing hoops searing the skin. She laughed. "My name is Sirileth Helsene, and I will make you remember me!" They were not the words of a brainwashed zealot trying to bring a monster to our world. There was hatred in those words. Anger. Vengeful spite. She was anchoring herself to the ground with Geomancy, reaching out with Ingomancy and Kinemancy and pulling on something as she laughed at the Maker. Above, the great eye in the rift darted about, frantic, searching.

Kento screamed with new pain. I turned to see her rip the dagger from her leg, lurch forward a step, throw it at Sirileth. I had no time to form a kinetic barrier. No time to do anything but...

I am the shield.

I threw myself to the side, felt the dagger sink into my chest. Pain blossomed from the wound like ink dropped into a pool. I hit the water at Sirileth's feet.

"No!" That word, screamed. A word of agony, pain, regret. It didn't come from Sirileth, she was too focused on her struggle against the Maker. It didn't come from Imiko. It came from Kento. I saw her limping through the water, sloshing towards me, hand outstretched. Well, at least she would regret killing me.

I turned to stare at the rift and the great eye. If I
was going to die, I would at least watch Sirileth's victory,
whatever form it took. The eye roved about. Tendrils picked
at the sides of the portal, frantically pulling at its boundaries.
Sirileth shouted, still tugging on something.

In the sky, beyond the great rift, our moons shifted.

CHAPTER
THIRTY FOUR

IT WAS SURREAL. I HURT EVERYWHERE, THE
pain in my chest the keenest, but it all felt distant somehow.
Like listening to sounds underwater. Muted and indistinct.
It happened sometimes, down in the Red Cells. I'd
occasionally found that point where the pain was fuzzy and
the world seemed smaller, further away. It helped. Not with
the Emperor and his beatings and cuttings and knives and
the screams, but with the in-between times. Aching, hurting,
waiting for the knives to come again. In those moments,
the distance was a welcome thing, almost like leaving my
bruised and battered body behind.

I floated in the water at Sirileth's feet, watched her
pulling an invisible rope, wrenching on it. I watched her
pull the moons from the sky. No. Not the moons. Just one
of them. Just Lursa. Only one, as if that somehow lessens
the magnitude of such a feat. Sirileth fought through the

rejection that was killing her and poured all her power into her goal. She tore our two moons apart. Lokar and Lursa had been locked together for thousands of years, since they collided and freed both the Rand and the Djinn. For all that time, they had been slowly grinding into one another. Now, Lursa broke free of Lokar's stifling embrace. Sirileth liberated her. It was an oddly silent catastrophe. So far away, it looked small. Lursa's cracked red bulk left Lokar's blue behind. Chunks of rock split off like cracked ice floating away on a still lake. And then Lursa started growing larger, obscuring Lokar as she left him, as she raced joyously away from her jealous lover. As the larger of our twin moons hurtled towards Ovaeris. Towards us.

The fuzzy distance in my mind vanished. It was unfortunate as all the pain was waiting to make itself known, the knife in my chest most pressing. I may have cried out. I'm not proud of it, I like to think I'm capable of taking a bit of pain without mewling, I certainly used to be. Unfortunately, in my dotage, I was no longer used to the regular beatings of my previous life and was unprepared for the agony. Aras Terrelan's ghost would probably have revelled in the scream the knife in my chest earned, maybe have made a note about which of his twenty-two screams it was and the exact placement of the knife. But he wouldn't get the chance because long ago I sealed Aras Terrelan's ghost in the shell of his corpse and left him there while his body rotted. No doubt he was buried underground somewhere by now, anchored to his bones forever. Good. Fuck him!

Kento reached me, fell to her knees by my side, pulled me floating towards her. "Eska. I..."

I looked up into my eldest daughter's face and saw

none of the anger from earlier. Only concern and fear warred there now. "Ow!" I said.

Kento placed one hand over the wound and gripped the dagger with the other. She didn't even warn me about what she was doing. She just ripped the dagger out of me. I screamed, then choked as heat flooded my chest. I am used to being healed by Biomancy, the wash of someone else's magic inside me. Back at the Orran Academy of Magic, a lifetime ago, I was always injuring myself, either by my own foolishness or by Lesray Alderson's vicious design. Josef was ever there to heal me though. I Became so used to the touch of his magic it almost felt natural. Kento was different though. Her Biomancy was hot. So much so, it felt like it burned. I half expected to smell my own flesh sizzling, but then it would probably have been hard to smell it over the burning flesh on Sirileth's arms where the metal hoops were melting into slag.

As soon as my wound was healed enough, I could sit up, Kento gripped the dagger and surged to her feet. "What have you done?" she screamed at Sirileth.

"Careful, sister," Sirileth said, still not taking her eyes from the moon slowly plummeting towards us. Or perhaps it was moving quickly. There is a distance where perspective becomes confusing. "I'm saving us. I mean, if you kill me, nothing will slow Lursa's descent." She grimaced as the top hoop on her left shoulder began melting, molten metal sloughing down her arm.

Kento ground her teeth, dagger trembling, then looked at me, shaking her head. "What do we do, Eska? What's happening?"

We had quite an audience already. Terrans and pahht from all over the oasis, both those who were passing through, and the mad ones who called the place home, were gathering, staring, pointing, whispering. Ten, twenty, thirty of them. There was nowhere else for them to go, nowhere to flee to but the desert, so they flocked to the spectacle at the centre of the oasis.

I stared at the rift and the moon growing larger behind it. Sirileth was right. She had dislodged Lursa from Lokar, pulled it from its orbit to plummet towards us. It was happening now, and nothing could stop it. Sirileth was no longer pulling the moon, but pushing it, slowing it, guiding it. And that was when I finally realised why.

"You're trying to close the rift," I said.

Sirileth looked away from her struggle with Lursa for just a moment, smiled at me past the pain of her burning arms and the blood streaking from her eyes and nose. "I told you to trust me, Mother." She turned her attention back to the moon. "I'm not... I've done my research," she growled. "I have. The rift is essentially a giant, stable portal. It's growing larger by the day as the Maker tears at it. We can't close it because that thing is holding it open. But all portals are Sourcery and the ore our moons is made from disrupts Sourcery. In sufficient quantity, it was enough to contain the Rand and Djinn." She coughed, blood spraying from her lips into the lake. "If I can pull Lursa through the portal, the moon will reset it."

"Reset the rift?" Kento asked.

Sirileth groaned, struggling against some pressure, some force I could neither see nor help her with. "I mean, make the rift so it leads nowhere instead of the Maker's realm."

"I don't understand," Kento said.

Sirileth growled, but it turned into a whine of pain as

one of the hoops on her left ear started to glow hot. Her skin
burned. "I don't have time to explain realms to you, sister. I
will, but... not now. Please."

Kento looked at me and shook her head, eyes wide. I
had no idea what Sirileth meant about realms, but I thought
I grasped what she was doing. She was trying to close the
rift, cut the Maker off from our world.

"What do we do, Eska?" Kento asked again.

Lursa was still growing larger behind the great rift.
As big as the rift was, the moon dwarfed it. The eye of the
Maker was frantic, darting about. Angry. Somehow, I knew
it was angry, but it wasn't only feeling anger. It was filled
with the rage of a God of gods, beyond anything mortals
could hope to experience. Well, I was fine with that. I had
plenty of contempt for our gods, so I was happy enough to
share it with theirs too. I had trusted Sirileth so far, and I had
been right to. She was not trying to bring the Maker into our
world but stop it once and for all. She was trying to prevent
the Second Cataclysm, not cause it.

Purple lightning rippled across the surface of the
great rift. A moment later, a bolt streaked towards us.
Luckily, I saw it coming. Also, I know a thing or two about
lightning and how to direct it, or in this case, misdirect
it. I threw my arm out and unleashed my own bolt of
lightning. The jagged purple line arcing out of the rift forked
sideways, connected with my lightning, then consumed it
and exploded into a tree, sending flaming chunks of wood,
soil, and screaming fruit flying in every direction. If only
it stopped there. The purple lightning then launched itself
along the shore and slammed into one of the onlookers, an
old pahht man with thinning, patchy fur on his cheeks. The
lightning struck him in the chest and purple fire spread from

the wound, winding outwards along his arms and legs, up his neck, across his fur like creeping vines.

The pahht was almost glowing purple when he opened his eyes and stared directly at us. His eyes smoked, burned. But they were not his eyes at all, they were the eyes of the Maker, colours beyond colour staring out at us. The old pahht screamed, his voice discordant sound, and I saw purple fire raging within his throat, tearing out of his mouth and scorching his lips. Then he charged us.

I grabbed hold of Kento's arm, used her to haul myself back to my feet, and thanked Isen's ghost that our daughter was as sturdy as her uncle. "Protect your sister," I said once I was upright.

Kento narrowed her eyes, glared at Sirileth for a moment, then turned and sloshed to meet the crazed pahht. She threw an invisible kinetic blast at him, hit his leg, knocked him face-down into the water. The pahht roared upright a moment later and lurched on, one leg broken and dragging behind him. His eyes were still filled with the Maker's colour, and purple fire ran beneath the cracks in his skin like lava, spewed from his mouth. He swung at Kento as they reached each other and she ducked under the swing, planted her little knife in his neck and ripped it out sideways. He fell into the red water, gurgling, blood fountaining out into the oasis. A lightning bolt ripped from his chest back towards the shore. It hit a terran woman wearing a green shawl over her face, tore out of her back and hit a Polasian man with a bare chest and yellow veil over his mouth. They glowed with purple fire as it spread through their veins, cracking open their skin. Their eyes smoked and swirled with the Maker's myriad colours. Then they screamed and ran for us.

Kento didn't hesitate. The Polasian man reached her first, hands snatching, fingers burning into bony claws. She brushed his left hand away, grabbed his right, twisted, slammed him down face first into the ankle-high water, then stood on his back to keep him under. As the terran woman closed in, eyes blazing behind her green shawl, she tried to rush past Kento toward Sirileth. Kento knelt, thrust her free hand into the oasis. The waters froze so quickly ice dust exploded into the air. The woman with the shawl was locked in place, trapped in a tomb of ice.

Purple lightning tore from the woman's back and streaked towards the shore once more. The woman's eyes turned black, burning in her skull. Another bolt of lightning shot out of the water beneath Kento, the bolt arcing into the air and then down upon more hapless onlookers. Four new enemies burned with the purple fire now, their eyes replaced by the Maker's hateful colours. Four more puppets waded into the waters, clawing towards Sirileth.

Kento and I fought to protect Sirileth side by side. I used my Sourcery, turned my storm on those attacking us, and dashed from my mind that they were people. Or had once been people. I believe that once the Maker had taken them, they were something else, something no longer terran or pahht, but a part of the god. I was exhausted, beyond it even, but I fought on because the alternative was something I could not consider. Kento formed a Sourceblade and showed as little mercy I did. Whoever had trained her had known their stuff. Kento possessed a skill I would have been hard pressed to match even in my prime. A dozen of the puppets fell before us, bleeding into the oasis, the crimson waters turning opaque and sticky. And for every one we killed, lightning sought two new hosts to turn against us.

Imiko waded out to meet us, staying close for protection, but taking no part in the fight. I did not blame her for that. She supported Sirileth, kept my youngest daughter on her feet when she almost fell. And Sirileth bent all her strength and power on dragging a moon from the sky, directing it through the great rift.

Despite everything we did to protect Sirileth, the puppets kept coming, beating us back. I formed a kinetic shield, pushed all my strength into it and dug my feet into the muck beneath us, rooting myself with Geomancy, holding the shield firm as a dozen of the Maker's puppets beat on the kinetic haze, clawed at it, screamed at me, pushed me back. The other side of Sirileth, Kento fought like a wild abban protecting its cubs. It seemed like all the oasis was throwing itself at us.

A horse wreathed in purple flames, eyes mad with colour, crashed out of the trees and into the water, charging at us. I could not turn to stop it, too busy holding back a whole family of pahht as they thrashed against my shield, adults and children both. Kento met the charge at a run, thrust her sword into the horse's neck, was thrown back by the force. Woman and horse fell together, rolling, thrashing. Kento screamed as the horse sank teeth into her shoulder.

All around us, drops of water started to rise into the air. I felt my stomach shift, lurch, bile rising into my mouth. The broad, red leaves of the trees bent upwards as if reaching for the sky. I glanced up to see Lursa dominating everything, her red bulk massive and looming, greater even than the rift she was barrelling towards.

Sirileth's voice was a breathy wheeze as she said, "You... will remember... me, God." The Source at the head of her staff cracked and shattered. Sirileth dropped the useless haft, reached with both hands as if she could take hold of Lursa, and gave one final pull. Then she collapsed into Imiko's arms.

Lursa collided with the great rift.

CHAPTER THIRTY FIVE

THE EYE OF THE MAKER BLINKED OUT OF existence. The puppets trying to kill us stopped, reeled, keeled over, and died, their eyes smoking, burning black within their skulls. Even the horse savaging Kento fell still. Kento ripped her shoulder from its mouth and staggered upright, blood streaming from the wound. We turned our gazes to the sky and watched.

Lursa barrelled through the rift, leaving a huge chunk of herself behind. No, not behind. Just gone. Swallowed by the rift. Our moon was many times the size of the great rift, but just passing through ripped a chunk out of her and sent it... Well, I don't know where. Wherever the rift led now it wasn't connected to the Maker's world. Or realm, as Sirileth had called it. I needed to ask her about that, but with a moon falling on top of us, now was not really the time.

Lursa continued falling towards Ovaeris. Her

surface cracked from the chunk ripped from her mass. Fire
burst to life all along her red bulk. Bits of her, chunks of
moon rock the size of houses trailed behind her. The world
seemed to lurch as though the normal rules that governed
it had stopped applying. I felt lighter, slower, as if I was
underwater. My hair floated around my face. Drops of
water and blood detached themselves from the oasis and
soared upwards. I wasn't the only one feeling it. Imiko
squeaked, clutched to Sirileth and pulled her close. Kento
limped towards us, moving slowly, her ripped coat pulling
upwards as if sentient and desperately trying to escape her.
The onlookers, those who hadn't been taken and killed by
the Maker, gathered at the water's edge to stare up at Lursa's
dominating form bearing down on us. Some of them tried to
run, but struggled to make it a few steps, as though their feet
found no purchase on the ground.

I was sweating. We were all sweating. It was the
middle of the night in the desert, but it felt like the sun was
up and beating down on us all. The air shimmered from the
heat, the oasis steamed in places and the water was starting
to get uncomfortable to stand in.

"Push it back," Kento shouted at Sirileth. She had to
shout to be heard over the roaring. I hadn't even noticed the
noise until then, but it was deafening and coming from all
around us.

Sirileth looked up at Kento. My youngest daughter
was so weary, she couldn't sit upright without Imiko's help.
Blood still leaked from her nose and ears, dripping down
dried tracks of the stuff. Her darklight eyes blazed in the
night but were half-lidded. All but two of the hoops piercing
her arms had melted to molten slag on her skin, and the
flesh beneath the metal was red and angry, still smoking in

SINS OF THE MOTHER

places. Sirileth simply shook her head at Kento.

Kento turned her icy blue eyes on me then. "What do we do, Eska?" Despair laced her voice. "What the fuck do we do?"

When the world is burning around you, people always turn to the pyromaniacs. First, for answers, and later, to blame.

I waved to the people standing on the shore of the oasis, waiting to die. "Get over here," I screamed. Kento quickly joined in, calling for the gathered merchants and mad folk to join us in the centre of the lake. Some started towards us, wading slowly through the water, fighting against gravity gone mad. Others ignored us completely, eyes fixed on Lursa as she fell, cracked, split open from the new wounds the rift had given her.

Ten people made it to us in time. A family of pahht, man and woman and two children. Three merchants, all terran, two men who held onto each and wept as only ill-fated lovers can, and a Polasian woman with a jaw like an anvil. A mad terran man with matted hair and no shirt. A pahht woman wearing all black, carrying a young terran child bawling for its mother. By the time the last reached us, the heat was almost unbearable. The waters were searing my legs, and all of us were struggling to breathe the hot, thinning air. There were others still wading towards us, struggling to get to what little safety we promised. I shared a look with Kento, and we both knew the truth. They wouldn't make it, and if I hesitated any longer, we would join them in death.

I raised my hand and formed a bubble from Kinemancy, Arcmancy, and Pyromancy all at once. The air was still too hot, the water scalding, but Kento thrust her hands into the red lake and used her own Pyromancy to cool the space inside my bubble. A terran woman with a dirty face streaked with tears reached us, hit the shield and rebounded off it, screamed at us, begging to be let in. I held her gaze, ignored the others inside my shield telling me to drop it and let her in. They would kill us all.

The roar became deafening, but I could do nothing about that. Lursa passed overhead so close I could make out the cracks running through her crimson skin, could see fires racing along them like blood through veins. She really was hollow inside and I saw all the way into her pock marked depths. A prison to trap the Rand, once broken and now falling upon us.

The waters around my bubble steamed, simmered, boiled. The trees on the edge of the oasis burst into flames, leaves burning, trunks charring. The woman who had pleaded with me to let her in staggered back, screamed, choked, melted. I turned away from the horrific sight and knew I would soon have a new ghost to unmake.

The air around us burned, fires sprang to life, then guttered out. I felt myself lifting, my feet no longer connected to the ground, then Kento grabbed hold of my leg with her blood-streaked hand, pulled me down. She knelt amidst the waters, one hand buried in the earth, radiating cold. Some of the others threw themselves to ground, but as Lursa passed overhead, people floated around my bubble as if unmoored from the world.

Lursa streaked slowly through the sky. Or, perhaps it wasn't slowly, but only seemed so. Huge chunks of her trailed in her wake, spinning, falling, crashing down around us, shaking the earth, and sending plumes of sand thrusting in the night sky even as it burned.

I felt my body regain its weight, my feet once more finding purchase on the ground. I kept my shield raised, infused with all my Sourcery to keep the burning world outside from destroying us.

A mighty crash buffeted us as the cracks and the fire and the stress of falling finally split Lursa in two like a cracked egg.

"Mother," Sirileth said. She choked on something, spat blood into the cool water sloshing around inside my bubble. The rest of the oasis was gone, the water had burned away in the friction of Lursa's passing. "Whatever you do, do not drop your shield." She was trembling, shivering, held upright by Imiko. "I mean, this isn't over yet. You have to protect us."

The others taking shelter in my bubble clung to each other, whispering about their fears, already starting to throw blame around. I heard the name Corpse Queen mentioned at least once, and something else too, a new title not aimed at me. The pahht called Sirileth Et-cera. I don't know much of the pahht language, but I know what that means. Et means end, cera means to bring. They called my youngest daughter the End Bringer, and I wasn't sure I could argue with them.

The terran child started wailing and I hissed at someone to shut her up. I will not lie; it was taking a lot of focus to keep my bubble raised and strong enough to withstand the pressures of the world trying to reassert itself. And a child's screaming is a wonderful way to shatter concentration.

Lursa, both parts of her, passed out of sight, over the horizon. We could see nothing but the chunks of her falling to the ground in her wake. But we knew when she touched down. The earth around and beneath us shook, bucked, twisted, warped. We felt it even through my bubble. Everyone else was thrown to the sloshing water at our feet. I stayed upright only because of Kento's support. Sirileth crawled towards me too, placed her hand on my back.

"Do not drop your shield, Mother," she reminded me. I felt... strength coming from her. I don't know whether she was truly lending me her own power, somehow transferring it to me through her touch, or whether it was just having my daughter close that leant me extra strength. Kento stood too, tall and strong behind me, her uninjured hand on my shoulder. I poured everything I had left into that shield. And side by side with my two daughters we watched the world end.

Fire lit the night sky almost as bright as day. A great plume of grey dust and ash shot into the air, impossibly tall and far away. The ground continued to tremble, split. I thought we would be swallowed by it, dropped into the depths of Ovaeris and crushed. Then the shockwave hit us. A wall of dust and rock and sand and... everything. It raced along the ground, reshaping the desert. When it hit my shield, I felt as though it would crush me even through the Sourcery. I stood my ground only through the support of my daughters as a storm I could never control raged around us. Sand, dust, rocks, other things that passed too quickly to identify. My bubble was battered again and again. And when it finally subsided, I realised we were buried. In my little bubble, no more than a dozen paces across, fourteen of us huddled amidst all that was left of the oasis, cool, red waters sloshing at our feet. And all around us, above and below, sand and dirt piled high. The only light came from the purple glowing haze of my shield, and from my eyes flashing, and Sirileth's burning in the darkness.

Sirileth had done this. She had ripped Lursa from the sky, closed the great rift, crashed the moon into Polasia. And now we were buried and I could not think of a way out. Also, the child started crying again. I couldn't really blame her given the situation, but it really wasn't helping.

The others started asking questions. The Polasian woman demanded to know what had just happened. The pahht still taking care of the child tried to calm the wailing brat. The crazy, shirtless fool laughed somewhere on the edge of hysteria. The male pahht left his wife and children, approached me, and started spitting insults in pahht.

Imiko was the only quiet one. She sat close by, alone, soaking wet and staring at nothing. It was so unlike my little sister, to be so silent and detached. I worried about her. I needed to go to her with whatever scant comfort I could provide, but I didn't have the time. I had to keep the bubble up or we'd all suffocate, buried alive, and there were too many other demands on my attention.

"Now what?" Kento asked.

"Give me a moment, sister," Sirileth said. She closed her darklight eyes and breathed deep. She knelt in the cool water, pressed her hand to the ground, frowned. "I can't reach outside your bubble, mother. I mean, with Sourcery, I can't... Your bubble disrupts it."

"That's kind of the point," I grumbled.

"I need you to drop your shield," Sirileth said tiredly.

"Being buried alive doesn't sound fun."

Sirileth opened her eyes and stared at me, the burning coronas terrible to look at. She looked so tired. "We're already buried alive, mother. I can't get us out of this without Geomancy."

"Everybody hold your breath," I said. "You may

want to cover the child's mouth." Then I dropped my
bubble. The baked earth rushed in around us, swallowed us.
The heat was uncomfortable to say the least. In that awful
dark embrace, terrible memories surfaced, ones I had long
thought left behind. Tied to a chair in the Red Cells, unable
to move, the Emperor of Terrelan driving knives into my
flesh. Half formed dreams Ssserakis had once shown me,
trapped, held tight, jaws of death closing in. My time in
the Pit, surrounded by darkness, running from Prig and
his friends as they chased me down with murder on their
minds.

The earth convulsed around me, shifted, rolled,
then spat me into a burning wasteland that had once been
a verdant oasis. I pulled my legs from the dirt and rolled
free, backing away from the spot as though a monster had
swallowed me and might try again. Others were climbing
free too. Kento and Imiko, the pahht family, the crazy terran.
One by one they all raised up out of the earth, scrabbled free,
and stared at the new world they now inhabited. Sirileth was
last. Bits of dirt stuck to the blood on her face and peppered
her dark hair.

We were surrounded by an ominous red glow. All
around us dust and sand and other debris floated, twisted,
rushed. We appeared to be standing in the eye of a dust
storm that was raging all around. Only the storm wasn't
moving. It was stable. Above me, the great rift was still open,
a hole in the world, a tear in reality. But it was empty. The
Maker no longer stared through it.

Nearby husks of trees, those with roots deep enough
they weren't ripped free and blown away, were still burning,
fire consuming them from the inside. There was no water
anymore, no trees or grass, no life at all, save for the fourteen

people I had protected.

"It worked," Sirileth said as she sat on the hot ground, leaned back and stared at the rift.

"What do you mean? It's still there," I said.

"Of course it is, Mother. It's a rift. A hole in the world. I couldn't close it. No one could. It... It is. Just is."

Kento turned on her sister, stalked forward. "Then what the fuck was all this about?"

Sirileth grimaced and leaned forward. Every time she moved, the metal streaking down her arms groaned with the stress, the wounds around it bleeding afresh. I realised she was using Ingomancy still, to move the metal, to move her arms. "I had to reset the rift," Sirileth said. "Right now, it's a hole in the world that leads nowhere. There's no other realm on the other side. There's nothing."

"What do you mean when you say realm?" Kento said.

"It's complicated, sister. We may not have time for me to explain it."

Kento took another step forward, towered over Sirileth. "Try."

Sirileth stared at Kento, then sighed, closed her eyes, pinched the bridge of her nose. "A lot of this I know from the Maker. When it took me, it taught me things about worlds and realms. Other things. But it... it didn't tell me everything. It didn't have time and there were things it didn't want me to know. I mean, things it thought I couldn't understand. The rest I've had to learn myself through research and experimentation."

Kento opened her mouth to speak, but I waved my hand in her direction to shut her up. No doubt she was going to raise a valid point about how her experimentation was killing people, but what good would it serve? Sirileth knew that. What was important now was knowing why she had done things the way she had, and what the rift now meant.

Sirileth took a deep breath, almost toppled over, but caught herself. "We exist within one realm."

"Ovaeris?" I asked.

She shook her head, winced, then opened her darklight eyes and pinned me with a stare. "Ovaeris is the world we live on. It exists within our realm. So do the moons, the stars, everything else. This is all our realm. But there are other realms."

"How many?" Kento asked.

"At least ten. I mean, that I know of for certain? Ten. But those are just the ones the Maker showed me. I believe there are more." She glanced at me and smiled, a look filled with terror and awe and excitement. "I believe there are a lot more."

"Like Sevorai?" I asked.

Again, Sirileth shook her head. "Ovaeris and Sevorai are one realm. One world. They just exist in different... um, spaces within it?" She sighed. "It's all... So, when the Djinn created Sevorai, they did not have the strength to create a whole realm. I mean, no one does. No one could. Not even the Maker could forge new realms. But the Djinn did have the power to create a world within this realm. Sort of? They, uh, twisted the laws, the, uh, fundamental laws that govern... everything. They made it so Sevorai exists here just as Ovaeris does within this realm, only it's also cut off from the rest of the realm." She stopped and shook her head.

I glanced at Kento. She looked lost and I took some comfort from that because I had to admit I was too.

Sirileth sighed, reached into a pocket, and pulled out a coin. "This stretch of dirt is our realm." She wiped a hand across the dirt before her, smoothing it out. "This coin is both Ovaeris," she held it up, the side facing us flat and without mark. "And also, Sevorai." She flipped the coin over and showed us a face with a single line gouged through it. Then she placed the coin in the dirt with the Ovaeris side face up. "We exist like this. As far as the rest of our realm is, uh, concerned, only Ovaeris exists. Sevorai is hidden. The other side of our world, but still there. Both part of and separate from all at once. It's... I don't..."

"A world within a world," I said as it started to fall into place. "That's what the Djinn did. When The War Eternal was at its most brutal and the Rand were sacrificing parts of themselves to make Aspects in a hope to trick the laws of our world—"

"Our realm," Sirileth corrected. "Our world doesn't have laws." She stopped, frowned, shook her head. "Not fundamental laws. Realms have laws. Worlds are just..." She picked up a handful of dirt and let it fall between her fingers. "Land. Water. People."

"Right, but the Djinn started created their own worlds within objects. Vainfold's crown, for instance. The crown has a world within in. It's a barely formed thing of fire and rock. It's small, but it exists within the crown."

Sirileth nodded, beaming a smile at me. "It exists within this world, but also separate from it. Sevorai is the same thing on a larger scale. I mean, it's genius. It's a world inside Ovaeris. Part of it. The other side of it." She flipped the coin over.

"What does this have to do with that thing?" Kento asked, pointing at the great rift. "And the Maker?"

"Rifts are more than just portals," I said. "They're holes in the world."

"Not world, mother. Realm," Sirileth said. "I had to do a lot of research around Portamancy and..." She laughed. "You wouldn't believe most of the stuff fool Sourcerers come up with. Terrans especially know fuck all. Tahren are a bit better, but all their research is centred around pointless religious dogma about the Maker coming to cleanse the world. I mean... I didn't do that. They believed it before me. I just..."

"Used them?" I asked.

Sirileth nodded. "I needed the staff and the ore. I needed their help, so I made them think I wanted what they did."

She closed her eyes for a long moment, took a deep breath, then continued slowly. "Portals are just that, created by Sourcery. They connect one place in a realm to another place in the same realm. Rifts are holes in the realm itself, they lead to other realms. Or, um, can... lead to other realms, I mean. When the Rand and Djinn clashed here during their war, they tore open a rift and by sheer dumb luck it led to the Maker's realm. The Maker is powerful enough to hold the rift open and started tearing at it, making it larger in an attempt to enter our realm. It was also strong enough that while it was connected to our realm through the rift, it could sometimes hijack portals. That's how it took me when I was young."

"But you..." Kento paused, winced, rubbed at the back of her neck. "You reset the rift to lead nowhere rather than the Maker's realm?" The way she said it, hesitantly, implied she either didn't believe Sirileth, or was struggling to understand what my youngest daughter was saying.

"Yes." Sirileth smiled at Kento. "Rifts are created using Sourcery. The ore in our moons disrupt Sourcery. So, I tested it. Experimented. I, uh, created smaller rifts leading to other realms, then brought them into contact with the ore. Smaller lumps of the ore were simply taken to the other realm. I mean, whichever other realm. But if the ore was larger than the rift, it reset the rift to lead nowhere." Again, she paused, winced as she tried to collect her thoughts.

All around us, the storm still raged. Lightning raced along it here and there, and though the winds and dust didn't reach us, the roar of the storm was like a lion thrashing at its cage, desperate to reach its prey.

"But the only rifts I was able to create were mere pinpricks. Too small to... It was like glimpsing another realm through a keyhole. But this one, the great rift, is more like an open door."

"That's a big door," Kento said.

"It is!" Sirileth agreed.

I sighed. "And the only clump of ore big enough to disrupt it was one of our moons."

"Exactly, Mother," Sirileth nodded, slumped, her shoulders sagging. "The Maker was going to keep picking at the rift. One day it was going to tear it large enough to slither through and kill us all. I know it. It... it showed me. Tried to make me help it. Tried to... This was the only way to stop it. I looked. I looked I looked. I looked for another way. I did. This was it. Our only chance."

The others were all still gathered around us. The mad terran was on his knees, hands raised to the rift, begging the Maker to return. The Polasian woman was pacing, staring at the storm around us, cursing. The pahht couple were arguing in their own language, the man waving his hands wildly. But their children, they were standing close by, listening to Sirileth. I am not good at guessing the ages of pahht, but if they were terran, I would put the boy at no more than six and the girl at nine or ten. The boy clung to the girl, and she held him tight.

"Why did the monster want to kill us?" the little girl asked in terran.

Sirileth stared at the girl a moment. She looked away from those darklight eyes, but didn't back away, even with the little pahht boy tugging on her arm to retreat.

"When I was ten years old, the monster kidnapped me," Sirileth said eventually. "It took me to its realm, cradled me, and showed me many things. It showed me what it intended to do, what it needed me to do to free it. I asked it one question, the same one you have. Why? I mean, what could be so important, so horrible about Ovaeris, our world... us, that the monster needed to destroy it?"

Kento shook her head, turned away and crossed her arms. She didn't walk away though. She was still listening.

"You see, every realm is different," Sirileth continued. "I know. I've looked in on a few. I've seen a realm where people worship the stars instead of gods. Another with a world swallowed by forest and fog. I've seen a world so bathed in bloodshed and war that the dead themselves have risen to stop it." She stared at me, eyes wide and shook her head. "But the realm of the Maker, the monster... It's empty. It's always been empty. There is nothing there but the Maker. Can you imagine how lonely that must be?"

I could. I have always hated being alone. But even in my most separated times down in the Red Cells, I was not truly alone. I had my guards and my torturers. I had the ghosts of all those I had killed. Even more recently, during my time in Wrysom, the people around had no idea who I truly was and that was certainly a loneliness of a sort, but I was never truly alone. The idea, the possibility of existing in a world, a realm with no one in it. To be utterly and inescapably alone... That was true terror.

The little pahht girl shook her head. "I'd like to be alone sometimes." She glanced down at the little brother clinging to her clawed hand.

Sirileth smiled at her, nodded. "Siblings can be tough. At least he hasn't tried to kill you yet." She glanced at Kento, but my eldest daughter did not even turn to acknowledge her words. The little pahht girl frowned, tried to pull her hand free, but her brother held on tighter.

Sirileth sighed. "The monster had no siblings, no parents, no friends. It had no one. It watched the other realms from time to time, its power was so great it could do that, but it found nothing like itself. Nothing that could understand it or communicate with it. So, it decided to make itself some company. It had children."

"With whom?" the pahht girl asked.

Sirileth chuckled. "With itself."

The pahht girl opened her eyes wide, bared her fangs. I knew from my time with Ishtar long ago that was the pahht expression of disgust.

Sirileth nodded, then turned her darklight eyes on me. "It created the Rand and the Djinn," she said.

I already knew this. I had figured it out years ago before Sirileth was even born. I think my daughter was testing me, trying to figure out how much I knew.

"It gave them bits of itself, of its power," she continued. "The Maker was trying to create companionship, but it was also trying to understand itself. It thought if it could remove bits of itself, put them into new things, new life, then maybe it could understand them, and through that understanding, understand itself too."

I scoffed. "Just like the Rand and the Aspects."

"Where do you think they got the idea?"

That made a lot of sense. Ssserakis had once told me the Rand and Djinn lacked any imagination. Everything they claimed to create was actually a recreation or alteration. Sevorai was based on Ovaeris, the creatures that populate it were ripped from the imaginations of terrans and pahht and the other sentient races. The Djinn cities, their very aesthetic was based upon the architecture of the garn. Even us, the terrans and pahht and tahren, who the Rand claimed to have created, are alterations on what was already here, the primitive races of Ovaeris.

"What happened?" the pahht girl asked. Her brother was clinging to her, sucking on one of his claws as I've seen terran children do with their thumbs. She draped an arm over his shoulder. "If..." she frowned. "If the monster made the gods, how did they come here?"

"Exile," Sirileth said. "The Maker's children were a rowdy lot. Siblings fight, as I'm sure you know, and the Maker's children fought constantly. Frustrated, the Maker sent them here, trapped them inside our moons. It had seen Ovaeris before as it watched the realms, and it already knew our moons were made of strange metal that resisted its power. Not enough to render it powerless, but enough to do that to its children who had nowhere near its strength."

The little girl stared up into the sky. Past the great rift, now a dark void in the sky, we could just about make out Lokar still hanging above us. He was a shattered husk of a thing now. His blue skin had never provided as much light as Lursa, but now that she had left him, he seemed darker, diminished. He was cracked open, innards torn out, turned towards Ovaeris so we could almost see inside him. Much of his surface was shattered, massive fractures running along every part of him. Huge chunks of his rocky flesh had been torn away and were suspended between him and us. There were some bits of Lursa still up there too, the red now so dark it was almost purple. This was what Sirileth had left us with. One moon crashed into the world, and I still could not fathom the consequences of that. The other moon was a cracked, shattered thing, spilling rocks from itself like guts trailing across the sky.

"I know all of this," I said eventually. There was still something niggling at me, a part of the puzzle that didn't fit. And damn Sirileth, but she knew the answer. She really was smarter than me, better at reasoning out the pieces and fitting them together. It was unfortunate that Kento did not share our love of puzzles. "What I don't understand is why the Maker needed the rift in the first place. If it was powerful enough to put the Rand and Djinn here, why did it need the rift?"

Sirileth pinned me with her blazing stare. "Exactly, Mother. I mean, why the rift? Why you? Why me? Why did a creature of such vast power need us lowly terrans?" She grinned, slightly lopsided just like my own. "Because it was a fucking idiot."

I laughed at that, pure and wild. Sirileth sounded so much like me. Me, but smarter. Me, but better. Me, but more dangerous. Sirileth hesitated a moment then laughed with me.

"The Maker gave the Rand and Djinn too much of its power," she continued, clearly more enthusiastic now.

"While they were still in its realm, it, um, had access to that power through them, because they were still a part of it. But then it sent them here, trapped them in Lokar and Lursa. It couldn't kill them; they were its children. But they needed to be taught a lesson. It left them here and retreated back to its own realm." She laughed. "Locked the naughty children in their rooms. The Maker didn't mean the exile to be permanent, it was just a punishment for obnoxious children. But when it retreated to its own realm, it realised it no longer had access to the power it had given the Rand and Djinn. It trapped itself in its own realm, but this time it couldn't travel to other realms, couldn't create more children. It had, uh, given too much of its power to them. It was alone again."

That was the final piece of the puzzle. I nodded. "Then the war between the Rand and the Djinn opened up the great rift."

Sirileth smiled at me. "Yes, Mother. Exactly. The Maker had been peering through the realms for thousands of years, trying to find where it had left its children because it wanted them back. It wanted its full power back. But watching the other realms was all it could do. Then the rift opened, and it latched onto it. But by then, so many of the Rand and Djinn were dead that even reconnected to the power it had given them, it wasn't strong enough to travel here or force the rift open fully. So, it picked at the rift endlessly, slowly making it larger."

Kento was watching now, still with her back to us, but turned just enough to peer over her shoulder, her eyes cold as ice. "Why you?"

Kento met her sister's gaze. "Because of her. I mean, because of Mother. Our mother."

I blanched at that. I had been waiting for the blame to

fall on my head.

"She caught the Maker's attention years ago when she accidentally visited it. Her and Ssserakis."

"Who?" Kento asked.

"Ssserakis," Sirileth said eagerly, looking from Kento to me and back again. "The horror from Sevorai."

I'd never told anyone about Ssserakis, and I didn't feel like breaking that tradition no matter how important it might be. I couldn't even say why really. I think, maybe it was because Ssserakis was mine and mine alone. The one thing that no one knew about me. Or maybe because I didn't want others to know how much of a monster I truly was, that the embodiment of fear itself had possessed me, made me its home, and we had been friends. More than friends. Partners in a way I could never explain. I missed Ssserakis, every day. And I was scared of what that meant, of what Kento would think of me if she knew.

"When you and Ssserakis came to the Maker's attention, Mother, it realised what the Rand had done. They'd used the power it had given them to make children of their own."

Kento was still staring at me, but I refused to meet her gaze. I stared, instead, at the storm swirling around us, around the rift. The shifting dull red and occasional flashes of lightning were mesmerising. "I don't think either the denizens of the Other World, or the Rand, would be pleased about being called children of the Rand."

"But they are," Sirileth said. "I mean, sort of. So, are we? Terrans, pahht, Aspects, Sourcerers. We were all created by the Rand, who were in turn created by the Maker. When you crossed over, Mother, the Maker realised that. It saw, uh, the fingerprints of itself in your, uh... in you. It took an interest in you, watched you through the portals. And then when I stepped through, it took a chance. On me, I mean. It showed me so much, taught me so much." She smiled bitterly.

"It thought it could control me. So, I let it believe it could. But I knew what it really wanted. It didn't care about us, or me, or Ovaeris, Sevorai, the Rand or Djinn. All it really wanted was its power back. And with so many of the Rand and Djinn dead, their power trapped inside Sources, the Maker knew the only chance it had would be to consume Ovaeris entirely.

"Everything I have done has been to this goal, Mother," Sirileth said. Her voice was a little higher than before, a child begging for approval. "The Rand called it the Second Cataclysm. That's what Tamura said. A prophecy of the end. I stopped it. I did."

I buried my head in my hand, pressed against my temples as my head began to ache. I felt a drop of blood run from my nose, tasted it on my lips. I'd used too much magic and was starting to reject my Sources.

"What's to stop the Maker from finding Ovaeris again?" I asked as I fumbled in my pouch for Spiceweed. "If it can still watch, peer through at other realms, surely it can just latch onto the rift again." I shoved a wad of damp Spiceweed into my mouth and sucked on it until the retching took hold.

"Yes," Sirileth said as I vomited up my Sources. "That's why we don't have long. I need to redirect the rift somewhere else. Once it's connected somewhere, anywhere else, the Maker can't pull the destination back to its own realm. I, uh... I think? I mean, I think I know."

"Idiot!" Kento snapped. "You haven't prevented the

Second Cataclysm, Sirileth. You've fucking caused it!" She turned, stalked toward her little sister, grabbed her by her collar and hauled her upright. I could only watch from the baking ground as I retched up my second Source.

Sirileth didn't resist as Kento dragged her in the direction Lursa had fallen, then gave her a push. Sirileth stumbled a couple of steps before she caught herself. I saw fresh blood running down the tracks the molten metal had seared into her arms. She turned to Kento and shook her head. "I don't understand. I stopped it. The Maker. The Second Cataclysm. I stopped it."

Kento shook her head. "Do you know how many people live in Irad, Sirileth? Lived there. Not anymore. That's where you brought down the moon." She stabbed a finger in the direction Lursa had fallen. "You fucking crashed a moon on top of a city." She threw up her hands in exasperation. "How do I even start to... A moon! No one survives that."

Sirileth shook her head again. The metal on her left arm squealed as she bent it to pull at her braid. "It's evacuated," she said. "I made sure. I... I mean, maybe a few thousand people left, those who couldn't get out."

"They didn't evacuate," I said. It was all I could get out before I retched again, bringing up my last Source.

"But..." Sirileth faltered, frowned, fingers rubbing at the hairs of her braid. "I told the prince to evacuate. Prince Jamil, I mean. He wouldn't just ignore me. He wouldn't..." Her certainty evaporated as quickly as the waters of the oasis had.

Kento spat, clenched her hands into fists, stepped forward and pushed Sirileth hard in the chest. Sirileth stumbled back another couple of steps. "Oh, the prince didn't ignore you, Sirileth. The royal family evacuated, sure enough. But they left the rest of the city to die."

"I... I told him to get everyone out," Sirileth said quietly. My poor youngest daughter. Always so good with puzzles, with numbers, equations, research. Always so bad with people.

Kento shoved Sirileth again, hard enough my youngest tripped and fell on her arse, crying out in pain. "He did get his family out. The royal family. You idiot. You fucking idiot. Why didn't you go to the queen? Why didn't you tell her? Why didn't you..." Kento stopped, turned, kicked the dust.

"She... she would have stopped me," Sirileth said quietly, uncertainly.

"Because you needed to be stopped!" Kento roared. She turned on me then, throwing out a hand and pointing at Sirileth. "You did this, Eska. You and her, you're both just as fucking responsible. Do you have any idea how many people lived in Irad?" She glared at me a moment, then turned her icy blue eyes on Sirileth. "Do you know how many people you just fucking murdered?"

"A hundred thousand," I said. "Two hundred?" Too many. Too damned many.

Sirileth stared in the direction of Irad, and I saw so many things cross her face. Dawning realisation, horror, grief, nausea, determination, acceptance. All in a few seconds. She struggled back to her feet, raised her chin in defiance. "It was worth it."

Kento went terrifyingly still.

"A hundred thousand dead," Sirileth said, her voice wavering, breaking. "The whole of Ovaeris saved." She lowered her darklight eyes, not meeting Kento's baleful stare. "Worth it," she said it so quietly.

Kento's fist struck Sirileth's jaw and sent her sprawling on the baking, dusty ground. Imiko launched to her feet, ran over to Sirileth, stood between my two daughters even as Kento moved to attack again.

"Leave her alone," Imiko snarled.

My eldest daughter stared at Imiko for a moment, her lip quivering.

"Do you really think it's going to end at Irad?" Kento asked quietly. "Look at this storm. The only reason we're alive is because the rift is somehow keeping it off us. Everyone else it touches will die. How far do you think it will reach? You dropped a moon on us, sister. A fucking moon!" She shook her head and sank onto her knees. I knew how she felt. When the anger is too much, when it leaves and only exhaustion remains. "Tsunamis, hurricanes, storms, this fucking dust blotting out the sun. Irad is just the start. This..." She threw up her hands, waving at the storm raging around us. "This is the Second Cataclysm. Not some impotent god watching through a rift. This!" She sobbed. "You didn't stop. You caused it. And now we're all going to die."

I shuffled to Kento. I had no words to comfort her but hoped maybe my presence could help. She gave me such a reproachful stare I pulled up short, knelt a few paces from her. I think I understood. She was angry, yes, furious even. But it was not her anger that was swallowing her, dragging her into the cold oblivion. It was fear. She was scared of what would happen to our world, what Sirileth's actions would mean. She was terrified her daughter, Esem, would die because of it. And also, that we were stuck in the desert. She was scared her daughter would die without her.

The pahht couple had retrieved their children, were keeping them away from us now. All the others were keeping their distance too. I didn't blame them. They had all heard us arguing and knew the truth. They knew Sirileth had just killed us all.

"Are you ready?" I heard Sirileth ask quietly. "Are you sure?"

"Yes," Imiko's voice, quiet, defeated.

I looked up to discover Sirileth was not yet finished destroying us.

CHAPTER THIRTY SIX

FOR AS LONG AS I CAN REMEMBER, SIRILETH was a restless sleeper. Even as a babe, she used to thrash in her cot and wake suddenly. It continued into her childhood and as far as I am aware, beyond. For a long time, I did not know why. I watched her occasionally, trying to determine the cause. She would twitch, then jerk, then thrash. No sound escaped her lips bar a hurried breath.

I could always tell when she woke though. Her thrashing eased, her breathing calmed. Her eyes opened, and even in the darkest room and without my nightsight, I could tell when Sirileth open her eyes. Her darklight lit up the room as surely as the flashing of my own.

I asked Sirileth if she had dreams, and she took her time considering the answer before telling me simply. Not that I can recall. An articulate little girl even as a child, though she sometimes struggled to find the right words. I wonder who she got that from, certainly not me.

Her restless nights continued and with no idea what
to do, I brought Hardt in the on the matter. He watched her
thrash and wake just once. Then he sat on the edge of her
bed and stroked her hair until Sirileth dropped back to sleep.
His gentle nature brought out a trust in Sirileth. Or maybe
she was simply emulating my unquestionable trust in the
big man.

Hardt pulled me aside once Sirileth had dropped off
once again. You really don't remember? He asked. I did not.
Well, that's not entirely true. I remembered just fine, but I
did not understand. They're nightmares, Eska. You used to
suffer from them too. Hardt stopped and chuckled. We all
suffered from your nightmares, Eska. Just after we escaped
the Pit. It started in the Forest of Ten, but you suffered for
years after that too. You used to thrash about, kicking up
a storm around you. Punched me in the jaw once or twice.
Then you'd snap awake, screaming like a hound was
chewing off your foot.

Oh yes, I remembered, all right. Those nightmares I
suffered from were not natural. They were inflicted upon
me by Ssserakis. Before we formed a true bond, came
to rely upon each other, even love each other, Ssserakis
had tormented me in my sleep with visions of the Other
World. But my little daughter was not me. Sirileth was not
possessed by Ssserakis.

Parents pass so much to their children. We often don't
mean to, and just as often what we do pass on we wish we
hadn't. We want our children to be stronger, better, smarter,
to have an easier life than us. Well, Sirileth hit two of those
four, at least. But despite all the comfort I tried to provide
her, all the love I thought I gave her, she did not have it

easier than I. Sirileth, my youngest daughter, my darling little girl, inherited my horror.

Imiko was on her feet. She reached down and pulled Sirileth up to join her. Both women looked nervous, but Imiko was smiling. Not the sharp smile I was used to seeing on her, but something softer and more real. As though she had always been wearing a mask, but now it was stripped away to reveal a vulnerability she kept hidden her entire life. Silva once told me that Imiko was forever running, chasing the spirit of adventure, her name written across the horizon. I misunderstood. We all did. Imiko had been running her entire life from a predator she could never escape: herself. Her own dark, churning thoughts that crept up on her every time she stopped. For a while I thought I had been the one to force her to stop running. But I never had that power over her. No. It was Sirileth who unwittingly forced Imiko to face that part of herself, to stop and confront it. It was Sirileth who gave Imiko a reason. A purpose.

They embraced. It felt a private thing. Imiko had been a mother to Sirileth in my absence. Probably a better mother than I ever was. I had to come to terms with that. Sirileth would always see Imiko that way. Sirileth wrapped her arms around Imiko, the metal squealing, the flesh beneath oozing as she used Ingomancy to her limbs. One of the final two hoops through her left arm was glowing softly, a hazy orange colouring it as it fought off the rejection that was even now threatening to undo my youngest daughter.

I don't know how long Imiko and Sirileth held to each other. I watched them, fighting the jealousy that bubbled within me. I have never been one to hide my emotions or run from them, but jealousy can be an ugly thing, so I pushed it down, told myself it didn't matter how close they were because I was Sirileth's mother, not Imiko. I really am an ungrateful bitch.

When finally, they separated, Sirileth reached up, caught Imiko behind the head and pulled her close once more until their foreheads touched. "Are you sure?" The words were barely more than a whisper. They should have been drowned out by the storm, but I caught them. Or maybe I just imagined them in my vain hope that my daughter is not what everyone thinks she is.

Imiko nodded. They pulled apart, clasped hands for just a moment. Clinging to each other again and again as though unwilling to let go. Imiko closed her eyes, grinned that sharp smile I was used to seeing on her. The mask slipping back into place. There were silent tears streaming down her face. She laughed once, hard and manic. I caught sight of a small Source rolling between her fingers. Then slapped her hand over her mouth and swallowed hard.

Why the fuck hadn't I seen it coming? So damned wrapped up in my own issues, I turned a blind eye on Imiko's. I had seen that self-destructive part of her rear its head back in Lanfall, but I hadn't found time to talk to Imiko about it, not really. We argued once and then... The timing had never been right. One more excuse.

The call of the void, that insidious little voice in my head telling me to end it and find peace in oblivion, had always been a constant companion of mine. Ever since Lesray Alderson planted the seed of suicide in there, perhaps even earlier than that. I have always felt it. I have always danced on the edge of it, dreamed of that nothing. I even leapt over the edge once. I like to say it was all to send Ssserakis home, but we all know that is only part of the truth. And I am not the only one who hears the call of the void.

For some of us, life is pain, the world is agony, and we drown in it every single fucking day. It's all we can do to tread water and keep our heads above the waves. We might hide it, from others and from ourselves, but it is always there, no matter how many smiles we paper over it. Some days it is easier, others are so so hard. Some days we dip below the surface, and there is always such a temptation to just let it take us. A few agonising moments of panic and pain and then blessedly nothing. Nothing ever again. I have been treading water all my life and I am tired of it. But that is no excuse. I didn't see the extent of Imiko's pain. I missed the intention, the desire. I honestly never thought she felt the call of the void.

I tried to get back to my feet, but my limbs had seized. My old flesh and bones ached and didn't move like they used to. Kento watched, frowning, not understanding.

Sirileth stood behind Imiko, tears flooding her eyes, sending shards of darklight sparkling all around, but not stopping Imiko. I saw Sirileth reach into her own Source pouch, hoped she was going for Spiceweed, to force it into Imiko's mouth, but Sirileth pulled out another Source, clutched it in her fist.

Imiko turned to me, opened her mouth to say something, then grimaced and doubled over, clutching at her stomach. Source rejection hitting her fast. She wasn't a Sourcerer, couldn't survive the magic. She gasped and I saw blood dripping from her face, quickly swallowed up by the thirsty soil.

"Lursa's Tears," she said in a trembling voice. "It really does hurt."

I struggled to my feet, snatched a pinch of Spiceweed from my pouch. "Imiko, take this." I held out my hand. My stupid fucking legs were wooden and stiff. She couldn't survive long. Source rejection would take less than a minute to kill her. It was already killing her even now. Even as I watched.

Imiko straightened, still clutching at her stomach. Blood streamed from her eyes, her nose, her ears. When she spoke, I could see it smeared across her teeth.

"Tell Hardt..." Imiko trailed off, shook her head, shrugged.

I staggered toward her, closing the distance. I would damned well force the Spiceweed into her mouth if I had to hold her down. For a moment, her skin went almost translucent, and I saw somewhere else reflected back at me. I saw Sevorai, the Other World. I knew then she had swallowed an Impomancy Source and if she broke down and rejected it, she would summon who knew what from that world. I couldn't let it happen. I couldn't understand why it was happening, what she was doing. Why was she killing herself?

Behind Imiko, Sirileth popped the new Source in her mouth and swallowed. Her face was grim, lines deeper than before, tears wet on her cheeks. She closed her eyes for a moment, grit her teeth, then pointed at the ground beneath Imiko's feet. There was a sound like ripping paper as a portal tore into existence below Imiko, and she fell through.

I staggered forward, dragging my left leg as it cramped beneath me. Sirileth snapped the portal shut and turned her face to the sky, staring up at the great rift. I reached my youngest daughter and clung to her, partly to keep upright and partly for... I don't know. To make sure she was still real? To drag her back into her right mind? To shake her until she made some fucking sense? I did none of those things. I just clung to Sirileth and snarled at her, "What have you done?"

Sirileth was rubbing her braid again, between thumb and fingers, tears dripping from her chin. "It was her choice," she said quietly.

I turned my eyes upward just as the rift pulsed, flashed, released a shockwave of force that knocked everyone from their feet. Everyone but Sirileth. My youngest daughter used her Geomancy to steady herself, stay rooted to the ground, not taking her eyes from Imiko's sacrifice even for a moment.

"It was her choice," Sirileth repeated so quietly, more to herself, I think.

The great rift flashed again and released another shockwave that pressed us all back to the ground, stirred up dust, and scattered the clouds above, shattering them into drifting bronze chunks. The great rift had changed slightly, the colour of it different. Through it, I saw a featureless sky.

"Shit!" I buried my head in my hand once more and sobbed.

"What happened?" Kento's voice, drawing closer. "What did you do now?"

"Me?" Sirileth asked, her voice oddly detached, almost dreamlike. "Nothing. Not really. She chose it, I just... I mean, I just gave auntie Imiko's death meaning."

"You killed her?" Kento said, the rage creeping back in. I didn't have the strength to stop it again. If my two daughters tried to kill each other now, I knew there was nothing I could do but get in the way.

"She killed herself," Sirileth said. She grunted with

pain, and I opened my eyes to see her doubled over, Kento standing over her. Sirileth sank to the ground next to me. Both remaining hoops pierced through her left arm were glowing now. The skin around them was red and angry. Sirileth reached for her pouch and pulled out a pinch of Spiceweed. She had staved off rejection for so long, but even she was at her limit with two unattuned Sources, Ingomancy and Portamancy, in her stomach. "I just gave her sacrifice meaning." Her voice broke on the words.

She shoved the Spiceweed in her mouth. A few moments later, she pitched forward and retched, her braid of hair dangling before her. I reached out to hold the braid back, but she slapped my hand away.

"I don't understand," Kento said. "Where is Imiko?"

"Gone," I said quietly. The world felt colder now. No. I felt colder. I wanted to hate, to rage, to grieve, to scream, to cry, to burn everything to ash. Instead, I was numb. Painfully, horribly numb. "She's dead. Suffered Source rejection. Broke down." I shook my head, still not quite believing it. It couldn't be real. Not Imiko.

"She chose it," Sirileth said between retching. "I mean, she wanted it."

I shook my head at my youngest daughter. "You gave her the Source, Sirileth. You..." I struggled to push the words past my constricting throat. Struggled to form them. Even knowing they were true, knowing they were real, somehow saying them, giving them voice made the entire thing undeniable. "You killed her. You murdered Imiko."

This time Sirileth didn't argue.

"Why?" Kento asked. She sank down to her knees with us. We sat together, myself and my two daughters. A strange, morbid wake. Kento opened her mouth to say something, closed it again, shook her head. "Why?"

"To redirect the rift," I said. Sirileth nodded, still retching up her Sources. "When she passed the moon through the rift, it reset it to lead nowhere." I dug my hand into the loose sandy soil, scooped up a handful and pressed my fist around it. I don't know why really, but it felt good to crush something. "But as long as it led nowhere, the Maker could find it again, latch onto it. All that experimenting Sirileth did, forcing people to reject Sources and break down, to create smaller, stable rifts, was to find a way to redirect this one."

Sirileth nodded again, wiped her mouth on her shoulder and sat up. Her arms hung awkwardly. Without Ingomancy to bend the metal that had fused to her skin, she could no longer move her arms without tearing the flesh open anew. She was stuck like that. "It worked, Mother. I mean, I did it. We did it. Imiko..."

"Don't you fucking dare, Sirileth," I snapped at her.

"I dare." Sirileth's voice shattered on the words. "She meant more to me than she ever did you." I glared my contempt at her and Sirileth's face crumpled. She turned away and sobbed. There is no more damning reflection than seeing yourself in the eyes of those you love.

Sirileth drew in a ragged breath. "She always talked about going after you, Mother. Imiko, I mean. I tried to push her over and over. Told her she should go. She should find you." She clenched her jaw, her voice turning tight. "She hurt so much and nothing I could do helped her. I couldn't... I mean, I didn't know how to fix her. What was broken in her. I hoped you could. She missed you." Sirileth faltered and she sobbed again.

I didn't know what to do with that. I didn't know

how to deal with the blame that was implicit in Sirileth's words. So, I pushed it away as I always do with my grief. "The Source Sirileth gave to Imiko was an Impomancy Source," I said to Kento. "When she rejected and broke down inside the rift, it changed the destination from nowhere to Sevorai." I looked up at the great rift and the grey sky within it, somehow light without light. "The rift is now the first ever stable portal to the Other World."

"A closed circle," Sirileth said in a small voice. "That is... I mean, no way for the Maker to find it." She was right. Of course, she was fucking right, she had planned all of this. Somehow, my daughter had planned everything down to the smallest detail, and it had worked. Sevorai and Ovaeris were one world, occupying the same space. A world within a world. The rift was more of a gateway between those two worlds now. It was genius. It was fucking monstrous. It was beyond anything I could have imagined, and Sirileth had engineered it.

We sat for a while in silence as the storm continued to rage around us, a dull roar close and yet far away. We sat in the eye of it, an unmoving eye. There was nothing around us. The impact of Lursa, the shockwave had scoured the desert clear, restructured it into solid earth beneath us. I knew the sun would rise soon, and there was no shelter from its glare. We would all bake here, trapped in the eye of the storm. But for now, we were all too exhausted to go on.

Eventually Sirileth toppled sideways, hit the ground with cry, and was still. Kento shuffled over to her, held a hand in front of her face, and declared she was alive, but asleep. I felt numb, raw, like flesh scrubbed too hard. I just ached everywhere but most of all inside. A place beyond skin and muscle and bone. I just fucking ached, and I knew nothing would ease it. Nothing would make it better. Only time could erode the sharp edges and make the pain distant.

I miss Imiko. Every day I miss her still, my little sister, my best friend. She was in so much pain and I didn't see it until it was too late. Until she was gone. She took her own life to end it, to be free, and though I was there with her at the end... I wasn't there for her when she needed me.

I miss her so much.

CHAPTER THIRTY SEVEN

THREE THINGS BECAME CLEAR TO ME AS WE camped under the new portal to Sevorai. The first was that the storm surrounding us was not likely to dissipate. At least, not anytime soon. It continued to rage, a wall of churning amber dust punctuated by savage forks of lightning. It roared like a distant monster tasting blood in the air. Something about this new portal to Sevorai kept the storm from closing in on us though. Despite that fact, I knew it would still kill us.

The sun rose, and as it reached for its zenith, we crowded inside a makeshift hut of dirt I raised from the ground with my innate Geomancy. It was little more than a lean-to without anything to lean on, but it provided us all with a little shade from the worst of the sun. But that leads me to the second thing that became clear.

We would soon starve to death. Well, unless we

resorted to eating each other, I suppose. We terrans certainly used to before the Rand changed us. The Damned, those poor unfortunate wretches who still exist as a vile mockery of our ancestry, don't give a damn whether the flesh they're eating is another Damned. Meat is meat, I suppose. Regardless, I like to think we have evolved somewhat since those days. Besides, a good half of our party was pahht and I imagined they would be quite stringy and probably taste strongly of pepper. I don't know why. It was very hot, and I wasn't thinking clearly.

We had enough water to keep us going, for a while at least. The oasis was gone, scoured away by that initial shockwave. What trees had managed to cling to the earth were charred husks half buried in the sand. The water was no longer rising to pool at the surface, but it was still below us. Kento could bring it up as a slow trickle with her Hydromancy. I formed a small basin in the earth, and she worked at it, despite her obvious exhaustion, and brought water up to quench us all. She didn't stop. Even barely able to keep her eyes open for more than a few seconds, she kept at it until we had something to drink. I will forever be impressed by my eldest daughter. Her strength, her unfailing will to keep going is something she got from me, I think. It certainly wasn't Isen. Her father was much more the give in to fate's whims type of person. Strong of body but weak of spirit. Then again, maybe Kento's will came from Mezula. The Rand had given my daughter her anger, but that didn't mean Kento hadn't learned other things sitting at the foot of the god.

My thoughts were detached things. They zipped through my head like fleas, of which I had no doubt we were all covered with. Sand fleas. Nasty little buggers determined to feed on the moisture of larger creatures. Unfortunately, we were the only large creatures around, so they fed mostly on us. Shade kept us from broiling in the harsh sun, but it also convinced the biting little arseholes to climb on out of the sand and give us a good nipping. Not that any of that mattered. As I have said, my thoughts were rambling.

Water, we had. But food, we did not. The oasis was gone, blown away by the shockwave, and all our supplies were gone with it. Perhaps some of it was caught in the currents of the storm, swirling around in the great madness of wind, but we would never know. We had no food. We had no way to get food. Our deaths would be slow and agonising. And itchy if the bloody fleas had anything to say about it.

As we huddled under my makeshift shelter, I peered out at the great rift. The portal that had claimed Imiko's life. I wanted to believe Sirileth. I wanted to believe that it was Imiko's choice. That she had committed suicide redirect the rift and save our world. It made her death a sacrifice; it meant something. I wanted to believe it, but I couldn't. I couldn't because... because if it was true, then I really had missed it. I had been through such deep depression myself; I had suffered through it myself. I should have been able to help Imiko. She had come to me for help, and I had been so caught up in chasing Sirileth and in my own struggles that I had missed it. I can look back at it now and admit the truth of that, but I was too close to it then, too busy running from my grief. So, I blamed Sirileth. I blamed my daughter for murdering my sister. And perhaps the worst of all, the most damning evidence against me, is that Sirileth needed me. She had just watched a woman she thought of as a second mother commit suicide, had helped her, even. Sirileth was in pain, and I should have been there to comfort her, not heap blame on her that was more rightly placed on my shoulders.

But again, I am getting distracted. The third thing I realised as I peered out at the great rift, is that it was growing larger. Like a hole in a blouse, it was slowly tearing, the rent ripping closer to the ground. When Sirileth had flung the moon through the scar, it had been high above us, sitting in the sky as far up as Ro'shan flew. But now... now the bottom spike of the rift was tearing so low it was a mere hundred feet from the ground.

At first, I thought Sirileth was somehow doing what the Maker had originally wanted her to do, enlarging the rift. But it couldn't have been. Sirileth hadn't woken. She had barely stirred since toppling over the night before. Even when Kento had dragged her into the shelter, Sirileth mumbled about the darkness coming, closing in, but she hadn't woken. Despite everything, I feared for her. The damage those metal hoops had done to her arms when they melted was severe. Streaks of metal had melted into her skin. There were wounds around the burns, sores. Wounds like that, in conditions like the desert especially, were likely to get infected.

Kento pitched forward, her eyes snapping open just in time for her to startle and get an arm beneath her. She pushed upright once more and slapped lazily at her cheek as if that little sting could keep her awake. She focused on the depression in the earth and placed a hand over it. A trickle of water seeped up to the surface and started pooling. The pahht woman with the terran child was waiting for a drink.

I caught Kento's eye and waved my hand at Sirileth. "Can you help her?" I knew I had no right to ask, but it was all I could do. I had no Biomancy, nor the knowledge to use it. The sad truth is, an untrained Pyromancer can create a fireball and destroy almost as well as a trained Pyromancer, but an untrained Biomancer is more likely to harm than heal. They need to understand how the body works to know how to fix it.

Kento finished pooling water in the depression and turned away as the pahht woman leaned down and sucked at it through parched, blistered lips. She glared at me, then shuffled over to Sirileth, and placed a hand on one arm. I watched, almost holding my breath I was so nervous. I expected to see... I don't know. Metal peeling from Sirileth's skin maybe? The flesh rejecting the ore melted onto it. I don't know. After a while, Kento sat back and slumped.

"I've done as much as I can, Eska." She paused, took a few moments to breathe, eyes closed, and shoulders slumped. "I've stopped any risk of infection for now, but that metal..." She sighed and laid back on the ground, her voice becoming hazy and dreamlike. "It resists Sourcery."

The pahht woman shuffled closer to Kento, tapped her leg with a clawed finger. When Kento opened her eyes, it was with such a glare I expected her to smite the poor woman. "What?" Kento snarled.

"The child is thirsty."

Kento glanced at the young terran for a moment. Then she heaved herself upright, held her hand over the depression in the ground, and pulled water up from far below. I wished I could take that burden from her, but she was the only one who could do it. She was the only chance we had of survival. Not that surviving the day would do us much good with nowhere to go and no way past the storm.

The day passed by in a baking heat haze. We were all waiting for a saviour that would never come. We were just waiting to die. Sirileth didn't wake. She dreamed, I think. She tossed and turned as much as she could with her arms locked in place. Occasionally she whimpered. I longed to bring her out of it, to throw water on her face or shake her until her eyes opened, but Kento warned against it. If Sirileth was going to survive her injuries, she needed rest, then she could die from starvation or exposure like the rest of us.

I spent most of the day watching the jagged line of the great scar creep towards the ground. No one else seemed to notice. I wondered what would happen when the rift met Ovaeris? Would it suddenly swallow everything? Would it recoil like ice from a flame? Would it lose its connection to the Other World and allow the Maker to find it once more and flop into our realm and devour everything? I think the heat and hunger and exhaustion was making me a little delirious. I was sitting around doing nothing, waiting for my own death and the deaths of the two people most important to me in the whole world. That's rather unlike me, so we can assume I was not thinking clearly.

As the bottom spike of the rift drove ever deeper, ever closer to the land we all sat on, I considered warning people. Perhaps warning Kento at the very least. I had no idea what might happen, and whatever it was, we should probably meet it united and on our feet. I didn't though. Just watched in silence and let my eldest daughter snatch a few more moments of sleep.

Part of me wished Sirileth would wake. I wanted her to sit up and explain it to me. I wanted her to tell me what was happening, how all of it factored into her plan. Most of all, I wanted her to give me a reason. Why Imiko? She was willing to kill thousands of people by dropping a moon on them, but she let Imiko choose to sacrifice herself instead of forcing it upon someone else? I wouldn't have made that choice. If I thought it truly needed to be done, I would not have allowed it to be her. I would have picked one of the others, the pahht man or the crazy terran. Maybe that makes me more callous than my daughter, or maybe we are just as bad as each other. A darker part of me hoped Sirileth would not wake. Then, perhaps, I never needed to come to terms with what she had done. I feared if she explained herself, I would never be able to forgive her. That is how vile a person I am. Part of me wished my daughter would never wake. I hated that thought, but it was there all the same. Luckily, we are not our darkest thoughts. We are made of our actions, not our impulses.

Bah! My mind was whipping about like a flag in a hurricane, snatching at subjects, running them through to any conclusion, then finding another one to flagellate myself with. I have never been good at being alone, and right then, I felt very much alone regardless of how many people surrounded me. I was torturing myself, tearing myself apart, finding reasons to despise myself. Easier to do that than confront the truth, the grief. The pain of losing her.

The sun was waning, slouching towards the horizon. My shelter no longer provided any shade where I was sitting, but I didn't move. I let the merciless ball of fire beat down on me and Sirileth both. My racing, delirious mind decided that we should die together. The world could be rid of the two greatest war criminals it had ever produced. I think, perhaps, I was a little dehydrated. Everyone else had slurped water out of the little depression. I had even wet a cloth and dripped it drop by drop between Sirileth's lips, but I hadn't drunk anything since... I didn't know. Couldn't remember. It didn't matter anyway. We were dying and the sooner I got on with it, the better.

Time dragged on. Moments lasted for lifetimes. Trapped in my own head with nothing to do but count my mistakes, ruminate over all those who had suffered because of them, because of me. My ghosts came to me. The new ones. A few at first, then more and more. Ten. A dozen. A hundred. I took them for the people of the oasis, those I hadn't managed to save. Some of them certainly were. I considered unmaking them, using my innate Necromancy to unweave the tenuous incorporeal energy that anchored them to the world and to me. To give the poor spirits the rest they deserved and would forever be denied.

But I didn't. I was too tired, too numb, too raw, too hot, too thirsty, too angry. I just couldn't bring myself to care. I watched them draw closer, mingle, separate, drift from the storm and flock toward me. So many of them. Too many. More than had been at the oasis. More and more still. And yet more again. The people of Irad. Hundreds of thousands of people murdered in an instant by Sirileth and now raised as ghosts by my guilt and my innate Sourcery. But that couldn't be right. They shouldn't have been my ghosts. I blamed Sirileth, I tried to tell the ghosts she killed them, not me. They didn't care. Of course, they didn't care, they were ghosts. They exist only as fragments of memory and emotion. I gave them ethereal form. Except, there were too many of them. I had only ever raised a few ghosts at a time. Or, at least, I had only made visible a few at a time. The ghosts gathered before me, before us, before the portal. They weren't my ghosts at all. It might have been my Necromancy that was making them visible, but they were Sirileth's ghosts. Yet even so, they weren't here for her. They were here for the rift.

The jagged line of the great rift crept closer, a tear in
the world, like ripping fabric audible even over the tumult
of the storm. Others noticed it too. The pahht children first,
tugging on their parents' arms, pointing, crying. Then the
crazy terran, slapping the ground and whooping as if it was
all part of the mad plan. Kento woke too, startled, cried out
for Esem. Then reality slapped her and she, too, stared at the
rift, eyed the ghosts. I watched them, watched the rift, the
ghosts, watched Sirileth. I felt oddly detached from it all. It
was happening, whatever it was, and there was nothing I
could do to stop it. That was why I was unsurprised when
the rift finally touched the ground and stopped.

Bit of an anti-climax really.

Sirileth woke, sat bolt upright, fixed me with her
darklight stare. "It's coming!" she whispered.

I nodded.

"You can feel it?"

I shook my head. A lie.

Everyone was up now, staring at the rift. The crazy
terran ran a few steps toward it, scattered some ghosts,
dropped to his knees, raised his hands in prayer. The pahht
family huddled under my shelter, the young boy crying
about the ghosts. The Polasian woman glanced about as if
looking for somewhere to run and hide. Kento stared first at
the rift, then at Sirileth. She approached with fists balled and
ready for a fight.

"What is happening now?"

Sirileth grinned at her sister. "It's coming. I mean...
You'll see."

I watched my youngest daughter and felt... Pity.
Sorrow. Saving the world from the Second Cataclysm,
defying the Maker, redirecting the rift to Sevorai. Had it all

been about this? Sirileth didn't understand. She was going to
be so disappointed. She was going to hate me.

"What is coming?" Kento asked.

Sirileth managed to twist a hand into her pouch and
found her Ingomancy Source. I took it from her and placed
it in her mouth. She swallowed hard and then smiled at me,
so wide and earnest and full of happiness. I wish she had
smiled more as a child. I wish I had given her a childhood to
smile about.

The others were pointing at the rift now, not to where
it touched the ground, a thin crack in the world, but above
where it loomed large, a gaping hole.

"What is that?" Kento asked.

Darkness flew from the rift. In the lazy afternoon sun,
it plummeted toward the ground, shadow steaming from it.
I turned away from the sight, watched Sirileth instead.

"It's coming," she said again. She took a step forward,
opened her arms in welcome. "Come to me."

Still, I stared at her. If I could have changed things, I
would have. So many things. I would have talked to Sirileth
more. Made her understand, even as a child, what she was
and where she came from. Perhaps even more important, I
would have made her understand who I am, and why she
should never try to emulate me. But it's too late for that now.

"I am so sorry, Sirileth."

She didn't even turn to look at me. I'm not sure she
heard me. She took another step forward, her darklight eyes
a beacon shining at the darkness hurtling down toward us.
She opened her arms wide. "Come to me, Ssserakis."

The ancient horror screamed as it flew. Perhaps in
excitement, anticipation. Perhaps in pain from the searing
sun. Ssserakis screamed right up until the moment it flew

straight past Sirileth and hit me in the chest.

CHAPTER THIRTY EIGHT

ESKARA! Ssserakis screamed in my head. An icy cold settled inside of me, wrapping around my chest, filling me up. I shivered despite the baking sun of the desert. Believe it or not, it was a welcome sensation.

Sirileth turned to me, her face contorting into a hundred different expressions too fast to catch. Hurt, maybe. Betrayal, jealousy, anger. Confusion. I understood it now. All her life, Sirileth thought she was missing something, a piece of herself. I understood, because I felt it too.

Ever since I took my own life and threw Ssserakis out of my body back into its own world, I felt like I had carved off a piece of my soul. Worse even than losing my left arm, sending Ssserakis away had felt like a true loss. And now I realised Sirileth felt it too. Only worse. She had never known what it was like to have Ssserakis within her. She just knew she was missing something. Something that could never be hers because it was mine. My horror. My burden. My darkness. My fear. My anxiety. Ssserakis and I had found within each other soul mates. The perfect jagged pieces to fit into each other's' broken spirits.

"I'm so sorry," I said. The words felt meaningless. Were meaningless.

Eska, I missed you.

"You were never meant to know about it." I shuffled forward on aching legs as I said the words. Sirileth backed away, staring at me like I had just stolen her last meal.

You're weak, Eskara. I'll help.

New strength flooded me. My limbs grew lighter, my aches dulled, my head cleared. Oh, but I had missed this feeling. Ssserakis was fear incarnate. A horror that fed on the terror of others. And it had always had the ability to share its power with me. How many times had I survived only on the strength it lent me? How many times had I drawn out the fear in others to feed the horror? We were despicable. But we were made for each other.

I reached for Sirileth, and she stared down at my hand in fear or revulsion or anger. I realised then I had reached out with my left hand. I had a left hand again. It was a skeletal thing. Like all the flesh had been stripped from bones made of shadow. Each finger ended in a black talon.

What is happening? What's wrong with your body, Eskara? I thought you were dead. Why won't you talk to me?

Sirileth stared at me, her face twisting in pain, tears in her darklight eyes. She tugged on her braid, shook her head, then turned and fled. There was nowhere to go, but she fled away from me.

Eskara? ESKA? Talk to me. Please.

I sighed. I wanted to go after Sirileth, but what could I

do? What could I say? She had crashed a moon into Ovaeris, defeated a god, murdered hundreds of thousands of people. And still the one thing she had wanted had gone to me. I would hate me too.

"It's alright, Ssserakis," I said wearily. "I'm here."

"Who are you talking to, Eska?" Kento asked.

Who is that?

"It's Kento," I said.

Kento frowned. "What?"

I shook my head. "I'm talking to..." My old instincts clamped down and I shut my mouth before I could tell anyone that Ssserakis existed. Not that the horror was a secret anymore.

The Aspect said your daughter was dead.

"She lied."

"Who lied?" Kento asked, clearly frustrated.

I knew it. A creature of the Rand. They cannot be trusted.

"Kento is an Aspect now," I said.

Then she, too, cannot be trusted. Why is our other daughter sulking? I was being pulled in too many directions at once and Ssserakis' words did not sink in as they should have.

"Eskara," Kento said slowly. "Who are you talking to?"

I dismissed her question with a wave of my shadowy hand. Kento stared at it and like a child with a stolen toy I tried to hide it behind my back.

How are you still alive, Eska? I felt you die.

"Hardt brought me back."

The big terran was always a useful one. Where is he now?

Kento glanced back toward the rift, then skewered me with a suspicious glare. "Eskara, what came through the portal?"

How much to tell her? How much could I trust her? She deserved to know something.

She will tell the Rand, Eskara.

"Enough!" I snapped. "Both of you, just shut up!"

"Both..." Kento started, but I held up a hand to stop her.

"Give me a minute, Kento." I took a deep breath, closed my eyes, and found Ssserakis waiting for me in the darkness of my own soul. Despite everything that had just happened, despite Sirileth's obvious hurt and Kento's suspicion. Despite it all, I was so glad to feel my horror again. I would have hugged Ssserakis if it had a body, but I didn't need to. My horror felt it through me.

I missed you too, Eska. What happened to you?

"I got old, Ssserakis," I said out loud, not caring that Kento and anyone else could hear me. "We terrans do that. Me faster than others."

I had forgotten how frail you terrans are. Undo it, like the Iron Legion.

"It's not that simple." I stopped, sighed, shook my head. "I looked for you. So many times, I looked for you in Sevorai. I couldn't find you."

I was busy. Eska, you must come with me.

"What? Where?"

My world. Our daughter has opened the portal and now both our worlds are in danger. Quickly. I wasn't strong enough alone, but we have always been more powerful together.

There was an urgency in my horror's voice that brooked no hesitation. I opened my eyes to find Kento still watching me, jaw clenched.

"I have to go," I said. I really wasn't sure Ssserakis was right about us being stronger together. I was old and weak and frail, a far cry from the woman I had been when we had fought to beat the Iron Legion. But my horror needed me, and I would not deny it. Besides, we were all going to die in the desert. I thought, perhaps there was something in Sevorai that could help. At the very least, I could kill a Khark Hound and bring it back for us all to eat.

Your age is nothing but a door you hide behind to say it is too hard to try. You were never one to fail before even attempting, Eska.

"You're right," I said, smiling. "Better to kick down the door and say, 'fuck you' to whatever waits."

Kento sighed, pinched her nose. "What are you talking about, Eskara? Go where? Why? With whom?"

"Sevorai," I said with a smile. "With Ssserakis. Ask your sister, she knows who it is." I turned toward the portal, stopped, glanced over at Sirileth. She was facing away from us, had sunk down onto her arse and was hugging her knees out on the sun-baked sand. "Look after her, Kento," I said quietly. "Please."

Kento shook her head wildly, hair pulling loose. "What?"

She'll figure it out. We have to go.

Huge, shadowy wings burst from my back and unfurled. Ssserakis gave them an experimental flap and I saw the other survivors cry out in shock. The pahht couple pulled their children further away from me. Even Kento took a step back.

"I'll be back," I said. I think it was more to myself than to Kento. A promise I made on behalf of myself and Ssserakis. No matter what we encountered in Sevorai. No matter what danger we needed to face together. I would come back for my daughters.

We will come back for our daughters. Ssserakis corrected me.

Books by Rob J. Hayes

The War Eternal
Along the Razor's Edge
The Lessons Never Learned
From Cold Ashes Risen
Sins of the Mother
Death's Beating Heart

The Mortal Techniques novels
Never Die
Pawn's Gambit
Spirits of Vengeance

The First Earth Saga
The Heresy Within (The Ties that Bind #1)
The Colour of Vengeance (The Ties that Bind #2)
The Price of Faith (The Ties that Bind #3)
Where Loyalties Lie (Best Laid Plans #1)
The Fifth Empire of Man (Best Laid Plans #2)
City of Kings

It Takes a Thief...
It Takes a Thief to Catch a Sunrise
It Takes a Thief to Start a Fire

Science Fantasy
Titan Hoppers

Science Fiction
Drones

Ingram Content Group UK Ltd.
Milton Keynes UK
UKHW010741260323
419068UK00006B/194/J